HOT
Italian
NIGHTS

JACKIE ASHENDEN **JANE PORTER** **SUSAN STEPHENS**

MILLS & BOON

CONTENTS

The Italian's Final Redemption

Jackie Ashenden

Books by Jackie Ashenden

Harlequin Modern

Crowned at the Desert King's Command
The Spaniard's Wedding Revenge

The Royal House of Axios

Promoted to His Princess
The Most Powerful of Kings

Shocking Italian Heirs

Demanding His Hidden Heir
Claiming His One-Night Child

Visit the Author Profile page
at millsandboon.com.au for more titles.

Jackie Ashenden writes dark, emotional stories with alpha heroes who've just gotten the world to their liking only to have it blown apart by their kick-ass heroines. She lives in Auckland, New Zealand, with her husband, the inimitable Dr. Jax, two kids and two rats. When she's not torturing alpha males and their gutsy heroines, she can be found drinking chocolate martinis, reading anything she can lay her hands on, wasting time on social media or being forced to go mountain biking with her husband. To keep up-to-date with Jackie's new releases and other news, sign up to her newsletter at jackieashenden.com.

To JA. For true leadership.

CHAPTER ONE

LUCY ARMSTRONG HAD planned her own kidnapping meticulously.

Something simple, that wouldn't cause a fuss, and that would ultimately allow her to get away from her controlling father once and for all.

It wouldn't be easy. She was a valuable commodity to Michael Armstrong, and not for being his daughter, no, that was the very least of it. A tutor her father had hired for her had discovered she was a genius with numbers and had understood money from an early age, and had passed that discovery on to her father. He'd soon found a use for her, making sure she laundered all that ill-gotten money, and he would definitely not let her go without a fight. He guarded her assiduously and jealously, the same way he'd guarded her mother.

However, Lucy only needed an hour's physical freedom, long enough for her to implement stage two of her three-stage plan.

Stage two being to throw herself on the mercy of her father's enemy.

Stage three to request that he kidnap her and hide her for the short amount of time it would take to ensure that she disappeared without a trace so Michael would never find her again.

It wasn't the best plan she could come up with—she didn't

like relying on other people—but her mother's death could not be in vain. Lucy had made a promise to her mother before she'd died, that she wouldn't let herself be kept a prisoner the way her mother had been. That she would get away from Michael, no matter what the cost. And of the few other scenarios she'd run, this one was most likely to keep her out of her father's clutches for ever.

Or so she hoped. She'd allowed for all kinds of variables, and could predict most things with surety, but she couldn't account for everything.

The main variable being him.

Vincenzo de Santi. Her father's enemy number one.

She'd done her research. The de Santis were an old and infamous Italian crime family for whom her father had once worked—at least until the matriarch had been imprisoned and her son, Vincenzo, took over. Then his crusade against the big crime families of Europe began.

One by one Vincenzo had taken them down and turned them in, including his own mother, it was reputed. The de Santi business empire—once a hotbed of white-collar crime—had been cleaned out, all sources of corruption and illegal activity removed. Now it was the very model of a business that excelled. Legally.

Vincenzo de Santi had been ruthless in his quest to drag his family back over to the right side of the law, and with other families in his sights he'd made a lot of enemies. Including her father, who hated him and had sworn to take him down.

Which made him both the perfect target and the perfect refuge.

Lucy peered up at the old, graceful ivy-covered building opposite the bus stop she was currently sitting in.

She'd managed to get hold of de Santi's schedule, and his visit to London to check on several of his family's businesses was timely, not to mention useful—for her plan to work she had to talk to him directly and not be dismissed by flunkeys. Right now he was checking on one of his family's auction houses and she'd decided this was the perfect place to throw herself on his mercy. Far less security than the big skyscraper near the river and it was in a quieter area of the city.

Still, she didn't have a lot of time. The security detail that followed her wherever she went had no doubt already figured out that she hadn't gone to powder her nose after all and were tearing up the cafe she'd insisted they stop at trying to find her.

And find her they would, she had no illusions about that.

Which meant she needed to get to stage two of her plan, and quickly.

Keeping her head down, Lucy hurried across the road to the de Santi auction house and pushed through the ornate double doors.

It was cool inside, her footsteps echoing on the marble floor as she walked towards the reception desk. A nearby waiting area was furnished with richly upholstered couches, but there was no one currently waiting. There were pictures on the walls, sculptures on the tables and various other precious items displayed in cases. Silence permeated the place. The kind of silence that only the astonishingly rich and important could buy.

Lucy ignored the art the way she ignored most things, keeping her attention on what was in front of her, since what was in front of her was always the most important thing, and approached the large and obviously antique reception desk.

A beautifully dressed young man sat behind it, looking intently at a paper-thin computer screen, and he glanced up as she approached, his expression pleasant and professional. 'Can I help you, miss?'

Lucy gripped the strap of her handbag tightly, her heart beating very fast. 'I need to speak to Mr de Santi immediately, please.'

The man's pleasant expression didn't change. 'Do you have an appointment?'

This part of her plan was always going to be difficult.

All she had was her name, and even though most people didn't know it, they surely knew of her existence. Or at least, Vincenzo de Santi would know of her existence.

'No,' Lucy said. 'But he'll want to see me. I'm Lucy Armstrong.'

That clearly meant nothing to the receptionist. His smile changed to one of polite refusal. 'I'm sorry, Miss Armstrong, but if you don't have an appointment I'm afraid you can't see Mr de Santi. He's a very busy man.'

She'd have only twenty minutes now. Twenty minutes and then they'd find her. They'd track her down and then she'd be dragged back to Cornwall. She wouldn't be allowed back to London again, and then her mother would have died for nothing.

Ice collected inside her, small tendrils of frost working their way through her veins. She'd become adept at ignoring her emotions, at not seeing anything but the task in front of her, which was generally numbers on a screen, the financial markets she lived and breathed. And for years that had worked very well.

But with freedom so close and the loss of it approaching fast, the fear she'd been trying to suppress was battering at the box she'd locked it in, trying to get out. It had taken her years to muster the courage to put this plan into motion. It *had* to work. She wasn't going to get another chance.

'It's Armstrong,' Lucy said, hoping her voice was firm and not shaking. 'Lucy Armstrong. I'm Michael Armstrong's daughter.'

The man's expression still didn't change. Her father's name meant nothing to him.

She swallowed, the chill inside her deepening. She'd expected de Santi's gatekeepers to at least know of her father, but it was obvious that wasn't the case.

The fear was reaching higher, cold floodwaters threatening to drown her.

Her mother lying on the floor, blood pooling on the carpet where she'd fallen as she'd grabbed Lucy's hand.

'Promise me,' she'd gasped out. *'Promise me you'll survive long enough to get away from him. Escape, have a life, be free. I want you to be happy, darling. I don't want you to end up like me...'*

She'd promised and her mother had died right there in front of her.

Think.

Right. She couldn't freeze, couldn't let the fear get the better of her. Concentrate on the immediate problem and figure out a solution.

Although there didn't seem to be any security around, she wasn't fooled. De Santi's security team were legendary, which was part of why she'd chosen him to start with. If she made herself a threat in some way, she'd be instantly grabbed and hustled away somewhere secure.

Maybe that would be the way to go.

She was just sorting through that option, when a door behind the reception desk opened and an expensively dressed older man strode out. 'And I'll see you in hell, de Santi,' he flung over his shoulder before storming over to the exit.

The receptionist was halfway out of his chair, no doubt to soothe the other man's ruffled feathers, and Lucy saw her chance.

She was good at remaining unnoticed and, since the door to de Santi's office stood open, she moved quickly, heading straight to it.

No one stopped her.

She went in, her heart beating far too fast for comfort, turning and shutting the door quickly, and locking it for good measure. Then she turned around.

The atmosphere of luxury and astonishing amounts of money was here in this office too. No marble on the floor this time, but a thick, deep carpet in midnight blue. Dark wood panelled the walls, the lighting of various paintings on it discreet and subtle. Bookcases and display cases, a couch, a low coffee table and a huge oak desk.

There was a man behind the desk. And he was looking at her.

He said nothing.

Lucy's heart thundered in her ears. The minutes were ticking away and yet somehow she'd lost her voice. As if the man behind the desk had struck her dumb.

He wore a dark suit that had clearly been made for him, but it wasn't the suit that Lucy noticed first. It was his height and the broad width of his shoulders, and the hard plane of a very muscular chest. He was strength incarnate, the epitome of power. Although he lounged in the big leather chair as if waiting for a boring meeting to finish, one ankle resting on the opposite knee, he radiated that power like a king, all determination and purpose and casual arrogance.

She blinked, a feeling of safety filtering through her.

Yes, she'd been right to come here. If there was anyone on earth who could protect her from her father, it was this man.

He still didn't say anything, watching her with eyes so dark they verged on black.

He wasn't handsome, though he possessed a powerful and undeniable charisma. It was there in his deeply set eyes, in the hard cast of his jaw, high cheekbones and straight nose. An aristocrat turned crusader. The air of ruthlessness around him made him utterly compelling.

Are you sure you were right to come here?

But Lucy shoved the thought away. She couldn't start second-guessing now.

This was Vincenzo de Santi himself and it was time to implement the next stage of her plan.

She forced herself to walk forward to the desk, stopping in front of it just as someone rattled the handle of the office door.

'Mr de Santi!' a voice called from outside.

She swallowed and said very quickly, before Security came

bursting through that door, 'Mr de Santi, my name is Lucy Armstrong and I'm here because I need your protection.'

De Santi ignored the shouting and simply watched her with no more than minor curiosity. And said nothing.

'Mr de Santi!' The door rattled again. 'I'm calling Security right now!'

He stirred, as if only mildly bothered. 'No need, Raoul,' he called back, his English lightly accented, his voice deep and cold. 'Security are already aware.' He sounded bored.

Except the black gaze that speared her was not.

He is dangerous.

Fear moved through her again and she had to force it down hard. That was the problem with strong men. Strength meant safety but it could also mean danger, as she knew all too well. Especially for her.

He was a fanatic, the rumours said. He couldn't be swayed and he couldn't be bought. He was incorruptible and merciless against his enemies.

You are his enemy.

She was. But she had no other choice. She couldn't go to the authorities, not when she was a criminal herself, and that limited her options. Vincenzo de Santi was the only one who could keep her safe, she had no doubt. Anyway, though he was dangerous, he couldn't be more dangerous than her father, surely?

'Mr de Santi,' Lucy said, preparing her speech again, in case he hadn't heard her the first time, 'my name is—'

'I know who you are,' he interrupted in the same bored, calm way.

'Oh.' She was a little nonplussed. If he knew who she was already, then shouldn't he be more...interested? Wouldn't the daughter of his enemy simply walking into his office make him pleased? Certainly he should have been asking her questions. Except he wasn't. He was simply sitting there, at his leisure, in that big black leather chair. Staring at her.

It was unnerving.

Lucy shifted on her feet. She wasn't used to being stared at the way he was staring at her. As if those dark eyes were X-rays and they could see right through her clothes to her skin and deeper, right through her flesh, down to her bones.

You're freezing again. Don't get distracted, keep your attention on the goal.

That's right, she had to concentrate. The minutes were ticking away and she didn't know what would happen when her father's men burst in here. They might drag her away and she didn't want that, at least not before she'd put her proposition to him.

Steeling herself, Lucy pushed her glasses up her nose and stared right back. 'If you know who I am then you'll also know who my father is. I need your protection, Mr de Santi, and I'm willing to pay handsomely for it.'

'I see.' He didn't look at all surprised at this, nor one whit less bored. 'Please explain why I should give you anything at all.'

But Lucy didn't have the time to answer questions. She knew what she was bringing to his door in coming here: a war. No more and no less, and he needed to know immediately.

'I'll explain when you've agreed. You probably have ten minutes before my father's men track me down and come pouring through your door ready to drag me home.'

Vincenzo de Santi didn't react. He remained in his chair, his hands loosely clasped in his lap. Her father favoured big gold rings, but this man wore no jewellery. He was austere as a monk. Except monks generally did not have eyes that glittered like polished onyx; he reminded her of a great black panther about to pounce.

Time was going faster and faster, and the fear was harder and harder to contain. She gripped on to the strap of her handbag for dear life, her nails digging into her palm, the slight pain holding panic at bay.

This was obviously deliberate, this silence he was giving her. Hoping to rattle her possibly. Well, she wouldn't be rattled and she wouldn't panic. She'd got this far and she couldn't allow herself to fail.

Failure was her mother dying in a pool of blood after trying to protect her from her father's wrath, and she couldn't let that death be in vain. She wouldn't.

'Please,' she said. 'I am throwing myself on your mercy.'

The young woman—it was difficult to tell her age, given the quantity of dark hair covering most of her face, but he thought she was a woman rather than a girl—was plainly terrified, yet trying very hard not to show it. The knuckles of her right hand where it clutched the strap of a ratty brown leather handbag were white, and her skin was very pale. Her eyes behind her glasses were very large and an indeterminate colour between brown and green, and she wore a shapeless dress of the same muddy colour.

Vincenzo eyed her. Silence was a useful interrogation tactic and so he used it often. People didn't like it. It made them uncomfortable. It made them want to fill the dreadful quiet any way they could, letting slip all kinds of interesting information.

Not that Miss Lucy Armstrong was someone he was interrogating.

At least, not yet.

'Mercy,' he said, tasting the word, because it was strange to hear it used in conjunction with himself. 'I'm afraid if it's mercy you're wanting, Miss Armstrong, you've come to the wrong place.'

Her gaze, for all that it was trapped behind two pieces of thick glass, was startlingly direct. In fact, he couldn't recall a woman—or, indeed, anyone—staring at him the way she was staring at him. People were generally too afraid to look him in the eye, and with good reason.

She should be afraid too. Especially being Michael Armstrong's daughter.

He'd tried to take down that particular piece of scum for

years now, but the man had evaded all Vincenzo's attempts to bring him to justice. And Vincenzo had tried *very* hard to bring him to justice. A couple of centuries ago, when crime families warred against each other, the war was carried out physically and brutally, and the authorities left well alone if they knew what was good for them. It had a certain...efficiency about it.

These days though, the battles were conducted on twenty-first-century battlefields; online, in the financial markets, in numbers and money. In shell companies and tax havens.

Vincenzo had tried many times to shut down the lucrative money-laundering business Armstrong had going on, since money and all the ways to hide it was a relatively easy way to take down someone's illegal empire. Yet every time Vincenzo thought he had Armstrong, the man managed to get away. It was puzzling.

Armstrong wasn't a subtle man and Vincenzo was almost positive he didn't have the kind of understanding required to evade Vincenzo's team of financial forensic specialists, yet somehow he did. One would almost suspect that Armstrong himself was far more sneaky than anyone thought, but Vincenzo didn't think he was. What Armstrong had was help. And Vincenzo thought he knew who that help might be.

The woman standing in front of his desk right now.

There had been many rumours throughout the European underground about Armstrong's daughter. That he guarded her closely, jealously, because she was the secret of the success of his empire. She knew numbers and money, was a genius with computers, could hide anyone's digital tracks with ease...

A dangerous woman. Yet she didn't look very dangerous. She looked very small, her body hidden away behind that awful, shapeless dress and thick, dark, frizzy hair hanging over her face. Her features were mostly hidden too, behind those thick glasses, but he thought he could see a scattering of freckles over her nose.

Not dangerous, perhaps. Just very, very unremarkable.

Interesting, though, that she should come here. That she should blunder through his doors seeking him. His security had informed him of her presence the moment she'd set foot in his family's auction house and despite his inclination to have her instantly taken and imprisoned, since her arrival was the kind of windfall he couldn't pass up, he'd decided to let whatever she was here for play out.

Raoul needed the practice in dealing with difficulties anyway.

Lucy Armstrong took another step forward, still holding his gaze. There was a certain ferocity to her, a determination that on another day he might have admired.

But he wasn't going to admire her. She was Armstrong's partner in crime, fully complicit in his evil empire, and so he would use her instead. Get her to reveal all her father's secrets, and once Armstrong was in prison, where he belonged, she would join him.

'Mr de Santi—' she began yet again, her voice low and slightly husky.

'Don't worry, Miss Armstrong,' he interrupted. 'Your father's men won't even get through the front door. My security is excellent.' And it was, because it needed to be.

When you were conducting a crusade against the most powerful crime families in Europe, having people try to kill you was an everyday occurrence.

It didn't bother him. If people were trying to kill him it meant he was doing something right.

'You don't understand,' she said. 'He will—'

'No.' Vincenzo didn't raise his voice, didn't put any emphasis on it. Just let it cut across her, cold as an icicle. 'He will not.'

Her mouth opened then closed. It was, Vincenzo couldn't help noticing, a rather full and soft-looking mouth.

'Now,' he went on, dismissing the observation and nodding at the chair near his desk. 'Sit.'

She frowned, a deep crease between two straight dark brows, and he thought she might be working herself up to argue with him. But, clearly thinking better of it, she did as she was told, holding her worn handbag protectively in her lap.

He tilted his head, studying her. She was still very afraid. He could almost smell it on her. He was a connoisseur of fear. He knew how it worked and what it did to people, and how it could be used to manipulate them. He himself didn't use it that way, since that was an approach he loathed above all others. But he wasn't averse to people letting themselves be manipulated by their own emotions. And he was constantly amazed by the fact that they did.

Another reason, if he needed one, that it wasn't a gun that would kill you, it was fear. Or hate. Or anger. Or love. Emotions were far more dangerous than any weapon.

'Explain,' he said, finally breaking the silence that had fallen. 'Why are you here, Miss Armstrong? Apart from throwing yourself on my non-existent mercy?'

She was sitting in the chair completely rigid, almost vibrating with tension. 'But my father's men will be here any minute.'

Fear, again. And she was right to be scared. Coming to him directly would be a betrayal her father would not forgive.

He glanced at his computer screen and, sure enough, she wasn't wrong. Some of Armstrong's thugs were already at the doors of the auction house.

Vincenzo touched a button on his keyboard and swivelled the screen around so it was in front of her. 'Top right-hand corner is a camera feed of the front of the building. As you can see, your father's men are already here. But they are being dealt with.'

It was clear he'd get nothing out of her until she was satisfied that she was safe from her father, so he might as well let her watch the proceedings. It would also serve as a good reminder to her that he was no less dangerous.

She watched the camera feed avidly, her eyes unblinking

from behind her glasses. She didn't move, clutching her hand-bag and looking like nothing so much as a small brown owl.

Fanciful of him. And he wasn't given to fancies. Nor was he given to mercy for small, unremarkable women, who also hap-pened to be accessories to the crimes committed by their father.

Really, he didn't know why he was letting her sit there watch-ing a feed of his security team dealing with her father's men. Especially when what he should be doing was to call his head of Security and get Alessio to hand her over to the British police immediately. After all, if his crusade against the crime fami-lies of Europe had taught him anything it was that immediate action was the best kind of action.

Then again, she could be useful to him in all kinds of ways, especially if he wanted to eventually bring Armstrong down. Perhaps he wouldn't be calling Alessio quite yet.

'Seen enough?' he asked, watching her.

She glanced at him, frowning ferociously. 'How do you know that your security dealt with it? You didn't look once.'

'I don't need to. My team is the best there is.' He swivelled the screen back. 'Your explanation, if you please.'

She took a little breath. 'Okay. So, as I said, I'm here be-cause I need your protection against my father. I managed to get away from him, but he'll never let me go free. He'll come for me whether I want to go back or not, and the only way to stay safe from him is to have someone to protect me. Which is where you come in.'

'Lucky me,' he said dryly. 'Presumably you know who I am, Miss Armstrong? I mean, you didn't wander into my office at random looking for a place to hide?'

The look she gave him was almost offended. 'Of course I know who you are. I planned my escape meticulously, including coming to you. You're my father's enemy number one. You're powerful and strong, and you have a great many resources. You don't owe my father anything and apparently you can't be bought.' She pushed her glasses up her nose again in what was obviously a nervous gesture. 'You're incorruptible, which makes you perfect.'

She had done her homework, hadn't she?

'I'm not as perfect as I'm sure you'd like me to be,' he said flatly. 'What's to stop me from taking you direct to the authorities right now, for example? You're an accessory to a great many crimes, Miss Armstrong, and, as you're no doubt aware, it is my stated aim to make sure people like you and your father are brought to justice swiftly.'

Her frown turned into a scowl. 'I am *not* like my father.'

'And yet you're complicit in a number of illegal activities if my sources are correct, and they usually are.'

She went even whiter than she was already, making the dusting of freckles across her nose stand out, and highlighting the shadows beneath her eyes.

Now the little owl wasn't just afraid, she was terrified.

Vincenzo had a reputation for ruthlessness, and some would have called him cruel. He supposed they could be correct about that. His world was a very black and white one, and it needed to be, since his personal mission in life didn't allow time to debate moral quandaries or sort out grey areas. He turned everyone over to the authorities and let them sort the innocent from the guilty, which could be interpreted as cruelty by some people.

It didn't bother him. He didn't care how other people interpreted his actions.

And he wasn't sure what the strange tightness was that whispered through him when he looked at the terrified young woman sitting across his desk. But it was there all the same. It was almost like...pity.

Her chin came up then, her narrow shoulders squaring slightly, as if she were facing down a firing squad.

'Yes,' she said. 'You're right, I am complicit. But prisoners don't get choices, especially when they're being threatened, and I didn't have the luxury of refusing. Believe me or don't, it's up to you. Just promise me that you will keep me safe from my father.'

She was wrong. Everyone had a choice, even if you didn't like the choice you were given.

'And why would I promise you a single thing?' he enquired, keeping the question casual.

Her gaze turned ever more determined. 'Because I can give you everything you need to take my father down.'

CHAPTER TWO

LUCY HAD KNOWN nothing but fear for most of her life and was used to it. But the fear that gripped her as she sat opposite Vincenzo de Santi was unlike any she'd ever known.

And she couldn't work out why.

Her father's men had been dealt with efficiently—she'd seen just how efficiently on that camera feed—and so there shouldn't have been any reason for her to remain scared. Yet she was, and now it had less to do with her father than it did with the man sitting opposite her.

He was still lounging there in that casual pose, to all intents and purposes bored. But his eyes glittered like black jewels and they did not move from her face, not even once. He was all coiled menace and a ruthlessness that she could almost feel like ice against her skin.

She hadn't expected to be confronted about her own crimes, not so soon, though in retrospect she should have. But she didn't like having to think about the things her father had made her do and, since she was very good at not thinking about certain things, she'd simply pushed it out of her head to be dealt with later.

Except later had now come. And Vincenzo de Santi calmly

stating that she was complicit in her father's crimes wasn't something she could deny.

But she'd told de Santi the truth. She hadn't been given a choice. It was either she did what her father asked, or there were consequences. Survive, that was what her mother had told her and so that was what she'd done, any way she could.

Maybe one day there would be time to address her crimes, but she would see her father taken down first if it was the last thing she did.

Yet it wasn't her guilt or otherwise which scared her. It was something else. Something about Vincenzo de Santi himself that she couldn't put her finger on.

She wasn't used to men. Her father kept her secluded in Cornwall, her every move watched by the guards he employed twenty-four-seven. She had a few online friends, but she made sure any identities she used online were heavily cloaked. She didn't really see anyone but the guards in real life, and she kept away from them, because they made her uncomfortable. It would have been a lonely existence if she'd let herself think about it, but she didn't ever let herself think about it. Never let herself see the bars of the cage she was locked in. Never contemplated the tightrope she walked between being useful enough for her father so he'd keep her alive, and refusing to do certain things that would anger him and make him deal out the same punishment he'd given her mother.

Her attention must always be on what was directly in front of her, never looking right or left, or anywhere else. Otherwise she would lose her balance and fall to her death.

She stared hard at Vincenzo de Santi, not letting her focus waver, not paying any attention to the new fear that lived inside her, just under her skin. An electric, prickling kind of fear that made her heart beat fast.

'Of course, you will give me everything you have on your father,' de Santi said easily, as if that had always been a fore-gone conclusion. 'Immediately, if you please.'

Lucy eyed him warily. 'And you will then hand me over to the police?'

He lifted one powerful shoulder and she found herself watching the way the fabric of his suit jacket pulled in response to the movement. She didn't know why. She already knew he was strong; she didn't need to watch him in order to confirm that.

'Naturally.' He put one hand on the arm of his chair, one long finger tapping out a soundless, slow, meditative rhythm. 'I should imagine the police would be very happy to get their hands on you.'

They probably would. But she didn't want to go. She hadn't survived for years waiting for her chance to escape, only to be put back in yet another cage. That wasn't what her mother had wanted for her.

But you have committed crimes. You deserve prison.

It was true. And to a certain extent she'd protected herself from the knowledge of what she'd done by not enquiring too deeply about where all her father's money had come from. Because she knew, if she did, she'd discover things that would make her life even more untenable than it was already. So she hadn't enquired. She'd only done what she was told. She'd made some money disappear into offshore accounts, pouring the rest into other investments, making her father's bank balances grow.

It had been survival, pure and simple.

But did survival really deserve a jail cell?

Because Vincenzo de Santi would hand her over to the police, that was obvious. She could see it in his mesmerising, compelling face. He was her judge, jury and executioner, and she couldn't look away.

Her hands tightened on her handbag and the laptop hidden in it. The laptop that contained all the information he required. But not the passwords he would need. Those were all in her head.

'When you say you will hand me over to the police, when will that happen?' It was very difficult, but she held his gaze. Because she had to know. His handing her over to the authorities had always been a possibility, but she'd held out a tiny sliver of hope that perhaps he wouldn't. That he'd help her disappear into obscurity somewhere in the US, far away from her father. Where she could make sure her mother's death hadn't been in vain.

He tilted his head and she had the impression that he could see every single part of her. From her guilty conscience to the fear she lived with every day. Every aspect of her small, narrow, confined existence.

'You give me the information I want,' he said in that easy, casual voice, 'and then I will notify the authorities. This afternoon probably. The quicker you do it, the quicker I can take your father off the streets for good.'

Perhaps he'd meant that to be encouraging, or maybe an incentive for her. But it wasn't.

And her expression must have given her away, which was a shock in itself, since no one ever noticed her emotions, because he said, 'This does not please you?' His mouth curved slightly and she found herself watching that too, as if she was compelled. 'But Miss Armstrong, if you'd done your research you would know that I do not care for criminals. And, as I've already told you, if it's mercy you're looking for, you'll find I have none.'

She'd underestimated him. She'd thought that perhaps she would be unimportant to him. That her father would be his ultimate goal and he'd let her slip away to pursue her own redemption far away from the constant fear.

But she'd been so fixated on her immediate plan she'd miscalculated.

That's always been your greatest failing.

Yes, that was true.

She shifted her hold on her laptop, her fingers nervously gathering up the fabric of her dress and pleating it.

Okay, she told herself, *so don't think about what he was going to do, don't think about police cells and having to survive for years in a prison with fear your only companion yet again. Don't think about your mother dying in a pool of blood, begging you not to end up like she did.*

Only think about how to change his mind.

She steeled herself, met his black gaze head-on. 'It'll take some time to give you this information, since I don't have all the data yet. Probably, say, a week.' Was a week long enough to change his mind? She didn't think she could push for more. And the reality was that she'd have to work with whatever he gave her.

If he even gave her anything at all.

One black brow rose. 'A week?' he echoed, as if it was the most preposterous thing he'd ever heard. 'Forgive me, Miss Armstrong, but I've heard all the rumours about you. I know what you're capable of. You could get me that information in ten seconds if you wanted to.'

'But I don't want to,' she said flatly, before she could stop herself. 'A week, Mr de Santi. A week and I'll give you all you need to not only take my father down, but his entire empire along with him.'

De Santi's eyes narrowed, an obsidian blade getting sharper. So sharp it might cut. 'Why would I wait a week? In ten minutes I can make you tell me anything I want to know.'

The icy flood of fear inside her rose higher. His ruthlessness was legendary, as was his single-minded determination. He'd betrayed his own parents to the authorities, it was rumoured, which meant he would have no qualms about torturing her into giving him whatever he wanted.

Lucy gripped on to her courage, held it tight, and didn't look away. 'You can torture me all you like, Mr de Santi, but I'm not going to give you a thing.'

If being accused of potential torture bothered him, he didn't show it. 'And what makes you think you can hold out against torture, Miss Armstrong?'

Well, that was the problem. She didn't think she could. Then again, she'd doubted she'd ever be able to escape her father and yet she had, so anything was possible.

'I have a very high pain threshold,' she said, because that was true. Certainly her father wouldn't let her have painkillers, so she'd had to deal with severe period pain and migraines by herself. 'You can put glass under my nails or break my fingers, but I won't tell you a single thing.'

De Santi blinked once. 'Glass,' he murmured. 'Break your fingers… Hmm. Both good options that yield results, certainly. But I could just take that laptop you're clutching on to and save myself the drama.'

'You could,' she allowed. 'But it wouldn't do you any good. All the information on this laptop is encrypted, and the passwords are all in my head.'

The edge of his stare was pressing against her skin, cutting her.

She gritted her teeth, refusing to give in and look away. She might not know much about men, but she did know that strong men liked to test that strength on others. She'd seen her father do it with his associates and his enemies, and he enjoyed it. When he was in the mood, he even appreciated strength in others, too.

Perhaps de Santi was the same. In which case maybe letting him test his strength against her determination might buy her the time she wanted. Maybe it would even go towards him changing his mind about handing her over to the authorities.

Whatever, it was clear that remaining unnoticed and slipping beneath the radar the way she normally did wouldn't work with him. In which case, if he was going to notice her, then she couldn't allow him to see her fear, her weakness. And, since she wasn't particularly strong, she'd just have to be determined instead, and if there was one thing she was it was determined.

'Looking at me ferociously won't make me any more likely to tell you,' she said, clutching tighter to her laptop. 'I can hold out against you.'

He tilted his head, his eyes gleaming from beneath surprisingly long, dark lashes. 'I'm sure you can. But I've broken hardened criminals, and I'm sure one small, soft one would be no bother at all.'

Was he mocking her? She couldn't tell. The expression on his brutal, aristocratic face was utterly unreadable, his gaze absolutely opaque.

He frightened her. And yet she realised that, even though she was frightened, the prickling feeling she got between her shoulder blades whenever she thought about her father had gone.

De Santi had dealt with him for now. For now, at least, she was safe.

That thought steadied her.

'You can try,' she said, glaring at him. 'I'm not afraid of you.'

'Yes, you are.' His voice was very deep and very cold, his gaze as merciless as the man himself. 'You're terrified of me.'

It was obvious she didn't like him pointing that out to her. Anger glittered in her eyes, her delicate jaw getting a stubborn cast. She opened her mouth, no doubt to deny it, but he forestalled her.

'Don't lie to me, Miss Armstrong. I can smell a lie a mile off. And I have a feeling you're not very good at it anyway.'

She bit her full bottom lip, small white teeth worrying at it. He found his gaze had fixated on that soft mouth for absolutely no reason that he could see. He liked a woman's mouth, but unless it was doing something interesting to him he wouldn't tend to notice it in the general scheme of things. Certainly not when the owner of said mouth was a criminal he was hoping to bring to justice.

He took his pleasures with women only when it suited him and did not allow himself to be subject to the whims of his body. It was true that he'd been too busy for female company the past month, mopping up the last of the St Etienne family and their drug empire, but that didn't concern him. His body might protest but he rather enjoyed such exercises in self-control. It kept him sharp.

Regardless, even if he'd been desperate he wouldn't have let his interest fall on the woman opposite. He preferred his lovers less…unkempt. And definitely not criminals.

Especially criminals who had the gall to accuse him of using torture. Which he didn't. He would never stoop to using the same tactics his own family had once employed, even if only in centuries past. He didn't need to now, anyway. When it came to information gathering, the team he'd assembled to assist him was the best in the world, and most of the time he didn't even need his quarry to be physically present. He collected the information, handed it to the police, and let them do the rest.

Miss Lucy Armstrong continued to glare at him, while at the same time her knuckles were white as she simultaneously clutched her laptop with one hand, the other gathering and releasing the fabric of her shapeless dress. 'Well?' she demanded in her sweetly husky voice, ignoring what he'd said about her fear. 'Will you give me a week or not?'

'Why should I? I can take your laptop and turn it over to my forensic specialists right now. They can crack any encryption within—'

'No, they can't,' she interrupted flatly. 'Not the encryption I put on the information on the laptop. No one can crack it except me.'

An unaccustomed irritation rippled through him. Being interrupted was not what he was used to and especially not being interrupted by people he was going to turn in.

Most especially when those people were small women who were afraid of him and yet couldn't quite stop themselves from challenging him.

It…intrigued him that she couldn't and spoke of a certain courage. Unless she was stupider than he'd initially suspected. But no, he didn't think she was stupid. A woman who'd escaped a violent crime lord like Michael Armstrong would never be stupid.

'Then you won't mind handing it over and letting my specialists take a look,' he said mildly, deciding to let the interruption go.

'Any attempts to access the data without the passwords will result in all the data being deleted automatically.' She glared owlishly at him from behind her glasses. 'So I guess if you want to risk losing it all, then that's up to you.'

No, definitely not stupid at all.

Vincenzo's irritation deepened, along with the curiosity he'd been trying not to pay any attention to. It stretched out inside him, lazy and subtle, making him think of questions. Such as, how had she managed to escape her father? And why had she come to him now? What made her think he would protect her? If she'd done her research, she must have known he'd simply hand her over to the authorities, surely?

You could give her a week. What would it matter in the long run? You'll turn her in eventually. And in the meantime you can get everything you need to know from her about Armstrong.

It was true, he could. And there were other things he could get from her too. If she was indeed the reason Armstrong had evaded all his traps, perhaps he could use her to entrap others. Because, after all, he had a long list. And hadn't he made the decision to employ hackers in his IT section to make sure their own online security was watertight? Use a criminal to hunt down other criminals... Why not?

He was a patient man. A week was nothing.

Vincenzo studied her carefully, taking his time. He kept his finger tapping on the arm of his chair and saw her attention zero in on it. A useful distraction technique.

She was still hunched in her chair, narrow shoulders collapsing in on themselves like the wings of a bird trying to hide itself beneath its own feathers.

It didn't surprise him. Armstrong was a man much given to

casual cruelty and there had been many rumours about his first wife and her death years ago. Rumours that only made Vincenzo even more determined to bring the man down.

He didn't have any particular sentimentality towards women—he knew that they could be just as ruthless and cruel as men, and he'd had personal experience of this—but he despised physical cruelty. It was the weapon of the weak, in his opinion, and he had no doubt that Michael Armstrong was one of those weak men who needed to use it in order to enforce his power over people.

Had Armstrong used it on his daughter? Was that why she was hunched in her chair trying to make herself small? Was that why she was so afraid of himself?

Why are you thinking about her like this? She's his daughter and a criminal, and now she is a tool you can use.

All very good points.

He moved, sliding his ankle off his knee and leaning forward, elbows on the desk. He watched her reaction as he did so, observing how her eyes went wide and how she held herself very still in her chair, her knuckles whitening even further on her handbag.

Yes, this little brown bird was very afraid. And of him.

Yet, for all that, she watched him very intently, as if he was a large cat stalking her. And, yes, there was fear, but it was clear to him that she also had a stubborn, determined spirit that wouldn't let her give in. An interesting combination.

Why? Since when are you intrigued by the people you bring to justice?

Vincenzo ignored that thought, since he didn't have an answer to it. Instead, he held her fixed hazel gaze with his and said, 'You are enterprising, Miss Armstrong. I'm impressed. Your encryption might hold out against my experts or it might not. But perhaps I'm not in the mood to wait for them to break it. Perhaps I'm in the mood to make a bargain with you instead.'

Her gaze was ferocious. 'What kind of bargain?'

'Your skills are obviously valuable and I could use them, and not only to take your father down. There are plenty of other men and women just like him around. Those who need to be behind bars, and I think you could prove very useful in helping me bring them to justice.'

Those small white teeth worried at her bottom lip. It was very red now and very full, and it had the sweetest curve. A vulnerable, soft mouth. Would it taste as sweet if he took a bite out of it himself?

Why are you thinking about her mouth, fool?

The thought was sharp and bright and shocking. He had no idea why he was thinking about her mouth. None. He shouldn't have even noticed it.

'Why would I want to do that?' she asked bluntly, not noticing his sudden stillness. 'I'll help you with my father and that's all.'

Irritation rippled through him once again, his temper not helped by his own wandering thoughts. 'I'm afraid you do not have a choice.' He kept his voice flat and cold. 'If you want a week before I hand you to the authorities it will be in my custody and you will do anything I ask. That is the price. If you don't want to pay it then I will get my security team to hand you over to the police immediately.'

She bit at her lip, the expression on her face—what he could see of it behind all that hair and those big glasses—turning angry. 'But you won't be able to take down my father if I don't help you.'

'Of course I can take down your father without you.' He made a negligible gesture. 'It would only take longer. Your help would expedite the process, but it's not necessary.'

'Then why bargain with me at all?'

Another good point. She was astute, he'd give her that. Because he really didn't need to bargain with her. He could make her do whatever he wanted, since he was the one with all the power here. But doing so would make him no better than those he brought to justice, and he would never use those kinds of tactics.

'Because, although you are not necessary, you could prove to be useful,' he said, just as blunt as she was. 'And a tool is only useful if it is not broken. I have no wish to break you, Miss Armstrong, believe me.'

'But you want to use me.' There was no anger in her tone, only a kind of…resignation. As if the situation she now found herself in wasn't unfamiliar.

And it wouldn't be. She was as much a tool for him as she was for her father and he was very aware of that fact. Not that it bothered him. Not given what was at stake.

The old crime families of Europe were like a disease, rotting the body from the inside. Corrupting everything. That corruption was inside himself too and he knew it. Knew his own family's history and the stain they'd left behind them over the centuries.

He wasn't exempt from that corruption, but at least he wasn't here to hasten its spread. No, he was a surgeon and he would cut it out completely.

'No, *civetta*,' he said, because a surgeon needed a sharp scalpel, 'I do not want to use you. I *will* use you. If you want your week of freedom, then you must pay for it and that is my price.'

She continued to stare at him, frowning, as if he was a problem she wanted to solve. 'When you say "freedom", what exactly do you mean?' she asked. 'Because you won't be letting me go, I assume.'

'No, I'm afraid not.'

She only nodded, as if that was the answer she'd expected. 'Well, I suppose if I were truly free that would leave me unprotected, which would undermine the whole point of me coming to you in the first place.' The line between her brows seemed etched there, marring her pale skin, and he found himself idly wondering if that skin was as soft as it looked. Whether it would be as soft as her mouth. 'I wouldn't like to be in a cell,' she went on. 'My father kept me in his house in Cornwall with a lot of guards. I could walk in the garden but that was it. It was by the ocean, but the house had no view so I couldn't see it. I could hear it though.' A thread of some emotion he couldn't place crept into her voice. 'I'd like to be able to see the waves.' Her gaze had turned distant, looking through him as if he wasn't there. 'In fact, I don't think I've ever seen the ocean. How ridiculous is that? When we live on an island?'

Slowly, Vincenzo leaned back in his chair, studying her. A strange criminal indeed to escape her father, throwing herself on his non-existent mercy then demanding his protection despite her obvious terror, only to talk with wistfulness about an ocean she'd never seen.

Perhaps it was an act. One could never tell. People of her ilk were liars and used all kinds of emotional tricks to get what they wanted. Already he was thinking odd thoughts about her mouth and about her skin... Thoughts he'd never normally have about a woman like this one. He'd encountered women who'd used seduction as a way to get close to him, either to murder him or manipulate him for other reasons. Women who weren't aware that their techniques wouldn't work on him. He was impossible to manipulate, especially when it came to emotions, because he didn't have any.

A lesson he'd learned the hard way. From his mother. A lesson this woman, this little brown owl, would soon learn too. Also the hard way.

So what are you going to do with her, then?

A good question. She was either exactly what she seemed and relatively harmless apart from the information she carried in her head, or she was far more dangerous than she appeared. Either way he would need to watch her closely.

'Prisoners do not get to determine what cell they prefer,' he said after a moment. 'That is what being a prisoner means.'

The line between her brows was deep, a carved furrow of worry or of concentration. Or maybe both. 'I know what being a prisoner means, believe me. I guess it's too much to ask for a week of a normal life.'

Vincenzo frowned. 'A normal life? Is that what you were expecting when you came to me? That I would simply let you go?'

Her gaze behind her glasses wavered, colour staining her cheeks, softening the drawn look on her face. 'Yes. I was hoping that you would help me...disappear, if I gave you the information you want.'

'Disappear?

'You give me a new identity, help me get to the States or somewhere else, away from Dad. And then I could vanish where no one would ever find me.'

For a second all Vincenzo could do was stare at her, conscious of a certain shock echoing through him. Did she really think he would help her? That she, a known criminal, would put herself in terrible danger simply on the expectation that he would do exactly what she asked? She was either very stupid or very arrogant, or maybe a combination of both.

Then again, as he'd already thought, she wasn't stupid. And the woman huddled in her chair in an ugly dress with her hair in her eyes definitely didn't seem arrogant either.

Perhaps she's telling the truth. Perhaps she genuinely thought you would save her.

A foolish belief. He wasn't in the business of saving people. He was in the business of delivering them to justice. And if she thought she would be different, then she was wrong. Mercy was a luxury he couldn't afford.

'Then I'm afraid you're destined for disappointment,' he said, keeping his voice hard. 'You should have been more thorough with your research, Miss Armstrong. I keep telling you that I am not a merciful man. You should have listened.' He pushed himself out of his chair and strolled around the desk towards the door.

Her eyes had gone very wide and she didn't move, obviously

frozen in place by fear. A gentler man might have felt sorry for her, but he had no gentleness left in him.

He crushed the ghost of that strange emotion he'd suspected was pity. Crushed it flat completely. Then he unlocked his office door and opened it. 'Get Security, Raoul,' he ordered casually, not raising his voice. 'This prisoner needs a cell.'

CHAPTER THREE

LUCY SHIVERED. A cell.

There had been a few times when she hadn't wanted to do what her father had told her, when she'd pushed against the bars imprisoning her, and his response had always been the same. Since she was too valuable for him to kill or maim, he would drag her down to the basement in that house in Cornwall—or get one of his guards to do it—and lock her in one of the tiny rooms there. The room had no windows and when the door closed the darkness was absolute. A crushing weight that stole her breath. She never knew how long he would leave her there, but it always felt like aeons.

She hated the darkness. Hated that room. And without fail, whenever he dragged her out of it, she would always do what he asked. Until eventually she learned to always do what he asked every time.

She'd thought that when she'd escaped her father she'd leave that room behind her for ever. It seemed she was wrong.

Vincenzo de Santi had always been the variable she couldn't predict and yet she should have been able to. She'd ascribed to him a morality that it was clear he didn't have, and in retrospect she didn't even know why she'd thought he would help her in the first place.

He was everything the rumours had said about him. Cold, incorruptible, ruthless. Without a shred of mercy. He stood there staring at her, so tall, so powerful, a certain cold, brutal beauty to him that her stupid brain couldn't help appreciating even as everything inside her felt as if it was collapsing in terror.

You're not brave, not like your mother.

No, that was true. She wasn't. She was made of fear instead and that fear in turn had made her stupid. She'd thought that the knowledge in her head would be worth more to him than her physical presence. More than the weight of her own crimes.

She was wrong.

'Please.' The word was a scraped thread of sound, which was all she could muster up. 'Not a cell.'

Begging now?

Her mother hadn't begged. Her mother had been fearless, stepping between her and her enraged father, taking the blow that had been meant for her.

She could only dream of being that brave, that strong.

The sound of footsteps came and two security guards dressed in black appeared in the doorway. She knew how skilled they were. She'd watched them in the camera feed de Santi had shown her. There was no escape for her. There never had been.

Always, in every way, she was trapped.

Fear had locked all her muscles, her breathing getting faster. They would drag her away, wouldn't they? Drag her into a hole, into the darkness, and she would be trapped there. It was like dying, that darkness. A weight that would crush all the life and the breath out of her…

The guards came towards her and her vision wavered, turning black around the edges. The darkness was coming for her. It would swallow her whole.

She opened her mouth to scream but there was no air in her lungs, no air anywhere, and she was falling, falling into that blackness, and there was no end to it…

'Breathe, *civetta,*' a deep, cold voice ordered in her ear. 'Breathe.'

It was to be obeyed, that voice. It brooked no argument. So she tried, sucking in air, pushing back against the crushing weight on her chest and the darkness pressing in.

A wave of dizziness caught her, making her tremble. She was so cold. She couldn't feel her fingers or her toes.

'Breathe,' the voice ordered again, and so she did.

More dizziness and she was trembling even harder. But something was around her, something strong. Something hot. Holding her. The heat made her feel less cold and she was held very tightly, which seemed to ease the shaking.

A warm scent surrounded her, cedar and sandalwood, oddly comforting, and she could have sworn she could hear the beating of someone's heart. It was strong and steady and slow, and she found herself trying to breathe to match that rhythm. In fact, if she concentrated, it steadied the frantic race of her own heartbeat too.

Gradually the tight pull of her muscles relaxed and the cold feeling in her hands and feet began to ease, the weight on her chest lifting. Everything was still dark, but as her consciousness returned she gradually realised that it was because her eyes were closed.

And then she realised something else: that the thing holding her was a person and the strong bands around her were arms. That the warmth was someone's body. She was lying against someone and it was their heart she could hear beating.

Shock rippled through her.

'Breathe,' the voice reminded, a deep rumble in her ear.

So she breathed and kept on breathing as she became conscious of more, that she was being held by someone very strong and very hot, and that the warmth of their body was helping her to relax, making the panic—and it had definitely been panic— recede.

Strange how the fact of being held made her feel safe, because she definitely did feel safe. And that was an unfamiliar feeling in itself, since it had been a long time since she'd felt safe anywhere. So she held on to it, kept it tight in her grasp, not wanting to move, not even wanting to breathe in case the feeling disappeared.

But she had to breathe and she kept on breathing, and she became aware of where she was. Of what had happened. Of whose arms surrounded her and who it must be holding her so tightly.

Vincenzo de Santi. Who was going to put her in a cell.

Lucy opened her eyes.

She was sitting on a sofa in the same expensive, luxurious office she remembered, in the lap of the same man who'd stared at her so intensely from across that big desk. A man with black eyes and the face of a warrior angel.

His powerful arms were around her and she was leaning against his chest as if it were her favourite pillow. Her glasses were gone and everything was blurry, but she remembered those eyes and that face. They would haunt her dreams.

She must have had a panic attack. How humiliating.

And then she realised that two other men were standing in front of the sofa, dressed in black uniforms. Tall, powerful men… The guards, come to take her away.

Instantly cold fear poured through her veins, her hands clutching on to de Santi's shirt, and she was pressing herself against him, as if he could keep her safe.

You idiot. He's the one who wants to imprison you.

Her fingers were going cold again and she could hear the frantic rush of someone's frightened breathing. Hers.

'Out,' de Santi ordered flatly, then said something else, deep and low in fluid Italian.

The guards instantly turned and left the office, closing the door behind them.

'Keep breathing,' he murmured. 'Relax your muscles.'

Helpless to do anything else, Lucy did what he said, leaning against his very hard chest and cushioned by the expensive wool of his suit. His body was so warm and the beat of his heart was in her ear, a steady, relentless sound. She concentrated on that, since it had worked so well before, and her breathing slowed, her muscles losing their rigidity.

It was strange to be held like this. She couldn't remember the last time anyone had held her. Not since her mother had died, certainly. She'd been around seven then, so…a long time. And definitely not by a man. Were all men this hot? This hard?

You're an idiot. He wants to put you in a cell.

The thought made her stiffen again, his arms tightening in response.

'No,' he said casually and without emphasis. 'Be still.'

And, since those arms gave her no other choice, she did so. Yet, though the panic lost its bite, the fear wouldn't go away. Not now she was fully aware of who held her and where she was. And what he was going to do.

'What happened?' she asked, her voice rusty-sounding. 'Did I faint?'

'Very briefly.'

The low rumble of his voice was oddly comforting, though she had no idea why. 'Why are you holding me?'

'Because you were shaking and you'd gone very cold.' He shifted slightly, the movement of his powerful body beneath her sending a bolt of some strange sensation through her. 'I removed your glasses for safety's sake.'

She blinked, remembering something. 'And my computer?'

'It's on the sofa beside me, along with your handbag.'

A brief silence fell.

Lucy closed her eyes again, suddenly exhausted. She'd been operating on nothing but adrenaline since she'd woken up this morning with her plan in place, and now, the panic attack having burned through all the rest of her reserves, she had nothing left.

She was literally in the arms of her enemy, the prospect of a cell in front of her, and all she wanted to do was sleep.

Pathetic. Do you really want your mother to die for nothing? Pull yourself together.

Lucy gritted her teeth and forced herself to ignore her own weariness.

'Do you have panic attacks often, Miss Armstrong?' he asked after a moment.

'Not usually.' She hadn't had one for weeks, not since she'd stopped resisting her father. But did the nightmares count? Maybe they didn't.

'What is it about a cell that frightens you?'

She hadn't wanted him to know the depth of her fear, but that ship had long since sailed. And perhaps, if he knew, it might make him more sympathetic towards her. Useful, given the fact that she was still hoping to change his mind and have him not hand her over to the police.

'There's a room in the basement of our house in Cornwall. My father locks me in there sometimes when I won't do what I'm told. It's dark. There are no windows.' A shiver coursed through her, making de Santi's arms tighten once more.

'I see,' he said, his tone very neutral. 'And do you not do what you're told often?'

As a child, she'd been fearless and curious, always getting into things she wasn't supposed to, which had made her father angry. Her mother had shielded her from the worst of his rages—until she hadn't been able to shield her any more and Lucy found out just how much her mother had protected her.

'I used to,' she said, because there was no need to get into that. 'Not so much any more.'

'Except for escaping from him.'

'Yes, except for that.' She had relaxed against him fully now, the warmth of his body stealing through her. How could such a cold man be so warm? It didn't make any sense. 'Why are you so hot?' she asked, opening her eyes again. 'Are you sick?'

His face was blurry and she couldn't read it, but she could feel his muscles tighten beneath her as if in surprise. 'No, I'm not sick.' There was a thread of something in his tone, marring the casual sound of it, but she couldn't tell what it was. 'Are you dizzy? Still a little faint?'

'No. I'm okay now, I think.'

Instantly he moved, gathering her gently without a word and shifting her off his lap and onto the sofa. The whole of her left side where she'd been resting against him felt hot, the withdrawal of his arms like a loss, which was very strange and she didn't understand it, not one bit. A wave of sudden vulnerability flooded through her, and she fussed with her dress, hoping he hadn't noticed.

It seemed he hadn't though, because he moved over to the desk, picking something up off it and holding it out to her. Her glasses.

'Thank you,' she murmured awkwardly, taking them and putting them back on.

De Santi was leaning against his desk, his arms folded, his dark gaze fixed on her with unnerving intensity.

Lucy wanted to stand up, not have him loom so threateningly over her, but she wasn't sure if her legs would even support her, so she stayed where she was and lifted her chin instead. 'I suppose you're now going to put me in a cell?'

'I haven't decided,' he said.

An echo of fear shivered through her once again, but she borrowed some of her mother's courage and steeled herself against it, meeting his gaze head-on. 'If it's to be a cell, then you'll have to either drug me or knock me unconscious, because I won't go in there willingly.'

'Clearly.' He continued to stare at her for a couple of moments longer, then he muttered to himself in Italian again, and abruptly reached into the pocket of his suit trousers and brought out a slim, complicated-looking phone. Pushing a button, he raised it to his ear, then began to speak in rapid Italian, his gaze still resting on her.

The feeling of unease widened. What was he going to do

with her now? Would he really drug her or knock her unconscious and put her in a cell?

Then again, he'd obviously had every intention of doing just that before and he hadn't. She'd had her panic attack and, instead of simply picking her up and dumping her in whatever holding facility he'd intended to put her in, he'd held her in his lap instead. Calming her down, soothing her.

Perhaps he isn't as merciless as he told you he was?

Certainly a merciless man wouldn't have held her like that and eased her fear. A merciless man—and she knew all about merciless men—would have dumped her in that cell and left her there, panic attack or not.

Something hard inside her, a knot that had pulled so tight it felt as if she'd never get it undone, relaxed slightly. Perhaps there was hope, then. Perhaps she might change his mind after all. Perhaps she might be able to make good on the promise she'd made to her mother after all.

She swallowed, and smoothed her dress again, keeping her gaze on the green fabric while listening to the fluid lilt of his voice.

Eventually, he stopped speaking and she looked up at him. He slipped his phone back into his pocket, his dark gaze impenetrable. 'You can relax. There will be no cell for you.'

Relief swept through her and it was a good thing she was sitting down, otherwise she would have fallen. 'Oh?' she managed thickly. 'Then where will you keep me?'

'I have a house here in London. You will be going there.' His gaze was as hard and sharp as obsidian. 'It's not a cell, Miss Armstrong, but believe me, it is still a prison.'

She didn't doubt that, not for a second. Yet somehow the knot inside her had become a little less tight. It wasn't freedom, no, but at least it wasn't some dark hole where she would be left for hours on end.

'I didn't think you had any mercy left,' she said, which in retrospect probably wasn't the wisest of things to say to him.

He only looked at her, his expression as neutral as his tone. 'As I said, I don't like my tools broken. And you're no use to me if you're catatonic with fear.'

Lucy swallowed again. Perhaps she was wrong after all. Perhaps the way he'd held her and soothed her had purely been from self-interest.

Why do you care what his reasons are? You're safe. That's the only thing that matters.

It was true. And she didn't care about his reasons. She only wanted to know so she had hope that she might be able to change his mind about handing her over to the police. That hope was still there, especially if he thought of her as useful.

In which case, she would make herself as useful as she possibly could for as long as she possibly could.

'Thank you,' she said.

'Don't thank me yet.' His gaze was very intent. 'You're not going alone.'

Vincenzo took a dim view of people's emotional...difficulties. He'd encountered them many times in his little crusade for justice and they always left him cold. Some people pleaded with him, weeping and going to pieces, while others got angry, throwing punches and shouting curses. Some even did what Miss Lucy Armstrong did, collapsing in fear as their lives unravelled before their eyes.

He was always impervious. He didn't let any of those emotional storms touch him, refusing to be manipulated by tears or curses, or white-faced panic. Much of the time it was all for show anyway, people thinking they could get him to change his mind with a few moving emotional scenes. They were always wrong.

His mother had been the queen of emotional manipulation and he could see through such fakery very easily.

So he wasn't sure what had made him gather Michael Armstrong's daughter up in his arms as her eyes had rolled back into her head and she'd nearly fallen off her chair. It was just the kind of thing that some people tried to get his sympathy or his pity, and so he should have let her fall onto the ground. Or let his security drag her off to the small office bathroom he'd planned on locking her in.

Yet he hadn't. No, he'd darted forward as her glasses had fallen off her nose and she'd started to list to the side, pulling her into his arms and going to sit on the sofa with her in his lap. Holding her tight as she'd shivered and trembled. She'd been so pale, and without her glasses guarding her face he was able to see clearly the scattering of freckles across her small, straight nose. A delicate, vulnerable face, with a decidedly stubborn, pointed chin and that luscious, full mouth. Not beautiful and yet not without charm. Her lashes were long and thick and dark, the same as the untidy mass of hair flowing over his arm. And he'd been surprised by the feel of decidedly feminine curves against him. He could have sworn she'd be very slight and skinny, but she definitely wasn't. No, she was warm and soft. And then when she'd come to and had seen his guards, and had clutched at his shirt, trying to press herself closer against him, as if he could protect her...

His chest had gone oddly tight and he'd sent his security away before he'd even had a chance to think straight.

Why had he done that? Why had he held her so tightly? What on earth was the feeling that had coiled inside him, because he could have sworn he was immune to both pity and sympathy? He should have ignored her and had her dragged away, treating her panic like the award-winning performance it no doubt was...

Yet he didn't think it was a performance. Her panic had been real.

He watched her as the unmarked, nondescript car he'd used to transport them both to his house in one of the quieter parts of Kensington drew up to the kerb. Since assassination attempts were a daily part of his life and since Armstrong would now no doubt be aware of where his daughter was, Vincenzo had sent a decoy limo heading in the direction of the city, while he'd bundled Lucy and himself into another car out the back of the auction house.

There had been no incidents in the short trip and nothing out of the ordinary now as his bodyguards checked the quiet square where his house was situated. He had a few in London and he changed where he stayed with each visit.

So far no one had worked out that this place was his and so it was relatively safe. He still hadn't decided what he was going to do with her though. He had to fly back to Naples in the next couple of days to deal with a few issues with one of the de Santi business subsidiaries, and hadn't expected to be dealing with Michael Armstrong's notorious daughter. Hadn't expected to be giving her a week's reprieve from justice, either.

It interfered with his plans and he didn't like it.

The bodyguards pulled open the door and Lucy got out. He followed, striding past her and up the stairs to the front door. It opened immediately, one of his housekeepers having been alerted to his presence on the drive over.

Lucy was hustled inside and directed to the lavishly appointed sitting room at the front of the house, with the opaque windows that made looking inside very difficult.

His housekeeper had put some refreshments on a small tray— tea and some expensive chocolate chip biscuits—on a table next to one of the armchairs and Vincenzo guided Lucy over to the chair and made her sit down.

She glared crossly at him from underneath her curtain of hair, her hazel eyes looking very green behind the lenses of her glasses.

A strange woman. Almost catatonic with fear one moment then angry the next. Was this another performance for his benefit? Or had her fear been the performance? But no, it couldn't have been. He'd already decided it wasn't, hadn't he?

'Drink the tea,' he ordered. 'And have a biscuit. You could probably do with the sugar.'

'I don't want a biscuit. Or the tea.' She continued to glare at him for no reason that he could see. 'What are you going to do with me?'

He turned away, pacing over to the fireplace and stopping, laying a hand on the marble mantelpiece.

It was a good question. What *was* he going to do with her? He could leave her alone in this house for the next week, which would be the most logical thing, and have his security team get the answers he required from her. And yet...he was strangely reluctant to do so.

He'd told her that he hadn't wanted a broken tool and he hadn't lied. It had been the most likely explanation for his catching her before she'd fallen off the chair and holding her. It certainly wasn't because he felt sorry for her. No, if she was frozen with fear then he wouldn't be able to get any information out of her at all, so he'd had to do something. She was to be the scalpel with which he cut out the corruption that was Michael Armstrong, but one couldn't cut with a broken blade. That blade had to be sharp and whole.

His thoughts scattered then rearranged themselves with their usual orderly precision. If he wanted the information she held in her head, he would need to be careful with her. He would need to be subtle and delicate. His usual methods would break her, which meant he would have to try a different approach.

Leaving her to his security team ran the risk of breaking her and, since that couldn't happen, the most logical thing was to deal with her himself.

Something coiled inside him, a certain sense of...anticipation. He ignored it the way he ignored most of his emotions, since there was absolutely no reason for it. No, handling her personally would be the best option all round and, though he couldn't really afford the time it would take for a more delicate interrogation, he'd make time.

The information she held was valuable. Michael Armstrong was powerful in England and did a lot of work for several Russian families, as well as some for French and Italian families that he was also in the process of dealing with. Taking Armstrong down would be a blow and would effectively end their influence in England.

It would be worth it.

Are you sure that's the only reason you want to deal with her personally?

A sudden memory filled him, of the softness of her in his lap, her hair over his arm, her fingers clutching his shirt. She'd smelled sweetly of apples ripening in the sun, reminding him of summertime in the valley at his family's *palazzo*. Playing as a boy with Gabriella, before his mother had used him and changed everything.

'Mr de Santi,' Lucy said from behind him. 'What are—?'

'Drink your tea,' he interrupted, staring down at the empty fireplace, going over plans in his head. 'I will not have you fainting on me again.'

There was an annoyed silence behind him, then came the clink of a cup on a saucer.

He straightened and turned around.

She was holding the cup in her hand, sipping very pointedly on the tea, still looking highly irritated. A less perceptive man might have thought her fear had vanished, but he could see that it hadn't. Her knuckles had remained quite white and there was a certain darkness to her eyes.

Her father had locked her in a room in a basement with no windows when she wouldn't do what he told her...

Vincenzo felt something inside him shift and tighten. He'd asked her how often she refused to do her father's bidding and she'd said not very often. He could understand why if that panic attack was anything to go by. There were many ways to break a person's spirit, and leaving them alone locked up in the dark would certainly do it.

Except she wasn't quite broken, was she? There were glimmers of defiance and stubbornness in her hazel eyes, and certainly a broken woman would never have got up the gumption to escape her father in the first place.

Brave. He'd give her that at least.

'I'm drinking, see?' She lifted her cup again.

'Good.' He gave her a critical look, noting the colour in her cheeks. Probably she wouldn't faint again, and certainly not if he didn't threaten her with a cell. 'Are you going to give me the information I want?'

'About my father?'

'*Si.*'

Her gaze turned wary. 'I'm not sure. You might hand me over to the authorities if I do.'

A strange restlessness took hold of him and he wasn't sure if it was irritation or something else. 'I told you I would give you a week and I meant it.'

'A week of what?' She peered up at him from beneath her lowered brows, her wealth of dark hair curtaining her face again. 'A week of being in a cell?'

'There will be no cell, I've said so already.'

'But you didn't say what else there will be. I operate best with clear parameters, Mr de Santi.'

It was definitely irritation, he decided. 'Are you trying to bargain with me, *civetta?* Because I should tell you now that you are in no position to do so. You are only out of a cell at my pleasure and I can put you in one at any time.'

She continued to glare at him, but her hand was shaking a little, the tea in her cup rippling in response. And he had the oddest urge to put his own hand around hers to steady her. Or perhaps gather her into his arms again and hold her until she'd stopped shaking. Ridiculous. Where on earth were these urges coming from? He'd thought he'd put his protective instincts behind him a long time ago, especially when it came to women. Women were treacherous—more so than men, as he had good reason to know. His father had been ineffectual and weak, while it had been his mother who was the dangerous one. Small and exquisite and utterly merciless when it came to putting the de Santi name and its poisonous history before everything.

Even before her own son.

'But if you do that, I won't tell you anything,' Lucy pointed out. 'And you want me to tell you things, don't you?'

He gritted his teeth. 'I do not make bargains with prisoners.'

Lucy put her tea down, the saucer clattering on the table as she did so, tea spilling on her hand. She gave a little hiss of pain and he found himself instantly moving over to the table and reaching for one of the napkins on the tray, taking her small hand in his and dabbing the tea away gently.

She tried to pull her fingers from his, but he held on. He shouldn't give in to these urges and he knew it, but the hot liquid had burned her.

Because you are scaring her.

But he scared a lot of people. Why should scaring her feel so different?

'Let me go,' she murmured. 'It's just a little burn.'

He ignored her. Beside the tea and the plate of biscuits was a glass of water with ice in it, so he took one of the ice cubes out of the glass, wrapped the napkin around it and then pressed it gently against the burn on her hand.

'What do you want?' he heard himself ask, even though he'd told himself he wouldn't. That he definitely would enter into no negotiations with her.

Her hand trembled lightly in his grip and then, slowly, steadied.

'What do you mean?' she asked, her voice husky.

'You wanted a week of a normal life, you said. Is that the kind of thing you're talking about?' Her fingers were slender, her skin pale. Her hand looked very small in his. He couldn't think why he was tending to a tiny burn in this way. What was it about her that was making him do this? She wasn't beautiful and she wasn't charming. She didn't flutter her eyelashes and seduce him the way some women did. She didn't weep and she didn't scream. She was only scared. And wary. And guarded. Trying to stay in control even when he had all the power.

'You can't give me a normal life,' she said. 'You're going to hand me over to the authorities.'

He glanced up from her hand. 'You don't think you deserve to face justice for your crimes?'

Colour tinged her cheekbones and her gaze wavered. But he could read her very easily. She was ashamed and he thought that was genuine. Which meant she also thought she was guilty.

Your mother never thought she was guilty.

That was true, she hadn't. Not once. Not even when the police had dragged her away. It was a war, she'd kept telling him. And sometimes in a war there were casualties.

But it wasn't a war. Because if it had been, he'd have felt like a solider and not a murderer.

'No,' Lucy said, a little less certain now. 'I don't think that. I mean, I—'

'You have broken the law, Miss Armstrong. Numerous times.' Her hand in his pulled against his hold, but he didn't let her go, and he didn't look away. 'Do you think you should not have to answer for that?'

He could see her pulse beating very fast at the base of her throat, and as he watched she swallowed. She was radiating fear again and that angered him, though he didn't understand why. Because she had to fear him. She was supposed to.

As if she hasn't spent most her life being scared.

He didn't know if that was the case or why he should care even if it was. She wasn't any different from any other criminal. Her father might have forced her compliance by locking her in a dark basement, but that didn't change the fact that she had committed a crime.

Your mother used the same tactics on you, or had you forgotten?

No, that had been different. This little brown bird had only been locked in a room, fear keeping her in line, while his mother had used a far sharper tool. His mother had used his own love for her against him.

But Lucy didn't do what you did...

'I know I broke the law,' she said quietly. 'I know that. I hid his money for him and I helped him make more, and no I didn't do it legally. And I...' She stopped and pain flickered through her gaze. 'I know what he did with that money. But I was forced into it. I didn't *want* to do it, not any of it.' All the breath went out of her then and her shoulders slumped. 'I guess if that doesn't make a difference to you, then it doesn't. All I wanted was...a taste of what it would be like to be free.' Her voice had got soft, her fingers lax in his. She was staring down at her lap, all the defiance and mulishness leached out of her.

She looked defeated.

It should have satisfied him that he'd managed to break her, should have counted it as a win, and yet he didn't feel satisfied. And this didn't feel like winning.

This felt as if he'd destroyed something fragile and precious, and he didn't understand why. In fact, none of this made any sense. She was a criminal, regardless of whether she'd been forced into it or not, and as far as he was concerned she was guilty. He should have no feeling about her whatsoever. So why he should feel something tight in his chest and an anger in his soul he had no idea.

Perhaps it was only that he was annoyed with himself at his own clumsiness with her. He wasn't supposed to break her after all. He was supposed to be subtle. It wasn't his usual way—he preferred the direct approach, always—but he was going to have to try it at least, that much was clear. He didn't want her so terrified that she was useless to him, and if he carried on the way he was going that was exactly what she would be.

It was time for what the English called the 'softly, softly' approach.

'Give me your other hand,' he said quietly, and when she

did so without protest he laid it over the top of the hand he was holding, keeping the napkin pressed to her skin.

Then he released her and straightened, looking down into her pale face. 'I can give you a week. No, it will not be complete freedom, but I can give you a small taste of it none the less. The price, though, remains the same. All the information you have on your father and your expertise to take down anyone associated with him.' He hesitated then said, 'If you do this, I will put in a good word with the authorities. Perhaps it will help make your sentence lighter.'

Her forehead creased, her gaze still wary. But he could see something glowing in it, something that looked a little like hope.

Poor *civetta*. She shouldn't hope. Hope was merely a drug to ease the pain and it only made everything worse when it ran out.

'Okay,' she said slowly. 'How do I know that you'll keep your word, though? That you won't put me in a cell or hand me over to the authorities the moment I give you anything?'

'You won't know.' He was not in the habit of sugar-coating anything and he didn't now. 'My word shall have to suffice.'

CHAPTER FOUR

LUCY TRIED NOT to be excited, but she couldn't help it as the small private jet touched down in Naples. She'd never left England before, had barely even left Cornwall, and now here she was in an entirely different country. It was almost overwhelming.

De Santi had dealt with customs technicalities with astonishing ease. He'd somehow produced a passport for her, even though she'd never had one, and she'd barely had a chance to look around after disembarking the aircraft before she found herself bundled into a helicopter. Then they were in the air again, flying over the sprawling city of Naples and then over the deep blue water of the ocean.

She couldn't drag her gaze from the sight of it. She didn't know where they were going—de Santi hadn't told her—and she didn't care. All that mattered was the wide blue of the water below her.

Finally, the sea. She'd listened to the waves at night in her bedroom in her Cornwall prison, but the house had no views and so she'd never seen the source of the sounds. Never seen such an expanse of blue.

She didn't know why it hypnotised her but it did.

Liar. You know exactly why you're letting it hypnotise you.

Okay, so, yes, she did. Staring at the sea was infinitely better than being conscious of the man sitting so closely beside her. Tall and powerful and utterly silent. He hadn't said a word the whole trip, at least not to her. He'd spent most of it on the phone talking to other people or looking intently at his laptop. A busy man, was Vincenzo de Santi, with a vast family business to run—since both his parents were now in prison and he had no other siblings, he had to run it alone—and a personal mission to take down as many of the European crime syndicates as he could.

Except somehow he'd found the time to whisk her away from London almost as soon as she'd agreed to pay his price for a week of freedom, and into Italy.

Once he put his mind to it, things certainly got done, she'd give him that, and if this was part of the taste of freedom he was offering her, then she was going to take it.

She wasn't sure what had changed his mind back in England, because it had seemed as if he was hell-bent on handing her to the authorities immediately. And she'd just about given up. She hadn't wanted to mention her mother—that was a private pain she wouldn't reveal to anyone—and so she'd waited for his judgment, feeling her defeat sweep through her.

And then he'd said that he would give her one week. It hadn't been exactly what she'd hoped for, but it was better than nothing. And it might be enough time for her to get him to change his mind about handing her over to the police. Because if he'd changed his mind once, then maybe he could change it again. If she was...persuasive enough.

You will have to be.

The thought was a warning and it made her afraid, so she ignored it. She was very good at ignoring the things that scared her, at seeing only what was right in front of her, and, since the sea was right in front of her now, that was where she looked.

Except she couldn't quite ignore the presence of the man beside her, no matter how hard she tried. His warmth was distracting, as was his intriguing scent. She'd never even thought a man could smell intriguing, but he did. It was disconcerting, too, that she could still feel how he'd held her hand when she'd burned herself on the tea, the heat of his skin on hers and then the cold press of the ice.

She'd been afraid of him then and she still was, yet she was drawn to him as well and she didn't understand how that could be. His strength and his power were both attractive and terrifying, as was the merciless way he looked at her, the cold ruthlessness of him, and yet how tightly he'd held her when she'd panicked.

No, she didn't understand how she could find him so fascinating and yet be so terrified of him at the same time. He was a panther, sunning himself on a rock, and she couldn't help wandering closer, wondering what it would be like to run her hands over his fur...

You're thinking of touching him now?

Lucy stared hard at the ocean. No, she definitely was *not* thinking of touching him. He was her enemy. He didn't care that she hadn't wanted to do any of the things her father had forced her into doing. In his eyes she was guilty and he would hand her over to the police once this week was done.

A creeping sense of cold threatened, only to vanish as the helicopter eventually soared over a big jewel of an island, all green with soaring cliffs and lots of expensive and very grand-looking mansions.

Ten minutes later they were coming in to land on a rolling flat green lawn that seemed to stretch to the edge of the ocean itself, an old, sprawling building constructed out of white stone sitting in the middle of it. There were lots of terraces and balconies, beautifully laid-out formal gardens and winding paths, the sun glittering off the sea beyond.

De Santi got out of the helicopter, ducking his head beneath the lazily turning rotors as he held the door open for her. She slipped out into the cool, salty air, the hot sun providing a delightful contrast. She wanted to just stand there and look around, but de Santi's fingers gripped her elbow and she was being guided along one of the paths and up some stone steps towards the big house.

A few people in uniform met them on a beautiful terrace that overlooked the sea, guards and probably housekeepers, all greeting de Santi in rapid Italian. He issued a few of what sounded like orders and then ushered her through some open double doors and into a large white room with big, deep sofas upholstered in a thick, textured white fabric. The floor was parquet and worn, as if centuries of feet had walked over it, the walls were white, with a few pieces of artwork here and there, decoratively displayed. A few antique pieces of furniture—shelves and a sideboard—also displayed various other artworks as well as being stuffed full of books and other knick-knacks.

The place was cool and quiet, and she could hear the sound of the sea. It might have bothered her, that sound, reminding her of things she didn't want to think about, but it felt different here. The air smelled different, was hotter, drier, and she could see the sea right there in front of her.

'Where are we?' she asked, as de Santi finished speaking with one of the uniformed women.

'Capri,' he said shortly. 'This is Villa de Santi, my family's holiday villa.'

She blinked, staring around the room. 'A holiday villa? This is…pretty amazing.'

'It's built on the remains of a historic Roman palace and has been in my family for generations. My family's actual estate is inland, near Naples, but I thought you would prefer to be near the sea.' He gestured towards the doors. 'You may wander at your leisure around the grounds, and don't worry, you'll be completely safe. My security is excellent.'

As if she'd needed any extra confirmation of his power… He had another house—no, estate—somewhere else on the mainland. But then, her research had confirmed that his resources were vast. An auction house in London was only the tip of the iceberg.

You will never escape him.

It was a strange thing to think when escaping him wasn't what she actually wanted, or at least not right now. She only wanted to change his mind about handing her over to the authorities.

Even though you deserve it?

No, she didn't. That was her fear talking. She ignored the thought. 'But only around the grounds,' she asked, to clarify. 'Not anywhere else?'

His eyes were dark as midnight and just as impenetrable. 'Of course not anywhere else. Your freedom is of a specific kind, *civetta*, and entirely at my pleasure.'

Not that she expected a different kind of answer. And this was already better than the house in Cornwall. Yes, she was still a prisoner, but at least she could see the sea. She could maybe even swim if she was lucky.

'Why do you call me that?' She frowned at him, distracted from swimming for a second. 'What does it mean? Is it "filthy prisoner" in Italian?'

An odd expression flickered over his face. 'No. It's nothing.'

'If it's nothing, then why say it?'

'It means "little owl".' He turned abruptly away. 'We will have a late dinner out on the terrace there. Martina will show you to your room and collect you when it's time to eat.' He was already moving towards the door. 'My staff do not speak English, so do not attempt to use them for any escape plans.'

She wasn't thinking of escape plans. 'Little owl?' she echoed blankly.

But he'd already vanished through the doorway.

How strange. Why would he call her that? Was she particularly owl-like? Perhaps it was an Italian term of disdain?

She had no more time to think of it, however, as one of the

uniformed women bustled in, letting out a stream of musical Italian and gesturing at her.

Lucy followed her as the woman led her through the echoing halls of the house. It was a wonderful place, the ancient walls whitewashed, giving it a light and airy feel. Sometimes the flooring was smooth tiles, sometimes it was parquet, but there were always beautiful artworks on those whitewashed walls and richly coloured rugs on those floors. It was an intoxicating combination of simplicity and richness, the scent of the sea everywhere and the sound of the waves permeating the house. And she felt the hard knot inside her loosening a little further.

Martina showed her to a big room on the next floor, with that warm wood on the floor and those lovely white walls. Gauzy curtains hung over big windows that looked out over the intense blue of the sea, and there was a big, dark oak bedstead covered in white pillows and a white quilt against one wall. Through one door was a blue-tiled bathroom, and through another what looked like a dressing room.

Martina, still talking, disappeared then came back with a length of lustrous red fabric thrown over one arm. She laid it across the bed, gesturing emphatically at Lucy's dress. Lucy frowned then looked down at what she was wearing. 'What? I don't understand.'

Five minutes later it was apparent what Martina wanted, her firm hands briskly divesting Lucy of her handbag and then her dress. Shocked, Lucy could only stand there as Martina draped the red fabric around her shoulders, then tied it around her waist with a long red sash. The housekeeper stepped back, gave Lucy a satisfied look, then, holding Lucy's dress between one thumb and forefinger, as if it were something nasty she'd picked up after her dog, she went through the door and closed it behind her.

Well, that was interesting.

Lucy took a breath, looking down at herself again. It appeared that she was wrapped in the most gorgeous Chinese robe made out of thick, brilliant red silk and embroidered all over with gold dragons.

Clothes hadn't ever interested her, mainly because she had no one to dress for. She'd never cared about her appearance, didn't even think about it. But there was something...cool and delicious about the feeling of the silk against her skin.

Not sure what else to do, she poked around the room, picking various things up and examining them before putting them back down. And when she'd examined everything thoroughly, she went into the bathroom and examined that too.

The shower was vast and, since the journey had been a long one, she decided a shower was in order. Half an hour later, feeling better than she had in the past twenty-four hours, or even longer than that, she towelled herself dry and then considered her dirty underwear. She didn't really want to put it back on, so she didn't, wrapping herself up in the red silk dressing gown again and wandering out into the bedroom.

De Santi had mentioned something about a late dinner, which meant she had a bit of time beforehand, judging from the light outside the window. She stared at the door for a moment, then crossed over to it and gingerly tried the handle, expecting it to be locked.

It turned easily.

A wave of some emotion she couldn't identify washed through her. So she wasn't locked in, the way she was at home. He'd genuinely meant what he said when he'd told her she was free to wander.

Lucy stepped back from the door, the knot inside her almost coming undone. Then she turned and went over to the bed, got onto it and lay back, curling up on the white quilt. She felt tired, and now she knew the door wasn't locked the urge to get out and explore had left her for the moment. She closed her eyes instead, only for a second.

At least, it should have been a second.

When she opened her eyes again the light had changed, long

streaks of twilight painting the white walls in vivid pinks and reds and oranges. She lay there a second, getting her bearings, remembering where she was and what was happening. Then she slipped off the bed.

She felt hungry now and ready to eat, so she went into the bathroom to get her underwear, looking around to see if Martina had brought her dress back. But not only had the dress not been returned, her underwear had gone too.

Lucy frowned, wrapping the silk robe more tightly around her. Annoying. She felt underdressed wearing only a dressing gown with nothing underneath it. There was nothing to be done about it, however, and, left with little choice, she eventually had to venture out of the bedroom wearing only the robe belted tightly at her waist.

The house was quiet and she encountered no one as she retraced the route Martina had led her on earlier, back into the big white lounge and out to the stone terrace again. It was beautiful in the twilight, the white stone glowing, the view framed by ancient olive trees, the table set for dinner.

Lucy stared at the table for a second, her chest feeling a little tight. There were candles and a white tablecloth and pretty wine glasses. It looked special. Not like a table set for a criminal and a prisoner.

Was this his doing? Or his staff? Did they know who she was? Perhaps they thought she was his girlfriend or his lover...

The tightness inside her twisted, making her feel hot. Disturbed, she turned away from the table and went to the edge of the terrace bounded by a low stone parapet. She sat down on it and looked out over the sea, taking in the amazing view.

There were so many boats, yachts with white sails and launches creating wakes, big super-yachts—floating palaces for the rich and famous—and smaller fishing boats. She imagined being on one and heading out to sea towards the setting sun, leaving everything behind to disappear over the edge of the horizon...

Maybe that would be her one day, finally escaping.

You think you really deserve to escape? Your mother didn't, so why should you?

Despite the view and the peace of the twilight, a chill whispered over her skin, curling through her soul.

Then a footstep sounded on the rough stone behind her, and she turned, thankful for the distraction, even though she knew who it was already.

It was him. De Santi. He'd obviously come through the French windows from the lounge area, and now he stopped as he approached the table, his dense black gaze flicking over her.

He'd removed his suit jacket, his white business shirt open at the neck, his sleeves rolled up. His skin was a smooth, dark olive, the muscles beneath it lean and sinewy. He should have looked casual and relaxed, but he didn't. Somehow the open shirt and rolled-up sleeves only served to make him appear even more ruthless, even more intimidating. The warrior angel ready to do battle.

He said nothing as he pulled a chair out and sat down, his movements loose and fluid. The setting sun bathed the almost medieval lines of his aristocratic face in gold, which should have softened him. Again, though, it was as if his presence rejected any attempts to mitigate it and instead the light simply illuminated even more strongly his dark ruthlessness.

He frightened her. Mesmerised her. Compelled her. She didn't know why. Yet again, she couldn't understand how a man could scare her and yet make her want to keep looking at him, as if she'd miss something if she glanced away.

Kathy, her mother, had been afraid of Lucy's father, she knew that much. It hadn't always been that way, Kathy had told her once. He had used to be a good man. But the years had turned him darker and he'd fallen in with bad people, and she had become afraid. Lucy had asked why they couldn't go away and live somewhere else. Her mother had only looked sadly at her and said, 'I love him.' As if that was explanation enough.

Lucy had never understood that. All it told her was if love was staying with someone who hurt you, then that was something very much to be avoided.

Not that love had any place here, with this man.

'Don't be like me,' her mother had said and yet here she was, inexplicably drawn to a dangerous man, and that scared her too.

He leaned back in his chair, his gaze still roving over her in a way that suggested he was hungry and she looked like something good to eat. It brought colour to her cheeks, made a strange, buzzing tension collect in the space between them and then go crackling over her skin like sparks.

Her cheeks were hot, her breathing oddly short, and the sound of her heartbeat echoed in her head. What was happening to her?

You know. You are more like your mother than you thought.

Lucy dragged her gaze away, back to the boats, an unfamiliar fluttering sensation in the pit of her stomach. No, that wasn't true. She didn't know enough about men to have any opinion on whether she was like her mother in that regard. Why would she? The only contact she'd had with them had been to be threatened by them. None of them had ever made her feel like…this.

'Sit at the table,' de Santi ordered coolly. 'Now, if you please.'

He didn't know what was wrong with him. Miss Lucy Armstrong was sitting on the stone parapet, the long twilight falling over her like gold dust, setting fire to the scarlet silk of the dressing gown and making the dragons embroidered on it dance. The colour made her skin look like porcelain and she must have done something to her hair because instead of the mat of dark brown, there was a wealth of glossy chestnut curls falling down her back. The gold in the embroidery of the robe picked up glints of gold in the depths of her hazel eyes and somehow, within the space of a few hours, this small, dull *civetta* had turned into something of a siren.

He couldn't take his eyes off her.

She slipped off the parapet she was sitting on, fumbling with the silk of the dressing gown as a bit caught on the rough stone. One side slipped a little off one shoulder, revealing a quantity of pale skin, and it was clear she wasn't aware of it because she didn't put the material back in place. Instead, she tied the belt tighter and came over to the table, pulling out the chair opposite him and sitting down. The movement made the fabric that should have covered her shoulder slip further down her arm, making it very apparent she was not wearing a bra.

Perhaps that was understandable. She had no clothing except the ghastly dress she'd been wearing when she'd appeared in his office, and there had been no time for her to get any more. At least some of the afternoon he'd spent in his office had involved ordering her various items via one of his assistants. The villa didn't contain much in the way of female clothing or anything else, since he never brought any lovers here, or, indeed, anyone.

He was still puzzled as to why he'd brought her here. He'd told himself that it was because, although the de Santi *palazzo*, deep in the Campania countryside, was a much better place for a prisoner, being, as it was, built along the lines of a medieval *castello* rather than a palace and thus very secure, it was also a place that she might find frightening with its ancient walls and dark rooms. This villa was brighter, airier, and being on the sea with cliffs on one side made it easily defensible, not to mention the fact that Capri was an island and therefore it was less likely that she would escape.

All very good reasons and justifications for bringing her here, where he never brought anyone. And yet all he could think about was her voice telling him that she could hear the waves from her house in Cornwall and yet had never seen the sea.

You are getting soft, perhaps? Tired of the crusade?

No, of course not. And he would never tire. He needed her unafraid of him and willing to share the information in her head, that was all. And all of this was in aid of lulling those fears, making her relax, and who knew? Perhaps he could even get her to trust him?

She was staring down at her plate, her hands fussing with the silk of her robe as if she didn't know what to do with either them or herself. He made her uncomfortable, that much was clear. She'd blushed before, when he'd looked at her, and had glanced away, as if she'd felt the sudden tension between them too.

There is tension now?

Vincenzo gritted his teeth, trying to force the thought from his head as Martina and a couple of other staff members bustled over bearing quantities of food. Olives and bread and cheeses. Plates of fresh pasta with the excellent oil that she made from the olives in the gardens, and a tomato sauce to go with it. And a bottle of a very good red wine from the de Santi vineyards themselves.

The consummate professional, Martina arranged the food, poured the wine, then left, taking her staff with her.

Silence fell and he still couldn't take his gaze from her pale, uncovered shoulder.

Lucy reached for a piece of the fresh bread, but his patience was thinning, and when the robe slipped even more it ran out completely. He shoved back his chair and rose to his feet.

She looked up at him, her eyes wide and startled behind her glasses, and he knew he shouldn't do this, but he couldn't stop himself. He moved unhurriedly around the table to where she sat and paused beside her chair. Then gently he lifted the slipping fabric of the robe up and over her shoulder, covering her. A better man wouldn't have touched her, but he'd always known, deep down, that he wasn't a better man, so he allowed the backs of his fingers to brush over her bare skin. It was warm and even softer than the silk that covered it.

Her eyes went even wider, that vulnerable mouth of hers opening slightly as her breath caught. Colour flooded her cheeks, making her freckles turn pink, though he was more interested in the row of goosebumps that rose as he touched her.

It would be so easy to push that silk away instead of lifting it up, to uncover instead of conceal. Examine the curves he'd felt when she'd rested in his arms in his office, caress them, see if they were as satiny as the curve of her shoulder.

She was staring at him as if she'd never seen anything like him before in all her life, and though there was fear in her eyes there was also something else. Something that he'd seen in the eyes of other women who'd stared at him just like this one.

She was attracted to him, it was clear.

Perhaps you could use that to your advantage?

The thought streaked through his brain, bright and clear as a comet at midnight, but he dismissed it almost as soon as it had occurred to him. Those were his mother's tactics and he would never stoop to using those. Just as he would never indulge himself with her. Seduction was not and would never be one of his weapons. He was better than that. He had to be.

He turned away, ignoring the tight feeling in his body as he headed back to his chair. She was still staring at him, a bewildered look on her face.

It occurred to him, as he sat, that the slipping of her robe might have been purposeful, but one look at her expression told him it hadn't. She seemed to have no guile at all, which was definitely a rarity in a criminal.

'Why did you do that?' she asked, her voice slightly husky.

He ignored her. 'I have ordered clothing for you. It should arrive tomorrow. In the meantime you can continue to wear that robe.'

She frowned and he thought she might push, since he hadn't answered her question, but she didn't. Instead, she reached for the bread she'd been going to have before he'd interrupted her.

So, she was uncertain about this...chemistry between them, was she? It certainly seemed that way. She'd had no trouble speaking about other subjects, but she didn't want to push him on this. Interesting. Perhaps she was inexperienced. He wouldn't be surprised, given how her father had kept her prisoner.

'Why are you doing this?' she asked after a moment, small

fingers tearing apart the piece of bread. 'With the candles and the food. This beautiful house.'

'What do you mean?' He reached for his wine and picked up the glass, swirling the liquid around inside it.

That deep crease between her brows was back. 'I'm a prisoner. A criminal. Yet there are candles on the table.'

'I did tell you that you wouldn't have a cell.' He leaned back in his chair, sipping his wine, letting the flavour warm him, since nothing else did much these days; justice was a cold mistress. 'The candles were Martina's idea.' They were not. They were his. He'd been concerned about the incipient darkness and wanted her to have some light, because he didn't want a repeat of her panic attack, that was all. But he didn't want to tell her that. It felt like giving away an advantage. 'You don't like them?'

'Oh, no, they're lovely. I just...' She stopped. Then lifted a shoulder as if the subject was one she'd lost interest in, and began layering some of the dip onto her bread with a knife. 'This smells very good,' she offered after a moment. 'I'm quite hungry.'

'That is obvious,' he observed dryly as she ate the piece of bread with small, precise bites then proceeded to get herself another. 'Are you ready to give me some information yet?'

She ate the other piece of bread then picked up her wine glass and took a sip. 'Is that why there are candles and nice food? You're hoping to bribe me into giving you what you want early?'

Irritation gathered inside him. It was true. He had promised a week. 'No,' he said shortly, even though he had a suspicion that was a lie as well. 'The candles and food are an added bonus. I do not bribe anyone, nor do I manipulate. You will give me what I want because I ask for it. Because we have made a bargain.'

She sipped again at her wine, frowning at him from behind the thick lenses of her glasses. 'Why is taking down my father so important to you? Did he do something to someone you know?'

'He's a criminal who has hurt others. He's a murderer, *civetta*, in case you didn't know. That's all the reason I need.'

An expression he couldn't read flickered over her face. 'Oh, I know what he is, believe me. But is it him in particular? Or merely the fact that he's a criminal?' She regarded him curiously. 'Why don't you let the police deal with it?'

Was she really expecting him to tell her his reasons? To justify himself to someone like her? She'd be waiting a long time in that case, because he did not have to explain himself to anyone. Rumours followed him, naturally enough, but he didn't concern himself with them. The facts were his own and he gave them to no one.

No one else, for example, needed to know how his mother had seduced his father into the de Santi family 'business'. Or how she'd manipulated Vincenzo himself into doing the same thing, using his love for her against him.

He'd been her creature through and through. Her perfect boy, her heir. Her tool. There was a war, she'd told him, and their family had enemies that they had to defend themselves against. All lies. Lies he'd been too busy basking in her attention to see. Too busy being the chosen de Santi prince to care.

You knew. Deep down, somewhere inside, you always knew.

Some nights he lay awake in the dark, going over and over the things she'd told him to do, searching for signs he'd somehow missed. Signs he perhaps should have noticed—a cruel glint in her eye or a betraying curl to her lip. Something that would have told him that what she'd said about wars and soldiers and fighting were lies.

But there had been nothing. His mother had spent years perfecting her lies and he'd been sucked in completely. It was an evil he could never be free of and so all he could do was mitigate the damage by pursuing justice relentlessly.

No, he couldn't tell her that.

'I do let the police deal with it.' He kept his voice level and without emphasis. 'I give them the evidence they need, and they do the rest.'

'But isn't gathering the evidence their job?'

Annoyance gripped him. He didn't want her questioning him. 'They miss things. And they do not have the resources or the knowledge that I do. In some instances the police are corrupted by the very people they're trying to bring to justice.'

'You don't trust them, then?'

'No one can be trusted.'

'No one except you?'

Vincenzo realised he was holding his glass far too tightly and that if he held it any tighter the slender stem would snap. With a conscious effort he relaxed his fingers, staring across the table at the woman opposite.

There was nothing sly or knowing in her gaze, only curiosity. She wasn't goading him, it seemed; she genuinely wanted to know and obviously hadn't picked up on his irritation.

'You're not very polite, are you?' he observed casually, turning the conversation back on her.

Her eyes widened as if the statement had surprised her. 'Aren't I? Is asking questions wrong?'

'You are my prisoner, *civetta*. And a prisoner does not interrogate her captor.'

Colour tinged her cheekbones, giving her face a rosy flush. She really was quite pretty, now he thought about it. Which was not at all helpful.

'No, I suppose not.' She took another piece of bread. 'I just don't get to talk to people very often.'

'Why not?' he asked, since what was clearly sauce for the gander could also be sauce for the goose.

She looked down at the piece of bread in her hands, tearing it once again into tiny pieces. And stayed silent. Her shoulders had hunched, her glossy hair a curtain over her face. The chestnut colour gleamed almost auburn in the fading twilight.

He was trespassing on painful subjects, it was clear, and no wonder. If her father had locked her in a dark basement, then what else had he done? But then, Vincenzo knew already. There were rumours about her, as there were about him; her father kept her well-guarded, deep in the English countryside. No, not just well-guarded. Her father had kept her prisoner.

The strange sensation in his chest that he'd felt earlier when he'd held her trembling body in his arms shifted again. A constriction.

He didn't like it and he knew he should let the subject alone, move on, even get up from the table and leave her here to finish her meal alone. Yet he didn't. Something compelled him to remain in his chair and to look at her all wrapped up in red silk, with her dark hair everywhere. Small and vulnerable and very, very alone.

'He kept you prisoner,' Vincenzo said, voicing his thoughts aloud to see her reaction. 'Didn't he?'

Her fingers shredded the bread to crumbs. 'I was too valuable to be let out, or at least that was what he told me. It was for my own protection. There were a lot of people who wanted to use me or kill me, and so I was safer in the house with the guards.'

The sensation shifted again, getting tighter.

'So you had no one at all you talked to? No friends? No family?'

'No. I had some online friends he didn't know about, but no one in real life. The only people I could speak with were him and my guards. But I didn't like speaking to the guards because they were...' She stopped.

But he could fill in the blanks. 'They frightened you?'

She lifted a shoulder, clearly not wanting to admit it.

'How long have you been a prisoner?' he asked, even though he shouldn't want to know, that it didn't matter. That being a prisoner was no less than what she deserved.

'Since I was seven.' Her hands rested beside her plate, still and tense.

'And how old are you now?'

'Twenty-two.'

Fifteen years she'd been her father's prisoner. Fifteen years. He was aware that another sensation had joined the tightness in his chest, something hot that felt like anger, though it couldn't have been. Because she was a criminal and needed to face justice, and it seemed that she'd served fifteen years of equivalent jail time already. A just sentence. Especially when she would have been committing even more crimes in that time.

She has been alone all her life. Like you have been alone.

No, it was not the same. And he wasn't alone. He had his staff and business colleagues, and anyway, he didn't need anyone. The path he'd chosen for himself was one he could only walk himself. No one else could walk beside him and he'd known that when he'd chosen it.

You are serving a sentence just like her.

He ignored that thought. His own guilt had nothing to do with this and he didn't need that contributing to the already tangled knot of emotions inside him. Emotions that he would have told himself even a day ago he no longer felt.

He was a fool. He shouldn't be sitting here talking to her about her life. He had better things to be doing with his time.

Vincenzo put his glass down on the table with a click. 'None of that matters, of course. You are guilty, Miss Armstrong. And at the end of the week you will pay for your crimes.'

CHAPTER FIVE

LUCY COULD HEAR the certainty in his deep, cool voice and it sent yet more chills through her. Clearly he'd finished making conversation. And he had been making conversation, that was obvious.

She shouldn't have asked him all those questions. She'd only been…curious about him and why this justice crusade he was on was so important, and she shouldn't have been. Curiosity had always got her into trouble and she shouldn't indulge it.

Sadly, he hadn't given her reasons for his crusade, though that was understandable. As he'd said, a prisoner didn't interrogate her captor.

And he's right that you should pay. You are *guilty.*

A shiver chased over her skin. If she was guilty of anything, it was of not standing up to her father. Of cowardice. Except cowardice didn't deserve a jail term.

However, he certainly seemed to think it did. She had to change his mind somehow, convince him to let her go.

Incorruptible, they said of him, but, as her father liked to remind her, every man had his price.

What was Vincenzo de Santi's?

Slowly she raised her head and looked at him, her heart thudding strangely in her chest as she met his inky gaze.

He was leaning back in his chair, the casual arrogance he carried around with him everywhere he went even more palpable. The menace that gathered like a cloak at his back even stronger. He was dark and he was dangerous and yes, she was frightened.

But she was always frightened. Of everything. She'd been frightened since she'd been seven years old and her mother had died right in front of her eyes.

Yet Kathy hadn't let fear of her husband stop her from protecting her daughter. She'd been brave; why couldn't Lucy follow her example?

You have other weapons at your disposal, remember?

She frowned, trying to puzzle the thought out, because what other weapon could there be?

He is a man and you are a woman...

A flash of heat seared her skin, passing over her so fast she barely had time to draw a breath before she could feel burning in her cheeks. Burning everywhere.

Because he *was* a man and the way he'd looked at her earlier, unable to tear his gaze from her bare shoulder, had been very much the way a man a looked at a woman. He'd been...hungry...

The heat deepened. She'd never thought of having a lover, had never liked the idea of getting that close to a man, not after what her father had done to her mother.

She had never regretted her decision. She didn't think of the future beyond her mother's promise. Have a life, Kathy had told her, but Lucy didn't let herself think about what that life would contain, because it was only the escape that mattered.

But if she *had* thought about it, a man wouldn't have featured anywhere. Yet a part of her now wondered if this would have been easier if she'd managed to find herself a lover.

Not that her father had given her any opportunity to find one, but still. Maybe if she had she might know what to do, how to use de Santi's definite hunger to her advantage.

Because she could, couldn't she? This could be a way for

her to take control, to get some power for herself. She could offer herself in return for her freedom. Some women did that, didn't they?

Of course, he could just take what he wanted from her whether she let him or not, but it was unlikely that he'd force himself on her physically the way some men did. Surely a man who'd held her in his arms while she'd been paralyzed with fear, who'd tended to her burn, wouldn't be physically violent, not the way her father had been. De Santi was a much more controlled man.

Her heartbeat had speeded up, her breathing becoming unsteady. He watched her as if he could read every thought in her head and knew exactly what she was planning, his eyes gleaming obsidian black in the night.

Was she really contemplating using her sexuality to get what she wanted? Hoping that she could earn her freedom that way? Because what did she know of seduction? Nothing. She was a virgin in every way there was, while he was a man of no doubt infinite experience. Plus, she was a terrible liar and an even worse actress. She wouldn't be able to pretend something she didn't feel.

Are you sure you don't feel it?

Her heart beat harder, fear like a fist slowly closing inside her. Yet…not only fear. Or maybe it was a different kind of fear, because this type didn't feel bad. No, it felt…like a fine electrical current, sparking over her skin, sizzling wherever it touched.

She wasn't a seductress. She didn't know how to do this with any subtlety or grace. Direct was the only approach she knew. So she took another sip of wine—it was more of a gulp really—and put down her glass. Then she made herself hold his dark gaze and put one hand on the knot of her sash. 'Are you sure I can't get you to change your mind? Perhaps there's something I can give you that might help.'

Then she pulled the sash and let her robe fall open.

The last rays of the sun had gone, leaving only a deepening

purple darkness that crept over everything. The candles flickered and danced, catching the gleam of his ink-black eyes as he stared at her. A breeze moved over her skin, making goosebumps rise on the thin strip of flesh she'd bared. Though that could have been the heat of his gaze.

She didn't look away, conscious that it wasn't only fear inside her now, but something more complicated than that. Like a delicate fabric shot through with threads of silver and gold, her fear had other things woven through it, emotions she'd barely felt before. A breathless excitement. The tight coil of anticipation. A nagging ache right down low inside her, between her thighs.

'What are you doing, *civetta?*' The question sounded idle, as if she'd done something mildly curious that he was puzzled about. But there was nothing idle about the tension that gathered around his powerful form. He was very still, the panther about to pounce.

Her pulse was loud in her ears and she wasn't sure if this was a good idea, but she'd taken this step and there was nothing to do but go on with it.

'Isn't it obvious? I undid my robe.'

'I can see that. Are you hot, perhaps?'

Had he misunderstood her? Were her seduction skills that bad? Or was he deliberately misreading the situation? Probably deliberately misreading it, surely?

'I'm not hot. I would very much like not to be handed over to the police at the end of the week and I thought that perhaps I could...change your mind.'

She wanted to cover herself, conscious of how the flickering candlelight was illuminating the bare curve of one breast. It wasn't the same as being wholly naked, but she'd never even been partially naked in front of anyone, let alone a man she was afraid of. A man she'd only known a matter of hours. A stranger.

It made her feel very vulnerable. But she was tired of feeling alone and powerless. Tired of feeling afraid all the time and so she didn't look away. He might be frightening, yet she refused to give in to her fear.

His face remained unreadable, his eyes glittering. 'Are you trying to manipulate me with sex, Miss Armstrong? Because I should warn you now, I don't respond well to it.'

She shivered slightly at the chill in the words. Clearly she was on dangerous ground. 'I...didn't intend it that way, no.'

'Then what did you intend? Do you think I'm a man who would be swayed by such things?'

The urge to cover herself returned, stronger this time as his gaze slid slowly down her body, dipping to where her robe opened. But she didn't move. She had the distinct impression that he was not...unaffected.

'I don't know,' she said, her voice hoarse. 'Are you?'

He lifted his gaze to hers again, unhurried. 'No. I am not. Especially when the woman concerned is afraid of me and doesn't want me.'

A little shock went through her. Did she want him? She'd never wanted anyone before, so how would she know? Was it possible to want someone you were afraid of?

But it's not just fear that you feel for him.

The shock deepened as she stared at him in the darkness, the light from the candles flickering over his strong features, touching on the harsh planes and angles of his face, shadowing the deeper darkness of his eyes and the hollow of his throat...

She wanted to tell him that she didn't think it was only fear that she felt for him, but her hesitation must have given her away, because he moved abruptly, shoving back his chair with some force. He didn't say anything, merely gave her one last, fierce look that she couldn't interpret, then turned and left her sitting there in the dark, with her robe open and the shock getting deeper and wider inside her.

Vincenzo didn't know what to do. He was furious, both with himself for wanting what he shouldn't, and with Miss Lucy

Armstrong for offering something he couldn't help wanting and in such a way as to ensure he could never take it.

Not only was she a criminal whose crimes had hurt people, but she'd also used her body as a bargaining chip. She'd said that she hadn't meant it that way, yet he felt manipulated all the same.

'Ask Gabriella out, Vincenzo,' his mother had told him all those years ago. *'Go to the cinema and have some dessert afterwards. Get her to tell you what her father's movements are, especially whether he's planning on returning home after the play on Friday night or whether he's going out. And if he's going out, we need to know where.'*

He'd been older then, eighteen, and starting to suspect that his beloved mother's casual requests were never as casual as they seemed, and so of course he asked why this was necessary. Why he couldn't just enjoy a date with his childhood friend and whom he was beginning to have feelings for.

'Oh, it's just some family business, my handsome boy. Nothing to be concerned about. I like to keep tabs on people. You know that.'

And she'd given him the most radiant smile, and he'd forgotten his doubts and suspicions. All he'd wanted was to make his mother happy.

Of course it was just business. Of course it was nothing to be concerned about.

So he'd taken Gabriella out and casually asked her about her father, then later relayed the information to his mother. And two days later, Gabriella's father had died in a hit. No one knew which family had been responsible, but Vincenzo had known. And so had Gabriella.

She'd realised Vincenzo had betrayed her. That he was the one who'd got her beloved father killed and that he'd made her complicit in it too. That the downfall of her own family was her fault, and all because a childhood friend had asked her a few seemingly simple questions.

He'd never forgotten the sound of Gabriella's devastated voice ringing in his ears as she'd called him the next day, confronting him with what he'd done, full of fury and grief. Nothing he could say would have made it better, because he knew what he'd done just as she had.

Afterwards, he'd gone to his mother as the shock of the assassination of a major player echoed through the crime families of Europe. She'd merely shrugged her shoulders.

'As I told you, Vincenzo. It's just business. So I would get used to it if I were you.'

She'd given him another of those radiant smiles.

'If you want to remain part of this family, that is, which I'm sure you do. You've already done so much for us as it is...'

But he knew he would never get used to it, just as he knew what his mother had issued with that lovely smile was a threat. She'd never done that before, but he understood what it was all the same. A reminder of his own actions, that he wasn't innocent and never would be, and that what she gave she could also take away.

It was in that moment that he'd realised what he was to her: not a son but a tool to build her empire. She'd never loved him. He'd never been her handsome boy. He'd been spoiled and pampered and paid attention to, but only so she could turn him into her creature. The way his father had always been her creature.

So that night he'd pretended to be her loving son, her yesman, just as he always had. Then he'd gathered what information he could about her activities and sent it to the police.

Two days later she and his father had been arrested, justice served.

But he would never again let himself be used the way his mother had used him. Never let his own feelings blind him to the truth. He would always listen to his conscience and never let his emotions sway him.

He would always do what was right, and sleeping with the little *civetta* because she offered, and because he wanted her, was wrong.

And he did want her. And he was furious about it.

He kept away from her the following day, to give her some distance and to give his recalcitrant body some time to rethink its choices. There were matters that needed his attention anyway. Her father was trying to contact him, no doubt to offer terms for her return, and Vincenzo was almost tempted to see what the man would say, but then, he knew anyway. Armstrong only used either bribery or threats, neither of which would work on Vincenzo. He couldn't take his daughter by force, either, since he didn't have the resources to touch her on Capri, not without getting allies at least, and that would take time.

Regardless, Vincenzo could afford to wait. He'd let Armstrong suffer for the next week, or for however long it took Lucy to give him the information he wanted.

So he closeted himself in his office in the villa, dealing with the thousand and one things he had to deal with, while his brain kept replaying the memory of her sitting in the dusk with her robe half-open, the shadowed curves of her body a temptation he hadn't envisaged. The rounded shape of one breast—fuller than he'd expected, given how small she was—and the graceful arc of one hip. Her skin had been such a pretty pink, highlighted by the red silk she wore, and his desire had risen, thick and hot. Shocking in its intensity.

He wouldn't have taken her even if she had wanted him, but he knew that she didn't. Her eyes behind the shelter of her glasses had been very wary, the fear glittering greenly in their depths.

It had angered him, that fear. His desire angered him. Her offer had angered him.

Everything had angered him and so he'd pushed himself to his feet and left before he did something he regretted, such as reaching for her and dragging her across the table and burying that anger between her thighs.

Yet even immersing himself in business didn't help. He felt restless and unable to concentrate, her presence an itch he couldn't scratch, and he was further annoyed that he had to wait until the week had ended before he'd get the information he needed to take down her father.

He would have gone back to the de Santi estate himself and left her here if he could have. But he couldn't. Even though his security was impregnable, he didn't want to leave anything to chance. He had to be here to keep an eye on her.

She might try to manipulate him again, of course, but if she was hoping that he'd change his mind about her she was mistaken. He would not be changing his mind. She needed to answer for her crimes so justice would be served.

The thought hardened his resolve, though it did nothing for the restlessness that coiled through him as the day progressed into night. He stayed in his office till midnight, and only then did he leave, stalking back to his bedroom in search of sleep.

He didn't find it, however, and after several hours of lying there, staring at the ceiling, he admitted defeat and slid out of bed, pulling on some jeans and prowling downstairs to the salon that led out onto the big terrace.

It felt hot and airless, so he went to the double doors and pushed them open, allowing the salt-soaked night air and moonlight to pour in. He stood in the doorway a minute and took a deep breath, trying to find his usual clarity of purpose, the bone-deep knowledge that what he was doing was right and necessary.

He couldn't allow himself to be distracted from it by an inconvenient attraction to the worst possible woman. He wouldn't. He must keep on with his crusade, right the wrongs his family had perpetrated over the centuries, that his mother had carried into this century too. It would end with him, that was certain.

Behind him came the sound of a soft footstep and a whisper of an indrawn breath, and he was turning, instantly on his guard. He normally had a weapon with him, but since the villa was well-protected he hadn't bothered with one tonight.

Not that he needed one.

A small figure stood in the darkness near the door to the

hall. There was enough moonlight for him to see golden drag-ons gleaming on red silk and the gloss of dark curls, of light reflected off the round discs of her glasses. The sweet scent of apples reached him and he felt himself go still, his entire body tightening in anticipation.

You're getting ahead of yourself. She didn't want you, re-member?

He remembered. She'd been made of fear, not desire.

'I'm sorry,' she murmured in her husky voice. 'I didn't know you were here. I'll go if you—'

'What are you doing up, *civetta*?' He shouldn't ask. He should leave her the way he'd left her the night before. Yet he didn't move.

'I…couldn't sleep.'

'Why not?'

'I don't know.' She shifted on her feet, silk rustling, sound-ing uncertain and nervous. 'I was just…restless.'

As he was restless.

Perhaps it's for the same reason?

Perhaps. But again, last night, he hadn't seen desire in her when she'd opened her robe. Only uneasiness and nerves.

You could be wrong.

A thread of heat wound its way through him and he found himself wanting to see her face, see what expression was in her hazel eyes.

'Come here.' He had to put some effort into not making it sound like an order, but he managed it. Part of him wanted to know if she would come if it wasn't a command. If she would come because she wanted to.

She hesitated, but only for a moment, and then she came slowly towards him, the moonlight moving over glorious red silk, dark curls, and pale skin.

He could see her face now as she stopped a few feet from him, laid bare in the light coming from behind his back. The moon had bleached all the colour from her cheeks, turning her eyes very dark. With the lenses of her glasses reflecting the light, she looked even more owlish than she normally did.

The night before when he'd told her that she didn't want him she hadn't denied it. She'd simply looked at him as if wanting him hadn't entered her head, even though she'd been fully prepared to offer him sex. And he couldn't lie to himself. The fact that she hadn't wanted him had angered him too.

'Yes?' The word was tentative, her gaze full of familiar wariness.

'Perhaps you can't sleep for the same reason I can't,' he said.

'I...' She stopped, and her hands moved nervously to the sash of her robe, touching it before falling away again. 'What reason would that be?'

He might have thought she was deliberately misunderstanding him if he hadn't known already that she had no guile whatsoever. But, as he was learning, she wasn't like his mother; her response had the ring of truth to it. She genuinely didn't know. Which meant that she had no sexual thoughts about him at all, or she was so desperately inexperienced she didn't recognise them.

Does it matter? You're not going to take her anyway.

It didn't matter. And of course he wasn't.

'Were you thinking of me?' he asked, not moving, not taking his gaze from hers.

Even in the moonlight he saw the flush rise in her cheeks.

'Yes,' she admitted hesitantly.

The confession hit him like a jolt of electricity, unexpected and raw as a lightning strike, making his hands curl into fists at his sides.

'Why?' This time he couldn't make it sound like anything less than a demand.

'I don't know. I can't work it out. I'm...afraid of you. And yet I can't stop thinking about you.' The blush in her cheeks got even deeper. 'That was too honest, wasn't it?'

But that was what she was, wasn't it? Too honest. And in ways he was only now beginning to understand. Honesty had been so rare in his life, he barely recognised it. Yet there was more to her than simple honesty. She was also wary and guarded, as if she didn't know what parts of herself she should be protecting.

He wasn't sure why that was, but one thing he did know. He didn't want her to be afraid of him. Thinking of him, yes. Scared, no.

He held her gaze. 'Honesty is rare these days and it is precious. Never apologise for it.'

She blinked, then her gaze dropped from his, down to his chest, which was bare, since he hadn't bothered with a shirt. And stayed there a second before she looked away, nervously fiddling with the knot of her sash.

She wasn't a seductress, he knew that already, and he knew, too, with sudden insight, that she would never have offered him what she had if she hadn't on some level been attracted to him. It simply wouldn't have occurred to her.

But she was attracted to him. Her problem was that she didn't know what it was, because she had no experience. She had no experience of anything at all.

'And are you afraid now?' He searched her vulnerable face. 'Afraid of me?'

Her fingers pulled at her sash. 'Yes.' She said the word tentatively, as if she wasn't sure whether she should reveal it to him or not.

That wasn't what he wanted, not here, not now. She'd been afraid for a long time and right now he didn't want her to be. Just as he didn't want to be only one more man who scared her.

Vincenzo didn't stop to question himself. He merely reached out and took one of her nervous hands in his and slowly drew it towards him. She tensed, looking up at him, her eyes widening. But she didn't pull away, allowing him to place that small hand palm down on his bare chest. Then he put his own over the top of it, holding it there.

The hiss of her indrawn breath echoed in the still darkness, her touch on his skin as warm as sunshine resting on him. Her eyes were wide, that soft, vulnerable mouth open.

'And are you afraid now?' he asked quietly.

CHAPTER SIX

LUCY WANTED TO tell him that she wasn't afraid. But she was. She was terrified.

Of the smooth, oiled silk of his skin. Of the heat of his body. Of all the hard muscle she could see clearly etched in sharp, carved lines all over his torso. Of the strength and power that hummed through him like electricity through a high-tension wire.

His eyes were the night itself beyond the terrace and his face was all brutal beauty and ferocity, a combination that mesmerised her.

She'd told the truth. She'd come downstairs, restless and unable to sleep, because she'd been thinking of him. She'd been thinking of him all day and she didn't know how to stop.

The words he'd said to her the night before kept revolving in her head, taking up space. Making her angry that he would dare to tell her what her own emotions were and yet also making her examine those emotions. Examine the fear that lived inside her and had done so ever since her mother had died.

Yes, she was afraid of him, but it was such a complex fear. And she'd never wanted anyone before, had never thought about physical hunger that wasn't for food. Had never felt drawn to anyone at the same time as she was afraid of them. It made her think of her mother and how afraid she'd been of Lucy's father. Yet she'd stayed with him all the same.

Love, that had been the issue, though, Lucy was sure.

And she didn't love Vincenzo.

The whole day she'd done her best to do her usual thing, which was to pay attention only to the moment as she'd explored the villa, to never think about anything else. Yet it gradually became clear to her as the day went on that she wasn't just exploring the villa. She was also looking for him. Wanting to see him, talk to him. Ask him how he knew that she didn't want him, because she wasn't sure that was the case.

She didn't think it was the case now as he held her hand to his powerful chest, the inky black of his gaze holding hers. She wanted... She didn't know what she wanted. Not love, that was for sure. In fact, she'd never want that, but sex? Maybe.

Sex wasn't a mystery to anyone with an internet connection and she'd looked up various things. It had all looked faintly ridiculous and like nothing she'd ever want to participate in, but what she'd seen on her computer screen had nothing to do with the reality of Vincenzo de Santi, half-naked, in the middle of the night in a villa on Capri, watching her with heat in those black eyes.

There was nothing ridiculous about him. Nothing ridiculous about the heat inside her either.

Why isn't he simply taking you?

A good question. Powerful men took what they wanted, as she knew all too well, but he wasn't taking her. He hadn't the night before either, even though she'd offered herself to him. In fact, he'd got up and left rather than reach for her, and that only added a layer to the complex puzzle he was turning out to be.

An incorruptible man, yet not a man without hungers. A man with a strong moral code who stuck by that morality regardless of what he might want for himself.

He is not your father. You don't have to be afraid of him.

Lucy swallowed, her mouth dry. It was true. He *wasn't* anything like her dad. And she wasn't anything like her mum. Once she'd been fearless like her. Brave and inquisitive and curious, too. But that had been before those things had led to her mother's death, so these days she locked them away. Fear kept her safe, after all.

Yet last night she'd realised that she was tired of being afraid, and now she realised something else. She was tired of being afraid of Vincenzo. The frightened little girl she'd spent so many years being wanted to pull her hand away and run to the safety of her bedroom. But the woman who'd spent a day near the sea, who'd smelled the salt and watched the boats, who'd opened her robe and offered herself to a dangerous man, didn't want to leave. Right now there was a fascinating and beautiful panther in front of her. And she was ruffling his fur and nothing bad was happening. He wasn't being violent. He wasn't hurting her. He was only holding her hand to his chest. And she was so very curious about what would happen if she stroked him...

You're not afraid of him. You're afraid of yourself, of what you want...

She took a breath, feeling something shift and turn inside her, a hunger of her own that she'd ignored. A hunger that there was no way of satisfying, held prisoner as she was in her father's house. So she'd ignored it, shoved it away. Forced it down.

But it was still there. And it was strong. And yes, it scared her.

'Yes,' she whispered and she felt him tense, the expression in his eyes changing, as if that wasn't the answer he wanted. 'Does it matter?'

A muscle in his jaw leapt. 'Of course it matters.'

'Why? Isn't my being afraid what you want?'

His hold remained gentle on her hand, but his gaze was not gentle in the slightest. 'No. You've been afraid for too long, *civetta*, and I don't want that for you. Not now. Not here. Not with me.'

She wanted to ask him what made now different. But that

was a rabbit hole she didn't want to go down, not with her hand on his warm chest and the hunger inside that kept on getting wider, getting deeper. That she was afraid of, because it felt bottomless. It felt as if it would swallow her whole.

'I don't think it's you,' she said. 'I think… I'm afraid of myself.'

'Oh?' His thumb moved on the back of her hand, a gentle caress that sent sparks glittering all over her skin.

'I'm afraid of what I want.' A shake was beginning in the pit of her stomach, a tremor like a small earthquake. 'I think I'm more afraid of that than I am of you.'

Tension was gathering in him, but his hold on her hand remained gentle. She could pull away at any moment. 'And what is it that you want, *civetta?*'

He knew, she could see it in his eyes. But he wanted her to say it.

You can't be so afraid all the time. You only have a week. You only have now. Tell him and let him give it to you. This chance won't come again.

And he would give it to her. He wanted to.

Lucy took a slow, silent breath and made herself hold his gaze. 'You were wrong last night.' Her voice was little more than a hoarse whisper in the night. 'I do want you. And I spent all today exploring the villa, but I think… I wasn't exploring. I was searching.' She tried to moisten her dry mouth. 'I was searching for you and I couldn't find you.'

The moon was behind him, glossing his black hair and throwing his face into shadow. But that shadow couldn't hide the flare of heat that leapt in his eyes. 'Well,' he murmured, and this time his voice wasn't cold or casual, 'you have found me.'

The tremble became deeper, wider, the tremor turning into an earthquake. 'Yes,' she said, unable to think of anything else to say.

His thumb moved on the back of her hand again. 'And now you have found me, what are you going to do with me?'

'I don't know.' Her pulse was getting louder and louder in her ears. 'I don't know anything. I've never... I haven't...' The hunger inside her felt too big to contain and she knew if it got any bigger it would shatter her. But she had no experience of this, had no idea what she should be doing. She could hide millions of dollars in offshore tax havens, make them disappear completely, but she had no idea how to touch a man. 'Please...' That one word was a request, a plea, an order. Encompassing everything she didn't know how to say.

An expression she couldn't read rippled over his face, then it was gone, and he was looking at her, the blackness of his eyes becoming the entire world. He raised her hand from his chest and brought her palm to his mouth, pressing a kiss to it.

She gasped, the feeling of his lips against her skin like a hot coal being held there.

Then, keeping her hand in his, he reached out with the other and slowly threaded his fingers in her hair, cradling the back of her head, drawing her closer. She was shivering now, but she didn't pull away; she didn't think she could even move.

And when he lowered his head and that burning mouth covered hers all thoughts of moving vanished entirely. Every thought vanished entirely.

His kiss had taken them all, including her fear.

Something opened inside her like a flower opening for the sun, a knowledge that had been sitting in her soul all this time. That she'd been waiting for this moment her entire life. Waiting for him. She was Sleeping Beauty and he was the prince waking her from sleep, and now he was here there was nothing to be afraid of. Nothing at all.

The trembling took over as he kissed her and so did her need, and her mouth was opening beneath his as if she knew what to do already, letting in his taste and his heat. It felt as if the kiss was a match, igniting her, and now she was burning so hot it felt as though the flame would never go out.

She hadn't meant to deepen the kiss, because he'd started off so gentle, but now his tongue was exploring the inside of her mouth, tasting her with more demand, and she didn't know how to hold back. She followed his lead, tasting him in return, taking in the rich, spicy flavour of him and letting it settle down into her bones. Into her heart.

One of her hands was still held in his, pressed hard to his chest, but she wanted more than that. More than his beautiful mouth talking to her in a language made of teasing kisses, gentle nips, and coaxing licks. She wanted the heat of that powerful body against hers, wanted to press herself to his velvet skin, explore what he felt like, because she didn't know and the lack of that knowledge was an ache inside her.

She moved closer, put her other hand on his chest, glorying in the heat of his body and the feeling of strength. It didn't frighten her, not any more. She knew to the depths of her soul that he would never use that strength to harm her, not the way her father did, and now all she wanted was to explore that strength. Touch that power. Have it turned on her to bring pleasure, not pain.

He released her hand and his arms were around her, pulling her close so she was where she wanted to be, pressed up against him. His mouth had turned hot on hers, the kiss more demanding, and yet even now expertly controlled. More and yet not more than she could handle.

She wanted to handle it though. Because, now she wasn't afraid, all that was left inside her was strength.

His hands slid from her hair down her back and suddenly she was lifted in his arms, held tight to his chest as he crossed the room to one of the long, low sofas. He put her on the cushions, sitting her upright, then came down on his knees in front of her.

She reached for him but he only took her hands in his, turning them palm up and pressing a kiss on each one. Then he put them on the couch and held them there, his gaze fierce on hers. 'Keep them there,' he ordered, his voice full of dark heat. 'Let me give you this, *civetta*. Let me show you how good I can make you feel.'

Lucy took an unsteady breath, shivering all over, held fast by the fierce, hungry look in his eyes. She nodded.

He took his hands away from hers then put them on her knees, easing them apart so he could kneel between them. She took another trembling breath as he came closer, his lean hips between her thighs, his bare chest inches away. He was so tall that, even sitting, she was barely at eye level with him, the breadth of his shoulders blocking out the night behind him.

Calmly he took her chin in one hand, holding her still as he leaned down and kissed her again, his lips hot, the kiss so achingly sweet that she moaned. He deepened it, his tongue dipping inside her mouth, and as he did so she felt his fingers slide beneath the silk of her robe.

Clothes had arrived for her that afternoon, but she hadn't gone through them all, and she hadn't been bothered to find any nightgowns or pyjamas. She'd gone to bed naked and now he knew that too, his fingers burning like a brand on the sensitive skin of her shoulder as he stroked her.

It felt so good that she trembled harder, shivering all over as his grip on her chin loosened and his fingers spread out along the side of her jaw, cupping it, his thumb stroking along her skin as he kissed her deeper. With his other hand he eased the silk of her robe aside, the tips of his fingers brushing down her side and lightly following the curve of her bare breast.

Lucy shuddered, the tips of her nipples abruptly achingly sensitive. She wanted him to touch them, but he didn't. He only caressed her side and then traced circles over her skin, teasing her, maddening her. His mouth left hers and trailed down the side of her neck, leaving kisses like fallen stars and nips like hot sparks. Making her shake, her fingers curling into the material of the sofa cushions, holding on tight.

She wanted more, so much more, but he was going so slowly and being so careful, and he didn't need to. She wasn't afraid, not of him. Not any more.

'Please, Vincenzo.' She'd never called him that to his face

before, but it felt right on her tongue. It felt perfect. 'Please...
I w-want—'

'Patience,' he murmured against her skin, kissing down between her breasts as his hands caressed her hips and thighs. 'I
know what you want and I'll give it to you, I promise. But anticipation will make it sweeter. And besides, I want to savour you.'

He did? Was she worth savouring? Her mother had died protecting her and sometimes, in her lowest moments, she wondered if her mother's sacrifice had really been worth it. Because
after Kathy had died her only value lay in what she did for her
father, her analytical brain and her facility with numbers. And
it was a value predicated on hurting others...

So no, sometimes she didn't think she'd been worth saving.
But now here was Vincenzo, telling her that he wanted to savour
her, making her feel almost as if she had been worth it after all...

Inexplicable tears collected behind her lids, but she blinked
them back fiercely. She wasn't going to cry, not while he was
doing this to her. And she wasn't going to protest, either. Not
while he was making her feel so good. She didn't want to be sad
with him, she only wanted this feeling, this pleasure to never
end. Because she'd never had it before. There were so many
things she'd never had before and all because of him.

He kissed down her stomach, his hands stroking, making
the sweet ache between her thighs become more acute, more
demanding, sending delicious chills everywhere. Then he was
pushing her thighs wider, his mouth moving lower, and she
found herself arching back, ready for anything he might give
her. It would only be good, surely.

His fingers stroked her inner thighs, his mouth finding the
hot, wet centre of her. Exploring gently, tasting lightly, and she
was shaking so hard she thought she might come apart, her
breathing loud, her heartbeat louder.

An ocean of pleasure rose up around her, hot and liquid like
honey, drowning her, but she didn't care. She wanted to drown.
She never wanted to come up for air again.

His hands slid beneath her thighs, drawing her close to the edge of the sofa, and she leaned back, gasping as he lifted her leg and draped it over one powerful shoulder, allowing him greater access, and then his mouth was back on her, tasting her deep inside as his hands caressed her.

There were lights behind her eyes, falling stars and supernovas, galaxies glittering, the end of the world approaching. And she had a front-row seat.

Until even that was lost as the pleasure took everything from her, leaving her with nothing, not even her name. But it wasn't frightening. She threw herself into it, happy to leave it all behind, the only anchor point Vincenzo's hands on her, holding her still, and his tongue working his magic.

And when the end of the world finally came she called his name as the galaxies exploded and she was exploding too, a star blazing in the night, her soul flaming before dissolving into bliss.

Her hands were on him, stroking his shoulders absently as she lay back on the sofa, her face flushed, her mouth curving in a smile as old as time—that of a woman well satisfied.

He couldn't look away from her. He had her flavour in his mouth, a salty sweetness that had to be the most delicious thing he'd ever tasted, and he was desperate for more. Strange, when he'd never been desperate for a woman before. Needing sex, yes, but not a particular woman. Not like this.

Everything in him was urging him to pick her up and take her upstairs to his bed, because he had protection up there and he wanted to be inside her more than he wanted his next breath. Yet he didn't move, because he hadn't seen her smile, hadn't seen her face when she wasn't scared, and the sight of that smile made his chest get even tighter than it already was.

He'd done that to her. He'd been the one to give her that smile. And he couldn't remember the last time he'd made anyone feel good, made anyone feel happy. All he ever did was cause pain.

They deserve it though.

Yes, there was no question that they did. But...looking at Lucy's smile, he found he liked that he'd been the one to give her that. And he liked that he'd given her pleasure, made her call his name. Wiped the fear from her lovely hazel eyes...

This is not what you should be doing.

No, but he was going to do it anyway. He'd crossed the line of his own control, and anyway, to leave her now would be cruel and he couldn't do it. This would all be so new to her and he wanted to show her what more there was, what more that lovely body of hers was capable of.

Don't pretend you're not selfish. You want her for yourself too.

Oh, he wasn't pretending. He did want her for himself. And even though allowing himself to want a woman like her, a criminal, went against his own moral code, he wasn't going to let that stop him. He'd denied himself many things in pursuit of the justice he craved, but she wouldn't be one of them.

Her robe had fallen open, the red silk in perfect contrast to her pale skin, and her hair was spread everywhere, lush, dark lashes lying still on her cheeks. She was naked and everything he'd imagined. Full, perfect breasts with hard, berry-like nipples. Rounded hips and thighs, soft and graceful, with the pretty little nest of dark curls between.

He was hard now, so hard, and he couldn't wait any longer.

Vincenzo leaned forward and gathered her into his arms. Her eyelashes fluttered, her eyes opening as he straightened, holding her close.

'Where are we going?' Her head rested against his shoulder, her body utterly relaxed. She didn't sound concerned and her gaze was only curious.

'To my bedroom,' he said, unable to keep the roughness from his voice. 'We could go to yours, but there is no protection in your room.'

'Protection?' Her forehead creased. 'Oh... Oh, of course.'

A shy little smile turned her vulnerable mouth. 'I was hoping that we might… That you would… I mean, I would like you to be my first.'

That soft confession shouldn't have affected him. It shouldn't have made his chest ache or cause bitterness to gather inside him, and yet it did both. An ache for the gesture of trust that it was, and bitterness because, God knew, he didn't deserve that trust.

He was going to hand her over to the police at the end of this week and nothing would change his mind. He would be giving her to people who would put her in a cell and there would be no one to hold her if she panicked. No one to soothe her fear.

That thought shouldn't have been so bleak, shouldn't have made him feel so hollow inside. Shouldn't have made him so angry. But it was and it did. And he didn't understand it. If he'd had any sense at all, he would have put her down and walked away.

He wasn't going to, though. He was going to make love to her, because he wanted her. And he wasn't going to mention anything about the police or a cell or her guilt, because he wasn't going to scare her.

Tonight he didn't want her to be afraid of anything and, even though he had no idea why that would be important to him, he was going to accept it.

'There are better men for your first,' he said shortly.

'There might be,' she agreed. 'But I don't want them. I want you.'

Her honesty…it killed him. Made the knot of feelings inside him tighten unbearably, drawing attention as it did to his own failings and the gaps in his morality.

You're a hypocrite and you always have been.

Perhaps he was. After all, only a hypocrite would set himself on a course of justice, all the while knowing that he was a criminal himself. That the only reason he'd escaped paying for his own crimes was that he'd handed over his parents instead.

'You look so serious.' She leaned against him, looking up at him. 'What are you thinking about?'

But he wasn't going to talk about the past. That had no place here.

'You,' he said, and it wasn't far from the truth. 'Naked and in my bed.'

'Why? What is it about me that you want?'

He should tell her lies. Tell her that he had no idea why he wanted her, that she must have drugged him or bewitched him to make him so hard for her.

Yet he couldn't do that. He might be a liar and a hypocrite at heart, but he couldn't lie to her. Not about this. Not when she was small and soft in his arms, and the scent of apples and musk wove around him, making his groin ache. Making him want to put her down on the stairs right here, right now, and have her.

'You're beautiful,' he said, and again this was the truth. Her beauty was a secret thing, slowly revealing itself like a photo being developed, a gorgeous picture gradually coming into perfect focus. 'And you're very brave. And you're honest.'

'Beautiful? No, I don't think so. And I'm certainly not brave. I don't know if I—'

'Those things are all true,' he interrupted and not without gentleness, because she wasn't to argue with him on this. 'Whether you believe them or not.'

The look on her face softened and she reached up, her fingertips brushing his cheekbone in a touch that felt like fire against his skin. 'You're really very kind, aren't you?'

Kind. She thought he was kind.

He was nothing of the sort, but that was something else that he wasn't going to tell her. So he stayed silent instead as he came to his bedroom, kicking the door shut behind him as he went through the doorway. Then he carried her over to the big white bed and laid her down on it, before stepping back and stripping off his clothes.

She watched him, her glittering hazel eyes alive with curiosity and fascination and hunger, and when he was naked she reached for him in instinctive welcome.

That stole his breath, made his heart feel heavy in his chest. There was an affectionate, caring, and generous spirit beneath her wariness, and he was uncovering it, bit by bit.

You don't deserve it. You don't deserve her trust. You'll betray her like you betray everyone.

Vincenzo shoved that thought from his head as he reached for the protection in the bedside drawer. And locked it away as he prepared himself. Then he moved onto the bed with her, easing her onto her back and settling between her thighs. She made a small, throaty, satisfied sound as he did so, her body arching beneath his, pressing herself harder against him. Her hands were on his shoulders, stroking, as if she couldn't get enough of touching him.

'You're beautiful, too,' she murmured as he eased himself against the soft, damp heat between her thighs.

But he didn't want words now, not with her silky skin against his and the light, feminine musk of her scent intoxicating his senses, making the need hammer in his head so loudly that he could barely hear a thing. So he bent his head and took her lovely mouth, tasting the sweet fire that he was beginning to suspect lay at the heart of her. And she didn't protest, kissing him back, all shy inexperience and untutored hunger.

That sweetness felt unbearable to him all of a sudden, as did her inexperience. He didn't want any reminder of how vulnerable she was, or how alone and unprotected she'd been all her life. How she'd only ever been in the power of a man who'd hurt her. Scared her.

It made him feel things he didn't want to feel, emotions that he had no place for in his heart. He didn't want to protect her, care for her, keep her safe. All he wanted was to be inside her and this hunger for her sated.

He kissed her harder, with more demand, stroking down her body to the wetness that lay between her legs, his fingers circling the sensitive little bud. She gasped, trembling, her nails scraping over his skin. And that was better. That was much better than softness and vulnerability, better than the tightness in his chest and the ache in his heart.

So he kissed her harder still, deeper, nipping at her, biting at her until she moaned and her nails scratched him as she quivered and shifted restlessly beneath him. He was relentless, making her come against his hand, her breathing wild and ragged, and only then did he finally allow himself his own pleasure.

He wanted to thrust hard, show her that, though she might think him beautiful, he had no mercy to give her. That if she persisted in being soft with him, there would be nothing but pain in store for her. But he couldn't bring himself to do it. The thought of her pain in amongst this pleasure anathema to him.

So he pushed inside her slowly, carefully, watching her pretty face, searching for any signs of discomfort in the wide, dark eyes that looked up into his. She groaned, her gaze going even wider as he pushed deeper, but he saw no pain in it. Only a kind of wonder. As if he was a secret she'd always wanted to know, a secret that in the discovering was even better than she'd thought.

She was so hot. Slick. Perfect.

His brain blanked and for a moment he couldn't think of anything but her. Anything but the heat of her and the pleasure that was unfolding inside him, many-faceted and complex. Fascinating. Demanding.

He pushed his hands beneath her hips, tilting her, enabling him to go deeper, and she cried out, her hold on his shoulders almost painful. But she wasn't hurting, he could see that. She was as much in the grip of this pleasure as he was.

'Oh, Vincenzo,' she gasped, shuddering. 'Please, oh, please...'

And he moved, harder, deeper, his hands gripping her hips, losing himself in the tide of pleasure that washed over him, sweeping away the tightness in his chest and the poison in the centre of his soul. The corruption he could never escape, since it was part of him and would always be.

Sweeping away everything but the feel of her around him, the tight grip of her sex as she stiffened and arched beneath him, calling his name.

Everything but the pleasure that raced up his spine and exploded in his head, an excoriating fire that gave him finally what he hadn't realised he'd been searching his whole life for: a single moment of purity.

It wouldn't last, though, and deep down he knew it. Which was why this could never happen again.

CHAPTER SEVEN

LUCY WOKE THE next morning knowing exactly where she was: Vincenzo's bedroom.

Sunshine came through a gap in the heavy white curtains, leaving a trail across the crisp white sheets, making it abundantly clear that she was alone.

A thread of disappointment wound through the pleasant, lazy, sated feeling inside her. She wanted him next to her so she could explore that powerful, masculine body in the daylight, discover what made his breath catch and turned his black eyes to flame.

She shivered deliciously as memories of the night before flooded through her. Of the feeling of him sliding inside her, pushing in deep, and how strange it had felt and how wonderful too. There hadn't been any pain, only a momentary discomfort that had gone almost as soon as she'd felt it. And then there had only been the most incredible feeling of connection, of being so close to another person. She'd never experienced anything like it.

His face had been stripped of everything but hunger, a fierce need that had echoed in her own soul. And for a brief, crystal-clear moment before the pleasure had washed it all away she'd seen something vulnerable in him. Something lost.

But the moment had been so brief that now, in the sunshine

of the morning, she wondered if she'd seen it at all. Because what would make a man as strong and powerful as Vincenzo de Santi vulnerable? What would make him lost?

Curiosity tugged at her, that fatal flaw, but this time she indulged it. Staring at the ceiling, she remembered the research she'd conducted into him as she'd planned where to run to. The de Santi family was an old one, going back to medieval times when they'd been spies for a now lost Italian duchy, before an ancestor had found that there were more riches to be had in illegal activities.

In modern times they'd managed to stay one step ahead of the law, concerning themselves only with the jostling for precedence and constant need to earn respect among the crime families of Europe, fighting petty private wars and constantly stoking ancient feuds, and they probably would have continued in that vein if not for Vincenzo.

He'd betrayed his ancient heritage, his lineage, and reported his parents to the police in exchange for immunity.

Then he'd turned himself into the scourge of Europe, feared and loathed by the all the families who'd once considered the de Santis allies.

Lucy frowned at the ornate plastered ceiling.

What had made him turn his back on his family? Loyalty was the lifeblood of the old families, it was ingrained deep in their bones, but something had happened to Vincenzo. Something had shattered that loyalty. Or perhaps he'd never had it at all.

But no, that couldn't be. A man who held to such a difficult purpose as the one he'd chosen for himself wouldn't be a man with no loyalties or beliefs. If anything it was the opposite. But then, where did those loyalties lie? And to what? To justice? To making up for the sins of his family? Or was it something else?

What does it matter? In a week you'll be in custody and then you'll never see him again.

That thought hurt and so she ignored it in favour of slipping out of bed and heading for the shower in the en-suite bathroom.

She washed herself, enjoying the cool water falling on various aching parts of her body, and when she was done she wrapped the familiar red robe around herself—which was the only item of clothing to hand—and went back to her own room.

The clothes he'd bought for her that had arrived the day before had been put away by Martina, and so she had to pull open the drawers on the big oak dresser and hunt through them. They were all very expensive, in beautiful fabrics, and all her size, and she, who'd never been much of a clothes person, found herself smiling as she pulled out a light, gauzy dress made out of pale green silk.

It was pretty, and when she put it on she could see how the colour brought out the green in her eyes. Immediately, her first thought was about what Vincenzo would think if he saw her in it and whether he would like it.

Your mother would have liked it too.

Oh, she would. She'd loved dressing Lucy up and Lucy had loved it too, but after Kathy had died she'd lost all interest in her appearance. Faint glimmers of interest were returning, though.

Perhaps it was silly to want to look nice for a man, especially a man who was still her enemy in many ways, but she decided she didn't care if it was silly or not and kept the dress on. She attempted to do something with her mass of hair, but, since she wasn't sure what, having never paid much attention to styling it before, she left it loose. Besides, she was hungry and wanted some breakfast.

She went downstairs to the terrace, where all the main meals of the day were served, hoping to find Vincenzo already there. But he wasn't. The table was set and food was on it, but the place was empty.

The disappointment she'd felt on waking returned and she turned around to go back inside and search for him, only to stop.

Why was she going to find him? What did she think she'd say? They'd spent the night together, that was all. No promises had been made, nothing had been said.

He'd given her pleasure and it had been the most incredible experience of her life, but he was still who he was. That hadn't changed. Nothing had changed.

But perhaps you have.

A strange feeling pulsed through her, part certainty, part strength. As if last night he'd given her some of his, along with the pleasure.

Yes, she had changed. She felt...different. More sure. Less afraid. And maybe if she had the urge to find him, to tell him that she wanted him again, then she should do it. He'd told her to be honest, that it was precious, so why shouldn't she be honest with him?

Avoiding things and hiding was what she'd done in the past and that had kept her safe. But safety was beginning to look overrated to her now. He'd given her a night without fear, a night of pleasure and warmth, and she wanted more.

She only had a few days left of it, after all—if she couldn't change his mind, that was.

First, though, she would eat.

Fifteen minutes later, full of coffee, bacon and some delicious pastries, Lucy went to find Martina to ask where Vincenzo was. Through some emphatic gestures, she understood that he was in his office and wasn't to be disturbed.

That gave her a moment's pause. Did that apply to just her or did that mean he didn't want to be disturbed by anyone? She only needed five minutes. That was allowable, wasn't it? Deciding that it was, she made her way to his office.

It was at the other end of the villa and the door was closed, so Lucy gave it a discreet knock. When there was no reply she stood there a second, debating, but then, nothing ventured, nothing gained, so she opened it quietly and went in.

The room was large, with fabulous views out over another terrace, a formal garden below that led all the way to the edge of the cliff and then the sea. A big desk stood near a set of high, arched windows and behind it stood the tall, powerful figure of Vincenzo.

He faced the windows with his back to the door, talking on the phone in his beautiful Italian, his voice calm and casual-sounding. His usual tone.

He wasn't in a suit today, wearing a pair of well-worn jeans that sat low on his hips and a faded blue T-shirt. As casual as his voice. A man doing a bit of light work on the weekend.

Except there was nothing casual about the tension that gathered in his broad shoulders and back, and even standing where she was by the door she could sense it. Was something bad happening? Did it have to do with her father?

She slipped into the room and closed the door behind her, moving over to the desk and pausing in front of it. Obviously hearing her footstep, he swung around, his obsidian gaze catching hers, the ferocity in it driving all the air from her lungs.

Had that fierceness always been there? Had she simply not seen it? Or was this new?

No, it had always been there, the driving force of his will allied with the flame of purpose. A man who would stop at nothing to get what he wanted or to do what was right. Who wouldn't let anything get in his way, not mercy, not sympathy, not tenderness. No soft feeling at all.

Yet…last night he'd been nothing but gentle with her—at least initially. Until she'd shown him that she didn't need gentleness.

He kept talking, the tone of his voice not changing one iota, holding her gaze with his. She couldn't breathe, couldn't move. The seething tension that gathered around him held her fast.

Something was wrong. He was angry. No, more than that. He was furious.

Male anger was always something to be wary of. Her father's rages had been terrifying and she'd seen the consequences of that rage first-hand. After her mother had died, being in his vicinity had always made her go icy with fear and she tried to avoid him at all costs when he was like that.

Yet, even though Vincenzo seemed no less angry, she wasn't scared. His was a coldly controlled anger and the threat of violence that hovered around him wasn't directed at her. He told her he would never hurt her and she'd believed him then; she believed him now too.

She didn't back away and leave the room the way she might have done even a week earlier. Instead she lifted her chin and stood there, waiting for him to finish. She'd been going to ask him why he'd left her that morning, but now she wanted to know why he was so angry. Was it her father? Business? What?

Quite suddenly he disconnected the call and flung the phone back down on the desk with a clatter. 'What do you want?' There was an edge to his cool voice. 'I told Martina I wasn't to be disturbed.'

Lucy took a breath, studying the hard cast of his features and the black glitter of his eyes. 'Why are you angry?'

'Why do you think? I gave orders that I wasn't to be interrupted and yet here you are.'

'That's not why.' Something more was going on here, she was sure of it. The hot breath of his fury was too intense to be about a mere interruption. 'Is it my father?'

He muttered something vicious under his breath and looked away, the tension pouring off him.

The urge to go around the desk and put her hands on those hard, muscled shoulders to ease him was almost overwhelming. But they'd only had one night together and she couldn't presume anything. He probably wouldn't welcome it anyway.

She clasped her hands in front of her instead. 'Vincenzo?'

'You should leave.' The words were bitten out. 'I'm not in the mood for conversation.'

'Why? What's happened?'

He lifted his head, his gaze clashing with hers again. The darkness in it made it hard to breathe. 'You happened, *civetta.*'

Shock slid down her spine. She stared at him, not understanding. 'What do you mean, I happened?'

He straightened, a muscle in his jaw leaping. 'Last night you compromised my moral code and it cannot happen again.' The anger threading through his voice was like hot metal piercing a block of ice, making his accent more pronounced. 'I do not sleep with my prisoners.'

Oh. So that was the issue. *She* was the issue. And he regretted it.

A heavy disappointment settled in her stomach, though she knew she had no right to be disappointed. There had been no promises made, no indication that it would happen again. She'd just assumed, because it had been so good...

For you. But perhaps not for him.

Her mouth dried, the disappointment turning inward, growing sharp edges. 'I...see,' she said huskily. 'I didn't mean—'

'You didn't mean to sleep with me? Is that what you're trying to say? You didn't mean to compromise me? Or cause me to forget everything I stand for?' He gave a harsh laugh. 'You overestimate your charms, Miss Armstrong. It wasn't you and your lovely body, believe me. It was my own weakness.'

The edges were razor-sharp, cutting her, pain seeping through her. She wanted to turn away and leave the room, run away and hide. She'd thought that what had happened between them had been special, had been precious, and now he was looking at her as if it had meant nothing. As if she'd meant nothing.

He'd told her that she was worth savouring, but...had he not meant it?

Are you worth it, though? After what your mother sacrificed for you? You were where you shouldn't have been and that's all your fault.

The thought ran like acid through her. No, she wasn't going to think about that. Yet she couldn't pretend to herself that his opinion didn't matter to her, either. Pretending wouldn't change the emotion sitting in her heart. It did matter, because the night with him *had* been special and it *had* meant something. And maybe she was assuming that because it had been that way for her, it had been that way for him, too. But clearly she was wrong. While she'd felt changed on some fundamental level, he simply felt angry.

That hurt, she couldn't deny it. She didn't expect anything from him—an emotional attachment was the last thing she wanted—but she wasn't going to act as if it meant nothing either.

He'd told her to be honest and so she would, both with herself and with him, and if he didn't like that then too bad.

'Yet it's me you're apparently angry with.' She pushed her glasses up her nose. 'Shouldn't you be yelling at yourself in that case?'

He gave a short laugh that held no amusement. 'I should, yes.'

'You might regret what happened last night, Vincenzo, but I don't.' She lifted her chin, holding his ferocious gaze. 'I don't regret any second of it. In fact, that's why I came to find you. I wanted to know why you left and whether you wanted to—'

'No,' he cut her off harshly. 'I will not sleep with you again.'

But she didn't let his tone get to her. 'I wasn't going to ask if you would, only if you wanted to.'

The tension gathered tighter around him, like a fist closing, and all of a sudden it was clear to her what that tension was and where his anger was coming from: he *did* want to. He wanted to badly, because she knew that fierce look in his eyes. She'd seen it the night before as he'd moved inside her. It was hunger, fierce desire, and denial.

He was at war with himself and what he wanted.

The raw feeling inside her eased; she'd been hoping he might feel the same way she had about the night before, but she hadn't been sure. Now it seemed clear that, despite himself, it had been good for him. And that he wanted more.

Except she didn't know what to do, whether to let him put her at a distance or to close it.

'I do not want to,' he bit out, his whole posture rigid with tension.

'You told me honesty was precious,' she said quietly. 'And yet you're lying.'

There were black flames in his eyes, his temper a cold fire. 'Don't presume to know me, *civetta*. You have no idea—'

'You want me, Vincenzo. I can see it in your eyes.'

The muscle in the side of his jaw leapt again. 'It won't happen, Lucy. I've already told you that.'

'Then why are you still so angry?' She came closer, the width of his desk all that separated them. 'If it's not going to happen again, then why should what's already happened matter?'

He said nothing, staring at her, the panther starving for his prey.

She swallowed, the sound of her heartbeat getting louder in her head.

Perhaps she should leave after all. Perhaps it was selfish of her to force this issue with him. He was a man of strict principles and she was essentially asking him to go against everything he believed in. Then again, he was also a man of strong passions, passions that he hadn't given in to and yet clearly needed release from.

Would it be wrong to encourage him to release them with her? He'd already done so the night before after all, and a second time couldn't hurt. And anyway, when was the last time anyone had made him feel good? Did he even have anyone?

Lucy put her fingertips on the desk, steadying herself. 'Do you want to know why I'm here, Vincenzo?'

'No.'

She ignored him. 'I came to tell you that last night was special to me. That you made me feel...so very good. And so very safe. I've been afraid for so long, but I wasn't last night. I wasn't afraid at all, not for one second. And I...want that again.'

The flames in his eyes burned like cold wildfire. 'You are my prisoner.'

'So you keep saying. And I know you care about that, but I don't.'

'You should care. I'm going to hand you over to the police and they're going to put you in a cell, and there will be no one to ease your fear then, *civetta*. No one to hold you or calm you.'

Something vulnerable inside her shivered, but she ignored it.

You won't be able to change his mind. He'll never release you.

She ignored that too.

'I know that,' she said and didn't look away.

'You will get no gentleness from me. No mercy.'

Lucy arched a brow, her own temper stirring. 'Did I ask for any?'

He muttered something low and vicious in Italian, then continued in English, 'You don't know what you're asking for.'

She lifted her chin even higher. 'Then show me.'

There was only the desk between them. Only a paltry length of wood that he could have reached across and dragged her over the top of at any time. It was all he could do to stop himself from doing just that.

She looked so beautiful this morning in a green silk dress that made her skin look creamy and deepened the chestnut of her hair, making her eyes seem greener too. The fabric was sheer and he could see the curvaceous shape of her through it, and it made him so hard he could barely think.

Then again, he'd been trying to think all morning and been unable to, his mind full of her. He'd thought going to his study and burying himself in work would be the answer, but it wasn't. Even the news he'd just received, about how Armstrong wanted to do a deal for her return, hadn't distracted him.

The whole night had been a mistake and he knew it. That moment of clarity, of purity, when pleasure had annihilated all thought and he'd lost himself in the darkness of her eyes, had been the turning point. If it had only been sex between them,

if she'd been just another in the long line of women he'd had
before, then it wouldn't have mattered. He'd have taken his
pleasure as often as he could with her and the rest of the world
be damned.

But she wasn't just another woman and it wasn't only sex.
He'd known it wouldn't be the moment she'd told him that she
wanted him to be her first. And it certainly hadn't felt like only
sex when he'd touched her, when he'd buried himself inside her.

There was something in the way she looked at him, the way
she touched him, as if he was her white knight, a man who
would save her, not lock her in a cell. A man who would protect her, keep her safe. A man she trusted...

But he could never be those things for her. Not if he didn't
want to compromise his entire life up to this point. Justice had
always been his driving force and he didn't allow himself to
be swayed or manipulated. Wouldn't allow his emotions to be
twisted or turned the way his mother had twisted and turned
them. Yet somehow Lucy had done both.

Correction. She hadn't done it; he'd allowed it to happen. The
problem was him, not her. He'd been weak. He should be burning with the holy fire of justice, not the sensual flame of desire.

Yet that flame wouldn't go out and now she was here, so
close, offering him more of what his body so desperately
wanted, and the need inside him wouldn't be leashed.

She was a criminal, though. She'd broken the law. She was
his prisoner. She was everything he'd been fighting against and
he couldn't allow himself to have her.

*But why not? She wants you. And no one need know. You've
told her that you won't be kind and you won't show mercy, and
that you're still going to hand her over to the law, so she will
have no expectations. After all, you've already crossed the line
once...*

His hands clenched tight, all the reasons for holding back
suddenly seeming spurious. Maybe he was turning this into a
bigger issue than it needed to be. Yes, he'd thought the night

before had been about more than sex, but it didn't need to con-tinue like that. She wasn't a virgin any more. And besides, it would only be for another few days and then the time limit he'd imposed would be up. He would give her over to the police and hopefully by then this madness—because it couldn't be any-thing other than madness—would have left him.

The look in her eyes from across the desk now was all chal-lenge, an emerald glow glittering in the depths. A familiar em-erald glow. It had burned bright as she'd climaxed beneath him, his name torn from her all husky and raw.

Show me, she'd said, and so maybe he would. Maybe she needed to see what kind of man he was at heart.

He unclenched his hands and moved around the side of his desk, approaching her slowly. She didn't move, watching him come closer, her gaze steady. There was nothing wary or guarded about it now—she was an open book, her desire for him easily readable in her pretty face.

The urge to take that face between his palms and kiss her, give her more gentleness, was strong, but he resisted it. He'd told her he had no mercy and so he would give her none. And if she wanted to know what that was like, then he *would* show her.

'On your knees,' he ordered coldly.

She blinked, but after a moment's hesitation she knelt on the silk rug in front of him, her head tilting back as she looked up at him. Pink tinged her cheekbones, her eyes a deep, fascinat-ing green behind the lenses of her glasses.

His breath caught, the ache in his groin almost overwhelm-ing now. He reached down and took her glasses off, laying them carefully on the desk beside them.

'What do you want me to do?' she asked breathlessly.

There was no fear either in her voice or her expression, only a sensual curiosity that made his pulse accelerate. There were so many things he could teach her, that they would both enjoy, and why not? Why not take the entire day? If he was going to do this, he might as well commit himself whole-heartedly.

'I'll tell you.' He dropped his hands to the fastenings of his jeans and undid the button, drawing down the zip. Her gaze followed his movements, the pink in her cheeks deepening into red.

'Give me your hand,' he murmured.

She did so without hesitation and he took it in his, guiding her fingers to him, showing her how to draw him out of his boxers and jeans, then how to hold him in her fist. Her touch was searing and it was all he could do to make himself go slowly. Because even though he had no mercy, she was still new to this and he still couldn't bring himself to frighten her.

'Now,' he went on, his voice husky as the pressure of her fist around him sent pure electricity to every nerve-ending he had. 'Take me in your mouth.'

She obeyed, taking him in as if she'd been waiting her whole life to taste him, and the second the heat of her mouth encircled him he had to grit his teeth against the urge to thrust deep.

Instead, he dropped both hands to her hair and threaded his fingers through it, guiding her mouth on him gently and showing her what to do. Encouraging her with whispered commands to use her teeth and her tongue, when to suck and when to release, teaching her the rhythm he preferred.

She was eager and didn't balk at anything he asked of her, the softness of her lips and her inexperienced enthusiasm somehow making it ten thousand times more erotic than what he'd had from other women.

He watched her face, pleasure sweeping through him, making his heart race and the blood pump hard in his veins. The feeling of that vulnerable mouth on him was exquisite, something he'd never forget, and when she closed her eyes as if he was the most delicious thing she'd ever tasted, and made a soft, husky sound in the back of her throat, he knew he wasn't going to last.

His fingers tightened in her hair, pulling her head away from him, and as he did so her eyes opened. 'Oh,' she breathed. 'Did I do something wrong?'

But he was beyond speech.

He pulled her to her feet lifted her onto the desk and set her on top of it. Then he pulled up the hem of her dress, gathering all the green silk up to her waist, before pushing her thighs apart. He spent a breathless minute finding some protection in his wallet, ripping open the packet and rolling down the latex. Then he pulled her to the edge of the desktop and dipped a hand between her legs.

Her eyes were very wide, the hazel gone smoky and dark with desire. And as his fingers touched her slick flesh she shuddered, gasping softly.

She was soft and hot, and very wet, and when he positioned himself, pushing slowly inside her, she welcomed him with a sigh of satisfaction. 'Yes,' she murmured. 'Oh, Vincenzo... yes...'

And he felt that peace again. That stillness. As if he'd been in a room full of unwelcome noise and someone had shut the door, leaving him with blissful quiet.

Nothing but heat. Nothing but pleasure. Nothing but peace.

Her thighs closed around his waist, holding him tight inside her, and then her hands were in his hair, pulling his mouth down on hers, kissing him so sweetly, making him feel as if all of this was new to him too, new and wondrous.

The war inside him ceased and he let himself have this moment of ease, beginning to move, allowing the pleasure to set its own pace, slow and languorous.

She sighed and arched against him, and he paused once to pull her dress off over her head and get rid of her bra, getting rid of his T-shirt too, so that there was nothing between them, nothing but her silky, damp skin against his. And then he kept moving, the thrust of his hips driving them both closer and closer to the edge.

Her kisses became hungry and he gave her back the same hunger, gripping her hips so he could move harder and deeper, the easy pace becoming something more desperate. She tore her mouth from his, kissing his neck and his shoulders, her tongue tasting the hollow of his throat as if she couldn't get enough of him, frantic, feverish words spilling out of her.

He'd forgotten he was supposed to have no mercy and that he wasn't going to give her gentleness. Stroking her back and soothing her were automatic and instinctive, as was the need to ease her desperation. He took her hand and guided it down where they were joined, putting his fingers over hers and showing her what to do to increase her pleasure. She writhed as he did so, her body desperate for release, giving harsh little pants and moaning against his neck, so he pressed her finger hard against the bundle of nerves where she was most sensitive, allowing her to tumble over the edge.

And only when she convulsed around him, did he allow himself to thrust hard and deep and fast, letting himself fall over that edge too, tumbling end over end, and down into peace with her.

CHAPTER EIGHT

LUCY TRIED TO crawl out from under the blanket thrown over one of the sofas in the salon downstairs, only for a powerful male arm to hook around her waist and draw her back in again.

'No, you don't,' Vincenzo growled, pulling her up against his very hot and very naked body. 'I haven't finished with you yet.'

She gave a long-suffering sigh, running a hand down the warm, velvety skin of his back, loving the feel of all that hard muscle beneath her palm, despite the fact that she'd spent most of the day running her hands all over his body. 'But I'm hungry. Lunch was hours ago.'

He moved, settling himself over her, his weight a delicious pressure pinning her down. 'You're always hungry.'

'So are you.' She shivered as he pressed his mouth to her throat.

'It's true.' He moved lower, nuzzling against her breast. 'Luckily I have all the food I need right here.'

'Yes, but I don't.' The word ended on a gasp as he took her nipple in his mouth, the hot pressure making everything inside her go tight.

She couldn't want him again, surely? They'd done nothing else all day.

After the encounter in his office that morning, he'd been

insatiable, taking her upstairs almost immediately and laying her out across the bed, setting about exploring every inch of her body. He'd been slow and relentless and she was pretty sure she'd screamed. More than once.

He'd sent Martina away for the rest of the day after that and forbidden his security to come into the house. Then he'd made her lunch himself, feeding it to her as she lay in bed wrapped only in a sheet. Once lunch had finished, he'd taken her yet again, and she'd fallen asleep in his arms. She'd woken to find herself downstairs on the sofa in the salon, the doors open, and a naked Vincenzo sitting on the floor leaning back against the sofa, doing something on his laptop. He'd known she was awake instantly and had put aside the computer, joining her on the cushions. They'd lost another hour like that and now she was feeling well rested, physically sated, and ravenous.

In other words, she'd never felt better in her entire life. Apart from being hungry, of course.

She pushed at his muscular shoulders. 'Vincenzo. Food.'

Finally, he lifted his head and gave her a measuring look. 'Very well. But you let me organise it, yes?'

'Okay.' She had no problems with that. If he wanted to feed her the way he'd fed her lunch, she was more than happy.

But Vincenzo clearly had a bigger plan than a simple meal in mind, because he made her stay where she was for at least half an hour, before finally coming to get her and leading her down a couple of hallways and out to a small private terrace shielded from view by trees and potted bushes.

A big outdoor bath sat on the stone floor of the terrace and steam rose from the water. Candlelight leapt and flickered from holders placed on various surfaces, casting a gentle glow over everything.

Her chest constricted as he urged her towards the bath, his hand gentle at her back.

'This is beautiful, Vincenzo,' she said huskily. 'Is it for me?'

'Yes.' He eased the robe he'd put around her off her shoulders. 'There's no beach here and it's too late to swim from the rocks. We have a pool built into the cliff but it's a bit cool at night. I thought you'd enjoy being outside and in some warm water in case you're sore.'

She was slightly...achy. And parts of her that were a little chafed would like some warm water to ease them. She definitely would enjoy that.

Then again, she already was enjoying everything he'd already given her, just as she was very determinedly only thinking about what was happening now and not what would happen in a few days, when he handed her over. It wasn't relevant to this moment and, since this moment was all she had, she'd enjoy every single second of it.

She slipped naked into the bath, the water delightfully scented and warm.

'I'll be back,' Vincenzo murmured and disappeared into the house.

Sighing, Lucy leaned her head back on the bath, loving the soothing effect of the water and the sound of the waves at the base of the cliffs below the house. The stars studded the black sky, the candlelight flickering, and yet another moment presented itself. A moment of peace and tranquillity and utter safety.

Her father couldn't reach her here. No one could. She was protected by Vincenzo and he'd let nothing touch her.

He will give you up, you know this...

But that thought wasn't part of the moment and so she ignored it, counting the stars above her head and letting herself drift in the water.

She must have drifted to sleep too, because she opened her eyes maybe only seconds later, to find Vincenzo had returned and had set a tray of food plus a bottle of white wine and wine glasses down on a stone table near the bath. He'd pulled on a pair of jeans, but wore nothing else, and so she lay there for a few moments, watching the play of muscles moving beneath his tanned skin as he opened the wine and poured it.

And she didn't need to see clearly to know he was beautiful. Stunningly masculine and so physically powerful. Also so fierce and passionate, and not at all the cold, judgmental angel he'd appeared to be when she'd first met him.

He'd told her that he had no mercy and yet with her he'd been nothing but kind. Demanding, true, yet also gentle. And his ruthlessness hid a protective nature that she found almost unbearably attractive.

You feel something for him...

Lucy forced her gaze away, the water around her suddenly not quite as warm as it had been. She was only admiring him. It didn't mean anything emotionally.

Her skin prickled and she looked up again to find that he'd turned from the table and was now watching her, a familiar expression of hunger on his blunt, aristocratic features. 'I was going to ask if you wanted some dinner now, but maybe we could wait five minutes. I suddenly have a very strong urge to have a bath.'

She flushed at the heat in his eyes. 'Dinner first,' she said firmly. 'It would be very unfortunate if I starved to death at a vital moment.'

He stared at her a second and then, much to her delight, his hard mouth curved into one of the most glorious smiles she'd ever seen. It softened the stern lines of his face, making him seem much more approachable and incredibly sexy. 'That would, indeed, be unfortunate. Perhaps I'll wait, then.' He picked up a large white towel he'd draped over a nearby stone bench. 'Come, *civetta*. Get out of the bath and let me dry you.'

She could have done it herself, but she didn't want to, getting out of the bath and letting him dry her off and wrap her in the lovely red silk robe. It made her feel cared for, and it had been a long time since she'd felt cared for, so she would let herself enjoy it while it lasted.

Not that you deserve it. Not when your mother died because of you.

Lucy ignored the thought.

A few minutes later she was seated on one of the stone benches, cushioned by mounds of pillows, a plate full of cold meats, salad, cheeses and delicious fresh-baked bread in her lap. A glass of wine sat on the back of the bench at her elbow, while Vincenzo lounged in a chair opposite, ostensibly making sure her plate was full. To 'build up her strength' since it was apparent he had plans for the rest of the evening. Plans that obviously featured her.

'This is wonderful,' she said, picking up an olive. 'Thank you.'

He inclined his head in wordless acknowledgement, sipping on his wine as she slowly chewed the olive, relishing the sharp, salty taste.

'This whole place is wonderful,' she went on, gesturing around them at the villa and its grounds. 'Did you come here a lot as a child?'

'Not often. I do spend a lot of time here now, however.'

'Oh? Why is that?'

'The *palazzo* is…medieval and dark. I prefer this villa. It's much lighter, and being near the sea is pleasant.'

There was something in his voice she couldn't place. An edge. She wanted to ask him what it meant, but the mood between them was relaxed and easy and she didn't want to upset it.

'I think that was the worst thing about the house in Cornwall,' she said instead. 'It was near the sea, but it had no view. I could hear the waves but I could never see them.'

'You weren't allowed to go out at all?' This time there was no edge in his voice, the question utterly neutral. 'Not even for a drive?'

'No.' She didn't see the harm in telling him. It was only the truth, after all. 'Perhaps I could have argued for a trip to the beach, but I couldn't see the point. It would only make me want what I couldn't have.' The story of her life, really. 'Easier to take a virtual trip via my computer.'

Vincenzo frowned. 'So you never left the house?'

'Dad would sometimes take me to London.' She reached for her wine and took a sip herself, enjoying the cool bite of it. 'But not often. I didn't like going anyway. It meant meetings with some of his contacts and friends and they scared me.'

Vincenzo's frown became fierce, the glitter of his eyes sharper. 'Why? Did they hurt you?'

She could hear the promise of retribution in his voice and it set up a small, warm glow inside her, even though she knew it shouldn't. 'No. Dad wouldn't have been pleased with them if they had and they were afraid of him.'

'You were afraid of him too.'

'I was,' she agreed. 'I am.'

'And yet you escaped him.' Vincenzo tilted his head, his black gaze focusing on her as if he'd never seen anything so interesting in his life. 'What made you run, *civetta*? Was it opportunity or had you been planning it?'

They hadn't talked of anything personal the whole day and she'd been more than happy with that. But now tension crawled through her. Talking about this would involve explaining about the promise she'd made to her mother, and how her mother had died, and the reason for it...

Then he'll know exactly how guilty you really are.

A kernel of ice settled in the pit of her stomach. She didn't want to tell him. She wanted him to keep thinking of her as someone worth savouring, someone worth taking care of. She didn't want this warmth between them to end. There was still a chance she could convince him to change his mind about handing her over to the police, but if she told him the real reason for her mother's death, that chance would be gone.

She looked down at her plate, picking up a red cherry tomato and eating that to give herself a moment or two to think, even though her appetite had vanished.

No, she couldn't lie to him. He valued her honesty, which meant she'd have to tell him the truth, face his judgment. Accept her own guilt, because she couldn't hide from it any longer.

Lucy gathered her courage and met his gaze head-on. 'I ran because of a promise I made to my mother. She wanted me to survive, get free any way I could, but it took me a long time to be brave enough to do it. I killed her, you see. The story was that she tripped and fell against a window, sliced her arm, and bled to death. But that's not what happened.' Her jaw ached, but she forced herself to go on. 'Dad had a lot of secret meetings and I was curious about them. I'd always try and eavesdrop, pretend I was a spy, stupid things like that. I knew I wasn't supposed to. Mum warned me not to, that Dad would get very angry if he caught me, and there would be consequences. But… I couldn't help myself.'

She took a breath, her hands now in her lap, her fingers twisting. 'He did catch me that day. And Mum was right, he was furious. He was going to hit me, but she put herself between him and me, and caught the blow instead. It knocked her into a window, which broke, cutting a major artery.' She felt very cold all of a sudden, as if she'd been plunged head first into a pool of snow melt. 'Dad did nothing. He just walked out, leaving me to try and help her. There was so much blood…and I couldn't.' Lucy's throat closed up. 'She made me promise to escape, to have a life away from him. To be happy. And then…she died.'

There was no expression at all on Vincenzo's face, but a fierce light burned in his midnight eyes. 'Lucy,' he said softly.

'And you're right,' she went on, because she had to say it now. 'I am a criminal. I'm guilty of all those crimes I committed for my dad. But mainly I'm guilty of being the reason for her death. If I'd only listened to her, if I hadn't been so curious, so s-stupid, if I'd just done what I was told, Dad wouldn't have found me. He wouldn't have got so angry. And he wouldn't have tried to hit me, and then Mum wouldn't have died. I killed her, Vincenzo. It was my fault.'

Of course it is. And you deserve everything that's coming to you.

Fear came bubbling up at the insidious voice inside her head, a black wave of it, and she had to turn away, unable to face Vincenzo's dark gaze and the judgment that would no doubt be there, sticking like a splinter in her heart.

She didn't know when his opinion of her had begun to matter so much, but it did, and she couldn't bear it. She didn't want the way he looked at her or treated her, with so much gentleness and kindness, to change, yet it would, and she couldn't avoid that.

She deserved his condemnation, not soft candles, and delicious food, and a warm bath.

Face it like your mother faced her death, coward.

Lucy swallowed and lifted her head, determined now, forcing herself to look into his eyes. Because her mother hadn't hesitated to put herself in physical danger to protect her, and so she couldn't hesitate now.

'I appreciate everything you've done for me, Vincenzo,' she said, her voice hoarse. 'But I don't deserve it. Not any of it.'

She'd prepared herself to meet his judgment—that much was clear from the look on her face. And, given how pale she'd gone, it was obvious that she was expecting that judgment not to be in her favour.

He hadn't meant to have this discussion with her, not here, not now. But that was his own fault. He'd been the one to ask her why she'd escaped when she had. And, of course, she'd answered him with her customary honesty.

And he wasn't sure what horrified him more: that she blamed herself for her mother's death or that she expected him to blame her as well.

You told her she was guilty, that she was a criminal.

That was true, he had. But how could he think she was either? After that?

Her little chin was lifted, her eyes shadowed behind the

lenses of her glasses, the green lost in the darkness. She was brave to tell him what she had. And it had cost her. He could see the cost in the gleam of tears she was trying not to let fall, that fogged her glasses, and in the tension that surrounded her.

She'd sat up so straight on the stone bench, telling him in a steady voice about her mother's death. About how her mother had defended her, protected her, and in the end bled to death right in front of her. And for that, Lucy blamed herself.

'I don't deserve it. Not any of it...'

She was a criminal and she was guilty. The crimes she'd committed for her father couldn't be erased. But what she wasn't guilty of was her mother's death.

'How old were you when that happened?' he asked carefully.

'Seven.'

Dear God. She'd watched her mother die at seven...

His heart contracted painfully tight. He wanted to put his wine down, cross the space between them, gather her into his arms, take the pain he saw in her eyes away with his touch. But he had to make this clear to her first.

The law was a logical thing and emotion had no part in justice. And he wanted her to know, unequivocally, that, from a legal standpoint at least, she was blameless.

'And did you stab your mother with that piece of glass?' he asked.

She blinked. 'No. She fell against the window because Dad hit her.'

'She died of blood loss, yes?'

Lucy nodded and he could see her swallow. This was so very painful for her. Her jaw and shoulders were so tight. She looked very fragile, so very vulnerable.

His heart contracted even tighter, but he ignored it.

'You could not have killed your mother, Lucy,' he said in a neutral voice. 'If you had picked up a piece of glass and stabbed her with it, then that would be a different story. But you didn't.'

She shook her head. 'I didn't listen. I should have—'

'You were seven,' he cut across her gently. 'You were a child. What seven-year-old listens to everything their parents tell them?'

The look on her face was bleak. 'She was afraid and yet she still protected me. She stepped in front of Dad and took the blow meant for me. And if she hadn't she wouldn't have fallen against the glass and—' Her voice cracked.

Vincenzo put his glass down then and rose from his chair, giving in to his own instinct, because the sight of those barely suppressed tears… He couldn't sit there, letting her cry, and not offer any comfort. He couldn't.

Crossing to the bench she was on, he sat down and pulled her into his arms before she could protest, holding her the way he had days ago in his office in London.

Immediately she turned her head, burying her face against his chest, her shoulders shaking in a silent sob, and it made him ache that her instinct was to turn to him for comfort. It made him want to hold her tight, protect her, be deserving of the trust she'd put in him.

He disentangled her momentarily to take her glasses off so they didn't hurt her, laying them down on the arm of the bench next to him, then he gathered her in his arms once more and held her close, stroking her thick, glossy curls.

'She was only doing what any mother would,' he said. 'She was protecting her child.' His own mother, for all her faults, would have done the same. But not out of any maternal instinct. She would have done it for her own ends, not his.

'Sometimes I don't understand why.' Lucy's voice was muffled. 'Sometimes all I can think is why? Why did she protect me? What was it about me that was worth dying for? And if she hadn't protected me, then she wouldn't have died and maybe other people might not have got hurt. My father might not have used me—'

'You cannot think like that, *civetta*,' he interrupted quietly. 'The past is something you can't change, so there is no point in going over all the what-ifs and might-have-beens. You did not kill your mother. She made a choice to protect you and she made that choice because she loved you. If you are going to assign blame to anyone, assign it to your father. He is the villain here, not you.'

'A villain I worked for. I did everything he told me to and if I hadn't been so afraid…'

Vincenzo tightened his fingers in her hair, drawing her head back. Her face was wet with tears, her eyes red-rimmed and her nose pink. She looked so sad and yet so unutterably lovely. How had he ever thought her plain?

'You cannot blame yourself for that, Lucy.' He put force into the words. 'You escaped him. You were afraid, but you made a promise to your mother and so you didn't let that stop you. In the end, you were brave and you escaped, and that's the only thing that matters.'

But pain lingered in her eyes. 'If I had truly been brave, I would have stood up to him. My mother did. She knew he would hurt her and yet she stood up to him anyway. I should have done that. Should have refused to do all those things, gone to the police.' A tear ran down her cheek. 'And I didn't. I…allowed him to keep me prisoner because I was just terrified.'

He cupped her cheek in his palm, his thumb brushing away the tear. 'You had reason to be terrified, *civetta*. He is ruthless and violent and he would have hurt you very badly if you'd done any of those things.'

Even the thought of what Armstrong could have done to her made Vincenzo's blood run cold and a red haze of rage descend over his vision.

Does she really matter that much to you?

But he ignored that thought entirely.

Lucy shook her head. 'Mum was afraid of him, but she didn't let it stop her. She was so brave, while I just sat in my room cowering for years. She would have been so ashamed.'

'No,' he said flatly and with absolute conviction, tightening his fingers in her hair for emphasis. 'To see you now, she would have been proud. And she would have thought her death worthwhile if it kept you from harm.'

Lucy's lovely face was tearstained, and she looked at him, as if she was searching for something that only he could give her. 'How do you know that?'

He didn't, of course. He didn't know anything about loving mothers who protected their children. But he did know this little *civetta* and what she'd done for him. Because she had changed him. With her honesty and her trust, with the heat of her passion and the cold grip of her fear. With the heart she wore on her sleeve...

'Because you are worth saving, Lucy Armstrong,' he said quietly.

Lucy flushed and the pain in her eyes eased, and he found himself going on, for what reason he didn't know. Maybe because he didn't want her to feel alone.

'And because I have done things I regret too, things I cannot change no matter how I wish I could.'

She blinked, tears glittering on the ends of her lashes. 'What things?'

He shouldn't tell her. No one knew. And he hadn't thought he'd want anyone to know either. But somehow it felt wrong to hold this back, to let her know that she wasn't as alone in the world as she might think. That he understood in a way few other people would.

You weren't supposed to let your emotions become a part of this.

No, but it was too late for that now and he knew it. His emotions were engaged already. All he could do now was to make sure he didn't allow them to get in the way of what needed to be done.

'I never knew what my family was.' He kept his voice quiet, his thumb moving on her cheek. 'My mother maintained a fiction of the proud de Santi legacy, an aristocratic family of war-

riors fighting to protect what was theirs. I believed her. A proud
de Santi prince, she called me, and that's what I believed myself
to be. I was arrogant and spoiled. So sure of myself and my place
in the world. I didn't see what was wrong with that place until
it was too late. Until people died because of what I'd become.'

Lucy's eyes were very wide. 'What did you become?'

'I became complicit.' He couldn't stop the bitterness that
coloured his tone. 'Though I was always complicit, I just chose
not to see it.'

A deep crease lay etched between her brows. 'What did you
choose not to see?'

Even now he didn't like to think about it. But he couldn't
not tell her, not when she'd shared what had happened to her.

'My mother was beautiful and very loving, but she was also
a de Santi through and through. I wasn't a son so much as her
tool. She used me from a young age, mostly as a spy or a distraction, since children could be useful for manipulating adults
and since they were so easy to manipulate themselves. She told
me I was her brave soldier and that if I wanted to be a general,
I had to prove my worth and follow orders.'

He could feel the creeping dread of the night he never thought
about. The inexplicable dread that he always tried to hold at
bay, because nothing had ever really happened. Or, at least,
that was what he'd told himself. What he'd been telling himself for years…

'We were at the opera one night in Naples, and at the end of
the production my mother pointed to a woman in the theatre
foyer and told me to bring her to the alleyway a couple of doors
down from the theatre. She said that if I pretended to be lost,
and cry a few tears, no one would question it. I was seven and
I loved my mother with all my heart. I only wanted to make
her happy, and so I did what she asked.' Years ago now, and yet
that dread still wrapped around him and squeezed him tight.
'The woman was so kind. She hugged me when she found me
crying, and gave me a sweet, and she followed me when I told

her to come with me to the place I'd last seen my family. She held my hand and told me a funny story…' He stopped, took a breath, and then went on, 'There was a van in the alleyway. And when we approached, the door opened and some men got out. They grabbed her and pushed her into the van and drove off. She didn't even have a chance to scream.'

Lucy's gaze darkened. 'Oh, Vincenzo.'

He could hear the sympathy in her voice, but he knew he didn't deserve any of it. 'My mother was so pleased with me. And I felt proud that I'd done what she wanted me to do. And yet… I couldn't stop seeing that woman's face as they grabbed her. The look of fear on it. Even then I knew that something had happened to her, but I didn't let myself remember it or think about it. But that memory was always there, and then Gabriella happened.'

Lucy placed a hand on his chest, her palm a small ember of heat. 'Gabriella?'

He didn't want to talk about this either, but it was too late for silence.

'When I was twelve, Mama encouraged me to be friends with the daughter of a rival family. She was my age and wasn't afraid of me like the other kids were. I liked that very much. I didn't question why my mother wanted me to be Gabriella's friend, I just let her encourage it because it suited me too.'

'Other kids were afraid of you?'

'Because of my family. The de Santis were very much feared, though I didn't understand why at the time.' He paused, the bitterness sinking deeper into his heart. 'I liked that though. I liked being the de Santi prince that everyone was afraid of. And I was very loyal to my mother, wouldn't hear a bad word said about her. I ignored the rumours and doubts that I picked up as I grew older. That the de Santis were a family of murderers and traitors, and that my mother was the most feared of all, because of her reputation for brutality. I didn't believe them. Mama was small and beautiful and adored me. I couldn't even conceive of her being brutal.' Tension wound through him, though he tried not to let it. 'Then when I was eighteen Mama mentioned that we needed to know the location of Gabriella's father on a particular night, and could I perhaps find out? I knew, deep down. After that night in Naples, I suspected. There was a reason why she wanted that information and that the reason wasn't going to be good. But I was so completely her creature that I ignored my doubts. I took Gabriella out and I got the information I needed from her. I knew she had feelings for me, and I used them the way my mother used mine for her.'

His heart clenched tight at the memory. Of Gabriella's pretty face and the way she'd looked at him, as if the sun rose and set in his eyes. 'It was easy. She told me everything, because she trusted me. And I betrayed her. I passed the information on to my mother.' He'd been so oblivious. So stupid. So blinded. 'Two days later Gabriella's father was killed in a hit carried out by unknown assailants.'

Lucy's eyes widened and he could see the shock in them. Now it was his turn to face judgment, and it would happen. She would soon see his own special brand of hypocrisy.

'Gabriella knew what had happened. She knew that I'd betrayed her. But she didn't blame me. She blamed herself instead.'

Lucy's hand pressed hard against his chest, as if she could sense his self-loathing and wanted to ease the burn of it. But nothing would. Nothing would ever make that get any better. Only the fire of justice ever came close.

'I was complicit in her father's death,' he said flatly, so there could be no mistake. 'I'd ignored the doubts I'd had for years about my mother, too blinded by my love for her to think that everything she'd told me about our family, about myself, could be a lie. But after Gabriella's father died I couldn't ignore it any longer.' He remembered the weight of his own realisation. The crushing burden of understanding that had nearly annihilated him. 'I confronted my mother about it and she laughed. Told me it was just business. That if I wanted to remain part of the family I should get used to it. That I'd already done so much to help, after all...'

He gritted his teeth, remembering his mother's warm, familiar smile. And the cold, cold look in her eyes. 'It was a threat and we both knew it. A reminder that I was as guilty as she and that she had the power to do something about it if I became a problem.' His mouth moved in a smile, though there was no humour at all in it. 'It was common knowledge that there was only one way out of the de Santi family and that was in a box.'

Lucy's gaze was dark and liquid, but she didn't say anything.

'So I made a decision.' He could still feel the flame of that decision, burning hot and strong. It never went out. He couldn't afford to let it. 'I gathered all the pieces of information I could find on my mother's activities and I forwarded them to the police. I made sure I was at her trial to give evidence and I made sure she went to prison. She didn't look at me at all as they led her away. I was dead to her already.'

There were so many things that had scarred him in that moment. The knowledge that he'd negotiated his own immunity from prosecution by betraying his mother. An immunity he'd wanted so he could dedicate his life to pursuing his own justice.

The way she'd ignored him so completely. He didn't blame her in the end, but it had hurt all the same. Confirmation, as if he'd needed it, that he'd never been her son to love.

There was silence afterwards, but he couldn't hear anything above the pounding of his own heartbeat.

'If I can't blame myself for what happened with my mother, then you can't blame yourself for what happened with yours, Vincenzo,' Lucy said quietly. 'You weren't complicit. You were used.'

CHAPTER NINE

VINCENZO'S DARK EYES were full of fire. 'You think I don't know that?'

'I do think you know that.' The anger in his face told her that clearly. 'But you don't feel it, do you?' She'd phrased it as a question, but it wasn't meant to be one. Not when she knew the truth so intimately herself. 'You feel responsible.'

'Of course I feel responsible. I lured that woman to that van. And I used my friendship with Gabriella to betray her father. My actions caused his death, and I knew all along that something wasn't right about it. I knew all along that there was doubt. But I didn't listen to that doubt. I didn't listen to my instinct. And if I had—'

'If you had, what would have changed?' She didn't know why she was arguing with him. It was only that there was pain in his heart the way there was in hers, and that he blamed himself just as she blamed herself. They were so alike. Both children of monsters. It made her feel his agony as if it were her own. 'You might have saved him, but someone else might have got hurt instead. And if the past doesn't matter for me, then it can't matter for you. We can't be complicit when both our parents used us, and we can't change what happened.'

His expression had become hard, like stone, but his eyes

glittered, sharp as volcanic glass. 'No, I can't. Which is why the only thing of importance is what I do now. And that is taking down the people like my mother. Those families who have caused so much harm to so many people. Justice is the only way forward.'

And he was burning with it, that was clear.

Foreboding fluttered deep inside her, but she ignored it. She understood all too well where he was coming from and she could see how heavily guilt weighed on him. Gabriella hadn't blamed him, but he blamed himself, and that surely had to be an impossible burden.

You know about those too.

Oh, yes, she did. She'd carried the weight of her mother's death for a long time, after all. But this life he'd set out for himself, this crusade, had to be a lonely one. She knew better than anyone how difficult it must be, to be constantly on your guard, to never feel safe. Never to be able to trust anyone.

Her heart ached for him and there was nothing she could do. No words to make the burden he bore for the deaths of those people lighter, no way to ease it. All she could do was offer him understanding, because she carried those same burdens.

He'd told her that she wasn't to blame and that she was worth saving, but the feeling in her heart was still the same, the doubt and the fear.

He felt those things too.

Maybe, though, there was some help she could offer him…

She shifted in his lap. 'Wait here. I'll be a couple of minutes.' Before he could stop her or ask what she was doing, she'd slipped off him, going quickly into the house and to her bedroom. Her laptop was still sitting in her bag on the armchair near the bed, so she got it out and went back to the terrace.

Vincenzo had risen to his feet, that dark menace gathering around him again, staring at her fiercely. But she ignored him. She opened up the laptop and typed in her password, then opened up the files she'd encrypted only a week ago.

Then she held out the laptop to him. 'Here. All the information you need about my father is in this file. It's yours, Vincenzo.'

He didn't look at it or make any move to take it. 'You were going to give me that at the end of the week. That was the deal.'

'I know. But justice is important to you, and I don't want to cower in fear any more. I want to do something. I want to help.'

'But why now? Why not before?'

'Because I understand better now why you're doing it and where you're coming from. And I don't want to keep that information from you. More people could get hurt the longer I hold on to it, and I don't want that either.' She lifted her chin, held that fierce stare. 'Take what's on that laptop. Use it to put him behind bars for the rest of his life, because that's what he deserves. At the very least for my mother's sake. And at the end of this weekend I won't protest. I'll go quietly to the authorities.'

Still he didn't take the laptop.

'If I have the information now, what's to stop me from handing you over immediately?'

He wouldn't, though. She knew in her bones that he wouldn't.

'You won't.' She dared him to contradict her. 'You gave me your word and I think that's important to you too.'

Once again he said nothing, that look on his face like a judge debating a sentence. 'You're really prepared to give yourself up? Just like that?'

That he didn't deny it caused her heart to miss a beat, just once. But she ignored it, because what else could she do? After all the things he'd told her about himself and his motivations? His reasons for what he was doing? He was taking responsibility for his actions and trying to make amends, and she couldn't fault that. She couldn't pretend that she didn't have amends to make either because, although logically she knew she wasn't responsible for her mother's death, the guilt remained. And maybe answering for the crimes she'd committed afterwards would help ease it.

'You've devoted your life to justice, Vincenzo. You took responsibility for yourself and the wrongs your mother did, and you're making up for that harm by preventing harm to others. By stopping those responsible. Yet what have I done? I broke the law and my actions would have caused people pain.' That guilt was so heavy, weighing her down. 'I need to pay for that. I don't want to go to jail, but not wanting to doesn't put me above the law. And besides... I don't want to manipulate you into helping me escape. That would be forcing you to compromise your principles and I can't ask that of you.'

He had set her an example and all she could do was follow it. She couldn't claim a freedom that she didn't deserve, and she couldn't ask him to ignore everything he believed in just for her sake.

Slowly, Vincenzo reached for the laptop and took it from her. But even then he didn't look at it. He put it down on the stone bench and reached for her, drawing her close. He was so tall she had to tilt her head back to look up at him. Her glasses were still on the arm of the bench, but she didn't need them to see those burning, dark eyes, and the expression on his face, like stone.

What he was thinking, she had no idea.

She didn't know whether she still wanted him to change his mind, or whether she'd be happier in a jail cell. Either way it seemed she'd have to endure pain, so perhaps it was better that she didn't know what he was thinking. Perhaps it was better to just be in the moment with him, where there was only his warmth and strength. The way he looked at her and the way he touched her. Where there was no past and no future.

Only them. Together.

He lifted his hands and cupped her face between them, staring at her as if she was a book in a language he didn't know but had always wanted to learn.

'*Civetta,*' he said softly, 'why should my principles matter to you?'

Honesty was precious, he'd told her, and so honesty she'd

give him, even though perhaps telling him this wasn't wise. Even though she was still sorting through the implications of it for herself.

'It's not your principles.' Her voice was scraped and raw. 'It's you, Vincenzo. You matter to me.'

She wasn't sure when it had happened, when he'd suddenly become important to her, but he had. And perhaps she'd only come to the realisation in the last ten minutes or maybe she'd known subconsciously for days. Whatever, the when didn't matter. She only knew that she felt it now, like a fire burning hot and strong inside her. A fire that in the space of the last half-hour, as they'd shared their secrets, had only strengthened.

You cannot feel anything for him, remember?

Oh, she remembered. But this was merely a feeling of...kinship. Nothing more than that.

Shock flickered in his gaze and something else, an instinctive heat that made her breath catch. His palms were warm against her skin, resting there lightly, holding her gently. Yet there was nothing gentle or light about the way he looked at her. Angry, almost. As if he hadn't liked her answer one bit.

'Don't.' An underlying thread of ferocity wound through his cool voice. An order that he wanted her to obey. 'You can't let me matter, Lucy. You can't feel anything for me, understand? I negotiated immunity from my crimes so I could dedicate myself to bringing people to justice, and that's my sentence. And it's for life. I cannot be distracted from it, not by you. Not by anyone.'

It was a warning, but she didn't need it. She knew what was at stake already. Not that there was any kind of future for them even if she'd wanted there to be. He wouldn't compromise his principles and she would never ask him to.

Yet they could have this moment and perhaps a night. Perhaps even the next couple of days, too. Surely that wouldn't be too much to ask?

Her mother had wanted her to be happy, and she'd never been happier in her life than when was in his arms.

'I know,' she said. 'Believe me, I know. But I think we could have the next couple of days, couldn't we?'

An expression she couldn't name rippled over his face. 'Oh, *civetta,* I don't—'

'Please, Vincenzo.' She stared up into the inky darkness of his eyes. 'I've never been happy before, but you've given me a taste of it. And I wouldn't mind a little more to take with me when I go.'

He muttered something harsh under his breath, the glitter in his eyes full of anger and desire, heat and regret, and too many other things she didn't understand.

But she understood the demand of his kiss as he bent his head and took her mouth, hard and deep and hot. Knew, too, the taste of his desperation, because she felt the same. She put her arms around his neck, rose up on her toes, kissing him back just as desperately as he was kissing her. And everything suddenly became feverish and raw.

He swept her up into his arms, carrying her from the terrace and through the villa till they reached his bedroom, where he tore the robe from her body and laid her on the bed. He got rid of his clothes, found the protection they needed, then eased apart her thighs and settled himself between them.

He didn't wait and she didn't need him to. There was a yawning emptiness inside her, an echoing hollow space that only he could fill. And he did, thrusting deep and hard inside her. And this time he didn't treat her as if she was made of glass. He didn't go softly or gently, treating her as if she was vulnerable.

He gripped her thighs, hauling them up and around his waist, tilting her hips back so he could slide more completely inside her, and then he was moving in an almost savage rhythm, forceful and hard and demanding.

It felt so good. Exactly what she wanted. Because she wasn't the scared little girl he'd brought to Capri days ago. She was different now. She was changed. She wasn't afraid any more, not of herself and not of him, and not of what she wanted.

And she wanted everything. She wanted it all and now, because she didn't have long to enjoy it. Only a few days. But she would take those days and throw herself into them. Take as much happiness as he could give her and then come back for more. She wouldn't hold back and she'd deny him nothing.

She might not deserve it, but he did. Everything he'd given her she'd give back to him, because, whether he knew it or not, he needed it too.

So she put her arms around him and tightened her thighs around his hips, holding him to her, moving with him. And she kissed him, nipped him, licked him. Let him know how much she liked what he was doing to her, how much she wanted all the pleasure he gave her.

And when she'd reached the point of desperation, when her soul had been drawn so tight with pleasure she almost couldn't stand it, she stared up into his intense face, and felt everything inside her still.

It was as if he held her in the palm of his hand, her whole being gathered up tight in his fist. Then he opened his fingers and her soul flew free, caught in a spiralling ecstasy. Only to fall into the hot darkness of his eyes.

And drown there.

For the first time in his life, Vincenzo had no idea what to do. Always, his path had been clear to him. Always, he knew in which direction to turn and which route to take.

Justice was what he was after. Justice for the woman he'd lured into that dark alleyway. Justice for Gabriella and her father. And perhaps some justice for himself, too. For the way he'd been used and manipulated.

There had never been any conflict within him. He always knew that what he was doing was the right thing, and even when there had been protests and denials from the people he'd put away, he'd never doubted that they deserved what they got.

But now he was made of doubt and the path that had always been so clear was shrouded in fog.

Lucy had accepted that she was guilty of the crimes she'd committed for her father and that Vincenzo would turn her over to the police. And not just accepted it. She felt she deserved it.

Days earlier, there had been none of this conflict. Yes, she was guilty. Yes, she deserved it. But now...things were different.

He sat on a sun lounger under the shade of a big white linen umbrella, gazing at the woman who lay face down on the lounger next to him, her head buried in the crook of one arm, her mass of dark hair in drifts over her pale shoulders. Beyond was the cool blue of the pool built right on the edge of the cliff, and beyond that the deeper blue of the sea dotted with white sails.

The past couple of days they'd done nothing but make love, eat, talk, swim, before starting back at the beginning again. He'd wanted to take her for a tour of the island, but the safety concerns were significant and he didn't want her to feel hemmed in by his security staff, so he'd organised to take her out on his small yacht, which at least gave her the illusion of freedom and meant they could be by themselves, even if his staff followed along behind them in another launch at a discreet distance.

She'd loved that, sitting out on the deck in the sun with the wind in her hair. Then he'd got her to take the wheel while he stood behind her, his hands guiding hers as she steered the little yacht. She'd laughed with delight, leaning back against him as they guided the yacht through the waves. The wind had been up and they'd moved fast, which had thrilled her.

Afterwards, after they'd talked more, sharing pieces of their childhoods that weren't too fraught as they'd eaten the lunch Martina had given them, he'd anchored in a sheltered, private bay and they'd gone swimming off the boat. Then, still wet and salty from the water, he'd taken her down onto the deck and made love to her under the sails as the boat rocked gently.

'I've never been happy before,' she'd told him the night she'd handed him her laptop, *'but you've given me a taste of it...'*

He'd given her a taste of that happiness. He, who'd only ever delivered justice, had made someone happy. And she'd wanted more of it, so she'd have something good to take with her when she went to jail...

The thought of that was unbearably painful for reasons he couldn't describe even to himself. Because why should he care whether she was happy or not? And why did he want to be the one who gave her that happiness?

Why did he even think she deserved it? She'd hidden her father's money and had enabled him to make more, helping him build the crime empire he now commanded whether she'd been aware of it or not. She'd helped him evade the law and she'd known that was wrong.

Yes, she did deserve a prison cell.

But she'd also watched her mother bleed to death. A death she held herself responsible for. And she'd lived in fear for years afterwards, threatened and terrorised, deprived of companionship and love and happiness, everything that made life worth living.

She'd been forced into doing things that went against her loving, loyal and honest nature, things that might have broken another person. But Lucy hadn't broken. She'd made a promise to the mother who'd died to protect her and had survived any way she could. He couldn't fault her for that. But it had left scars on her. The weight of a guilt she couldn't escape, just as he couldn't.

Lucy sighed and stretched on the sun lounger. She'd been wearing a swimsuit, but after their last swim, when he'd stripped it off her and had her up against the wall of the pool, she hadn't bothered to put it on again, and so was lying there naked, her pale skin flushed in the sunlight.

His beautiful *civetta*...

She doesn't deserve that cell and you know it.

His chest felt tight, as if his heart was pressing hard against his ribcage, a strong, steady ache. He felt as if he was looking through a window that had once been crystal clear, but had fogged up, rendering the view indistinct and out of focus. He couldn't even work out what he was looking at now. A badly hurt innocent or a criminal who deserved prison?

She was both, and that was the issue. That was why he didn't know what to do.

She is you, you realise that, don't you?

Vincenzo abruptly shut the laptop he'd been working on, the constriction in his chest getting tighter. No, surely not. She wasn't him.

She didn't have a history of corruption of her own family and she hadn't actually led people to their deaths as he had.

You think she should pay for her crimes while you escape having to pay for yours?

He *was* paying for his crimes. What he'd told her that night was the truth. He was serving a life sentence, using his contacts and his knowledge to help the police. Dedicating his life to the pursuit of justice.

He'd put a lot of people behind bars, more than if he'd been rotting in a cell himself. And it wasn't as if the life he had now had anything to do with freedom. Yes, he had money and a life of ease, but he lived in a cage all the same. A gilded one. Hemmed in by security, since not a day went by when someone didn't make an attempt on his life. Isolated, since he could trust nothing and no one. Curtailed in everything he did because, as far as he was concerned, everything had one point and one point only: justice.

He had paid and he was still paying. He'd be paying for the rest of his life.

Fine, but do you really think she should? Hasn't she paid already?

Putting the laptop down on the table beside him, he got off the lounger and paced over the green lawn towards the stone parapet that stood between him and the cliff face.

Her life had been a misery, spent in fear and loneliness, and so really she *had* paid. She'd been forced into committing offences and, regardless of what he'd told himself about choices, Lucy hadn't had one. Was she really guilty? And did she really deserve to be handed over to the authorities?

But then, what would he do with her if he didn't? She'd asked him to help her escape, find a new life for herself in the States...

Or you could keep her.

A fist closed around his heart, squeezing him tight, making it so he could hardly breathe.

He could keep her. She could live here in the villa. With him.

Slowly, Vincenzo turned around, his gaze settling on her where she lay on the sun lounger, a primitive sense of possession filling him. Perhaps he wouldn't give her up. Perhaps he would keep her. She would be there whenever he wanted her, warm and silky and sweet. Giving him her honesty and her passion. Her loyalty and her trust. He wouldn't have to be alone any more. He would have her.

And why not? He was paying for his crimes, but why couldn't he have something for himself? And it wouldn't be only for himself. It would be for her too, because she'd told him that he was important to her, and surely staying with him was more important to her than being imprisoned in a cell?

Is that really what she needs, though? And isn't being trapped on this island with you really just another cell?

A chill washed over him, burning away the burst of possessiveness. It was true, he could keep her here with him. And he could make her happy, he was sure. In fact, perhaps he even should, since with her help he'd be able to take down even more people than he would on his own.

But what kind of life would that be for her? She'd be in constant danger from those looking to use her to get to him, unable to go anywhere without security. It would be a curtailed, narrow sort of life.

It was the life she'd escaped when she'd run from her father. The life her mother had told her to get free of.

You can't do that to her.

Over on the sun lounger, Lucy sighed and turned her head, her hair trailing down her back. He could see her face, naked without her glasses, and for the first time he didn't see vulnerability and fear there. Her eyes were closed and her mouth was curved slightly in a satisfied way, and she looked at peace. She looked…happy.

He could give her more of that here, but not for ever. She was curious and intelligent and he could imagine her living a life without fear, where she was free to explore everything that interested her. Where she could put those impressive financial skills to better use in a way that would fulfil her, not cause her guilt and pain.

But that life wasn't with him. He'd chosen his path and it was a solitary one; he couldn't make her walk it with him. And if he couldn't trap her in a cage here with him, he couldn't trap her in any other cage either.

The knowledge filtered through him, not fast like a lightning strike but slowly, like the sun rising.

He couldn't give her to the authorities. He couldn't let her go to prison.

Yes, she'd broken the law but there were extenuating circumstances. She'd lost so much and there was so much good she could do out in the world. So much good she *would* do, because of the kind of person she was.

What things could she do if she was allowed to follow her own passions? What kinds of things could she create if she weren't hemmed in by fear?

What kind of person could she become?

Ah, but he knew already. She would be amazing.

He couldn't keep that from her. He wouldn't.

It went against everything he'd thought justice was, but maybe there were more forms of justice in this world than he'd previously thought. And besides, it would be a greater injustice to put her back in a cage than it would be to take her out of it.

Determination sat inside him, a new sense of purpose.

He'd never wanted anything more from this life than to bring down the people who hurt others and he would keep on with doing that. She'd brought him a little space of peace and he would remember that for ever.

But she wasn't his and she never would be. And the greatest gift he could give to the world would be to let her go.

Lucy sighed again and rolled over, glancing to where he'd been sitting. She frowned when she didn't see him, sitting up and looking around.

Then her gaze found his and her face lit up, and she smiled.

No, *that* was the sun rising. That was the lightning strike. Her and her smile, and the way she looked at him. As if he was a sight that made her happy and gave her joy.

Then she held out her arms to him and he felt something inside him crumble and fall away, like a narrow cliff path collapsing under his feet. There was nothing to stop him, nothing to hold on to. One moment the path was firm and solid, the next he was in the air and he was falling.

It was dizzying, terrifying, a rush of intense happiness and hope, along with a despair that he hadn't felt since he'd betrayed Gabriella.

He didn't know how he was ever going to give his *civetta* up.

But he was going to have to.

CHAPTER TEN

LUCY PAUSED BESIDE the bed and briefly debated whether to grab the book she'd been reading to bring down to the pool, or the financial magazine Vincenzo had given her. The book was some nice escapism, but the magazine had some interesting articles, and she wasn't sure what she was in the mood for. Both, perhaps?

She picked them up and turned to the door just as Vincenzo strode in.

A delicious shiver worked its way down her spine the way it always did whenever he was near, her heart beating faster, tension and flutters of heat collecting in the pit of her stomach. Along with a desperate, tight feeling she couldn't shake.

He was in a perfectly tailored midnight-blue suit today, with a black shirt that only emphasised his compelling, dark magnetism. With his inky hair and obsidian eyes, the harsh planes and angles of his face, he was the most beautiful man she'd ever seen in her life.

Don't feel anything for him. You can't.

No, of course she didn't. She was just…admiring him. And she liked being near him and touching him and having him look at her. She was happy whenever she was in his presence, so happy…

But it was nothing more than that. And it certainly wasn't love.

She smiled and took a step towards him, but he didn't smile back. And he didn't reach for her the way he normally did. The expression on his face was carved from stone, his black eyes cold. He looked the way he had when she'd first seen him in his office nearly a week ago. Unyielding. Ruthless...

A chill crept through her.

'Is there something wrong?' She tried a smile, hoping he would smile back, let her know that everything was fine. 'I was just going down to the pool and—'

'It's time to pack, Lucy.' His voice was cool. 'You'll be leaving in an hour.'

She was aware of a rushing sound in her ears, her vision tunnelling, darkness creeping in around the edges. 'What do you mean, leaving? You gave me your word that—' She stopped dead as he thrust out his hand.

He held something small, square and blue.

A passport. A United States passport.

The rushing in her ears grew louder, her vision wavering, her breath coming short and hard. She didn't understand. Why was he giving her a passport?

You know why.

She had an inkling. It was what she'd asked for when she'd initially come to him: an escape. To disappear to a new life in the States. With a new name and identity so no one would ever find her. Where she would be safe at last, just as her mother had wanted.

But that was before she'd realised he would never let her go the way she'd hoped. Before she'd accepted the weight of her own guilt and her need to make amends for the crimes she'd committed for her father. She'd accepted that her future was a cell and, if she wasn't exactly happy about it, she wouldn't balk at it either.

Except this was...not a cell. This was the escape she'd come to him to help her find.

'I don't understand.' Her voice sounded hoarse. She glanced at the passport in his hand and then at him. 'What does this mean?'

'What do you think it means?' There was only granite in the words, the hard edge of stone. 'I'm not handing you over to the authorities, Lucy. I've organised a passport for you with a new identity, visas, social security numbers, everything you'll need to start a new life in the States. Your father will never find you, I'll make sure of it.'

She began to shake, the tremors starting in her stomach and moving outwards, to her hands and knees. This surely couldn't be happening. He couldn't be giving her freedom. Not after everything he'd told her about justice and making amends. About guilt and the law and taking responsibility.

'But...' She tried to make sense of what was happening. 'I was going to be handed over to the authorities. That's what you were going to do and I—'

'I changed my mind.' His voice was like a blade, cutting her off. 'I'm not going to hand you over to the police.'

'Why not?' She searched his face to find some signs of his reasoning, but there was nothing. His features were stone. 'You were very clear that's what you were going to do. I don't understand why you're changing your mind.'

'You were forced into doing those things for your father, Lucy. You had no choice. And even if you had, you've paid many times over for those crimes.'

'But I haven't,' she said hoarsely.

'Haven't you?' His gaze cut like a knife. 'Weren't the years you spent as your father's prisoner a jail term? Wasn't that house he kept you in a cell? He took your mother from you, *civetta*. And that is a life sentence.'

She felt as if the ground had shifted under her feet. As if she were walking in quicksand that would suck her down at any moment. She'd never thought he'd change his mind. Never thought he'd present her with the freedom she wanted, enabling her to keep the promise she'd made to her mother long ago. A freedom she didn't deserve...

Is that really true, though?

Something hot swept through her. He'd told her she wasn't responsible, that she couldn't blame herself, that she was worth saving, and then, over the course of the past couple of days, he'd shown her. He'd taken care of her, made her feel valued, made her feel precious, and more—he made her feel worth the sacrifice her mother had made for her.

'You are worth saving, Lucy Armstrong...' he'd told her, and he'd believed it. This beautiful, passionate, strong man who'd changed her, healed her...

She stared at him and the ground kept shifting, the landscape kept changing, that hot, bright emotion continuing to sweep through her, crushing everything in its path. It was raw and intense and it filled her with strength, made her feel ten feet tall and bulletproof.

And she knew what it was. She knew the truth deep in her heart, in her soul.

The feeling was love.

Was this what her mother had felt when she'd protected her? This sweep of power? Blinding and sure and so utterly certain. A burst of purity, filling her with a confidence she'd never dreamed she'd have.

She'd been so afraid of this feeling all this time. Afraid of its power. The kind of power that made someone stay with someone who hurt them. That made them give up their lives for someone else. But she understood now, she got it.

Love wasn't something to fear, it was something to embrace. Because love was strength and it was courage, and that was what her mother had drawn on to take that blow to protect her. Her love for her daughter.

Lucy's eyes filled with sudden tears. She couldn't let that sacrifice be in vain. Her mother hadn't just wanted a life for her, she'd wanted her to be happy. And that was the best monument, wasn't it? Happiness? Not just for her, but for him too, because they'd both been through terrible things and they deserved it.

They deserved to have a future. And it would be love that would give them that future.

She met Vincenzo's hard, midnight gaze. 'No,' she said.

He ignored her. 'Pack your things. You'll be leaving in an hour.'

'No,' she repeated.

Vincenzo's expression became even harder than it already was. 'No? What do you mean, no?'

Lucy looked him in the eye. 'I mean no. I'm not leaving. I want to stay.'

The expression on his face darkened. 'This was what you wanted, Lucy. A new life. That's what you promised your mother.'

'Well, that's not what I want now.' And she didn't hesitate. She gave him the truth, because that was always what she gave him. 'What I want is you.'

A muscle flicked in his jaw, tension gathering around him like a storm gathering electricity. *'Civetta...'*

'I want the moments I'd planned. I want another day. I want more than that. I want a future, Vincenzo. I want a future with you.'

The tension around him became even more electric, a subtle vibration in the air. 'No.' The word left no room for argument. 'You will go and you will go now.'

'Why not?' She took a step towards him, holding his black gaze. 'Don't you want a future too?'

'No.' Something broke in him, the stillness shattering.

He threw the passport onto the bed suddenly, then he closed the distance between them in an explosive movement, reaching for her, his fingers closing around her upper arms and holding her in a grip that bordered on painful. It might have frightened her once, but there was nothing about him that frightened her now, and certainly not with the emotion blazing in his dark eyes, a black fire that nearly swallowed her whole.

'Yes,' he said roughly. 'Yes, I want that. I want a future. I want for ever with you, *civetta*. But if I take even one day I will *never* let you go. Do you understand now?'

Her heart was full, emotion flooding out of her, and she didn't hide it. She let him see what was in her soul.

'Then don't.' She leaned into his strong grip and his heat. Leaning into him. 'Don't let me go.'

For a second the fire in his eyes blazed so hot it nearly burned her to the ground, the grip he had on her searing her. But that was okay. She wanted to burn. She wanted to burn with him.

But then, as abruptly as he'd grabbed her, he let her go and stepped away, leaving her swaying, leaning into a warmth that was no longer there. The fire in his eyes had gone, the blaze doused. He was cold again, expressionless. Emotionless.

'You say that,' he said, casual. 'But you don't understand what your life would be like with me. People want to kill me every day. I'm a target and so you'll be a target too. You won't be able to go anywhere without a security detail or without planning your every movement. Your life will be curtailed. The only place you'll ever have any freedom is here in the villa, with me.'

'So?' She smiled, wanting him to understand. 'None of that matters, Vincenzo. Don't you see?'

His eyes were black stars, glittering cold and sharp. 'No, I don't see. And you may not think it matters, but it matters to me. I don't want you to be a prisoner with me on this island. I don't want you to have a life limited by safety concerns and security. You should be free to explore the things that interest you, that excite you. And, more than anything, you should be safe. And I can't give you that. I can never give you that.'

A crack ran slowly through her heart, sharp and jagged. Because it was obvious that he didn't understand. And why would he? He'd been betrayed by someone who loved him, the person who'd mattered most. No one had protected him the way her mother had protected her. She might have lost her mum, but she'd known that Kathy had loved her. Had he had anyone who'd cared about him?

He was so hard, so cold. So shut down. All the passion she knew lived in him locked away... No, he hadn't.

'Vincenzo—'

'I don't want to hear it. That is my decision, whether you like it or not.'

She studied him, sensing the battle in him. He'd been at war with himself the whole time she'd been here, torn between his principles and his passions. But he didn't have to choose, couldn't he see that? Didn't he know? He could have both. Love was big enough.

He's afraid.

The insight came almost forcibly and she saw it, because she knew fear, knew it intimately. It was there in his eyes, in the lies he was telling himself and her. And they were lies. He was afraid of what was between them and he didn't know what to do.

'If you really wanted me, you could have me,' she said quietly. 'It doesn't have to be a choice, Vincenzo. It's not one or the other. It's not black and white. And all this stuff about keeping me safe sounds good, but it's just a convenient excuse, isn't it?'

He said nothing, the tension around him almost humming.

The crack in her heart became deeper, wider, and her eyes prickled with tears. Because he was desperate, she could feel it. He was fighting so hard, her poor Vincenzo, and she didn't know what to say to reach him. To show him that he had nothing to fear.

She took a step closer, but he didn't move, towering over her, his gaze utterly forbidding. Intimidating. Yet she knew better now what that aura of menace actually was. It was his armour, his protection. His heart had been broken into pieces once before and now he was desperately shielding it.

'It's okay,' she said softly, trying to calm him the way he'd calmed her days ago. 'It's all right. You don't have to be afraid.'

His eyes glittered, cold as the depths of space. 'I'm not afraid.

You deserve freedom, Lucy. And what I deserve is freedom from you. You're a distraction. You're getting in the way and taking up my time. I have more important things to do than sleep with you.'

It might have hurt her badly if she'd been the same Lucy that had come to Capri days before. But she wasn't the same Lucy. She was changed, and he'd changed her. He'd shown her where her true strength lay, and it wasn't running and hiding, it was in embracing what was in her heart. And she knew he was lying. That what he was doing was protecting himself. He was a city under siege and he would do anything he could to keep the invaders out.

And she could storm those walls with anger and pain, but she knew that wouldn't work. It would only make him call for reinforcements. No, if she wanted to crack his defences she was going to have to drop her own.

Lucy reached out and gently touched his cheek, the faintest brush of her fingers. 'I've fallen in love with you, did you know that?' The words were soft, yet the power of the feeling inside her vibrated in every syllable. 'You make me so happy.'

And just for a second the walls around his city looked as if they might shatter as shock flickered through his black eyes. The defenders putting down their swords, the battle inside him pausing.

But only for a moment.

'I don't care,' he said in a voice made of ice.

The crack through her heart became a chasm. He couldn't see, he couldn't understand. Because he didn't want to.

Vincenzo de Santi was a man with an iron will and he'd made a decision and nothing was going to sway him, still less the woman who loved him with everything she was.

He was happy in his cage. He didn't want to see that she was handing him a key.

Anger and pain would accomplish nothing. Only love could scale those walls. Only love would help him overcome his fear.

But it was something he would have to come to in his own time. He would have to open the gates of his heart himself— she couldn't force him.

It hurt. It hurt so much. But her pain wasn't for herself, it was for him. This beautiful, powerful, passionate panther, stuck in a cage of his own making. Too afraid of the open door standing before him to take a step through it.

All she could do was give him what she always gave him: the truth. And hope that somehow it would stay with him. It would be her last gift to him.

'If that's what you choose to believe, then fine,' she said quietly. 'But know this. All the justice in the world won't change the feeling inside you. It won't do anything for the guilt or the grief. But you can allow yourself to have something good. You can let yourself be happy. You deserve it, Vincenzo. And so do I.'

He said nothing, cold radiating from him so fiercely he might as well have been made of ice, but she went on anyway.

'I think you do care. I think you love me as much as I love you. But you're afraid and I think I understand why. You were betrayed by the one person who shouldn't have betrayed you and now you're protecting yourself.' She wanted to touch him again, but she couldn't bring herself to do it, not when she knew it wouldn't help. 'But I need you to know right now that you can trust me. I won't betray you. I love you and you don't have to be worthy of that love. You don't have to be pure. You don't have to be just. You don't have to prove yourself, not to me. The only thing you have to be is you.'

The silence that fell was deafening.

Vincenzo's gaze had turned flat and black and depthless. 'Are you done?'

'Yes,' she said and her voice didn't shake, even though her heart had cracked into pieces in her chest.

This time he said nothing.

He simply turned on his heel and left.

* * *

He didn't want to see her pack up her meagre belongings. Didn't want to see her tears or hear her husky, sweet voice telling him things he didn't want to hear. Telling him that he was afraid. That she loved him.

So he left her standing there, going down to his office and slamming the door.

Rage burned in his heart. At himself for what he couldn't let himself have and at her for all those things she'd said. Because he wasn't afraid. And he really didn't care. And as for worthiness...

Vincenzo strode to his desk and sat down, preparing to focus on some work, trying to shove all those thoughts from his head.

But it was impossible.

'You don't have to be worthy,' she'd said, as if he'd been trying to make himself worthy all this time. Which wasn't true. He *knew* he wasn't worthy. What he was doing was trying to atone. For himself and for his family. Pursuing justice was the only way he could make up for what he'd done, for the weight of guilt that crushed him.

'All the justice in the world won't change the feeling inside you...'

Ah, but she was wrong about that too. He'd wait until she'd vanished to the States and was safely ensconced in the new life he'd made for her, letting her father believe she was still with him on Capri. And only once she was settled would he make his move.

And that *would* make him feel better. Delivering justice to the man who'd hurt her.

You, you mean?

Vincenzo gritted his teeth. Yes, sending her away had hurt her, but he'd had to do it. And it wasn't because of fear. He'd told her the truth; he couldn't allow her to distract him from his true purpose, because what else would he be without it?

A liar. A murderer. A traitor. A tool to be used, not a son to be loved.

'You were betrayed by the one person who was supposed to love you...'

His *civetta*. She knew exactly what to say to appeal to his traitorous emotions. And they were traitorous. He couldn't trust them.

But she loves you. She won't betray you.

A spear of ice caught him in the chest, the pain so sharp he could hardly breathe, along with a raw, desperate feeling that made him want to run from his office and find her. Hold on to her. Cup her white face between his palms and kiss away the tears on her cheeks and the pain in her eyes. Give her those moments she wanted, give her the happiness she deserved.

But he'd told her he didn't care that she loved him, and he'd told himself. And he believed it. He *had* to believe it.

So he stayed where he was, his hands clenched in fists on his desk.

In the gardens outside, he could hear the sound of the helicopter's rotors. His security staff would be leading her to the helicopter that would take her to Naples. From there, she'd take the jet to New York. Everything had been organised for her. He wasn't going to leave her in the middle of a foreign city with nothing.

There was a heavy, aching sensation in the centre of his chest. It hurt. He'd never been shot in all the years he'd spent destroying organised crime, but perhaps it felt something a little like this, a bright, pure agony reaching every part of him.

He ignored it. Because she was wrong. Justice *would* cure this pain. He just had to be more focused, concentrate solely on his mission. He had to work harder.

There could not be any more distractions.

He could hear the rotors spinning faster now, faster and faster, and his whole body tightened with the urge to go to the windows and watch the helicopter take off, watch her fly away from him. But he didn't move. Because he didn't care. He wanted her, yes. Needed her, maybe. Love her? No.

She'd told him she loved him as if love was a truth, but she was wrong.

Love was the greatest lie of all.

Love had controlled and manipulated him. Love had blinded him. Duped him. Love had betrayed him.

He would never allow love to have that kind of dominion over him again.

The noise of the helicopter became deafening now as he heard it lift off from the garden, heading into the sky.

Vincenzo closed his eyes as the sound became more and more distant, listening until, at last, it faded away. And there was nothing but silence in his house.

Silence in his heart.

She was gone.

CHAPTER ELEVEN

HE ENDED UP waiting a month. Just until the people he had keeping an eye on Lucy told him she was settled. Her father, naturally, thought she was still with him and had contacted him a number of times, offering all kinds of things for her return.

Vincenzo had ignored all of them.

Once he had confirmation she was safe, he contacted Scotland Yard and gave them everything they needed to bring in Armstrong. And put him away for life.

The news of Armstrong's arrest came swiftly after that, and afterwards Vincenzo sat on the terrace, staring out over the sea, a glass of wine in his hand and the peace of the evening closing in.

It should have been satisfying, but it wasn't.

All he could think about was how empty his villa was. How quiet.

How he wanted to look across this table and meet a direct hazel gaze, large and dark behind the lenses of her glasses. How he wanted a pair of warm arms to welcome him, and a curvy, silky little body to press itself against him.

How he wanted her smile. Her honesty. Her understanding. Her bluntness and her direct manner.

He wanted her and she wasn't here.

'All the justice in the world won't change the feeling inside you...'

His fingers tightened on his wine glass, the memory of her voice playing in his head.

Over the past month he'd thrown himself into his work, spending hours holed up in his office, sifting through information, looking for his next target.

It should have made him feel better. It should have cleaned the memory of her right out of his head. But it didn't matter how hard he worked, the ache inside him wouldn't go away.

If only that ache was guilt, because that was easier to deal with. But it wasn't. It was her and her absence, the silence around him not one of peace, but of loss.

You made her happy and you sent her away.

Pain deepened in his chest. Happiness. What was that anyway? He didn't need it himself. He didn't want it. He had a vocation, a calling, and that fulfilled him. It brought him all the satisfaction he required.

'You can let yourself be happy...'

No, he couldn't. Happiness and peace weren't for men like him and she was a fool if she thought they were.

He raised his glass and took a sip, wanting to savour it, but it tasted of nothing. Even the food he ate these days had lost its flavour, just as the world had lost its colour. The sun its warmth...

She'd taken even those small pleasures left to him.

Anger began to burn in his gut, unexpected and fierce, an anger that he'd thought he'd put behind him. And the more he tried to force it away, the more it grew.

She'd done this to him. She'd taken all the little things that had made his life bearable. She'd shown him what peace felt like, what it was to be free of guilt, what it meant to be able to smile at something amusing. She'd shown him how to take a moment and enjoy every second of it.

You made her happy, but she also showed you happiness and now you can never forget it.

The anger burned hotter, flaming high and wild, incinerating everything in its path.

She'd been right, hadn't she? She'd been right all along. Justice would never be enough for him, not now she'd shown him what else he could have, and because he could never have it she'd doomed him.

Vincenzo shoved his chair back so hard it fell over. He rose to his feet, the rage inside him a column of fire, burning him alive. The wine glass was still in his hand, and before he'd even realised what he was doing he'd flung it to the stone floor, crystal exploding in glittering shards.

It was her fault. She'd made him feel like this. And now he'd be Tantalus for ever, desperately thirsty and unable to drink. Starving and unable to eat.

Or you could just accept that what she said was true, that you can let yourself be happy.

Rage coursed through him. How could he accept that? How could he be happy? When he'd hurt people? When he was as guilty as his mother? She was in jail at least, but he wasn't.

You thought Lucy had served her sentence and deserved freedom. Haven't you served yours?

He was shaking, staring unseeing at the remains of the wine glass, glittering in the last rays of twilight. Years he'd spent pursuing his crusade. Years. And still he felt the crushing burden of guilt. That hadn't eased one bit, no matter how many people he had put away. She hadn't lied about that, had she?

No, there had only been one thing that eased him and that was her. Being deep inside her, looking into her eyes. Feeling her arms around him, holding him. Making him feel as if he was more than his mother's broken tool. More than a ruthless, merciless crusader, fighting to fill the gaping void inside him.

The void his mother had left when she walked away from him without a backward glance. The void left by betrayal. Left by love.

He sucked in a breath and then another as the knowledge

filtered slowly through him, another truth that Lucy had given him that he'd thought was a lie.

'You're afraid...'

Was he? He hadn't thought he was, but... What if that was true? What if he just hadn't wanted to believe it? And if that *was* true, then just what the hell was he afraid of?

You know...

Vincenzo closed his eyes. If he didn't have justice, if he didn't have guilt, if he didn't have atonement, then what did he have? Who was he?

Just his mother's tool, her weapon. The puppet she pulled the strings with. An empty void. Unworthy of even her tainted, conditional love.

Fear curled through him, so sharp and bright he shuddered. He didn't want to face it. He wanted to turn and go to his office, lose himself in doing something, anything so this fear didn't choke him. The fear that he was nothing and no one. That he was unworthy, undeserving.

She loves you. She believes you deserve happiness.

What if...she was right? What if his *civetta* had told him the truth? Ah, but then, of course it was the truth. She'd always given him that. So maybe the question wasn't what if she was right? Maybe the question was more what if he believed her?

Something shifted inside him, the urge to run back to his office and bury himself in his crusade. But he knew, with a sudden flash of insight, that if he did that, he'd be doing exactly what he'd been doing for years. Escaping.

Escaping pain. Escaping betrayal. Protecting himself...

Ah, *Dio*, that was what he'd been doing all this time, wasn't it? Running from his fear, running like a coward for decades. Using his justice as his shield and righteousness as his sword.

But he wasn't just or righteous. He was a man cowering in fear. Afraid of his own emotions. Afraid of pain and betrayal. Afraid of the most powerful emotion of all: love.

'I think you love me as much as I love you.'

Vincenzo took a ragged breath, his heart raw, chewed up and spat out, scarred and full of holes, beating hard in his chest as the greatest truth of all settled down inside him. His skin was sensitised, as if the slightest breath of air would cut him to shreds.

Yes, he loved her. He'd loved her for days, for weeks. The entirety of his life had been spent waiting for her and the rest of it would be spent aching for her. She was his fate and his destiny. She was his truth.

And he'd been afraid of her. Afraid of her honesty. Afraid of her strength. Afraid of her courage, because she had more courage and strength in her little finger than he had in his entire body.

And when he'd sent her away he'd been afraid of her love. Afraid of the power of it, of the acceptance and understanding in it. The absolution he could sense it would give him and the happiness and peace it promised him.

He didn't deserve any of those things, but she thought he did. She thought he deserved happiness. She thought he deserved peace. And really, in the end it was a simple choice. He either trusted in her belief, or he didn't.

Ah, but was that even a decision to make? He knew the answer. It lay in his heart, in his soul.

Of course he trusted her. He loved her.

This time, Vincenzo didn't run. He faced his fear. And he accepted her love. Felt it flow through him like a purpose, like a vocation, a calling. Yet so much stronger, so much deeper. So much more complex.

And it wasn't a flame, burning through dry paper, only to crumble to ash when there was nothing to feed it. It was a glow, steady and bright and unending, self-sustaining. True strength in its purest form.

It would never flicker and it would never die. It would be with him always.

Peace came over him, easing the anger, dissipating the last remains of the blaze, cool and soft like Lucy's touch on his skin, a balm to his wounded soul. Bringing with it an absolute certainty.

He would find her. He would lay his heart at her feet. He would give her everything she ever wanted and if what she wanted was to never see him again, he would leave and count it a privilege to have even known her.

It would hurt and he might not survive it, but then, he wouldn't survive without her anyway.

She was more important than justice and she was certainly more important than fear. She was the most important thing in his life and he couldn't let another day pass with her thinking that she wasn't.

Vincenzo reached into his pocket and grabbed his phone, punching in a number, his hands now steady, the path before him clear and true.

'Get the helicopter now. I'm going to New York.'

Lucy had eventually found herself a little house by the sea in Cape Cod. It wasn't Capri, of course, or the Mediterranean, but the wild Atlantic wasn't far from her door, and there was a beach. And she could walk along that beach, have sand under her toes.

It was a lovely place and she had a job with a small finance firm that enabled her to work from home. It wasn't the most challenging of positions, but she was able to earn a living, which was all she required. She was starting to think longer term, now she had a future ahead of her, and had been toying with the idea of a financial crime consultancy business, but that was still to be decided.

She might even have been happy if it wasn't for the fact that she was missing one thing.

Vincenzo.

She had everything she'd promised her mother she would have. A life away from her father, a life of safety, of freedom.

But she didn't have him. And because she didn't have him,

she could never be truly happy. Her heart remained broken and always would.

It was late in the day, the sun going down, and Lucy walked along the beach as she did most late afternoons, her feet sinking into the sand.

She shouldn't give in to these long, solitary walks, because they gave her too much time to think. Too much time to remember how she'd let him turn his back and walk away a month earlier. How she'd collected her things and followed his security staff out to the helicopter, not even watching as it lifted off and flew away because she'd been blinded by tears.

She couldn't force him to see what he didn't want to, and, though love had given her strength, it didn't shield her from the pain of her heart breaking.

Pain for him and what he couldn't allow himself to have.

She remembered the flight to the States and the tears she'd cried for him, weeping herself into sleep at last. Then arriving in New York with an aching throat and gritty eyes.

A kind woman had met her after she'd got off the jet, giving her all the information she needed and showing her to some accommodation in the Village where she could spend a couple of days acclimatising.

She didn't remember that either.

All she remembered was the hollow feeling inside her. Which made sense in a lot of ways, since she'd left her heart in Capri, in Vincenzo de Santi's strong and capable hands.

You just let him have it. You gave it to him and then you walked away.

Lucy bent and picked up a shell, brushing the sand off it.

Of course she had. He'd wanted her to leave and even telling him that she loved him hadn't changed his mind. And not because he didn't want her, but for all those lies he was telling himself. About keeping her safe. About being distracted. About justice.

It was fear and she knew all about fear, how it could get inside you, trap you. And she'd confronted him with his own. But he'd refused to see it. And if he refused to see it, what more could she do? There was nothing.

She stared at the shell, her chest aching. Her throat tight with grief for the lonely path he'd chosen and the life he'd trapped himself in. He was a prisoner just as much as she'd once been, but his cell was one of his own choosing.

It made her ache.

She lifted her wet face to the sky, letting the tears dry on her cheeks in the wind. And then her gaze narrowed as she saw the tall figure of a man coming down the beach towards her.

It looked like… But no. It couldn't be him. It couldn't be Vincenzo.

She should walk on. The sun would be going down soon and she needed to get home. Yet she didn't move, watching the man walk towards her instead.

Her heart began to speed up, beating wildly in her chest, because it knew who he was, even as her mind balked. And her body tightened, because it knew too. The easy, powerful way he walked. The darkness of his hair. The hard, carved angles of his face…

Lucy stilled. Afraid to move in case he disappeared. Because surely he couldn't be real. Surely he couldn't be here on a beach in Cape Cod. With her.

But he came closer and closer and soon it was apparent that it was him, and he *was* here, and her heart raged behind her breastbone and she couldn't breathe.

All she could do was stand there as he came to her and, without saying a single word, swept her into his arms.

She stiffened, pushing hard against his solid chest. This couldn't be real. She was dreaming. She'd offered him her heart and he'd refused it.

'Vincenzo? What are you doing here?' And then anger in a cleansing fire hit her and she struggled. 'Let me go.'

He shuddered, as if in pain, and then abruptly his arms opened and she was free. His face was taut with some vast, passionate emotion burning just beneath the surface of his skin, his black eyes blazing with it.

'I need to say something, Lucy,' he said, his voice raw and rough. 'Will you let me?'

She was trembling now, half of her desperate to throw herself back into his arms while the other half was desperate to send him away.

'Say what?' she demanded, shaken and unable to hide it. 'Didn't you say everything you needed to back on Capri?'

'No.' The word was hoarse. 'I didn't. What I said to you then were lies.'

Shock washed through her, the trembling getting worse. 'What lies?'

Vincenzo's gaze was full of something hot and vital, burning steady as the fire at the centre of the earth. 'That you were a distraction. That I didn't care. That I wanted you to leave... You were right, *civetta*. Right about so many things. And it took me a while to see them, to accept what you were trying to tell me, but I know now.' His hands were in fists at his sides, his whole body radiating a familiar tension. 'You told me I was afraid, and you were right. I was. And if you want to know why, it's because of this.' He paused, his great, powerful chest heaving as he sucked in a breath. 'My mother betrayed me. She manipulated me. She took my trust in her, my love for her, and she broke it. She broke me. I was the tool she used to make herself powerful. Not her heir and not her son. Nothing. No one.'

Her heart quivered at the desolation in those words, her eyes filling with tears. 'Oh, Vincenzo. That's not true.'

'I was afraid it was, though, so afraid. I filled my life up with justice, with a crusade, and used it as an escape, a way to hide. So I didn't have to face the truth that she didn't love me. She never loved me. And perhaps there was nothing in me to love.'

A tear rolled down her cheek, the cracks in her heart aching. 'That's not true,' she said hoarsely. 'There so much in you to love.'

'I didn't believe you back on Capri. I used so many excuses to run from what you were trying to show me. But... I'm tired of running. I'm tired of not believing, of not trusting. I'm tired of filling my life up with something that changes nothing. I want something else, I want something better.' He paused, his eyes dark and full of heat. 'I want you, Lucy Armstrong. You were brave. You facing your fears helped me face mine. And if there's one person in this world I know I can trust, it's you.'

Her throat closed up at the certainty in his face and voice; she couldn't speak.

'You and your honesty and your strength, my *civetta*. You helped me find peace, you gave me a taste of happiness, and I... I want that more than I have wanted anything in my entire life.' The desperate, burning look in his eyes had dissipated, and there was something else there: a steady, bright glow. Calm and sure and certain. 'I'm afraid of being nothing more than what my mother made me, of being no one, and I thought justice would somehow make that feeling go away. But it didn't. It was you who made it go away, Lucy. It was you all this time.' The glow in his eyes became brighter, hotter. 'I love you, my *civetta*. I love you so much. And I know it took me a long time to understand and you will never know how sorry I am that I hurt you, but I can't bear another day of you not being in my life.' Slowly, he raised his arms and held them out, his soul laid bare in his eyes. 'Will you come to me, Lucy? I would very much like you to be mine. And I very much want to be yours.'

There was no thought, only certainty. Only the truth of the feeling that had burned in her heart so long it was part of her.

Lucy closed the distance without hesitation, giving him her answer.

And when his mouth found hers, she knew she'd found everything she'd ever wanted, right there in his arms.

The perfect moment to find her for ever.

The for ever they both deserved and the happiness they'd finally found.

Together.

EPILOGUE

THEY HAD SO many plans. Lucy had informed him of her idea to use her financial skills to help institutions combat fraud and other financial crimes, and so he'd helped her set up a consultancy. As for himself, he'd decided to step away from his crusade. He was going to devote more of himself to his family's auction house and the other various businesses he had. It should keep him busy until they started a family, which they would. After all, someone had to be around to look after the children, and he fully intended to be that someone.

And if he passed on a few titbits that he'd heard through the grapevine to various law enforcement agencies on occasion, then it was only what a fine, upstanding citizen would do.

But the most important plan of all was the wedding Vincenzo had insisted on the moment they returned to Capri.

And that was where he married her, at their villa, the place where they'd both discovered what happiness was. And they discovered it anew as they said their vows to each other in front of the priest.

Lucy wore the most beautiful wedding gown of ivory silk that hugged her curvaceous form, a veil tumbling over her glossy dark curls. They'd been left loose down her spine, but some combs held it back from her lovely face.

No, she was more than lovely. She was beautiful.

She'd given up her glasses today for contact lenses, and not for vanity but because her glasses fogged whenever she cried and she was apparently going to cry a lot—or so she told him.

But she wasn't crying now as he held her small hand and pushed his ring onto her finger. Only looking at him with so much love he could hardly meet her gaze.

Yet meet it he did as he made her his and he became hers.

And he wasn't unworthy or undeserving. He wasn't nothing and he wasn't no one.

He was her husband and he had a new purpose: to love her for the rest of his life.

So he did.

* * * * *

The Price Of A Dangerous Passion

Jane Porter

For my editor, Megan Haslam,
so good to have you back!
You're a dream to work with.

PROLOGUE

New Year's Eve

SHE HAD RULES. Rules she never broke. There were no excep-
tions. Charlotte never mixed business and pleasure, never. She
wasn't ever tempted, either...regardless of the value of her clients. All her clients were VIPs to her, clients who came to her
for her sterling reputation. They trusted her to make the best
possible decisions for them. They came to her because they
needed her expertise in sorting out image issues, public rela-
tion snafus and social media nightmares. How could they trust
her judgment, if her judgment was faulty?

If her judgment lost sight of the objective?

If she forgot why she was there in the first place?

Charlotte Parks knew all these things, and yet Brando Ricci
was making it almost impossible to remember why these—
her—rules were so important. She'd wrapped up business weeks
ago, well before Christmas. All conversations and concerns
with the Ricci-Baldi family had been handled, settled, put to
bed. She was here at the Ricci family's grand New Year's Eve
party because they loved to throw lavish parties and loved to
include everyone who had helped them. And Charlotte had
helped them, having spent the entire autumn in Florence, work-

ing to smooth tensions following intense, negative media attention arising from the family's struggles with power, and issues from succession.

Not all issues were completely settled, but much of the tension was gone, and the family had come together to present a unified face to the public once again. Tonight's party was part of that unified face.

She shouldn't have come tonight. Her part was done. She'd been paid—well paid, too. There was no justifiable reason to have returned to Florence for a party.

The music changed, slowed, and Brando pulled her closer, his hand settling low on her back, her breasts crushed to his tuxedo-covered chest. "You're overthinking," he murmured, his breath warm against her ear.

"I am," she agreed. "Or perhaps I should say, I'm thinking. And I should be thinking. You are dangerous."

"I would never hurt you. That is a promise."

And she knew that. She knew he'd be amazing—in bed, out of bed. The chemistry between them was electric and had been there from the moment they'd met last September. But the chemistry is what also troubled her, because she'd never felt a pull like this... She'd never even considered throwing caution to the wind. And yet here she was, a half hour from midnight, wrestling with her conscience, wrestling with desire.

"I shouldn't be here," she whispered, fingers curling around his, her heart thumping too hard, her body warm, sensitive, exquisitely aware...aroused. She hadn't made love in over a year... perhaps two years... She hadn't felt this attracted to anyone... ever. Part of her was so tempted to give in to the heat, while the logical, disciplined part warned that it was a mistake, a mistake that could jeopardize her career, her reputation...

Her heart.

She looked up into his handsome face again. He was gorgeous...truly handsome, but it wasn't just beautiful bone structure. He was smart, fascinating, compelling. During the months of working with the Ricci family, Brando was the one who drew her, time and again. Even though he was the youngest in his family, he had the most wisdom and insight, and she'd come to trust and respect his point of view, even going to him when Enzo, Marcello and Livia couldn't agree on anything, hoping Brando could find a diplomatic way to bring his fractious siblings together. And he had. And he did.

She'd returned tonight to Florence for him.

For this…

Whatever this was.

"What are you afraid of?" he asked now, his narrowed gaze sweeping her face.

His scrutiny made her face tingle, setting countless nerve endings alight. "Losing my head. Losing control."

The corner of his mouth lifted ever so slightly. His hand slid lower on her back, nearly cupping the curve of her butt. "We're two consenting adults."

She could feel his sinewy strength pressed against the length of her. His hard chest, his waist, the powerful thighs. "Yes, but business and pleasure should always be kept separate—"

"We're no longer working together," he reminded, his head dropping, his lips brushing the side of her neck.

She shuddered, and closed her eyes, trying to ignore how her breasts tightened, nipples pebbling, desire coiling within her. It was becoming increasingly difficult to keep a clear head. All she wanted was his mouth on hers, his hands teasing, exploring the length of her. It had been so long since she'd been with anyone and yet she wanted him…wanted his weight on her, wanted his body filling hers, wanted the pleasure she knew he'd give. The pleasure she craved…not from just anyone, but him. Brando Ricci. Vintner. Entrepreneur. Billionaire.

Lover.

No, not her lover, not yet.

"We shouldn't do this," she whispered, air catching in her

throat as his thumb stroked the side of her neck, lighting little tongues of fires just beneath the surface of her skin.

"We've done nothing wrong," he murmured. "We're simply dancing."

Done nothing wrong yet, she silently corrected, with *yet* being the operative word.

Charlotte tipped her head back to look up into Brando's mesmerizing silver eyes that were anything but cool, or cold. The heat in them scorched her now and she felt a shiver race through her. She'd fought this attraction for months, fought the sizzling awareness, suppressed the hunger, but tonight she was losing the battle. Just being in his arms was making her breathless and dizzy. Her body hummed, aching with awareness. Hunger.

"It's nearly midnight," she said, glancing over his shoulder at the enormous clock that had been mounted on the wall of the palace ballroom for tonight's New Year's countdown.

He glanced at the clock, too. "Ten minutes."

Her gaze took in the orchestra on the stage playing everyone's favorites, and the throng of beautiful people filling the dance floor. The seventeenth-century ballroom was packed with some of Europe's most glamorous, wealthy people. They were having a wonderful time, laughing, dancing, drinking, celebrating. When the clock struck midnight, the celebration would become deafening.

She'd always hated crowds, and normally avoided parties, but when the invitation came to attend the Riccis' party, she didn't say no. She couldn't say no.

"What are you thinking, *cara*?" Brando's deep voice was a caress.

Cara, darling. She felt another helpless shiver race through her.

She'd come tonight for him.

She wanted only him.

And yet, her rules. Her stupid rules.

She dampened her lips with the tip of her tongue. "I don't mix—"

"Business and pleasure," he completed for her. "I know. But tonight is not business. We're done with business, done with the family, done doing what others want us to do."

His lips brushed hers, a fleeting kiss that felt as if he'd set a thousand butterflies free inside her heart and mind. Wings of hope. Flutters of possibilities.

She always lived so alone, so controlled, so contained, but tonight... Tonight she felt as if maybe, just maybe, she belonged somewhere, to someone. Even if it were for one night only.

"Just tonight," she said hoarsely. "You must agree this is just one night, and nothing more than that. Promise me, Brando."

His lips brushed hers again. "Fine. Tonight is ours. Tonight belongs to us."

"And tomorrow—"

"We won't worry about. It's not here."

CHAPTER ONE

CHARLOTTE PARKS TUCKED her long pale hair behind an ear, straightened the lapel on her fashionable coat and rang the doorbell on the tall, handsome seventeenth-century building in the heart of Florence, just steps from Ponte Vecchio. Originally constructed as a palace, the building had been turned into several private homes, including the town house for Italian tycoon Brando Ricci.

She'd been here twice before, once for business last October, and once for—well, *not* business—New Year's Eve. It was a large, lavish town house with three separate floors and the sheer size of it meant that it'd take a moment for someone to come to the door, and so she waited calmly, expression serene.

Charlotte was skilled at serene. She'd mastered stress and pressure, having learned how to adjust to instability and conflict early in life, as the next to youngest in a big, rather famous British family, her affluent, aristocratic parents marrying and divorcing with rather joyous abandon, giving her a dozen siblings, half siblings and stepsiblings. She'd been born in England, then hauled to Los Angeles for ten years with her mother when she married the roguish film director Heath Hughes, and then bounced back to Europe at fifteen for finishing school in Switzerland.

Charlotte's siblings and stepsiblings were quite famous in their own right—models, actresses, race car drivers, as well as beautiful, envied English socialites. The Parks-Hughes-horpe family even had their own reality TV show for a bit, before certain members of the family decried it as too common, too crass, too American. It didn't help that nearly half of the family was now American, and full of plans and ambition. Charlotte, having spent twelve years in America, the ten with her mom, and now the past two on her own with a lovely house in the Hollywood Hills, had come to appreciate American bluntness and the efficiency with which Americans tackled problems. Well, maybe that was overstating things. Affluent Americans, inevitably image conscious, were very good at hiring help for damage control, and Charlotte was very good at damage control, so good, she had her own little company that had become a very successful PR company with global clientele.

Her ability to solve problems is what brought her to Florence. She'd met Brando Ricci nine months ago when she was hired to sort out a public relations nightmare involving the legendary Ricci family, one of Italy's most famous families, known for their wine, their leather goods, as well as their modern fashion house.

The Ricci family business dated back to the turn of the century, when making a great Chianti was their claim to fame. Following World War II, the family expanded, adding fashion and luxury leather goods to their business. The three Ricci brothers, grandsons to the founder, grew and nurtured the business until they ran into a rather common problem—how would succession work in a family where the three brothers had been almost equals, and yet each brother had two or three children each? It was one thing to share leadership among three, but a corporation couldn't have eight leaders. She'd stepped in late last August to smooth over some of the negative publicity stemming from the internal family struggles, generating new media coverage that focused on the family's cohesiveness, but behind the scenes, the family was still rather fractious as succession hadn't yet been truly addressed. But she'd done her part. The Ricci family was out of the tabloids, and she'd been given a very generous payment for services, and that should have been that.

Except it wasn't.

Charlotte, who rarely made mistakes, made a critical tactical error on New Year's Eve. She shouldn't have spent a night with Brando Ricci. Yes, it had been an extraordinary night, but letting down one's guard, and breaking one's rules, had staggering consequences.

Now she was here, but she dreaded the moment she'd be face-to-face with him. Brando was brilliant, powerful, perceptive, exciting. He'd made her feel all kinds of things she'd never felt before, and that was while still on the dance floor.

Returning here, being carried up to his bedroom, had been earth-shattering. She wasn't a virgin but she'd never felt anything as exquisite as what she felt in his arms, in his bed. It was without a doubt the most amazing night of her life. The sex had been so good, so unbelievably good, that she'd flown home dazed and dazzled and completely swept away.

Thank goodness there was a huge distance between them—6,188 miles to be precise—a trip that required at least one or two stops, depending on the airline and route, so it wasn't easy, or convenient to jet over to say hello. She returned home determined to focus on the future, not the past, or the bliss of being with a man who knew how to make a woman feel like the most glorious thing in the world.

There would be no reunions, no weekend escapes. They'd had their fling, and yes, it'd been the most exciting, sensual thing she'd ever experienced, but she wasn't going to lose her head over incredible sex with the sexiest, most sensual, most overwhelming man she'd ever met. That would be plain foolish, and she might be slightly, *slightly*, secretly besotted with Brando, but she was no fool. He was completely out of her league, and she'd told him so when he'd phoned to say he'd be in Los Angeles and hoped they could get together.

Just hearing his voice on the phone slammed her back to the night she'd spent in his bed in Florence. She felt his heat and strength again, and could picture his head between her thighs, his mouth on her where she was oh, so sensitive, his tongue finding every delicate nerve so that when she came, she came hard, and completely fell apart, dissolving into tears because he made her feel, so very much, and it was actually too much. She might live in California now but underneath she was still quite British and didn't enjoy being flooded with quite so much emotion. Emotion was wonderful in tidy bites and measured doses, but the emotion Brando made her feel, well… Really, there was no place for it, and no room in her life for dazed, dazzled and befuddled.

Which brought her to this exact moment, where she waited on Brando's doorstep, her elegant swing coat hiding her secret, a secret she had to share, because there was no hiding it any longer. It was one thing to keep a secret when there was no physical evidence, but her bump was impossible to hide now, so here she was, steeling herself for a conversation she did not think she'd ever have. Because she'd been on the pill, and he'd used a condom, and yet…

And yet…

Charlotte's heart staggered and she exhaled hard, before drawing in a slower calming breath and ringing the doorbell again, pressing on the bell a little longer, and more insistently, than before.

The last time she was here Brando had almost made her believe in miracles. But there were no miracles, just bruised principles, and broken rules, and heart-wrenching consequences.

The front door suddenly swung open, revealing a tall slender young woman with long, dark tousled hair, red lips, her naked body barely covered by a white silk robe, the fabric so sheer, her dusky nipples shone through.

Charlotte recognized the model immediately. She was an Argentinean beauty taking the fashion world by storm.

"Sì?" Louisa drawled as her robe slid off her shoulder and down her slender arm, fabric no longer covering one jutting breast.

Charlotte ignored the nipple. *"Brando è disponibile?"* she asked, utilizing the Italian she'd learned at her Swiss finishing school.

Louisa looked her up and down, a sly smile curving her full lips. *"È un po legato."*

He's a little tied up, Louisa had said, and from the model's smug smile, Charlotte had a feeling the words were literal.

"Would you be so kind as to untie him?" she said politely in Italian. "Let him know Charlotte Parks is here. I'll be waiting for him in the grand salon," she added, stepping into the house and heading for the formal room halfway down the white marble hall.

Charlotte heard the door close hard, and then footsteps on the curving staircase that led to the second floor. Brando's bedroom was up there. Charlotte knew, because she'd been there, during that second visit to this house when he'd stripped her naked and turned her into a mass of quivering need. She'd been far too intrigued by him, and she'd been far too confident in her ability to manage him, just the way she managed everything else in the world. But one didn't easily manage Brando Ricci. He was a force to be reckoned with.

That force, all six foot two inches of him, entered the salon, dressed, thankfully, and looking casually handsome in faded denims that wrapped his muscular thighs, and a silver-gray cashmere V-neck sweater that hugged the hard planes of his chest. The cashmere sweater perfectly matched the color of his silver-gray eyes and paired a little too well with the espresso black of his hair.

He was tall, lean, honed and even more beautiful than she remembered. Her heart jumped, a quick staccato that did nothing for her sense of calm. Just that little glimpse of skin at his throat made her remember what it had felt like to be naked against him. His body didn't just look magnificent, he knew how to move it, and when he'd been inside her, she'd felt satisfied, more satisfied, more…everything…than she'd ever felt in her life.

Being intimate with him hadn't been just physical pleasure. She'd experienced a feeling of peace and wholeness, which made no sense since Brando had a history of breaking hearts. He didn't do long relationships. He didn't want commitments.

Which was why he should be fine with her proposal, relieved to hear that she would handle everything.

"Charlotte," he said, approaching her, and leaning down to kiss each of her cheeks. "What brings you to Florence?"

"You do." She smiled up at him. "I hope I haven't interrupted anything."

He gave her an amused smile, indicating he was aware that she was aware she'd obviously interrupted something.

"Shall we sit?" he suggested, gesturing to the chic armchairs in the white room with red and coral accents.

"Yes, thank you." She took the chair opposite his, the chairs a little closer together than she preferred, but it felt good to be off her feet as her heart had begun to race and all her cool, calm confidence deserted her now that he was here. Brando was larger than life, humming with an energy that she found potent and strangely addictive. Her family was filled with beautiful people, but Brando exuded a physicality and a virility that was all his own.

He'd more than impressed her with his virility six months ago in this very house.

New Year's Eve. What a life-changing night…

Heat rushed through her at the memory, and her stomach did a wobbly flip. The last thing she wanted to do was relive those intense memories now, here, with Brando within arm's length and his lover upstairs waiting for him in bed. "I imagine Louisa must be growing impatient," she said.

He smiled, a lazy, almost indulgent smile. "Louisa is good at entertaining herself." He was still smiling, but his silver gaze narrowed, expression sharpening. "When did you arrive in Italy?"

"Today actually. I've left my bags at the hotel, but haven't yet checked in."

"That eager to see me?"

"I wasn't sure if you'd be here, or at the country house. If you were in the countryside already, I was going to rent a car and drive out to meet you."

"I'm heading to the villa tomorrow." His gaze skimmed over her, studying her intently. "You look well."

"Thank you. I feel well." She hesitated, struggling for words, her carefully rehearsed speech forgotten. She'd convinced herself that he wouldn't care about her news. She'd convinced herself that he'd be relieved she was going to handle everything and do everything. Suddenly she wasn't so sure and her heart had begun to race, anxiety pulsing just below the surface. "Do you mind if I take off my coat? It's very warm."

"Yes, your cheeks are quite flushed."

The moment her coat came off, he'd see. He'd know. She hesitated, hands no longer steady, her confidence shaken.

What if it didn't play out the way she anticipated? What if he—

She stopped herself there, unable to imagine any other scenario than the one she'd planned on. He was a bachelor. A playboy. He wasn't father material. He wouldn't be interested in the domestic details.

"Charlotte, are you all right?" he asked.

Tell him. Just tell him now.

Instead, mouth dry, heart racing, she slowly, carefully eased her arms from the sleeves and then allowed the coat to slide off her shoulders and fall back onto the chair.

Her emerald dress was slim fitting, the soft knit clinging to her small frame, highlighting her bump. The baby gave a hard kick just then and she touched her bump, not sure if she was soothing the baby, or herself.

"I'm six months," she said quietly, steadily. "It's been an easy pregnancy, and there have been no complications. I didn't want to say anything until I'd made it out of the first trimester—" She broke off, took a quick breath and plunged on. "I wasn't showing until recently and then I just popped. I couldn't hide it any longer, and I didn't think I should."

"Should I be offering my congratulations?"

"If you'd like to include yourself in the congratulations."

There was a beat of silence. "Is this your way of saying it's mine?"

"Yes."

"And you're sure it's mine?"

"Yes."

His gaze held hers, the silver gray piercing. There was no judgment in his eyes, no censure, no shock, not even disappointment. "We took precautions, both of us."

"It seems we have a child that very much wants to be part of the world," she answered, sitting tall, shoulders straight.

"A child with determination," he replied.

She smiled, her most charming smile, aware that they were now both playing the same game. "It's an admirable trait."

"Agreed." He hesitated. "You never considered an abortion?"

"No." She eyed him cautiously. "Would you have preferred me to end the pregnancy?"

"I'm Italian. Catholic. So, no."

"I'm neither, but it was never an option."

His gaze held hers. "And now you're here."

"Yes." Her chin lifted, and yet she kept her voice even. As long as she maintained control, she'd be fine, and he'd be fine. Really, it was just a matter of needing time to work through the shock that he must be feeling. "It seemed best to tell you in person. I knew you would want to know, and you deserve to know. It didn't seem fair to just make all the decisions without consulting you."

Brando arched a brow. "And yet you haven't consulted me."

"I am now. That's why I've come."

Silence stretched and the silence made her pulse do an odd, uncomfortable thudding in her veins, a thudding she felt all the way through her. This was not the Brando she'd last seen. In fact, this was not a Brando she recognized. They were like strangers, and yet the last time she'd been with him they'd been incredibly intimate. She'd given herself all of him and had never regretted it...not until she discovered there were consequences for that night of passion.

"The pregnancy stunned me," she said after a moment. "It wasn't part of my plan, and it took me a few weeks to sort through all my feelings, but I'm actually now very much looking forward to motherhood."

"This consultation... What is your goal? You want money? Financial support?"

"No."

"What, then?"

Her plan was to offer him exactly what he didn't want—a chance to be a father. She'd give him the opportunity to co-parent, an opportunity she knew he wouldn't want, and when he balked, she'd gently offer to do it all herself, and he'd be relieved, and accept. Brando was handsome and brilliant but not ready to settle down. His sister had said so more than once. Brando was the least committed to family. Brando was the rebel and valued his independence. She understood that, though. Charlotte valued hers.

"I want you to be this child's father," she said quietly, "*if* you want to be his or her father, and if not, I am sure one day I will fall in love and marry a man who will raise this child as his. In the meantime, I recognize your rights, and I respect your rights, and would like to include you in the decision-making, should you want to be included."

"You were pregnant when I was in Los Angeles earlier in the year."

"Yes."

"Why didn't you tell me then?"

"It was early in my pregnancy, and I wasn't sure that the pregnancy was viable. My sisters have miscarried in the first trimester, and they warned me that it could happen to me."

"Your family knows, then?"

"No. I've managed to hide the pregnancy so far, but it's impossible now. I'm obviously expecting."

"Why haven't you told your family?"

"It's none of their business." She put a hand to her bump again, feeling another fluttery shift inside. "And if I was going to share the news with anyone, it should be you."

Charlotte Parks was every bit as beautiful as the last time Brando had seen her, naked in his bed, her long golden hair splayed across the pillow, her mouth swollen from his kisses. This morning she looked impossibly self-contained, as well as impossibly glowing. Pregnancy suited her. Her skin appeared more luminous, her eyes bluer, brighter, her long, golden blond hair shimmering in the sunlight that poured through the tall windows.

When Louisa had come upstairs to tell him there was a woman at the door, demanding to see him, he'd arched a brow, but hadn't been concerned. When he discovered it was Charlotte in the salon, he'd been intrigued. Charlotte, fascinating Charlotte, never made demands, and yet she'd been pure pleasure in his bed. But now he wasn't as sanguine. Apparently, she was pregnant. With his child.

He'd heard this before, years ago. Thankfully he'd asked for a paternity test, and the test had turned out negative. He couldn't have been more grateful.

Now… Now he didn't know what to think and Brando's gaze swept over Charlotte, skimming her fair hair, high elegant cheekbones, before dropping to her full breasts and her taut, round bump. She looked radiant, but not quite as serene as he'd first thought her to be. "Hasn't this been a difficult secret to keep?" he asked.

"No."

"Really?"

She shrugged. "I'm not one that needs to discuss things to make decisions, and I've never turned to others for advice. What I needed was time, and I had that time, which is why I'm here, ready to discuss the future."

"And yet this is all news to me."

Color swept her lovely high cheekbones, and her head dipped. "True." Her chin lifted and her gaze met his. "I expect you'll want a paternity test. I've already checked into clinics that do the testing here in Florence. It's a simple procedure, just a blood draw for both of us and then we wait for results." She hesitated a moment. "If possible, I'd like to get it done today. That way we'll have the results sooner than later."

"And if I am the father?"

"Well, you are the father, but please let me reassure you that I have things well in control. I'm not asking for anything from you. In fact, nothing in your world needs to change. I just wanted to be courteous—"

He laughed, a low husky sound that stopped her midsentence.

She glanced at him, winged eyebrows arching higher, her color even more heightened. "I wasn't trying to be funny," she said rather stiffly.

"Maybe not, but I found it comical when you said nothing in my world needs to change. *Bella*, everything in my world will change. It's already changed, if I'm to become a father."

"I'm obviously going to become a mother. But you... You don't have to do this...or be part of this. I'm quite comfortable parenting on my own."

"Which would be fine, if it wasn't my child, but if it is my child, then I'm going to be involved."

Her lips parted and then pressed together. She glanced to the tall windows framed by large red-and-white-check silk curtains, the checked fabric a contrast to the marble terra-cotta parquet floor. She suddenly looked anxious and appeared to be struggling to find the right words.

"I'm surprised you're taking this so well," she said at last, looking over at him, her blue gaze clear. "We had one night together, little more than a fling, and yet you seem ready to embrace parenthood."

"I've always taken precautions to prevent an unplanned pregnancy, and yet now that we're here at this crossroads, it's not a tragedy, not something that needs to be overcome. We're mature and independent, able to provide a safe, happy home for our child."

Again, her lips parted, and again they pinched closed. Color washed through her cheeks, her eyes shone overly bright.

It struck him then that he'd caught her off guard. What had she imagined he'd say? No thank you, and goodbye?

That he'd wash his hands of his child?

"But maybe it's not mine," he said, thinking back to that other time where a woman had tried to trick him.

"No, it's yours. Without a doubt. But I didn't expect you to believe me. Why should you? We spent only one night together. Which is why I want the blood test done today. I'm only here for the weekend, and then Monday I head to England for a week, but we should get the results in seven business days, or three, if we pay to rush the results." She drew a breath. "I'd prefer to pay the rush fee, so I could return here and draw up custodial paperwork before my flight back to California."

"Custodial paperwork?" he echoed, thinking she'd certainly mapped it all out.

"The baby will live with me."

Her calm, crisp answer stirred his temper. "It seems we do have things to discuss."

"I just want to reassure you, Brando, that I have no intention of sharing the baby's paternity with anyone. This isn't anyone's business but ours, and the secret will be safe with me."

He lifted a brow. "Our child isn't to know I'm his or her father?"

"Do you want to be a father?" she asked bluntly.

"I don't understand the question, *cara*. If I'm the father, I am the father."

Fresh color swept through her face. "I suppose that is the part we need to discuss."

Was she seriously wanting to cut him out? Was she envisioning him as a sperm donor, but nothing more? He felt a surge of temper, but swiftly checked it. "It seems you and I do have a great deal to discuss," he said, "but I'd prefer more privacy. Now isn't the ideal time, not with Louisa here."

Charlotte glanced up to the ceiling, as if she expected Louisa to be there, on the hand-blown glass chandelier. "True." She slipped her coat back on, opened her handbag and drew out a slip of paper. "This is the nearest clinic that can do the blood draw. They can get you in this afternoon. I'll be going straight there when I leave here. If you could just call and make an appointment for today? Would that be possible?"

"I see no reason for us to delay the test."

"Good, thank you." She rose and tucked her purse beneath her arm. "And I apologize for barging in on you like this. I should have realized you might have a guest."

"It's fine. This was important." He couldn't imagine anything being more important, nor could he imagine any woman more beautiful than Charlotte Parks. He'd wanted her from the very first meeting. She'd been the elusive one, but he hadn't given up...not until she'd returned to Los Angeles and ghosted him.

He walked her to the front door now. "Where are you staying?"

She gave him the name of her hotel, a five-star property overlooking the river. It's where she had stayed before. There were smaller hotels, more affordable hotels, but this one took such excellent care of her the last time she was in Florence, it's where she wanted to be this time.

"Let me call a taxi for you," he said.

"I think I'll walk." She forced a faint smile. "The fresh air will do me good and maybe then I can get some work done."

"You're still working?"

"But of course." She flashed a smile. "It's what I do best."

"It's not too much at this stage of your pregnancy? It won't hurt the baby?"

"No. Everything is good."

The baby, Charlotte silently repeated as she walked back to her hotel. He'd referenced the baby in such a way that emotion fluttered in her, little wings of pain and heartache.

It was strange talking about her pregnancy. She'd kept the news to herself all this time, carrying the secret within her, just as she carried the baby, close to her heart, protective of the world's reaction. And yet in a matter of minutes she'd shared her news, and Brando had knocked away the walls of secrecy and made the news...matter-of-fact.

She paused at the curb, checked for traffic and dashed across, grateful for the brisk walk, needing the quick pace to help her process everything she was thinking and feeling.

All this time she'd thought she was most concerned about the pregnancy, about becoming a single mother, but seeing Brando had stripped away the pretense.

Seeing him made her feel naked and nervous and incredibly vulnerable.

She didn't have feelings for him, and yet...

Charlotte exhaled hard, and blinked even harder, and wondered why she felt so terribly discombobulated. Seeing Brando made her feel...strange.

Raw.

Hurt.

Which didn't make sense as he'd been nothing but polite,

and respectful considering how shocking her announcement had to have been. She was grateful there had been no drama and he'd been quite cordial about taking the paternity test. The lack of drama made her suspect, though, striking her as too good to be true.

Maybe Brando was in shock. Maybe he wasn't as sanguine as he appeared, and underneath his veneer of calm, he was secretly rattled.

Or maybe he didn't believe her and was just waiting for the test results before challenging her...

Or maybe he wasn't even thinking about her news anymore and maybe he was back in bed with Louisa.

She blanched, and her stomach rose.

Oh, why, oh, why did Louisa have to be there today? And why, oh, why did Charlotte have to know about her?

Brando left the clinic across the street from Maria Beatrice Hospital and called Charlotte. It took her a few rings to answer the phone.

"It's Brando," he said when she answered. "Am I interrupting anything?"

"No. Just trying to write a press release but can't focus. I didn't sleep well last night."

"You should try to nap."

"Maybe," she said.

"What are you doing later?" he asked. "Do you have plans for dinner tonight?"

"No. Just more work."

"Have dinner with me."

"Did you have the test done?"

"I did, and we should have results in the morning. There is a lab here in Florence that will expedite testing for us."

"How? I heard three days was the fastest—"

"Unless you pay enormous sums of money to get something done."

"Ah."

He heard the wary note enter in her voice. "So, dinner?"

"What about Louisa?"

"She's not invited."

"Brando."

"Can we just focus on you for the time being? You're here, six months pregnant. Isn't it time we finally started communicating?"

CHAPTER TWO

BRANDO WATCHED CHARLOTTE emerge from the hotel's elevators and cross the marble lobby. Unlike this morning's form-fitting dress that had outlined her shape, she had chosen narrow black trousers and a stylish white tunic that skimmed her stomach, the tunic's natural fullness making the bump harder to detect.

Suddenly he flashed back to a different pregnancy with a different woman. It was years ago and when confronted by the news of her pregnancy, he'd been horrified. They'd had a brief relationship, and it had ended when he discovered she was not at all what she seemed, her vivacious, sparkling beauty a cover for an insecure, unkind, manipulative personality. It filled him with dread to think of her raising any child of his, and yet he'd promised her he'd support her and the baby…if the baby truly was his.

Thank God, the blood test came back negative. The child wasn't his. Adele had cried and protested, claiming the DNA blood test flawed.

It was only much later that he'd learned she'd manipulated some other wealthy man to marry her.

The pregnancy scare had been a wake-up call, and for a while Brando didn't date, choosing to be celibate over risking paternity claims. But after an eight-month celibacy period, he began dating again, and now here he was, waiting for the results of another DNA test.

He didn't like comparing Adele to Charlotte, though. They were nothing alike, and to be honest, Brando didn't need a paternity test to prove he was the father of Charlotte's baby. She wouldn't have come here, to him, if she hadn't been certain. Charlotte had money of her own, as well as a successful career. She'd even said earlier that she wanted nothing from him, and was planning on raising the baby in California, apart from him.

Which would be fine if it was someone else's child, but if the baby was his, since the baby was his, Brando was not going to be forced to the sidelines.

He'd taken the paternity test this afternoon to fight for his rights. He was going to be part of his child's life, and not as a distant figure on the periphery, but as a hands-on parent who was present from birth.

He moved toward Charlotte now, meeting her near the reception desk. "You look lovely," he said, greeting her with a kiss on the cheek.

She stiffened at the kiss, shooting him a suspicious look. "No need for compliments. This isn't a date."

"Would you prefer I had said something along the lines that you're very punctual?" he replied mockingly.

"Yes."

"Charlotte, good to see you. You're very punctual tonight."

She shot him another disapproving glance. "It's discourteous making people wait."

"You must have hated it when Marcello showed up an hour late for our first meeting."

"I wasn't impressed, no." And then her expression softened a fraction. "But you were on time. You're always on time."

"Speaking of time, we have a reservation in ten minutes. We can drive there, or walk, if you're feeling up to it. The restaurant isn't far." He glanced down at her feet. She was wearing pumps with a stylish kitten heel. "Would you prefer to drive, or walk?"

"I'd love to walk."

"Good. I was hoping you'd say that." Brando placed his hand lightly on her lower back and steered her out the front door, where he handed the keys of his car to the hotel valet.

Charlotte was exquisitely aware of Brando's hand on the small of her back as they left the hotel. He'd smelled heavenly when he'd kissed her in the lobby. It had been just a brief kiss on the cheek, and yet the warm brush of his lips and the light spicy scent he wore made her stomach curl and breath catch. He was sin on two legs, and her undoing.

"Where are we going for dinner?" she asked, trying to distract herself.

He named a restaurant she wasn't familiar with and for a few minutes they made small talk about Florence's cuisine. It was an inane conversation, she thought, as superficial as it could be, but also better than talking about what was really at stake.

The baby, and the future.

"You really think they will have results from the blood test tomorrow?" she asked, glancing from the golden sky to Brando.

"They said they might be able to rush something tonight, but we'd know for sure in the morning."

Charlotte wasn't worried he wasn't the father. He was the only one she'd been with in years, but she didn't expect him to take her word for it. After all, she'd slept with him on the first date. Why should he not think she did that all the time?

"Are you nervous?" he asked.

Her brow furrowed. "About the results? No. I think I'm more overwhelmed just seeing you again. It's...surreal."

"You had no plans to see me again, did you?"

She glanced up at him again, her gaze skimming his handsome profile. "No," she answered honestly. "I didn't. I don't mix business and pleasure, and once I'd slept with you, I wasn't going to be able to see you, or work with you, again."

"Why did you sleep with me, then?"

She mustered a small, tight smile. "I think you know the answer to that."

"If I did, I wouldn't have asked."

"I found you quite irresistible," she said, her voice lightly mocking. "And I thought, why not, just once, live a little? I should have remembered there are always consequences—" She broke off, stumbling, her toe catching in one of the cobbled stones lining the street. She didn't fall, though. Brando's arm tightened around her, keeping her upright.

"I've got you," he said.

He certainly did. His arm felt like a hot brand around her waist, his fingers sending forks of lightning through her middle. He was so very close and she felt completely overwhelmed by his nearness, creating an aching awareness she didn't want or need. Brando was already her kryptonite. If she wasn't very careful, she'd implode.

"Maybe," she said carefully, as she stopped walking, "I would be steadier without you."

"I don't want you to trip."

"I'm klutzy because you are close. I'd feel surer of myself if you didn't touch me." She tried to keep her tone light. "It must be a pregnancy thing where my center of balance is changing."

He looked skeptical, his silver gaze penetrating. "I was barely touching you."

Heat rushed through her, his words reminding her of the night where he did touch her, all over, giving her endless pleasure. She'd never felt anything like that, and doubted she'd ever feel anything like that again. He'd taken sex and elevated it to an art form. Making love with him had been transcendental… transformative.

"Nonetheless, I find it unsettling." The words sounded harsh, and so she added, "Take that as a compliment if you can. I might be six months pregnant, but you're still you, and apparently, I can't help responding to you."

Brando faced her on the street. "What we had was good, wasn't it?"

"Too good. I didn't trust it." She realized they were blocking the sidewalk and people were having to walk around them, some glancing at Brando and nodding, recognizing him. "We should keep walking."

Five minutes later they arrived at a building tucked off a hidden street not far from one of the famous squares. They took stairs down into the cellar. The walls were frescoed, the floor covered in thick tiles, the beams of the ceiling stenciled in shades of blue, red and gold. There were perhaps a dozen tables, almost all booths framed by rich burgundy velvet curtains. Italian glass chandeliers hung over each table, creating a mosaic of glittering light within each cozy booth.

They were seated at a table in the far corner away from the other guests. No one had paid them any attention when they arrived and Charlotte was happy to be off her feet, tucked into their booth, the cushion covered in rich, midnight-blue brocade with hints of gold thread, and yet her pulse raced and butterflies filled her. She couldn't remember when she'd last felt so worried. She hadn't been nervous when she'd arrived in Florence this morning, but ever since leaving Brando's house, she'd struggled. "I didn't think this would be easy," she said bluntly, "but at the same time, I didn't think it would be quite so difficult."

"Have I been difficult?"

"No. You haven't. But at the same time, I'm rattled."

"What is troubling you?"

She didn't know how to put her worries into words. She didn't know how to explain her feelings. They weren't making sense to her. How could they make sense to him?

She hadn't come to Italy expecting a declaration of love from Brando. She hadn't come imagining that he would even want to be part of her future. They'd had a one-night stand, and that was really all it was, and she'd had realistic expectations about what he'd say and do. And yet for some reason, seeing Louisa at the front door in that sheer negligee had maddened a small part of her brain, torturing her with a jealousy she couldn't, *shouldn't*, feel. There was no relationship between her and Brando, and certainly no commitment, or feelings of any kind, so why should remembering Louisa make her feel heartsick, and anxious, and angry?

And why should remembering Brando appearing in the salon, handsome and sophisticated and oh, so very calm, make Charlotte feel almost impotent with need, and pain?

That was the part that baffled her.

Why had she been so upset today?

Why did she feel cheated?

How could she possibly feel resentful, and played, when Brando wasn't even hers?

"I can't read your mind, *cara*. You'll have to try to use words," he said.

"It's ridiculous. You'll think I'm ridiculous—"

"I won't."

"No," she corrected, "you will, because I find myself ridiculous right now." She fiddled with the trio of stemware on the table, adjusting the glasses, forming them into a line. "I'm usually incredibly confident, and yet I've been rattled by your girlfriend Louisa." Charlotte glanced at Brando and shrugged. "I'm sorry. It sounds petty—"

"No, it doesn't. You're pregnant and feeling quite alone—"

"I wouldn't go that far. I'm excited about the baby. But seeing Louisa at your door made me realize how weird this really is. I should have called you first. I shouldn't have just shown up."

"It's fine."

"Louisa must be upset."

"She doesn't know. I haven't said anything to her."

"That makes sense, especially as you need to wait for results from the DNA test."

"I'm certain the results will show I'm the father."

She nodded. "They will." She hesitated. "And then you'll tell her?"

"No one needs to know anything, not right now."

She sighed with relief and felt some of her tension knotting her shoulders ease. "Thank you. I'm not ready for the world to know."

"I agree."

Charlotte then had another troubling thought. "But Brando, if you keep the information from her, it's going to cause trouble, it has to."

"Louisa and I are having fun. It's not a serious relationship."

"Do you ever have serious relationships?"

He cocked an eyebrow. "Do you really want to discuss my relationship history tonight?"

Charlotte grimaced. "No. I'm quite sure that's more than I could handle."

Brando laughed softly, the sound low and husky. "Before we put the subject of Louisa behind us, let me just reiterate that Louisa is lovely and fun, but we're not serious, or exclusive.

"You and me being here, having dinner together, isn't problematic, nor is it deceptive. We're not going behind Louisa's back. She knows I'm out with you tonight, just as I know she's with others tonight. So, you don't need to worry about her, or fear that you're stepping on toes."

"And yet she opened your front door almost naked."

"She's a bit of an exhibitionist. She enjoys the attention. Don't let her overly upset you. You've come a long way to meet with me and address the issue of co-parenting—"

"Co-parenting? Is that what you're thinking?"

"I'm the father."

Charlotte's chest squeezed. Her pulse began to race. Panic set in. "What if you're not?"

He gave her a look that made her stomach somersault.

"You are," she said lowly, "but I didn't think...didn't assume..." She couldn't finish the thought. She felt sick. Her limbs felt cold. She struggled to find her center and breathe.

Keep calm, keep calm, keep calm. "You're a bachelor, living the bachelor lifestyle."

"You're single, as well."

"But I'm not dating others, and not sleeping around—" She stared at him horrified, and yet unable to take the words back. "What I mean is, we live really far apart. It's not as if we can fly a baby back and forth across the Atlantic."

He said nothing, but she felt the weight of her words between them as well as the accusation.

He was still sleeping with others. She was upset that he was sleeping with others. She hadn't even phrased it as nicely as that. She'd made him sound like a tomcat.

She waited for him to speak. And still he kept silent. She went hot and cold, hating to now be on the defensive. "You are a bachelor. You can do whatever you please. I apologize if I sounded critical of your lifestyle."

"Is that why you've waited so long to tell me about the baby?"

"No." She forced herself to meet his silver gaze. "No, I promise. I waited because… I didn't want to share the news."

"Share the news, or share our child?"

It felt as if he'd struck her in the chest. She inhaled hard, pain splintering her heart.

"I live in California."

"And I live here."

She picked through his words, processing the meaning. "Do you truly desire to be part of our child's life?"

"Absolutely. Any child of mine will be raised by me."

Another blow that made her throat thicken and her eyes sting. "By you?"

"My father was a hands-on parent, and I intend to be the same."

"How can you be so sure you want to do this?"

"I would never walk away from my responsibilities." He hesitated. "Would it make you feel better if I offered to be the custodial parent? I'd raise our child—"

"*No.* Not an option."

"Then why is it an option for you to be the sole custodial parent?"

"Because I'm making this baby. I'm carrying it right now."

"And you wouldn't be making a baby if it weren't for my sperm that found a way to reach your egg."

"I don't need the biology lesson, Brando."

"And I will not permit you to cut me out. I might not be carrying our child, but I am as committed to his or her future as you are."

Things had escalated quickly, she thought, dazed. She sat back, stunned, and uncertain as to what to say in response.

The waiter appeared with a bottle of sparkling water and after a few words from Brando, cleared away the wineglasses.

Silence stretched and Charlotte's eyes stung, hot and gritty. Six months ago, she'd had sex with Brando, sex that resulted in three unforgettable orgasms, and one very unplanned pregnancy. "I didn't want any of this to happen," she said quietly. "I've never mixed business with pleasure, never, ever, until you, and now everything is a mess."

"Not that much of a mess," he answered. "We're two capable adults. We will sort things out and come up with a plan that puts the baby's needs first, because in the end, that is the important thing."

It wasn't a question, but a statement. It crossed her mind that she was seriously in over her head, because she'd had a plan, a good plan, but he'd just tossed it out and now they were starting over, and she had a feeling she wasn't going to like the new plan at all.

"There's no reason to rush, though," she said after a length pause. "We should take time to consider all the different options. The baby won't be here for three months, and that gives us time to discuss the pros and cons of each option. The last thing we want to do is let our hearts overrule our heads."

He studied her from across the table, the glittering light captured in his narrowed silver gaze and casting shadows beneath his high, hard cheekbones. Brando was no longer smiling. His jaw was hard, lips pressed firm. "Time will not change what is right. My duty is to my child, and the needs of my child come first now."

"I just thought you might want more time… You've only just learned about the pregnancy today. I worry you're being impulsive—"

"You didn't expect me to assume responsibility?"

"I—" She broke off, glanced away, the tip of her tongue moistening her dry lower lip. "I thought you'd be more ambivalent. I thought there might be more resistance."

"Why, if it's my son or daughter?"

"It took me weeks to get to the place you've reached in hours."

"Sex is how babies are made. I've always been cognizant that sex, as pleasant as it is, leads to procreation."

The waiter returned and there was no menu to read. The waiter rattled off the house specialties and Brando recommended the *bistecca alla Fiorentina*, claiming it was the best Florentine steak in the city.

"I won't be able to eat very much," she answered, "and I'm craving pasta. I thought I heard *crespelle* mentioned. Is that the dish that's similar and stuffed with ricotta cheese and spinach?"

"Yes. It's good here, too."

"I'll just have the *crespelle* and salad."

Brando spoke quickly to the waiter, placing their order. The waiter topped off their water glasses and left them alone.

"You didn't order wine," she said.

"You're not drinking so I won't drink," he said.

"I don't mind if you drink. You're a vintner."

"I'm not giving up wine forever. I just don't need any tonight." He studied her, expression hard. "Did you really think I'd agree to let my child be raised on the other side of the world?"

"I thought you'd react differently, yes."

"What did you expect?"

"That you'd be noncommittal, ask for a pregnancy test and then make me wait while you came to terms with the fact that I'm truly carrying your baby."

"Did you ever think it might possibly be someone else's?"

It was a fair question. It shouldn't put her on edge. She felt defensive, though. "No. You have been the only man I've slept with in the past year."

There was a subtle shift in his expression, his black lashes dropping ever so slightly over his piercing gaze. "Why?"

"I only sleep with someone I'm profoundly attracted to." She lifted her chin, smiled wryly. "I was profoundly attracted to you."

"Surely there are other men who catch your eye."

"Apparently not often enough." She pushed back a long pale strand of hair, tucking it behind her ear. "On the plus side, it made the question of parentage easy. You've been the only one I've slept with this year, so, you're it."

"Yet we used birth control."

"My pill, plus your two condoms." She felt hot bands form across her cheekbones. "Obviously, my pill wasn't effective."

"Nor were the condoms."

"I blame myself," she said. "Not you. It's why I'm on the pill. So there are no oops, no mistakes."

"And yet we still have an oops baby."

Her eyes met his and held. "I'd like to raise the baby at my home in Los Angeles. I have a lovely garden and I'm close to the ocean—"

"I don't live in California, *cara*."

She ignored the endearment as she held her breath, silently counting to ten. She needed to remain calm. "Perhaps you could buy a place near me. Perhaps you could make Southern California a second home."

"But it's not, nor will it ever be."

"I'll be there, and the baby—"

"Or, I kidnap you, keep you locked up at one of my estates."

She waited for him to smile or laugh. He did neither. "You wouldn't do that."

"You don't think so?"

Her insides did a nervous flip. He was being outrageous and she wasn't worried he'd kidnap her, but she understood the point he was making. He wasn't just going to walk away from them. He was asserting his rights. Brando would be a permanent part of their lives, and that was what made her heart race, and her anxiety spike. Brando wasn't one to be managed. Brando Ricci tended to do the managing. "No, you wouldn't do something illegal," she said lightly, feigning calm. "It would be bad for business, and we both know you're very serious about your family business and protecting your family's reputation."

"But even more protective of my child. If I'd go to great lengths to ensure the safety of the business, imagine what I'd do for my son or daughter."

Her pulse jumped yet again and she felt downright nauseous now. This was not going well. She'd thought she'd been prepared for these conversations, but clearly she'd forgotten Brando's strength and focus. "The point being that you'd never do anything to risk your reputation, and that includes your child's."

"Which is why I should whisk you away to keep you out of the public eye until we've figured out what we're going to do."

"I wish I could say that being whisked away sounded appealing—and yes, it does have a certain *Roman Holiday* sound to it—but I'm only here through the weekend. I fly into London Monday early afternoon."

"So soon?"

"I was actually worried that three days was far too long." She glanced up at the hard planes of his striking face, her gaze briefly meeting his, the silver-gray irises piercing, before looking away. Just that brief look into his eyes made her feel hot and tingly. If she could go back in time and change the past, she would. She would have never given herself to Brando, never allowed herself to imagine that she'd be able to handle all the complications of a night spent with him. "Why did I need to be here for three days? We'd have a conversation, you'd get a blood test and then we'd talk after the results were in. But it's not going like that. We're talking now as if we know the results—"

"Because we do. It's my child."

"But that doesn't mean we have to decide everything tonight. We have months—"

"No. We're not putting this off, and we're not going to try to negotiate with you in California. We're going to come to an agreement now, while you're here, and we get it in writing, and notarized, so that it's legal and binding."

"I'm not a runaway bride, Brando. I'm not going to disappear on you."

"How do I know that?"

"Because I'm giving you my word."

"That's a start."

"You don't believe me?"

"You waited six months to tell me I'm going to be a father."

"As I said this morning, I wanted to be sure the pregnancy was viable."

He said nothing for the longest time, and then, "Are we going to need lawyers? Should we just take it to court—?"

"Why would you say that? We don't need lawyers, and we don't need anyone else telling us how to do this. We're smart and reasonable. Surely we can come up with a plan between us."

"So, you'd be willing to live here?"

"I don't think that's necessary."

"You'd rather a newborn baby spend its first year in the air, flying back and forth between Los Angeles and here? That must be eleven hours or more in the air, without connections."

"No, of course not. That's why I think the first year the baby should be with me."

"And then you hand the baby over to me for a year?" he asked, expression blank.

She shuddered. "*No.* I'm not ever handing my baby over, not to you, not to anyone."

"So, we do need lawyers."

"Don't go straight there. Can't we at least try to talk this out?"

"I think you should live here the first few years. Your work is flexible. Your work isn't tied to a place. Whereas I'm a vintner. I can't abandon the grapes."

"Not all your work is in Chianti. You have other business endeavors—"

"So, let me get this straight. You want me to know about my child, but not be involved. You don't want support, either. You just want me to pretend this child doesn't exist, and let you do whatever it is you want?"

Her stomach cramped. She balled her hand into a fist. "That's not what I'm saying."

"Then how are you including me? Where is the space for me, *cara*?"

She didn't answer the question, but then, how could she? Her answer wouldn't have been positive, or flattering, but at least Brando understood Charlotte's intentions. She was doing the correct thing—informing him of the pregnancy—but then she was shutting him out. She didn't truly want him raising the baby with her. She wanted to be mother and father on her own.

That wasn't an option, but he chose to change the subject to keep her from jumping up and leaving.

He asked about a publicity campaign she'd been part of last winter, and as the subject changed, so did the tension. After a few minutes, he could see her relax. They discussed friends they had in common, as well as what was happening with the Ricci business right now.

Dinner arrived and conversation died as they ate, but at least it wasn't an uncomfortable silence. If anything, Charlotte looked thoughtful. He caught her looking at him several times, her brow furrowed, lips pursed.

"I hope you know that I would have never not told you about the baby," she said quietly after Brando ordered a coffee. "I wouldn't have ever kept his or her existence a secret from you. I'm not duplicitous. I genuinely needed time to wrap my head around the pregnancy, and the ramifications. Being a single parent will take work, but we can make it work."

"Why didn't you ask me to come to you in California?" he returned.

"And what would I have said to lure you there?"

"That you're pregnant. That you need me."

She ducked her head, but he could see the wash of hot pink in her cheeks. "I don't generally need people," she said after a moment. "They need me."

Suddenly he understood her in a way he never had before.

Charlotte wasn't playing games. She wasn't trying to cut him out—not in the way he'd first imagined—but she truly believed she was better off trusting no one, relying on no one, and just taking care of everything herself. It wasn't out of cockiness, or arrogance, but survival. This was how she functioned. This was what had allowed her to be successful.

"People make messes and I clean them up," she added with a faint smile, but the smile didn't reach her eyes. "I'm good at problem-solving. Rather exceptional, if I do say so myself."

"It's why we hired you last summer," he answered. "You were exceptional."

"I still am."

This was why he'd been so drawn to her. She was smart, articulate, gorgeous and passionate. The one night only hadn't been his rule, but hers. He hadn't liked making rules, or liked letting her make the rules, but he'd agreed because he'd wanted her that much.

He still wanted her, but everything was different now. This, between them, was no longer about sex, but family, and commitment. He couldn't think of her as an object of desire, but as the mother of his child.

"You might not like admitting it, but you do need me, *cara*," he said quietly, "and our child needs me, too. Let me in. Try to trust me a little bit."

"I will try, but it's not easy."

"You said you fly out Monday."

"Yes."

"It's Friday. That gives us the weekend to talk and make plans. Let's go to my house in the country. It will be quiet there, and we can discuss the future undisturbed."

She hesitated. "I don't know if that's a good idea. Being alone together created this situation we're now in."

"I'm not going to seduce you, if that's what you're worried about."

"I don't expect you to, not when there are other women in your life now, but I think we have to be clear in our intentions. Yes, I'm carrying your child, but I'm not yours, and you're not mine, and we don't have a relationship. We've never had a relationship. We had sex."

"Your point being?"

"One night of intimacy doesn't equate a relationship, so it's going to be very difficult for me to imagine a future where we do anything together, but I will try provided you realize that I'm not going to give up who I am, and what I want to do, just to please you."

Charlotte tried not to fidget as they waited for the bill to be brought. Her pasta had been excellent, but her nerves had kept her from eating too much. Their waiter, who had been attentive during the meal, now seemed to have disappeared, perhaps going on a dinner break of his own. Worse, she and Brando weren't speaking.

They sat at the table looking in opposite directions when he suddenly reached for his phone, tapped the screen and read something.

"The results are in," he said, his tone without emotion. "I am the father."

"There never was doubt at my end," she answered.

"Nor mine." He put away the phone. "But at least we have definitive confirmation, because people will ask."

"You mean, your family will ask."

"Of course they'll be interested."

"Even though it's none of their business?"

"That's where you're wrong, *cara*. It is their business. My child will become part of the business. You of all people, having worked with my family, should know that."

After returning Charlotte to her hotel, Brando drove home, and parked his car in his garage, but couldn't make himself go inside, his thoughts too tangled, his emotions intense, to the point of being overwhelming.

He was going to be a father.

A *father*.

It wasn't a hoax this time, or a game. The paternity test was positive. Charlotte was carrying his baby.

His.

Brando pocketed his car key and walked away from his house, heading toward the Arno, which flowed through historic Florence on its way to the sea. He walked along the riverbank to the medieval Ponte Vecchio with its multitude of shops.

Brando knew Florence intimately. He'd grown up here, not far from this very spot, just as his father had, and his grandfather before him.

Now he'd be a father, and he could raise his child here, too, or maybe in the countryside, maybe at his *castello* in the Chianti Valley.

Either way, his child would know and love Tuscany, just as he loved Tuscany, and the soil and grapes of Tuscany.

It was what it meant to be a Ricci. Passion. Perseverance. Commitment.

CHAPTER THREE

CHARLOTTE SLEPT BADLY, her sleep restless with dreams of Brando. Kissing him, making love with him…fighting with him, hiding from him, dreaming one dream after the other.

And now he was back at her hotel, driving the same classic sports car he'd driven to her hotel last night. It was a sleek glossy black car, a collector's car no doubt, a car that matched his sophisticated style and impossibly handsome face.

"I left the roof up," he said, "but if you prefer, I can put it down."

It was a beautiful early June day, the warm weather hinting at the summer heat to come. There would be no rain, nothing but gorgeous blue sky all day. "Is it too much trouble to put it down?" she asked.

"Not at all. You won't mind all the air?"

"I'd like it. It might help blow the cobwebs out of my brain."

"You didn't sleep well?"

"I'm having a hard time adjusting to the time change. I don't usually. Not sure what's changed," she said lightly.

"I do," he answered, "and I think you do, too. Maybe it's time to stop pretending everything is 'normal.' Nothing is normal. Nothing will ever be quite the same again, either."

She stiffened, even as dread swept through her. What did he

mean by that? It sounded so ominous, and yet Brando wasn't negative, or pessimistic. Perhaps she was just overreacting. Perhaps her exhaustion was making her overly prickly. "There will certainly be some changes," she answered, "but nothing problematic. Nothing I can't handle," she added.

"That's a good attitude," he said.

Charlotte fought the urge to scream. She was losing control, wasn't she? It wasn't her imagination. Brando was slowly seizing the upper hand, bit by bit, smile by smile, encouraging word by encouraging word.

She'd come to Florence expecting tension, and drama, especially after the results of the paternity test came in, but Brando was anything but tense, or angry. He wasn't cold or detached. He was kind...calm. Solicitous. He was managing her, versus the other way around, and that would end badly. She knew it'd end badly. She'd seen how he worked, and how he turned situations to his advantage.

She should have had a better plan.

She should have remembered how smart he was. How strategic.

"I was worried about you flying at this stage of your pregnancy," he added, his hand light on her back as he walked to his car, and yet the possession was clear. He was acting as if she was his, and the baby was his. He was acting as if they belonged to him. But they didn't.

She stepped away from him and gave him a pointed look. "No touching," she said under her breath. "Remember?"

"*Cara*, I do this for every little old lady, including my grandmother."

Annoyed, she bit her tongue and gave her head a short, sharp shake.

"I might as well be a cane," he added soothingly.

She wasn't soothed. Her nerve endings tingled. She felt hot all over, hot and incredibly aware of him, as well as aware of the night spent together. It wasn't all that long ago. Just months ago. And it had been the most sensual, memorable night of her life, a night so full of passion and sensation that she didn't think she'd ever be the same.

She certainly didn't think she'd have to be here, now, dealing with him.

She'd allowed herself to do everything because she hadn't thought she'd ever see him again...

"What's wrong?" he asked. "Why are you aggravated?"

"I'm not aggravated. And I'm not a senior citizen, Brando, nor am I in need of assistance. I'm strong, and capable, and really happy not being helped," she answered tersely, hating herself for wishing his hand would return to her lower back, wanting the press of his fingers against the curve of her spine. Her body felt even more sensitive now that she was pregnant, and for some reason her libido was even stronger than before. She dreamed erotic dreams at night. During the day, she found herself wanting more, fantasizing about making love, and since that wasn't an option, she'd pleasured herself once, and the orgasm was so intense she'd worried that she might have hurt the baby, and so she hadn't done that again...even though she still craved touch and sensation. Satisfaction.

Brando opened the car's passenger door, and she settled into the sports car's low seat, feeling decidedly awkward. Her center of balance was changing, and her narrow skirt hindered her movement. Brando waited patiently, though, before closing the door behind her even as the hotel bell captain finished putting her bags in the trunk of the car.

Brando then went to work putting the convertible top down, which required just a couple of adjustments on his part, and then he was done.

"Was the international flight taxing?" he asked, returning to the driver's side and sliding behind the steering wheel.

He was dressed in a pale gray linen shirt and gray linen trousers, the shirt open at his throat, sleeves rolled back on his forearms. His throat and chest were tanned, the same burnished color of his arms. It took effort for her to focus on his words and not his lean, powerful body.

"I flew business here so I had my legs up," she answered, "and that definitely helped. But this is probably my last international trip until the baby arrives."

"Do you know if we're having a boy or girl?" he asked, shifting into Drive and pulling away from the hotel to merge into traffic.

She tensed all over at his use of *we* and she glanced at him, studying his profile as he focused on the congestion ahead caused by a truck delivering sleek modern leather couches to an interior design store. The truck was blocking a lane and drivers were honking. "Does it matter to you if I'm carrying a boy or girl?" she asked.

"No."

She wasn't sure she believed him. "Would you really love a daughter as much as the son?"

"I might love a daughter more," he said with a faint shrug.

She didn't know why but his words made her heart ache. Her father hadn't been unloving, but he hadn't been particularly affectionate, or attentive. She'd always thought if she was a horse he would have loved her more. He adored his horses.

She'd once wanted to be adored. She'd wanted him to miss her the way he'd missed them when away for too long.

He never did, though, and her mother had never really missed her, either, not even when she'd gone to Switzerland for boarding school.

Charlotte had learned to fill her time, and she'd learned the art of distraction. Don't think too much, don't feel hardly anything. Work, focus, achieve.

Those three things had become her mantra, and her mantra had made her successful.

She could still be successful as a mother. She'd certainly be a more devoted parent than either of her parents. She'd make sure her child knew he or she was loved and wanted.

Finally, Charlotte would have a family of her own. Finally, she'd have someone she could shower with love…

"There are no disadvantages to being a girl." Brando's deep voice drew her attention.

Charlotte glanced at him, heart suddenly too tender. "But there might be with a boy," she said.

He lifted a brow. "How so?"

She adjusted her seat belt around her middle and tried to make herself more comfortable. The interior of the sports car was small and Brando was close, his hand resting on the stick shift just inches from her knees. She could smell whatever he was wearing—aftershave, cologne, body spray. It was light, and sexy and very masculine. Between his heady scent, and the warmth radiating off him, she felt painfully aware of him. "I don't want to quarrel. I'm too tired today to quarrel—"

"Why would we quarrel?"

"Because if I'm carrying a boy, you might feel differently about being…involved. It might influence you somehow."

"How so?"

She swallowed hard. "This isn't the best time. I don't want to do this now—"

"Do what? Discuss the future?"

"Yes."

"But that's why you've come to Florence."

"But you're taking over, dictating everything—"

"You've had six months to be in charge. It's time I had a say, don't you think?"

She gritted her teeth, battling her anger, battling fear. She wasn't just losing control, she'd lost it. She'd been a fool to come to Florence without a proper plan, a fool to think it'd go any other way. For a split second she wished she'd never come to Italy, wished she'd never told him about the pregnancy, but just as quickly as the thought came, she smashed it. It wasn't right, or fair, not to Brando, and not to their child. Their child had a right to a father as much as a mother. "I hate this," she whispered. "I hate all of it."

He said nothing for a long moment, his jaw hard, his eyes narrowed as he concentrated on the road. And then after an interminable silence, he said, "You hate me."

Her eyes burned. It hurt to swallow. "I don't hate you." Charlotte blinked back the sting of tears. "I hate that we're going to be playing tug-of-war with our baby. I hate that he or she will never have what I always dreamed of—a stable, unified, loving family. A family that stays together, sticks together, through thick and thin."

Silence followed her words. Charlotte knotted her hands in her lap, feeling raw and exhausted. Was it only yesterday she'd arrived in Florence? Was it only yesterday she'd knocked on Brando's door, feeling confident of her plans?

"It doesn't have to be acrimonious between us," Brando said, breaking the silence. "There's no reason we can't be unified, and supportive of each other, and when the baby is with me, he or she will have a supportive and stable family. A loving family. The Riccis might argue over succession within the business—"

"Might argue? Brando, you all hired me because your fights were making headline news."

He shrugged dismissively. "We're Italian. We're passionate."

"It's more than being passionate. Your family is in the middle of a battle over leadership, and the Riccis don't separate business from family. You might call yourself the Ricci family, but it's truly about the Ricci business."

"Your point being?"

"I don't want my child to be dragged into that. I'd hate for our child to become part of that scramble for power and position."

"Any child of mine will automatically become of the Ricci family, and thus the Ricci legacy. Boy or girl, he or she will play a role in the family—"

"Business," she added.

His broad shoulders shifted again. "You're right, in my family, it is one and the same. Family. Business. We're one family working together to succeed."

"Except you all weren't working together. You were at odds with each other—"

"We were, until you came along and helped shift the focus on what we weren't doing right, onto what we were doing right. You helped us focus our vision, our mission and our internal communication." He glanced at her, lips twisting. "We're stronger than we were before, thanks to you."

His words gave small comfort. She put a hand to her taut belly, uneasy, and worried. "Will an American child be welcomed into your very Tuscan, old-world family?"

"You're not American. You're British."

"I like living in America, though. I plan on remaining there, raising the baby there, so yes, the baby will be—"

"No."

She stiffened at his brusqueness, and for a moment there was just silence before she said quietly, "You like America. You have many American friends, particularly in Napa Valley."

"Yes, I do, but I'll never agree to my child being raised apart from me. That's not even an option."

Her pulse kicked up a notch. "Since we're being honest, tell me. What would you do with a small baby?"

"The same thing you'd do." He glanced at her, features hard. "I'm an uncle to a half-dozen nieces and nephews and we get together a lot. I've been part of their lives since they were born."

"Being an uncle isn't the same thing as being a father. Parenting is full-time work—"

"Which is why we should do it together, not forcing the baby to bounce between us."

"Well, the baby won't be bouncing anywhere for quite some time. He or she will need to be with me since I'll be nursing."

"I have no desire to separate the baby from you, but no Italian court will decide to give you custody based on breastfeeding."

She gripped her hands tightly together to hold back the whisper of panic. She hadn't flown all this way to lose her child. She hadn't begun this trip to be told she'd have only partial custody, either.

In her heart, she believed that babies belonged with the mother. It was her mother who did all the heavy lifting when Charlotte was small. Well, her mother and the fleet of nannies and housekeepers who were employed to keep the family running.

She blinked hard, fighting emotion she didn't understand.

He shot her a swift glance. "You should have come to me right away, you know. You should have told me the moment you knew you were pregnant. Instead you've had all this time to imagine life the way you wanted it to be, versus what it must be."

"You don't have to want the baby," she said under her breath.

"But I do."

She turned away, glancing out at the river, and the light bouncing on the bridges and elegant historic buildings. "During the ultrasound, I was asked if I wanted to know the baby's gender, and I said I didn't, because it doesn't matter if I'm expecting a boy or girl. I'm simply excited about being a mom, and the goal is a healthy baby."

"Agreed," he said. "But that baby is going to need a family. A healthy family. Neither one of us can do that on our own."

Brando drove, concentrating on the road, and Charlotte watched the city suburbs give way to rolling hills of gold and green.

For the next forty minutes, Brando drove the narrow, winding road that connected Florence to Siena, a road famous for its scenic beauty through hills and valleys dotted with villages and vineyards, while Charlotte admired the beautiful landscape. This was the renowned Chianti Valley, an area famous for its wines, olive trees and medieval villages.

She knew about his estate, but had never been there, and

she was curious about the undulating hills, and the picturesque villages, each with its own bell tower rising above tiled roofs.

They were between villages when a tire blew in a loud pop and the sports car pulled sharply right. Brando slowed, and parked on the shoulder of the road, before climbing out to inspect the damage.

"It's just the tire," he said, opening her car door to speak to her. "Stay put. I can change it while you're in there."

She watched him roll his sleeves higher on his arms. His arms were sculpted of corded muscle. His skin the loveliest shade of bronze. "I heard it was dangerous to do that," she said, remembering how his shoulders had been equally powerful, and his torso endless lean muscle.

"You'll be safer in the car than standing on this narrow road."

"But what about you?" she asked, shading her eyes to look up into his face.

"Nothing's going to happen to me. You're the one I'm worried about." He closed the door firmly and she turned in her seat to watch him go to the boot and pull out the spare tire, the jack and tools.

He made changing it look effortless—well, except for the part where he lay on the ground, partway under the car to check the jack's position, and then he was out again and the car was up, the lug bolts off, tire swapped, lug bolts replaced and car back down. Brando stowed the flat tire, dusted himself off and returned to the driver's seat, flashing her a wry smile. "Hope I didn't keep you waiting too long," he said.

His olive cheeks had a dusky flush and his eyes were bright from exertion, but he looked sexier than ever, and she thought a man who knew how to do things with his hands was incredibly appealing.

"That was impressive," she said, smiling at him as he buckled his seat belt.

"You must be easily impressed, then."

"Actually, I'm not. I have very high standards."

He shot her an amused glance. "Then how did I get you into my bed last New Year's Eve?"

It was her turn to blush, and she felt herself go hot all over. "Can we blame the champagne?"

"You weren't drinking that night. Everyone tried to hand you a glass of something. You refused."

"I rarely drink." She wrinkled her nose. "It's not that I don't like alcohol, but I'm a control freak."

"I see. You lost control, hated yourself for it and then promptly ghosted me."

"I didn't *ghost* you."

"What would you call it, then? No calls, no emails, no communication?"

"We didn't have sex to start a relationship. We had sex because we were attracted to each other and we were curious to see if it would be good."

One of his black brows lifted mockingly. "I hadn't realized I'd left you disappointed."

"You didn't. You know that night was incredible. But it wasn't something that we could do again. I was hired to work for your family, not bed the rebel son."

"I'm no longer the rebel son. I've become the good son."

"Then why do Enzo, Marcello and Livia all work together at the Ricci headquarters in Florence and you have your own office? And why are they no longer involved in the wineries, and you alone manage that arm of the Ricci business?"

He shrugged. "Because I have an affinity for the land, and they don't."

"Marcello told me you're the smartest of them all, but they worry about you doing your own thing."

"Because I don't do things by consensus, I do what I think is best. They don't like it—"

"Because you're the youngest?"

"And because you've met them. You know how it is. Too much discussion. Too much tension. It's a waste of time and energy. If something needs to be done, I'm going to do it. End of story."

"You don't feel isolated?"

"No. I love it. It's far better now that they are out of the fields and winery, and they can focus on fashion, and merchandising."

"And yet I saw the report Enzo had prepared for our meetings last August. Your wineries are outperforming, and outearning, what the three of them do…combined."

"Now it does. It wasn't always that way."

"But you have to be pleased."

"I'm not competitive, at least, not with them. I like to be successful, but not at their expense." He glanced at her, black lashes framing those startling silver eyes. "They're my older brothers and my sister. I look up to them. I respect them. I just want to do my part now—" He broke off, drew a breath, "It's time to do my part, to ensure my family's success."

It wasn't a villa, but a proper castle, she realized as they turned off the main road and began driving up a hill to the castle with a square tower in front of them, while tidy rows of grapes covered the hillsides.

"That's your home," she said, because it was the only building nearby, and what an impressive structure it was. The tower was made of stone, while the plastered walls were a soft creamy yellow, surrounded by tall stone exterior walls.

"It is," he agreed.

The *castello* was positioned on a hill with sweeping views of Val di Greve, and with access to both Florence and Siena, it had most likely been a strategic stronghold for centuries.

"From the square tower, it must date back to the eleven hundreds."

"There are some disagreements regarding the age of the *castello* itself, but historians all agree that the central tower is from the twelfth century. Some sources claim the castle as it is today dates from the early fourteen hundreds. We know from ancient records that the *castello* has been inhabited since 1456, and it was during that time period it earned its name, Castello Mare Scotti, for a descendent of the Medicis."

"When did you buy the property?"

"It's been almost ten years. The castle and grounds were a mess, in need of serious restoration, and while the vineyards were still producing grapes, they also needed to be replanted. Overhauling the orchards made sense—and those have become quite profitable. The restoration of the *castello* is more of a labor of love, an ode to Tuscany. I've lived many places now, but nowhere else is like this place. Chianti Valley is without a doubt home."

"More so than Florence?"

"I enjoy Florence. It's elegant and filled with art and history, but I've discovered I prefer the country over the city. My family had a big estate outside Florence when I was growing up, and my brothers have divided it between them, but that estate has never resonated with me, not the way Castello Marescotti resonates. From the first time I walked the property, I knew it was meant for me." Brando flashed a wry smile. "The family said I was crazy. Livia emailed me a half-dozen listings of available properties featuring palaces and villas in excellent condition, many with land attached, but none of them were right. Marescotti was mine. I often spend weeks at a time here. One day soon I hope to live here full-time."

"What about your house in Florence?"

"I'll still go for a special night, or a weekend, but once I have children—" He broke off and shot her a meaningful glance as he slowed to pass through the ten-foot stone walls with the huge iron gate. "I'd like to raise them where there is space to run and play."

Staff appeared as Brando parked. Someone claimed the luggage. Someone else took the car keys and then the car. A housekeeper ushered them through the front door, offering to show Charlotte to her room, but Brando said he'd take her himself.

Sunlight poured through the windows flanking the front door, and the staircase rose in the middle of the great hall, the staircase three levels of dark gleaming wood against pale yellow walls. Framed oil canvases hung on the walls while an enormous Venetian glass chandelier cast sparkling light everywhere.

She followed Brando up a flight of stairs to the second floor. They walked down the hall to the second door on the left. Her bedroom was luxurious as well as spacious, with plastered walls and thick dark beams set into the ceiling. The rose silk curtains framed tall windows, and the bed was covered with a matching silk coverlet. Fresh roses filled a vase next to the bed, and more roses nestled in a low bowl on the antique dressing table.

"Would you like a brief tour of the house and gardens?" Brando asked. "Or are you too tired?"

"Not too tired. I'd love to see your place. I heard so much about it last fall."

They exited her bedroom, stepping back into the hallway, which was sunny and bright thanks to a trio of tall windows lining the wall. The windows overlooked fertile vineyards and tidy orchards.

"How much of this land is yours?" she asked, pausing at one of the hall windows.

"Almost everything you can see from this spot." He pointed to a distant hill topped with another castle. "See that *castello*? That is my nearest neighbor, and his property starts at the bottom of his hill and continues for one hundred and ten acres that way. Everything from here, to that hill, is mine."

"How many acres do you have?"

"A little over two thousand, but it's in chunks and clusters as I've purchased available property in the valley."

Her eyebrows arched. "That is significant land for this area, isn't it?"

"I've been buying land when I can. Most of it is devoted to grapes, but not all. I also have a large olive orchard, and we have bees, and produce honey, too."

He led her back downstairs through the reception rooms and grand salons and smaller sitting rooms, as well as through the dining room, and the kitchen staffed with a head chef and an assistant. They walked through kitchen gardens, their shoes crunching the gravel paths, before entering a small orchard with fruit trees. At the back of the fruit orchard were the bee-hives, and they found one of Brando's gardeners, who also was the chief beekeeper, just finishing repairing the rain cover on one of the hives. Brando greeted him warmly and introduced Charlotte before they continued, returning to the path with the worn tiles. The smooth red-tiled path led them away from the house to a small chapel with its own square bell tower. They peeked into the chapel with its stained glass and dark wooden pews, before he led her back down the path, cutting through rose gardens and a topiary garden to end up at an enormous infinity pool with a jaw-dropping view of the valley. Elegant wrought iron loungers lined one side of the pool while a fountain happily splashed away in a far corner, creating tinkling sounds.

The valley was that of dark green rolling hills and pictur-esque villages and grapes. The terrain was more rugged than Napa, with high mountains in the distance. "You have a bit of paradise here," she said.

"I'm quite partial to it. I focus well here. In fact, I enjoy my work so much that it doesn't feel like work."

"That's the best sort of work, when it feels more like a pas-sion."

"Do you feel that way about your work?"

"Sometimes. It depends on the clients. And the crisis." She flashed a smile. "Sometimes the crisis element overwhelms everything else and all I feel is adrenaline."

"Did you feel that way working with my family?"

"No. The Riccis are pragmatic. None of you liked the bad press, and you were able to come together to downplay the succession issue." She made a face. "Not that the issue has gone away. It's just smoothed over for the time being."

"I think we've at least begun to whittle away at the issue. We aren't burying our heads in the sand anywhere. Something has to be done."

"But you personally don't think Enzo's son is the one to lead the Ricci company in the future."

"I think he should be involved in management, but Antonio isn't a visionary, and he's overly cautious, which leads to a fear of making decisions. You can't have your CEO afraid to make a decision."

"And what of Marcello's and Livia's kids? Anyone there look promising?"

"Livia's daughter, Adriana, is brilliant. She's strategic and has this rather dazzling ability to 'see' the future while very much coping with issues of today. My vote would be for Adriana, but that won't be popular with my brothers. They both have sons and they're both grooming their sons to head the company." He paused and looked down at her. "And who knows what our child's strengths will be, but I'm hopeful he or she will also embrace the family, as loud and fierce and complicated as we are."

"Yet you all love each other," she said after a moment. "I think that is the thing that struck me most. You quarrel rather passionately, but that's because you all care so much." Her family was the opposite. The quarreling wasn't warm and loving. The quarreling was incredibly divisive, so divisive that Charlotte was more comfortable with her stepbrothers and sisters than her own siblings.

He shrugged. "We're family. Family sticks together."

Or not.

He looked at her, silver gaze assessing. "You don't agree?"

"My family isn't as neat and tidy as yours, so I'm not sure how I feel about 'family.' It's not a simple question, nor a simple answer."

His expression eased, and he smiled. "Then how about I pose a simple question. Are you hungry? Lunch should be served soon."

"I am hungry," she admitted. "Lately I feel like I'm always hungry."

"Then let's walk back to the house, and you can freshen up before we meet on the terrace for lunch."

Brando escorted her back to the sprawling *castello*, where he left her at the foot of the stairs—on her insistence, as she didn't need to be walked all the way to her bedroom door—but as she climbed the stairs to the second floor, she couldn't help thinking of what Brando had said when they'd first arrived, that Castello Marescotti is where he'd want to raise his children, because there would be room for them to run and play. He was right, there was plenty of room here, both indoors and out. The stone house was huge, almost too big for a game of hide-and-seek, but she'd been raised in such a place herself and had thought nothing of the grandness, or the sheer amount of space. It's what she knew. It was home.

In her room, she took a brush to her hair, combing through the long blond strands until they were smooth, and then touched up her makeup. As she reapplied her lipstick, Charlotte tried to imagine this house as her baby's home and felt an odd prickle of pain and her hand shook. She had to draw a breath and steady her hand before putting the cap on the lipstick. It wasn't that this grand medieval house wasn't comfortable, because the interior was stylish and yet welcoming, a place both grown-ups and children would be at ease, but rather it was the idea of the baby being here without her...that her baby would have a whole life without her...

Sudden tears stung her eyes and she blinked hard, clearing her vision. She wasn't usually emotional, and yet all she felt right now were emotions, strong, intense, overwhelming.

She loved her unborn child rather desperately, and every fiber of her being wanted to protect the baby. But how could she do that if she wasn't with him or her?

How could she bring a child into the world and then not be part of his or her life...even part-time?

She put away her lipstick and slid the makeup bag and hair-brush into the top dresser of the pretty vanity, and then squared her shoulders. She could do this with Brando. She could be civil, and calm, and make him understand that she wasn't going to let a baby grow up without her. She didn't know the answer to "sharing" the baby, she just knew she was going to be with her child full-time, end of story.

CHAPTER FOUR

BRANDO WAITED FOR Charlotte on the terrace, the sun warm overhead as he stood at the balcony overlooking the valley. It was perfect weather for lunch al fresco, the temperature warm, the air fragrant, smelling of roses, citrus blossoms and jasmine. The table was set for two, and a lush bouquet of pale pink and creamy white antique roses created a charming centerpiece, especially when paired with the fine china and delicate Venetian stemware.

It was a table setting that hinted at romance, but there was nothing romantic about his intentions. Brando had never been a man of romance—he was far too carnal, far too practical. He loved women and loved sex, but so far, he'd been careful to avoid commitments, much less serious entanglements.

And yet despite his best efforts to avoid entanglements, he was facing one now, an entanglement with lifelong implications.

He'd known that one day he'd have children—Italians were family oriented, and he had a wicked soft spot for his nieces and nephews, who made it clear they adored him—but marriage and children was down the road, far, far down the road, because marriage was forever. Marriage required complete commitment, as well as a suitable partner who one could grow old with, and hopefully, still like decades later.

His parents had had such a marriage. His parents married in their twenties, and had just celebrated their sixtieth wedding anniversary when his father passed away. Heartbroken, his mother had almost immediately moved to her widowed sister's house in Cinque Terre, where she and her sister found happiness being under the same roof. They missed their husbands but found endless opportunities to see their children and grandchildren.

Livia and Enzo had grumbled about their mother moving to the coast, to a place that wasn't easy to reach, but Marcello agreed with Brando that it was good for their mother to have an identity of her own, that she needed to have adventures and fun, adventures that had nothing to do with the rest of them.

Brando smiled thinking of his mother. She was a spitfire, full of endless energy, and she was always happy to see her family, but he respected her for not wanting to sit around her house, just mourning the death of her husband, and waiting for death to come. Life was meant to be lived. Life was meant to have passion, and gusto, and if anyone in the family had gusto, it was his mother.

But he also knew what his mother would say if he knew he'd gotten a woman pregnant. Her first question would be, "How will you make this right?" Not because a pregnancy was shameful, but a pregnancy represented life, and love, and family. He didn't think of himself as a traditionalist, but the idea of someone, *anyone*, having his child and raising that child far from him made his skin crawl. Maybe Charlotte was comfortable picturing a world where her baby—*their* baby, he corrected himself—shuttled back and forth between two homes, but he wasn't.

He knew her family had numerous marriages, divorces and out-of-wedlock babies in it. They took the idea of commitment far more loosely than his family did. There hadn't been a divorce in his family for generations. Nor had there been a baby born out of wedlock.

One of his older brothers had married when his girlfriend

was pregnant, and it had been a rather hastily arranged wedding, but they were still together, and had added three other children besides that first unplanned pregnancy.

Brando hadn't been thinking of marriage, nor had he thought he was ready to settle down, but if Charlotte was pregnant, this was serious. This was a game changer. This impacted everything. Either she would agree to give him custody of the baby—which he didn't see her ever doing—or she would agree to marry him. Those were the only two options he saw. He wasn't about to have his firstborn raised in a bohemian household in California, or at one of the sprawling estates owned by her family in England. Her family seemed to spend as much time in England as they did in France and that was not acceptable, not for a Ricci. His family was Italian, and proud of their heritage. He wanted his child—son or daughter—to be raised immersed in his culture, his language, his family.

Bottom line, he wanted his child to be part of his family.

And put like that, it did make him sound conservative, and old-world. But the Riccis were family oriented, and family came first, and last, and they understood what it meant to stick together, through thick and thin. It wasn't that her family or culture didn't count, but her culture was a mishmash of English, American, French, and then there were those years from the Swiss boarding school, years where he suspected young women were taught how to snare the world's most eligible bachelors, rather than how to live a successful, independent life.

Charlotte, though, was probably the exception. She'd started her own business and had created a name for herself. She was financially independent, and successful. She'd be a good wife. Once he convinced her it was the right thing to do.

He thought of her, stubborn, proud, confident—and then just like that, she was there, stepping through the glass doors out into the Tuscany sunshine, blond hair spilling down her back, a hint of rose in her cheek, fire in her eyes—and he knew it would take some convincing, to get her on the same page.

She wasn't going to want to marry him, but having weighed his options, it was the only real option before them.

Lunch was leisurely, with small courses being replaced by other courses, and the portions were perfectly sized so that Charlotte enjoyed everything as much as she could, considering Brando kept watching her with an intensity that she found dizzying. Every movement reflected his physical strength and grace. He was not a man of leisure. One didn't get a body like his without hard activity. She had a sudden flash of memory, of his hips arching against hers, his body filling her so completely that she wanted nothing more than to be his, again and again.

The vividness of the memory, the picture of his beautiful naked body above her, filled her with heat and a breathlessness that made it impossible to take another bite of her custard dessert.

She pushed the small plate away, hot, flustered, confused, and put a hand to her hot cheek, as if to cool herself.

"Is it too warm in the sun?" Brando asked, immediately noting her gesture. "Would you prefer to sit in the shade? We can move to the umbrella—"

"I'm fine. The sun is gorgeous."

He didn't appear convinced. "I don't want to fatigue you."

"I'm pregnant, not eighty, Brando."

"Yes, you're pregnant," he said darkly. "Which is why I won't have you overly tired. Perhaps we should go inside—"

"I'm *fine*. Trust me."

"You're flushed."

Yes, because I'm thinking about making love to you. Thinking about your body. Thinking about the amazing things you did with your body...

She didn't say it, though, but she blushed, exquisitely aware of him.

"If you truly are comfortable where we are, I think it's time we talked about why you've come to Italy, and what we're going to do." Brando's deep voice was firm, his gaze direct as it met hers.

"I suggest we marry. Soon. A simple ceremony, followed by an intimate dinner with our immediate family—"

"Excuse me?" she interrupted, brow creasing.

"The sooner the better," he concluded.

"Your wife?" She stared at him aghast. "Please tell me I'm misunderstanding you."

"No. You are understanding me perfectly."

"I am not going to marry you."

"Why not?" he retorted calmly.

"There's no reason for us to marry. We're not living in the Dark Ages, or the Victorian times. There is no reason we can't have a child without being married—"

"There is in my family."

"Maybe your family needs to adapt, then. Maybe it's time the Riccis evolved."

"It's not just about my family's values, or morality," he answered. "It's about the business. Our child won't have any hopes of heading the family business if we're not married."

"Well, I sincerely doubt our child would want to head your family business, not if it's that archaic." She gave him a long look. "And I know your family is archaic. It's why I was called in to mediate in the first place. The Riccis still live in the nineteenth century, but it's time they caught up with the rest of the world. Children do just fine in single-parent homes. Children thrive—"

"When raised in a stable home, with two loving stable parents."

She eyed him for a long moment. "You and I are stable, and we will be loving parents. But it's not necessary to be in the same house together. In fact, that's asking for disaster. I can guarantee that will create more instability than anything."

"Why?"

"We're not meant to be together, Brando, and regarding a single home, you don't live in just one house. You bounce between your properties, never in one place long."

"But you've already heard me say that this place is home, and this is where I intend to raise my children."

"You're not settled here yet, and babies are adaptable. Obviously it's different once children are in school, but that's years from now. Five or six years."

"I hadn't planned on settling down quite yet, but your pregnancy changes everything. It changes both of us. I'm prepared to make the necessary changes." He hesitated a beat. "Are you?"

She felt her shoulders rise, and a quick hot retort rush to her tongue, but she held the words back and forced herself to count to five, and then ten. "I already have. I'm preparing a nursery in my home. I've begun taking birthing classes."

"All without me?"

She choked on an uneasy laugh. "I'm not planning my future around you, no."

"You should be. I'm planning my future around you, or more correctly, I'm planning my future with you."

If her heart wasn't racing she'd get up and move. Flee. But as it was, she didn't feel steady enough to even get up and walk. "I don't think we're on the same page," she said hoarsely.

"*Cara*, my love, children need security, traditions and a familiar routine."

She suppressed a shiver at the husky rasp in his voice, as well as the endearments. She wasn't his darling, or his love, and she hated that he sounded so reasonable, so patient, when everything in her screamed in protest. "That's where we don't see eye to eye, Brando, as I had very two very different families and very different traditions with each family, and it didn't hurt me. If anything, it was good for me. I learned to be flexible, and adaptable."

"You say that now, but I'm sure you felt pain when your parents divorced, and then your mother remarried and moved you to California."

"It was a change, and yes, it was hard being ten with chaos all around me, but I'm stronger because I've had to deal with challenging circumstances."

"But if you had your way, is that what you'd wish on your child? Challenging circumstances? Or would you want to protect him, or her—"

"Now you're just being unfair. I would always want to protect my baby. I want to do what's best for the baby, which is why I'm here, trying to include you, but there's a big difference between including you and becoming your doormat!"

"How is marriage making you a doormat?"

"Because it's giving up everything I want, and need, to do what you think is best. But I don't believe it's necessary for us to marry, and I most definitely don't believe it's the best thing for us. We can provide stable homes independently of the other. You provide a home here in Italy, and I'll provide one in LA—"

"You can't possibly be serious about raising our child in Los Angeles."

"What's wrong with Los Angeles?"

"What is right about Los Angeles?"

She pressed her lips together, frustrated and unwilling to say more. She counted to ten, and then she couldn't remain silent any longer, and blurted, "There is much to like about Italy, and much to love about Tuscany, but you're a little too smug about being Italian—"

"I'm proud of my heritage."

"But it's not the only heritage in play here. I have my own."

"You've run away from yours. You left it behind. You're just like everyone else that has run to Los Angeles, looking to re-invent themselves."

His scorn stung and she bit into her lower lip, trying not to focus on his criticism. He was fighting for a place in their child's life. He was fighting to be included. She understood that. She respected that. But he was giving her no middle ground and middle ground is what she needed. "There is beauty in reinvention," she said quietly. "And beauty in change. I appreciate you wanting to do the right thing by offering to marry me, but I must decline, must most adamantly decline. I will not marry because it's the morally right thing. If I marry it's because I'm in love and want to spend the rest of my life with someone, rather than being trapped with someone out of duty or misplaced obligation."

"Now that is old-fashioned."

"To marry for love?"

"Love marriages end in divorce when the dopamine fades. You and I both know that. Children can help parents bond, and marriages can last because of oxytocin. We make a choice, and then choose to be committed, and we have a marriage that endures."

"For a moment, I thought you were speaking of grafting grapevines. That is another asexual propagation technique."

"Yes, but I believe our procreation technique was sexual. I believe you're pregnant because we couldn't get enough of each other."

True, true, true.

Charlotte closed her eyes, held her breath and prayed for something witty to say, because right now she just felt trapped.

"We still have two days," Brando said quietly, "two days before you fly to London. Let's say no more now, and let you have some time to yourself. We can discuss this again at dinner."

Her eyes opened and she looked at him a long moment before she gave her head a short, regretful shake. He was beautiful, and fascinating, but not the man she'd marry. Not a man she could plan a life with, either. He loved women, loved sex, loved his freedom. He'd be a terrible husband, and he'd break her heart because she wouldn't be able to share him, nor would she be able to forgive him for being in other women's beds. "My feelings won't change."

"Neither will the facts. We're having a baby. We have to put aside our differences—"

"I don't think we can."

"Let's leave it for now. We have tonight."

In her bedroom, Charlotte curled up in a chair near the window, pressed her fist to her mouth and stared out the window at the valley trying to calm herself and yet unable to relax, annoyed by Brando's high-handedness, and frustrated by his inability to listen to what she wanted and needed.

This was why she didn't date powerful men, or powerful, wealthy men, and this was why she didn't want to become part of a powerful man's family...or any family that made edicts and rules and told her how she was supposed to live and behave. She wanted to be herself. She wanted to be her own person.

How did she become so good at handling family strife? Because she'd grown up in it. Immersed in it. And would have drowned in it if she hadn't figured out how to rise above.

The point was, she understood family dynamics, and family politics. But just because she understood it didn't mean she wanted to spend her future answering to others. It was bad enough that she still had her own family to contend with, but to marry Brando, and to suddenly have to deal with the Ricci family, as well?

No.

It wasn't going to happen.

His family were not bad people, and she'd enjoyed them as an outside consultant, but Riccis were very strong and opinionated, and passionate, and forceful with their thoughts and feelings. Her family, on the other hand, were quieter, and judgmental, and distantly disapproving. One still had to measure up, but the interactions were different, and the expectations were communicated differently. She didn't know what was worse: the fierce, expressive discussions that took place in passionate families, or the cool, disapproving silence of her family. Either way, she preferred the calm of living alone, on her own terms, able to make the decisions that were right for her.

During dinner Charlotte felt as if she was on pins and needles, waiting for Brando to launch into another persuasive speech about why marriage was the right choice for them, but he didn't. Instead he asked her how much she knew about the wines of Tuscany, and when she said she knew very little other than Chianti was considered the most popular red wine from Tuscany, he gave her an interesting history of winemaking in Tuscany, explaining that Sangiovese, the most commonly plated red grape, and the basis for Chianti Classico wines, was such an ancient grape in Italy that many considered it indigenous to the area. "It's a grape that has a very long growing season, budding early, and then needs time to ripen. In the industry, we say it's slow to ripen."

"Not all grapes are slow to ripen, then?" she asked.

"We have mutual friends in Napa Valley, and their Chardonnay and Pinot Noir are both early ripening grapes. Cab, Merlot, Sangiovese are late varieties."

"Is that what brought you to California last year?"

"No." His gaze met hers and held. "You did."

"Me?"

"Mmm-hmm. I'd hoped to see you again."

She felt herself flush. "We agreed there would be just that one night."

"Most women don't mean it."

She grew hotter, her skin hot and prickly across her cheekbones, her lips tingling, too. And just the tingle in her lips made her remember how good his mouth had felt on hers, and how his kisses had drawn her in, pulling her under, seducing her like nothing she'd ever known before. "I'm not sure how to respond to that."

"You're remarkably good at compartmentalizing."

But ah, she wasn't, and she hadn't found it easy to put him behind her. She'd felt almost desperate with desire, and she'd craved him for weeks after her return to Southern California. The desire and her emotions had been so intense they'd scared her, making her feel alien even to herself. In the end, being with him that night hadn't been a release, but a bond, and now the ties to that bond were tightening. Her stomach did an uncomfortable little flip and she forced herself to respond, feigning a cavalier attitude she didn't feel. "You mean, good at compartmentalizing for a woman?"

"I'm not sexist."

"Oh, you most definitely are. You're the one expecting me to move here. You're the one that won't even consider other arrangements."

"Nothing is in stone. I'm open to discussion, open to suggestions. How should we make this work, *cara*?"

Again, she bristled inwardly at the endearment. He said them so easily, dropping them like overripe cherries, even as he neatly turned the tables on her. "There is no simple solution. It's one of the reasons I've waited to come to you. I needed to accept what's happening, and then problem-solve. And I'm here now, because I believe that at least for the baby's first year, the baby should be with me—"

"Then how will our baby bond with me?" he interrupted, his expression still pleasant but there was a new, steely edge to his voice.

"Fathers bond with their children later... They're never fond of the baby stage and tend to feel useless until babies are weaned and able to have more independence and mobility."

Brando looked at her for a moment before laughing, and not just a little laugh, but a big, deep laugh as if he'd never heard anything half so amusing. "I don't know where you get your information from, but it's wrong."

"It's common knowledge."

"Is it?"

Again, he made her hackles rise. "My father had no use for babies. My brothers are useless until the toddler stage, but even then, they hate it when the children cry for Mummy."

"Maybe it's cultural, then, because my father was very hands-on, from day one. My brothers all helped with the night feedings by changing diapers, bringing the newborn to their wives and then burping the newborn before returning to bed. Marcello and his wife have a young baby now, and they're in the middle of the sleepless-night phase. Marcello is exhausted but he said he wouldn't trade this stage for anything. It's when he feels closest to the bambino, and the most needed."

His words filled her with a strange yearning feeling, which was so strange since just a moment ago she felt fierce and angry. She hated the rioting within her making herself feel as if she were a living kaleidoscope. "You paint an idyllic picture."

"Well, I've left out the colic, and the baby that won't sleep at night, but insists on napping all day, or the exhaustion from trying to cope with an inconsolable infant who won't stop screaming."

She just looked at him, unable to think of a thing to say because it struck her for the first time that he might know more about newborns than she did.

"It's easier to parent as a team. I think we should work as a team," he added. "I think we'd be most successful as parents that way."

She suddenly needed air. She needed to move and breathe and she couldn't do it in the dining room, as elegant as it was. "Would you mind terribly if we stepped outside? I'm feeling overly warm."

"Let's step outside and walk a bit. It might be a little cool, though."

"I'm sure it'd feel good."

It was cooler outside, but not cold, and there was a light breeze that carried the fragrance of flowers, freshly cut grass and warm soil. It was rich and ripe and pungent and Charlotte breathed deeply, drawing the layered scent in, reminded of her family's country house in Sussex.

"How are you feeling now?" Brando asked her as they walked along the pea gravel path that led from the house and into a long, rectangular walled garden, the pale gray stone walls lined with neatly pruned boxwoods, the center dominated by an ornate fountain that looked as if it had been there for hundreds of years, and two ornate flower beds. The light was just now fading, painting the garden shades of lavender and plum.

"A little better," she said.

"That doesn't sound very convincing," he replied.

She didn't answer, and he said nothing. They walked the length of the walled garden in thoughtful silence, and then did another lap, completing a full circle of the garden.

"I'm just scared," Charlotte blurted, stopping next to the fountain. "I feel like everything is moving faster and faster, and I feel like I'm losing control."

"You're entering the final trimester. It won't be long until the baby arrives, and that is a loss of control. Everything will be different, for both of us."

The baby gave a kick just then and she inhaled and put a hand to the side of her bump.

"Moving?" he asked.

She nodded. Impulsively she reached for his hand, and placed it where hers had been, pressing his palm to the spot she'd felt the kick. For a moment nothing happened, and then it happened, a swift, little kick, or stretch. She looked up into his face to see if he'd felt it.

His jaw had firmed, and his lips pressed, but his silver gaze softened, and there was a look of wonder in his expression. *"Sorprendente,"* he murmured.

Amazing.

Her eyes burned, hot and gritty, and she blinked, chasing away the stinging sensation, but she couldn't erase the aching lump in her throat. Quickly, she let go of his hand, suddenly self-conscious, aware that she'd reached for him, creating an intimacy neither of them wanted.

"I'm glad you're here," he said huskily. "I'm glad you came now, so that I can be part of this. Thank you."

Her heart squeezed and she felt more of that terrible pain— yearning coupled with fear, longing layered with anger. Feelings were messy business. She preferred order and structure.

As if he could read her mind, he tipped her chin up, studying her face in the soft light of the rising moon. "Neither of us has absolute control," he said. "But then, no one has absolute control."

And then he dropped his head, his mouth covering hers, and kissed her. She'd imagined that maybe his kiss now would feel platonic, or reassuring, but no, the kiss was just as shocking and scorching as it had been New Year's Eve when his lips made her feel as if she'd touched a live wire, electricity coursing through her.

He must have felt her shuddering response because he drew her closer, his lips moving across hers, deepening the kiss. She thought she'd remembered the pleasure, but this was even more intense, more sensual, and she welcomed the pressure of his mouth, and his hand sliding from her waist down her hip. She leaned into him, giving herself over to him, and when he parted her lips, and his tongue swept the inside of her soft swollen bottom lip, she couldn't contain her sigh, or the desire humming through her.

He caught her soft lip between his teeth, and then his tongue stroked the inside of her mouth, reminding her of how his hips had moved as he'd thrust into her, filling her, making her body come alive.

She was coming alive now, feverishly alive, and she clutched

Brando, holding on, legs weak, heart pounding, veins full of honey and fire.

Then his head lifted and he gazed down into her eyes. "I suggest we marry as soon as possible."

Charlotte staggered back a step, dazed, senses swimming. "What?"

"I'll look into the paperwork tomorrow."

"Brando, no." She moved back another step, legs trembling, tension rippling through her. "Marriage isn't the answer, it isn't. There must be another way to make this work. I'll get an apartment in Florence...something not far from yours."

"We should be together, under one roof."

"Then give me a suite of rooms in your house. We'll be roommates."

"That will never work. There's too much chemistry between us. We'll drive each other mad."

"I'm not going to rush into anything. We have time. We have months."

"Let's not tempt fate."

"Months," she repeated firmly, smashing her panic, even as she turned around and started back to the *castello*, her gaze fixed on the tall, magnificent house glimmering with soft yellow light.

CHAPTER FIVE

THE MORNING SUN shone brightly, warming Brando's back as he walked from the house to the vineyard. The dark soil beneath his feet smelled fresh, the air around him fragrant. Summer was coming, and then it'd be fall. Brando was glad to be back on his estate, and he never felt more peace than when he was here, close to the vineyards, able to walk amid the vines. He checked clusters of grapes as he walked between the tidy rows. It looked like an excellent crop this year and he anticipated a good harvest come September.

But that wasn't all that would happen. By the time the grapes were harvested, he would be a father.

He hadn't quite yet become accustomed to the thought. It was still exciting, surprising. Even a little overwhelming. He hadn't been ready to settle down, hadn't imagined starting a family for another few years. Because the Riccis didn't divorce, they tended to marry late, and he was no exception. He'd planned on marrying in his mid to late thirties, but God had a different plan, and he was good with that.

Charlotte, he knew, wasn't.

Charlotte saw obstacles where he saw solutions. He wasn't worried, not yet. He'd find a way to make her understand, but it would mean he needed time, and there wasn't much time, not if she intended to be on a flight to London tomorrow.

He paused at the next row, fingers lightly brushing a leaf, and then the cluster of grapes beneath.

Time together was what they needed. If she was determined to still go to London tomorrow, then he'd go with her.

Better yet, he'd fly her there himself.

None of Charlotte's clients knew she was pregnant, and none of them knew she was in Italy, either. She woke up to dozens of new emails in her inbox, and her phone showed an alarming number of new texts and voice messages needing attention.

Work was good, she told herself, as she sat with her laptop at the breakfast table, responding to emails she could answer now, and making note of what she'd need to do to get back to people.

She had to survive only another day here, she told herself, and then she'd be in England, with her family—not that any of them knew she was coming, in part because she wasn't sure where she should go. But she didn't have to have that figured out yet. Tomorrow was tomorrow, today was today, and she'd devote the rest of her morning to work, and then eventually she'd have to face Brando, and hopefully by the time she did, she'd be more sanguine about the kiss.

The kiss.

Her fingers hovered over her keyboard as heat washed through her. The kiss...

Brando still had such an effect on her. There was something so elemental about him, them, and she couldn't resist him, not physically. Emotionally, that was a different matter. Emotionally, all she had to do was remember Louisa at the door of his Florence house, practically naked, clearly having come to the door from his bed, and that memory still made her recoil.

She knew she couldn't judge him for having others—there was no relationship between them. But how could she make the leap from "nothing" to wife?

It didn't make sense. She couldn't wrap her head around it… or her heart. And for marriage, she needed her heart.

She closed her laptop and pushed it away before crossing her arms over her chest, frustrated and indignant. It was a mistake coming to Florence to see Brando, and an even bigger mistake agreeing to come to this house in the country with him because everywhere she looked, it was his world. She didn't belong here, and she felt trapped right now, trapped in his big, sprawling *castello*, trapped by the beautiful pastoral views, trapped in his world that was both seductive, and consuming.

Brando wasn't like anyone else she had ever known, and she didn't know how to deal with him. She felt hormonal, and restless, agitated and confused. She should have just stayed in California and gone to her yoga class and eaten her healthy salads and worked at her desk and sent him a message that they needed to talk, that she had something important to tell him.

He would have come to see her.

She could have stayed put and made him do the traveling. Why didn't she?

That was easy. She'd secretly wanted the element of surprise. She'd wanted to discover for herself who he really was, not who she imagined him to be. She wanted facts. The truth. Because one night together wasn't anything, one night of sex was just a fantasy. After she'd returned to Los Angeles, she'd built him up in her mind, too, made him special, and wonderful…almost mythic…and she knew it couldn't all be true, that he couldn't really be everything she'd made him out to be. And so, she'd arrived in his world unannounced, shown up on his doorstep to see what she would see—not the fantasy, but the man.

And the man had a famous model in his bed.

The man probably had famous models frequently in his bed. But, why shouldn't he? He was ridiculously wealthy, and impossibly handsome, and he made love like a god.

He'd made her feel things she didn't know she could feel,

and he'd made her hope—as impossible as it was—that she was different. Special.

Seeing Louisa on his doorstep dispelled that hope. Charlotte wasn't special, or unique. What they'd done...experienced... New Year's Eve was no different from what he'd done, and shared, with countless other women. Unwittingly she thought of her family, and the affairs—hushed as they were—and the lack of commitment. Both of her parents had been unfaithful. Both of them had found it impossible to honor their wedding vows. If she married Brando, she'd be living with someone who wasn't that different from her father, and it filled her with pain.

But maybe pain was good. Maybe it was better this way, better to deal in facts.

Fact one: she was pregnant.

Fact two: the baby was due in three months.

Fact three: Brando Ricci, Italian tycoon, was the father.

Fact four: Brando didn't love her, but she, Charlotte Parks, might just be a little in love with him...

Footsteps sounded and she glanced up, hoping it was the housekeeper with her cappuccino. She'd had one earlier with breakfast but still craved another cup. Instead it was Brando, and he was carrying a tall bottle of water and a glass.

He twisted off the cap on the bottle and filled the glass with sparkling water before placing the glass in front of her. "Too much caffeine isn't good for the baby," he said. "Water is better for both of you."

"I didn't sleep well. I can't wake up."

"Go for a swim. That will be far more refreshing, and healthier, too."

"I'm not interested in squeezing myself into a bathing suit."

"There is no one to see. You'll have complete privacy."

"I have too much work to do, and sadly, I didn't bring a suit."

He dropped into a chair at the table. "Is there anything I can help you with?"

"No. You've done quite enough, thank you."

"Giving you water instead of coffee?"

"No, getting me pregnant. I think I'll handle everything else from here on out." She shifted in her chair, and drew a slow breath, trying to calm the butterflies in her middle and the tightness in her chest. Just his appearance set her heart racing, and now that he was seated close, she felt breathless. Because this was also a fact—her body liked him, very much.

And then she forced herself to remember Louisa, and Louisa was sleeping with him, and Louisa was his, or vice versa. But the point was, just two days ago he was with Louisa and now he was proposing marriage and the whole thing was ludicrous, and more than a little disturbing.

"How can you suggest marriage when you're still romantically involved with other women?" she said bluntly, unable to hold the words back. "And how can I possibly think marriage is an option when just days ago Louisa opened your door, practically naked?"

"I thought we talked about this."

"She answered your front door."

"She's a free spirit. She knew I didn't want her to, so she ran downstairs before I could."

"You like that?"

"She's playful. Fun."

Charlotte closed her eyes, aware that she was nothing like free spirit Louisa. In fact, Charlotte was the exact opposite of Louisa, and Charlotte couldn't imagine being wild and outrageous. From an early age, she'd recoiled from drawing attention…doing anything outside the norm. And the one time she took a risk, it had been a calculated risk, but still a risk, and Charlotte had ended up pregnant.

"I've told you this already. Louisa and I are not together," Brando said patiently. "There is nothing serious between us. She was in Florence and we met and had dinner—"

"Had sex."

"Yes."

"Probably lots of it."

He leaned forward abruptly, closing the distance between them. "Charlotte, what are you doing?"

There was a bite in his voice and she shook her head, feeling sick. "This is all wrong," she murmured, looking anywhere but at him. "Every bit of it."

"You must stop thinking about Louisa. She's not part of this equation. No one is, but us. She is completely out of the picture"

She shook her head again, feeling even more frantic. "I can't have your baby. I can't. You will never be faithful. Never be mine. Never—" She broke off and jumped up, neatly sidestepping his hand to escape to the other side of the balcony. "What a mess this all is."

He rose from his chair and followed her. "What's going on? What's happening?"

"I'm just realizing that I've been living in a fantasy world. I've been pretending it's just the baby and me, but it's not. There is you, and you don't fit into my life or my plan. Last night you said we should marry. You said we should raise the baby together, married, but how? It'd never work. You're a bachelor. A virtual playboy—"

"I object. I'm not a playboy and have never been that."

"You have lots of sex with lots of women."

"When I'm in a committed relationship, I'm only with that woman. But if I'm not in a relationship, and I'm attracted to a woman, and she's attracted to me, we might go to bed together. Why not? Sex isn't bad, or dirty. It's physical, it's pleasurable. It's a form of communication and connection—"

"But I don't have sex with every man that is appealing. I don't just make love because I'm attracted to him."

"You did with me."

"And what a mistake that was," she retorted grimly.

He stood in front of her, hands on his lean hips, studying her. "You didn't think so at the time," he said after a long moment.

"I regretted it almost immediately," she answered, glancing

at him, and then away, because it was too unnerving to meet his penetrating gaze. "I flew home kicking myself the entire way."

"That must have been a very painful flight," he said deadpan.

She rolled her eyes. "Of course you'd make a joke about it. You don't know me, and you don't understand the first thing about me, because if you did, you wouldn't have suggested marriage as if it were a cure-all. Marriage wouldn't make anything better, Brando. It would make everything worse."

"Explain."

"I just have no desire to be married, much less marry someone who I'm not compatible with. We had chemistry, but you have chemistry with every woman—"

"That's not true."

"And you enjoy your freedom, and the opportunity to be with different women, and I refuse to be the one who takes that freedom from you. You like being a bachelor, so be a bachelor. You can be a bachelor and a father. It's done all the time."

"Not in my family."

"Well, welcome to the twenty-first century, Ricci family."

He ignored the jab. "I was happy being single, but I will also be happy being married."

"I won't be."

"You don't know that, because you haven't even truly considered the suggestion. You've decided outright it's not for you—"

"Because it's not."

"But don't you think that's a little immature? Can you try to have an open mind? We're having a baby, and we need to come together for our child. I think you're using me as an excuse. I've told you I'm ready, and nothing will change my mind now."

Charlotte looked away, his words weighing heavily on her, eating away at her conscience and heart. She did want what was best for the baby, but the only reason Brando was suggesting marriage was for the baby. Not because he cared for her, and not because he thought it would be good for her, but it would be good for the baby, and the Ricci family name.

In Los Angeles she felt sure of herself, and confident of her place in life. Here...

Here she wasn't Charlotte Parks, but a woman carrying Brando Ricci's baby, the baby who would be his heir.

His heir.

Not hers.

"I liked my life as it was," she said finally. "And I don't think it's selfish or immature to say that I'm a better person on my own. Being independent has been good for me. Being able to be who I want to be, versus what others project onto me, has allowed me to become the me that is successful, and happy." She could feel his gaze on her and she glanced over her shoulder and looked at him. "At the same time, I'm aware that we must come up with some kind of solution, find some middle ground, but marriage isn't it."

"I didn't realize you're so opposed to marriage."

"Not opposed to marriage in general, but opposed to me marrying out of some archaic idea that marriage solves problems. Marriage doesn't solve problems. Marriage creates problems."

"If we were madly in love, would you still feel the same way?"

For some reason his question, in that slightly mocking inflection, made her smile. "I don't know. But then, I've never been madly in love. Have you?"

He moved to her side and leaned against the stone balustrade. "I don't think I've even been in love, period." He looked out toward the valley, his gaze on the horizon. "At least not the way you describe. I've had long and close relationships with women, relationships I cherished, but there was never a sense, or a feeling, of necessity. There was no feeling that it was a forever relationship, one that I couldn't live without. I've been sorry to see relationships end, but I've never felt devastated, or heartbroken."

"Don't you think it's odd that neither of us have been madly, passionately in love?"

"I think it's odder that people fall in and out of 'love' so easily. It makes me think it's not love, but infatuation."

"What do you even think love is?"

He shrugged. "I know familial love. Loyalty, respect, attachment, devotion."

"So, you love your family."

"I do, but that's an attachment formed over time." Brando shifted, faced her. "It's probably why I'm comfortable proposing marriage. I believe together we could raise our children with kindness and respect. We'll be devoted parents, and that devotion is binding...us to them, them to us, and for each other."

"That sounds dreadful. You know that, don't you? Every word you say just sounds dreadful."

"Dreadful, how? It's stability. It's honorable—"

"Devoid of passion, energy, excitement—"

"And yet, you yourself seem to avoid those very things," he interrupted.

She drew back. "What?"

"You deliberately avoid passion and excitement—"

"If that was true, I wouldn't be here, in this situation, now."

"And yet you've admitted more than once that our night together was a mistake."

She felt her face heat. "I don't do one-night stands," she said stiffly. "You were my first, and I realized belatedly that casual sex wasn't for me."

"*I* didn't blow you off, and it didn't have to be a one-night stand. I phoned you while you were on the way in the cab to the airport. I phoned you again after you landed in Los Angeles. You didn't return those two calls. Undeterred, I tried to see you again a couple weeks later, but you pushed me away, saying that while you'd enjoyed our night together, it wouldn't happen again."

"It couldn't, Brando. I've never mixed business and pleasure before. You were the first client I ever got...intimate...with."

"Why did you?"

"I liked you. I was drawn to you."

"And I liked you, and was very drawn to you, too."

"But I don't sleep with my clients," she said firmly. "It's bad business, and incredibly irresponsible of me."

"Don't work with the Ricci family anymore. Problem solved."

"It's not that easy, Brando. The Riccis are important clients. I can't alienate them."

"You can't alienate them, but you can alienate me?"

She sighed with frustration. "You're not helping, especially not when you twist my words. You know what I mean. I didn't have feelings for any of them… I had feelings for you, and that's a problem." And then realizing what she'd just said, she hurriedly added, "And now that I'm pregnant, we really have a problem. How do we raise this baby, and where?"

Brando was silent, his features shuttered, and then he rolled one thickly muscled shoulder. "Sometimes solutions come when you're not obsessing about them. Perhaps we need a break from talking and thinking. Perhaps we should go do something and just not think."

She arched a brow, curious. "Do what?"

"We could get in the car and drive to Greve, and then stop in Montefioralle, which is up on a hillside, and actually overlooks Greve. Montefioralle is a village that dates to the early nine hundreds and there are wonderful views of the valley from there. Many tourists like to walk to Montefioralle from Greve, but I wouldn't suggest it in your condition, but the drive is scenic and Greve has a charming, historic main square, and several nice spots we could stop for lunch."

Charlotte glanced at her laptop on the table and then out at the valley, and she knew what she wanted to do—escape. Not think. But being with Brando was incredibly problematic. "Can we really not discuss the baby and the future for the next hour?"

"I promise we won't discuss either for the rest of the afternoon. Let's leave serious discussions until later, and just try to enjoy the day. You're not in this part of Italy often. Try to enjoy it."

They drove to Greve in his low-slung sports car and parked in a small alley behind a creamy stone building, and then entered through the back of the building. It was cool inside, the thick stone walls keeping out the heat, while the interior smelled of oak and wine. "One of our tasting rooms," he said, guiding her past an office to the public rooms where he gave her a brief overview of the Ricci wines being sampled and sold in the shop.

After saying a few words to the staff, he escorted her through the front door, where they emerged onto the medieval town square, the square ringed with handsome buildings filled with picturesque cafés, art galleries and more wine tasting rooms. They wandered in and out of the different shops and galleries and visited a church where the stillness and flickering candles filled Charlotte with much-needed peace. Everything would be fine. She didn't have to panic or worry so much. Brando would be reasonable and they'd find a way through this.

After an hour and a half of exploring the town, they returned to Brando's car for the short drive up a steep hill to Montefioralle.

This time Brando parked at a small restaurant perched on the side of the slope with a breathtaking view of the valley and Greve below. "Hope you're hungry," he said as they were seated at a table on the small patio. "The food here is excellent, and the wine, too."

"Is it wine from your vineyard?" she asked.

He flashed a smile that was as sexy as it was sinful. "How did you know?"

She couldn't help smiling back. He was irresistible when he turned on the charm. "Just a lucky guess."

Brando had been intrigued by Charlotte from the first time he met her in August of last year. She was stylish, stunning, smart and incredibly confident. He was impressed she could hold her own during contentious meetings with his family, and admired her ability to say what needed to be said, even if it wasn't popular. Brando, himself, tended to be blunt, and it wasn't often he met a woman who'd go toe-to-toe with him, rather than shy away from tough topics, but she did. And then when the conflict eased, she'd smile one of her smiles, and maybe that's what had hooked him.

When Charlotte Parks smiled, she lit up a room. Her smile was brilliant and wide, and her blue eyes gleamed, too.

It wasn't until she smiled now that he realized this was the first time he'd seen her smile since their night together New Year's Eve.

He realized how much he'd missed that smile, never mind how much he'd flat out missed her.

Brando hadn't chased after a woman in years, but he'd wanted to see Charlotte last year, after she'd returned to the States. He'd very much wanted another night with her, although he suspected one more night wouldn't be enough for him. He'd gone to LA to see her, but she gave excuses about being busy, and in the middle of a tense situation with clients, but she hoped she could say hello the next time she was in Italy.

She was giving him the brush-off. He'd been equally surprised, and disappointed, because even though she'd said all along it would be one night only, he hadn't believed she meant it. But she had.

He admired that, too.

This wasn't a game for her, either. She truly valued her independence, and it was a refreshing change from the women he dated who were utterly dependent on him, craving attention, desiring to be spoiled, hungry for gifts, big and small. Brando knew he was as much at fault for cultivating shallow relationships. He preferred giving gifts over giving his heart. It was a tidier transaction. Fewer complications.

Only now the woman who didn't want him was here, pregnant with his child, and there would be no tidy transaction. Their situation was enormously complicated.

He leaned across the table and kissed her, a firm, slow kiss. Her mouth was warm and soft and he felt the quiver in her lips before he drew back.

Her face was pale with two pink blotches in her cheekbones, which only made her blue eyes brighter. He could see the worry in her eyes, though, as well as a question. She didn't know why he'd kissed her. He didn't know, either, other than he wanted her. He'd wanted her from the very beginning, and it crossed his mind that he would probably always be this attracted to her, and not just physically, but intellectually. She held her own with him. She was his equal in every way. She'd make an excellent wife.

"You'll make an excellent addition to the family," he said. "If I didn't know better, I'd think you were a Ricci already."

Charlotte stiffened, her shoulders squaring, spine straightening. "We'd agreed we weren't going to discuss the future," she said quietly, flatly, anger washing through her. "Those were your words, too."

He gave a casual shrug. "I'm not discussing the future. I'm talking about the present. You fit in. You're my other half. You belong with me," he answered.

"I'm not your other half. You are a whole, and I am a whole and there is no room in our individual lives for each other. We are too independent, too headstrong."

"We're smart enough, successful enough to know how to adjust."

She held her breath, unwilling to speak, afraid that whatever she said might be used against her.

"What other choice do we have?" He'd ordered a glass of wine with his lunch and he gave his goblet a slight spin and watched the ruby-red wine swirl. "Not if we're putting our child's needs first, and I don't know a lot about you, but I've heard enough now to understand that your family never put you first. That your fear of families is the fear of being lost, consumed—"

"That's putting it a little strong," she interrupted.

"But I'm right, aren't I? You like your space because you can breathe, and be free, something you couldn't do in your family."

Suddenly parched, she reached for her water glass and took a gulp. "I might need a glass of wine, too, if we're going to be analyzing me over lunch today."

His lips lifted faintly. "No one is trying to psychoanalyze you. I'm just slowly starting to understand you. I think it's important to understand you—"

"Then let me help you understand exactly what I don't want. I don't want to become part of another family. And as much as I enjoyed working with your family, I have no desire to become one of them. I mean no disrespect, and I apologize if I'm phrasing this badly, but your family is every bit as overwhelming as mine—and that doesn't work for me in any way."

"No need to apologize. I agree we are passionate, but there is no malice in any of them."

She didn't immediately reply. Instead she looked away, out across the restaurant's patio toward the verdant valley filled with orchards and vineyards. A vineyard ran down the hill below them, the afternoon sun shining brightly on the tidy rows of grapes, gilding the green leaves with burnished light.

"There's a reason I'm happy in Southern California," she said after a bit. "I'm on my own. I have my own place, my own identity. I don't have to answer to my mother, my father, or any of my stepparents. I can just be myself. It's taken me years to break free and I've no desire to give up that space, and independence."

"But isn't your mother still in Los Angeles?"

Charlotte shook her head. "This isn't something we discuss, but my mother and Bill have been separated for a couple of years. They may even be divorced by now. I don't know, and I don't really want to know. I figure when Mother wants to announce something she will, and until then I'm happy to leave her alone and let her do her thing, and I do my thing."

"Where is she living?"

"South of France at the moment, but I think that's a temporary thing."

"You don't see your stepfather anymore? I thought you two were once close?"

"I like Bill. He's a maverick and colorful and he always invites me to Hollywood parties, as well as his big film premieres. Sometimes I show up because he loves a good red carpet photo with his family all around him, but I haven't since he and Mom went their different ways. But I'm fine with it. I like Los Angeles because I can be no one there. I'm invisible and I like that. I also like the weather, I like being close to the ocean and I like that no one descends on me in Los Angeles. My father hates LA. My brothers and sisters hate LA, too, which delights me to no end. I'm happy with my little house and career. It suits me."

She felt him study her from across the table and it was all she could do to sit still beneath his scrutiny.

"Marrying me doesn't mean you'll lose your identity, *cara*. You will always be Charlotte Parks, even if you become Mrs. Charlotte Parks Ricci."

"What if I didn't want to take your last name? What if I simply wanted to be Charlotte Parks?"

His powerful shoulders shifted easily. "If that is what you preferred, I'd have no objections. You have a career, you have a perfectly lovely name. Marrying you is about giving our baby a home, a family and a family name." He paused. "Or do you take issue with our baby being named Ricci?"

She couldn't believe she was even having this conversation. She wasn't seriously considering marrying him, was she?

She sat silent for a moment, processing everything being said, and realizing she maybe had given an indication that she was open to marrying him... But was she?

Was she even considering this future he suggested?

As if able to read her mind, he added, "It's not as if I live in my family's back pocket. There are family business meetings, as well as periodic family dinners, holidays and birthday celebrations, but my brothers and sister are busy with their own lives and families. They certainly wouldn't be overly involved in our lives, nor would we be expected to be immersed in theirs, not as newlyweds with a young baby."

"You realize I haven't agreed to marry you, nor is it likely that I will accept your proposal," she said.

"Yes, that's understood," he answered gravely, and yet she could have sworn his lips twitched, as if amused. "So, let's just keep moving forward, and discussing options, aware that no commitments are being made, on either side."

"Fair enough," she said before looking him in the eyes. "How important is it for the baby to take your last name? Would it upset your family terribly?"

His jaw flexed, and he frowned into his wineglass. "I don't know if it would bother them. It would bother me. I'd very much like my son or daughter to have my name."

"I thought you were the rebel."

"I've been a rebel, but I'm older, and wiser, and appreciate my family, and our history here in Tuscany. Riccis have been making wine for one hundred years—"

"But you're the only one still making wine. The others have all shifted to other industries."

"All the more reason for me to want a son or daughter to carry on the winemaking tradition."

She didn't immediately reply, because there was nothing she could say. She understood him, and if she were in his position, she'd feel the same way. It was only later, as they drove back to his *castello*, and passed through the huge gates set in the high stone walls that she said quietly, "We don't have to be married for our child to take your name. You are the father. The birth certificate will reflect your name."

He glanced at her, lips compressing, but that was his only

response as they traveled down the private lane lined with tall cypresses.

Brando parked in front of the *castello*, turned the ignition off and faced her. "Do you still intend to go to London tomorrow?"

"Yes."

"I'll fly you there. It'll be easier on you physically. You won't have to deal with long lines and security."

His offer caught her off guard, and yet at the same time, it was a little bit tempting. All London airports were unbearable. You couldn't escape the crowds and lines. But why would he want to fly her back to England? "I'm not sure how flying me to England benefits you."

"Less stress on you is less stress on the baby."

Ah, of course. It was about the baby. She didn't know why she felt a stab of disappointment, but she certainly wasn't going to analyze the reaction here and now. "And there is no other agenda?" she asked, arching a brow. "You're not planning on announcing we're engaged, or something outrageous like that?"

He matched her arched brow with one of his. "How can I do that, when we're not engaged? Really, Charlotte, you have so little trust."

His smirk was galling. But then everything about him was frustrating. He was gorgeous and interesting and he made her feel alive and wistful and confused...

She hated feeling confused. As well as wistful. Both reminded her of being a child, which wasn't a period in her life she remembered with fondness. Being a child, she was forced to rely on others, and the chief lesson from her childhood seemed to be that people weren't dependable, that most promises made were never kept. "I don't trust people very much, no."

"You ought to begin trying to trust me, especially if we're to co-parent."

"I haven't agreed to that, either."

"*Bella*, fortunately for me, that one is out of your jurisdiction. The law gives us both rights as parents. However, if you feel like agreeing to something, you could agree to marry me so when I do meet your family tomorrow, I can be introduced as your fiancé, and the father of your baby."

"Maybe I should simply take my flight as scheduled. It would be far less complicated."

"Or, I fly you home and meet your family and you can introduce me as the father of your child. I think it would be reassuring for them to know you haven't been abandoned and won't be having to raise the child on your own."

For a split second she couldn't breathe, her chest squeezing, her heart suffused with pain. *That she hadn't been abandoned.* She blinked hard, clearing the hot sting of tears, trying to suppress the emotions that were threatening to swallow her whole.

"Surely your father would be reassured by the news," Brando added, brow creasing. "As well as your brothers and sisters."

"Everyone is quite busy," she said, forcing a smile. "I don't think my pregnancy will trouble them one way or another, but you suddenly appearing with me would cause a fuss. And we don't need the fuss, do we?"

He gave her a long, considering look. "What happens when the gossips discover you're pregnant with my child? That will get lots of tabloid attention, but if that doesn't worry you...?"

"We'll deal with it when we have to. Hopefully it won't be for quite some time."

CHAPTER SIX

CHARLOTTE WOKE SEVERAL times in the night, not feeling well. Her lower back ached. Her lower belly felt heavy and tight. She'd leave bed and walk a bit, and then stretch and eventually she'd fall back asleep.

But the heaviness in her lower back was far worse this morning, and the tightness in her lower belly had become a perplexing cramp. The cramping sensation had become strong, and regular, far too regular. She'd read about Braxton Hicks contractions and wondered if this was what she was experiencing. She even looked them up online, but these didn't quite meet the description. No, hers felt strong, and the dull pain was intensifying to the point she couldn't walk easily anymore.

Something wasn't right.

The cramping was frightening, and the pain was becoming excruciating.

Charlotte had left her cell phone unplugged during the night after researching contractions, and now it was dead, the battery dying in the night.

Limping to the door, she prayed she'd spot one of the staff nearby. Fortunately, one of the maids was walking down the hall with a stack of freshly laundered towels.

"I need Brando," Charlotte said in Italian, panting and wincing as another sharp contraction hit. "Tell him something's wrong. I think the baby is coming."

"You must lie down," the maid answered. "Let me help you to bed, and then I'll send for help."

Brando was there at her side in less than five minutes. He was wearing jeans, work boots and a thin knit shirt, indicating that he'd been out in the fields again this morning. He leaned over her, his gaze searching hers. "What's happening?"

"Strong contractions. It doesn't feel right."

"You think the baby is coming?"

"I don't know, but I'm scared. It's too soon."

He reached for her hand and gave it a reassuring squeeze. "I've sent for my pilot. He should be here soon. He'll get us to the hospital quickly."

"What if there's something wrong? What if the baby—?"

He gave her hand another warm, firm squeeze. "We're only thinking positive thoughts, *cara*. Be positive, be strong."

Brando stayed with her until the pilot texted that he was on premises and the helicopter was ready. There was a small hospital in the valley that served the local population, but Brando was taking no chances. They were going to go to Florence where there were specialists and a neonatal unit, just in case one was needed.

The moment the pilot indicated they were good to go, Brando scooped Charlotte into his arms and carried her downstairs to the helipad, feeling her contractions as they hit, and soothing her when she expressed pain, and then fear and alarm. "It is all good, all fine," he said, looking into her eyes, letting her see his calm, and confidence.

"Can the baby survive at six months? I think so, but I'm not sure."

"This baby is fierce, and strong, it wanted to be conceived, so yes, I think this baby can survive. Absolutely."

She smiled even as she blinked back tears. "It is a stubborn little thing."

"Maybe because its mother is stubborn, too."

She smiled a little bigger, the smile still wobbly, but he found it hopelessly endearing. "And you're not?"

"I'm the most reasonable, rational man you'll ever meet."

"You forgot arrogant. As long as the baby's okay—" She broke off, eyes filling with tears.

"The baby will be fine. And you will be fine."

"And if something goes wrong?"

"If there are complications, you will know you are being seen by the best doctors, at one of the best hospitals in Europe, and I will be with you every step of the way. Have faith. Trust me."

"I'm trying." She gripped his hand tightly, desperately, as she searched his face. After a moment, she added brokenly, "I want this baby."

"I do, too."

The helicopter had them arrive in Florence in less than twenty minutes, and they were greeted immediately by a medical team.

As he'd promised, Brando stayed by Charlotte's side during the examination. He held his breath as the obstetrician checked her, and then performed an ultrasound. Thankfully, the baby's heartbeat was steady, and the baby looked fine.

Brando stared at the screen, taking in every detail. He hadn't seen many ultrasounds before, but unless his eyes were deceiving him, that was most definitely a boy baby.

His chest tightened and his throat ached with overwhelming emotion.

Charlotte was pregnant with his son.

"He's really okay?" Brando asked quietly.

Charlotte looked from the doctor to Brando and back to the physician. "It's a boy?"

The doctor nodded. "Yes, and your son looks good. He is fine. But you, Charlotte, are in preterm labor. We're going to try to stop labor, as the best place for your son is right where he is now, safe inside his mother."

"Can you stop the labor?" she asked.

The doctor didn't even hesitate. "Because you sought out treatment immediately, I think we have a good shot at it."

It was a long day, but by midafternoon the contractions had stopped, and finally pain free, Charlotte fell asleep, worn out from the worry and fear. Brando stood by her bed in her private room on the hospital's maternity ward, watching her sleep.

Her color was better than it had been this morning. Her long blond hair spilled across her pillow, her lips slightly parted in sleep.

The tension was gone from her face, and he felt as if he could breathe properly for the first time all day.

He'd been scared, truly scared, and he'd prayed not just for the baby, but for Charlotte, who seemed so determined to be an island and do everything, and manage everything, on her own. He'd seen her panic, and felt her fear, and for the first time, he saw a crack in that perfect, flawless mask of hers. She might not want anyone else to know, but she felt vulnerable, as well as alone, which perplexed him, as she came from a big family and yet it was a family she didn't seem to embrace.

His phone vibrated with incoming messages and he drew his phone from his pocket, scanned the texts and then checked his emails, and seeing nothing that required immediate attention, he pulled a chair closer to the side of the bed and sat down.

When he told her he would be there, with her, he'd meant it.

Charlotte and his son might be out of danger, but there was nowhere Brando wanted to be but here, with her. With them. His family.

His family, he silently repeated, mulling the words over, awed by the implication. He was going to have a son.

Warmth filled him and his chest felt tight with inarticulate emotion. Pride, hope, wonder.

Growing up in a close, overly involved family had made

him at times resent the family ties, and then during his early twenties, he'd had a falling-out with his family, particularly his father, whom Brando viewed as overbearing and interfering.

It didn't help that Brando did not feel wanted, or needed, by the family, and questioned why every family member was expected to go to work for the Ricci-Baldi company. He already had two older brothers and a sister working in the business, and they were content. Why was he needed? He wasn't. And the work he was being offered was menial at best. He found every aspect of working for the family to be boring and mindless— tasks anyone could handle. After a year of miserably working for the family, he realized he could go do this same pointless brainless work somewhere else and be paid a hell of a lot better than what he was earning working for his family.

He spoke to his father about his boredom, and his father dismissed Brando's concerns, stating that everyone was expected to prove themselves, and that as the youngest, he couldn't expect to ever be in a leadership position, not when Enzo and Marcello were already working their way up through management.

His father's answer didn't sit well with Brando, and in an act of utter rebellion, he returned the call from a modeling agency in Milan, and said he'd be open to meeting with the agency if they were still interested in him. During his teenage years, Brando had been approached several times about modeling, but he knew it wasn't something that would be viewed favorably in his family, so he'd turned the opportunities down. But now, in need of work, he went on his first go-see, booked the job and proceeded to book almost every other go-see he was sent out on.

Brando's father did exactly as expected—Brando was cut off from the family financially, but Brando wasn't upset. He was relieved. For the first time in his life, he was standing completely on his own and being successful. In six months, he made more money than he had in the previous two years, and by the time he turned twenty-five he was making so much money he needed to find investment opportunities, reluctant to leave that much cash sitting in the bank. He bought stocks, and purchased real estate, and when those proved to be good investments, he became a venture capitalist for two small technology start-ups, turning his hundreds of thousands into millions when one of the start-ups went public and became big.

At twenty-six he bought his first small winery. Within two years he'd bought another, and it was at this time his father came to him and asked if he'd come back to the family and work with them since Brando seemed to have a golden touch. Brando was still trying to decide if he would when his father died, and if Brando had one regret it was that his father died before Brando returned to the family, going to work in Florence with his brothers and sister, refocusing the Ricci brands and giving new life to the Ricci wines.

His mother used to say that she was sure Brando's father knew, but maybe it wasn't important that his father knew. Maybe what was important was that those living knew Brando would never shirk his responsibilities, or his familial duty, again.

Family came first, always.

Charlotte woke to the sound of murmured voices and, opening her eyes, discovered Brando at the foot of her bed in discussion with her doctor.

Brando was the one to notice she'd awoken and he immediately approached the bed, a question in his silver gaze. "How do you feel?"

"Better," she said, grateful the contractions had stopped, and there was no more pain. "What time is it?"

"Close to seven. Your doctor was just doing a final check on you before going home for the night."

She glanced over at the doctor as he approached her side. "Thank you for all your help today."

"My pleasure. I'm just glad you could get here quickly. Everything looks good right now," he answered, adding, "You'll be in excellent hands here tonight, and the staff knows I'm on call should you need anything."

Brando walked the doctor out before returning. "Are you hungry? You haven't had breakfast or lunch."

"I am starting to get hungry."

"Good, my personal chef is on the way now with dinner. When he heard we were back in town, he said there was no way we could eat hospital food. He's been cooking all afternoon, and I see you looking worried, but there's no reason for that. I've cleared the menu with the doctor, and the doctor said soup, pasta and a little bit of meat would help keep up your strength."

"You've thought of everything."

"I don't want you to stress. You're to relax, and eat dinner, and sleep well tonight, and tomorrow we'll see what the doctor says. Hopefully you won't have to stay here too long."

It was only then that Charlotte remembered her flight. "I missed it. My flight to London."

"Thank goodness you weren't in-flight. I don't think today's outcome would have been the same if you were on the plane."

"No, I don't think so, either." She slowly exhaled, trying to ease the tension in her chest. "I came close to going into labor."

"*Cara*, you were in labor. The doctors were able to administer medicine to stop it. But another thirty minutes… I don't know the outcome. We might have had our son with us tonight."

"I'm only twenty-three weeks along. I don't think the odds would be very good for him."

"I learned today that half of the babies born between twenty-three and twenty-four weeks survive delivery and have a shot at life outside the neonatal ICU."

"But that doesn't include all the complications premature babies have, does it?"

"No." His expression sobered, and he reached out to smooth hair back from her brow, his touch unexpectedly tender. "Which is why you need to rest and relax and give our son as much time as possible."

She watched the door after he walked out, apparently to make a call, or whatever it was he'd said, feeling raw and shaken. Not just from today's early labor scare, but from his kindness, and his strength, and his calm in the middle of a storm. She always tried to be calm during dramas, but she always felt like a fraud, not truly calm, not truly collected. It was an image she projected, aware that the world preferred strength, and people were drawn to success, but sometimes being strong and successful was isolating.

Sometimes being the one who had it together and needed nothing from anyone meant you had very little support from others.

Perhaps if she'd learned to ask for help, or was comfortable demanding attention, she might feel less alone. Perhaps if she was better at trusting people, she might have had proper relationships... Maybe she'd even be romantically involved with someone.

Instead she admired interesting men from afar, careful to never get too involved, careful to never risk her heart.

At least, until she gave in to her impulse and spent a night with Brando, and that night changed everything—and she wasn't referencing the pregnancy, but her hopes, and dreams.

She cared for Brando...a lot.

She also knew it was incredibly unrealistic to think he might have genuine feelings for her. He'd proposed because he was old-fashioned, and in his mind it was the morally right thing to do. She knew he would marry her, too, for the very same reasons. But he didn't love her, and she doubted he could be faithful, but she couldn't marry someone who didn't want her, not truly want her.

Brando returned to the room just then, entering with a man in a sharp suit, and the only indication that he might be Brando's chef was that he carried a large hamper in one hand, and an oversize insulated carrier in the other. The chef went to work spreading a small cloth over her table and laying out dishes, and Charlotte keep her attention fixed on the chef so that she didn't look at Brando even though she was incredibly aware of him, and that he was watching her.

No one had ever watched her the way he watched her.

No one had ever paid her as much attention or listened to her when she asked for space. He'd even let her go last winter when she wanted that, too.

Charlotte had met many powerful men, and a few handsome, powerful men, but she'd never met anyone who respected her desires the way Brando did. He could have tried to steamroll over her, but instead he appealed to her intellect and reason, and for that, she was grateful.

The chef was then gone as quickly as he'd arrived. Brando served her and then himself, and they ate the delicate seafood risotto, and while Brando had some of the main course of meat, Charlotte was satisfied.

She watched him as he cleared the dinner dishes, filling the basket before refreshing her water from the large bottle of sparkling water the chef had brought with him. "Thank you," she said, a lump in her throat because honestly, she couldn't remember the last time someone had done so much for her, never mind waiting on her hand and foot.

"My pleasure," he answered. "You do remember there is dessert. Mousse *al cioccolato*. Your favorite."

Chocolate mousse. It was her favorite, and he'd remembered.

They'd had chocolate mousse the night she'd stayed over, and she'd straddled him in bed, feeding him spoonfuls, before deciding it was far too good to share. She blushed, heat rushing through her. "Was this just a lucky coincidence, or did you ask him to make it?"

"I asked him."

Charlotte was dangerously close to tears. She clutched the covers in her hands, holding them tightly. "I'm overwhelmed."

"By mousse?"

"No, by you, today." She felt the hard thudding of her heart, and the strange prickly emotion in her chest, emotion that seemed to zigzag all the way through her. She hadn't been a virgin when she met Brando, and yet he made her feel naive, untutored, inexperienced in the ways of the world. He made her want to believe that better things existed, and that people could be good, and patient, and kind.

Today Brando also made her aware of just how much she needed him, even if she didn't want to admit it.

She didn't know what would have happened if she hadn't been with him when the contractions began. She didn't know how she would have managed without him today. He'd handled everything, and he'd been so incredibly focused, and calm, and strong. He'd said he wouldn't let anything happen to her, and he'd meant it. He'd been incredibly proactive, as well as protective. It was rather humbling to realize how good it felt to let someone else take charge. To let someone else be strong.

"Have I thanked you for today?" she said. "I don't know how I—"

"You have thanked me," he interrupted quietly. "But you don't have to thank me. I wanted to be here. There is nowhere else I'd rather be."

She gave a half nod. "I believe you."

The corner of his mouth lifted a fraction. "Are we making progress, *cara*?"

"I don't know if I'd call it progress, but you should know I appreciate everything, and am grateful, and our baby is grateful, too." And for the first time, the words *our baby* felt right. They felt true. It was their baby and there would be no shutting Brando out, and no fighting over custody. How could she do that to him? He would be a wonderful father, and she couldn't deny him the opportunity to be there every step of the way, or their son the security of a devoted father, either.

Brando misread her contemplative mood as fatigue, and insisted he leave for the night so she could get some sleep. "The nurse knows to call me if you want anything, or if you suddenly crave gelato, or if you're wide awake in the middle of the night and just want to talk."

She smiled crookedly. "I can call you just to chat?"

"If you're lonely or bored, have the nurse call me, and I will keep you company on the other end of the line."

"And if I wanted you to come back and keep me company here?" she asked.

"I'd get dressed and come straight away."

"What if I wanted you to stay here with me tonight?" The words popped out before she'd thought them through.

"Do you want me to? I've been told the little couch makes into a bed."

She eyed the small couch and then looked at him. He was over six feet two, and his shoulders were wider than the sleek Italian sofa. "You wouldn't be comfortable."

"I don't mind, not if it'd give you peace of mind."

She tried to picture him sleeping so close to her, his big body sprawled out, just the way he'd slept with her during their night together when they'd finally stopped touching and kissing and tasting—

"No, I wouldn't sleep a wink," she answered. "Go home and come back tomorrow...if you have time."

"*Cara*, I have nothing but time." He leaned over the bed, kissed her brow and then a fleeting kiss on her lips. "Can I get you anything before I leave?"

And suddenly, just like that, she didn't want him to leave.

Not just now, but ever.

The simmering feelings she'd had for him six months ago had become a fireball, exploding to life.

"No," she said, hating the thickness in her throat, and the aching pang in her heart. "I'm good. Go home, sleep well. I'll see you tomorrow."

Easier said than done, Brando thought, back at his elegant town house in the converted palace. He wandered through the second floor and then up to the third floor, which was his private office suite. Sitting down at his desk, he sorted through mail that had been left for him by his assistant, and documents requiring signatures. He signed where necessary and then leaned back and stared across the room, to the summer sky just now going dark.

He thought of nothing and everything, of Charlotte in the hospital bed, and the ultrasound earlier where he saw his son for the first time, the baby so tiny, but also so very perfect. Brando knew he would do whatever he had to do to ensure his son's safety, as well as his future. What mattered now was Charlotte and the baby. Everything else was secondary.

His phone pinged with an incoming text. He looked at it immediately, in case it had to do with Charlotte. Instead it was a text from Louisa.

Hello, handsome. I'm free now. Are you?

Brando picked up the phone and texted back.

Sorry, no.

He thought for a moment, before sending another swift text.

I enjoyed our time together, but I am no longer single. Ciao e abbi cura di te.

Goodbye and take care.

CHAPTER SEVEN

BRANDO WAS BACK at the hospital in the morning and Charlotte was sitting up in bed, looking anxious and restless when he arrived. "What's wrong?" he asked, leaning over to greet her with a kiss on her forehead.

"I need my phone, and my computer. I can't work without them." She gestured to the short stack of magazines on the bedside table. "The nurse brought me fashion magazines this morning but I don't want to read them. I need to check in with my clients—"

"Easy, slow down," he said, checking his smile as he pulled a chair close to the side of the bed. "You're supposed to be resting, not stressing out."

Charlotte drew a deep breath. "I know, and I agree. But I feel naked without my phone, and it's even worse not having a phone or computer. I'm not used to being completely out of touch."

"Do you want me to have someone drive them up from the *castello*? I can."

Her brow furrowed. "Am I going to be here long?"

"I don't know. That's something we'll have to ask the doctor when he makes his rounds this morning."

She was silent a moment and then nodded. "Obviously if me being here is the best thing, then I should be here. I just would feel better being here if I had my vanity bag, and briefcase with laptop, phone and chargers."

"I'm worried work will create stress for you, though."

"I'd be more stressed not being able to communicate with my clients." She hesitated. "I'll let them know I'm taking the next week or two off and will be in touch soon. I'd feel better about that than just not answering emails."

"Agreed."

She looked at him, brows still knitting together, expression still troubled. "I'm not flying anytime soon, am I?"

"I think it would be incredibly risky."

"I do, too." She looked past him to the window with its view of the city and the hills that framed the capital of Tuscany. "I don't want a repeat of yesterday."

"Neither do I."

"I was terrified."

He saw her bring her hands together, fingers laced tightly against the white hospital covers, and he reached out and covered her clenched hands with one of his. "Everything is good," he said quietly, firmly, determined to keep her calm. Relaxed. The baby needed her to be still, and relaxed.

"For now," she said, a catch in her voice. She glanced up at him, blue eyes shining with a film of tears. "But I can't stop thinking about the what-ifs. What if I'd been on the plane? What if I'd been going through customs at the airport? What if—?"

"But you weren't. You were with me, and we got you here quickly and the doctors were able to stop labor." He squeezed her hands. "And it wasn't all bad. Yesterday we saw the baby and he's healthy, and beautiful—"

She snorted. "I wouldn't go so far as to describe him as beautiful. I'm sure he will be—"

"He was beautiful to me. My son. *Our* son." Brando's voice deepened. "It's a miracle. I wasn't expecting a family and yet suddenly I have one, and I vow to take care of you both, always. Forever."

He hoped his words would reassure her, but instead tears trembled on her lashes before falling.

She pulled her hands free to wipe them away. "I hate crying," she said hoarsely. "Please don't mind me."

His chest squeezed, and he felt a peculiar pang near his heart. "You don't have to be an island," he said carefully, not wanting to upset her. "It's okay to have feelings and cry. Italian women are passionate, and emotional, but those emotions do not make them weak. Emotions are what make us strong."

She swiped beneath her eyes, drying them. "You seem to understand women quite well."

"Somehow you manage to make that sound like a criticism."

"In so many ways you seem so perfect, but then you don't want serious relationships. You aren't married—"

"If I was married, we wouldn't be here today. I would have never had that night with you."

She gazed up at him from beneath wet spiky lashes. "Lots of men have affairs."

"Are you thinking of that survey from a number of years ago that said in Italy, most affairs started in the office?"

"No, but interesting." Two bright spots of pink colored her cheeks. "I just know my parents divorced over affairs, and it was a problem between my mom and her last husband."

"I don't condone affairs. And I don't know if my father ever had an affair, but he cherished my mother, and taught his sons to protect your family at all costs, and you can't protect your family if you're damaging the marriage."

"So when you marry, you won't have one?"

"It goes against everything I believe."

"Then why haven't you married?"

"Because I hadn't found the one I wanted to commit myself to for the rest of time."

Charlotte's heart fell, and she looked away, teeth catching her lower lip to keep it from quivering.

Brando would marry her because it was the right thing to do, but she wasn't the one he would have married. And yet yesterday had made her realize she couldn't manage everything by herself. She'd been prepared to go it alone when she'd felt good and strong, but if there were complications, or if the baby came early, she realized she wouldn't be able to cope on her own. She didn't want to struggle alone.

"Remember when we agreed we'd be honest?" she said, stomach in knots, pulse racing.

He nodded.

"I'm going to be honest with you now, but it's not easy because I like my independence, but it's a problem." She glanced at him, trying to read his expression, but his silver gaze hid whatever he was thinking. "I was wrong. I can't do this on my own." She drew a quick breath and plunged on. "I can't even imagine what I would have done if I were in California when this happened. I don't know what I would have done yesterday without you. I was so scared, and in so much pain." She pressed her lips together, and counted a few counts, giving her time to gain control over her emotions, not easy when her heart felt bruised and she felt overwhelmed by the reality of her situation. "I try so hard to be independent and handle things, but Brando, I've never been so scared in my life. It was too soon for the baby to come, and I just kept thinking of all the problems he'd have if he was born at almost twenty-four weeks."

"It *was* scary, but you're fine, and he's fine—"

"For now." She looked up into his face, her gaze meeting his, and holding. This was serious. Important. She needed him to realize just how serious she was now. "But what if I go into labor again? What if the baby is born early? He could have serious challenges—" She broke off, swallowed and continued. "I was naive to think I could do it all, handle it all on my own. Honestly, it wasn't just naive, it was selfish. He isn't just my baby, he's yours, too, and you need to be part of his life."

"I will be."

She nodded, again biting down into her tender lower lip. For a moment there was just silence and then she added softly, "You were wonderful yesterday. You were such an advocate and so calm and so strong—" She broke off, fighting to hold back fresh tears, uncertain as to why she was falling apart now. She didn't cry and yet she felt as if she were a watering pot, tears springing free. "I realized I can't do this without you. I don't want to do this without you—"

The rest of Charlotte's thought was interrupted by the sudden appearance of the doctor with a nurse, and they entered her room in the middle of conversation, but the conversation ended as the obstetrician approached the bed.

"How are we today?" Dr. Leonardi asked, glancing from Charlotte to Brando and back again. "I understand it was a restless night for our patient. The night nurse said you were awake much of the night, but we need you to rest."

Brando looked at Charlotte, a black eyebrow lifting. She ignored it, and him, and answered the doctor. "I didn't realize hospitals are so noisy, and every time the nurse came in to check on me I'd wake up and then stay awake." She realized how that sounded and quickly added, "I'm not complaining, I'm just explaining why I couldn't sleep."

"You couldn't pretend it was a fine hotel?" the doctor teased.

"If it was a hotel, I would have phoned the front desk and complained," she answered with a wry smile. "I think I just had too much time on my own, and no way to distract myself. Brando has promised to send for my computer and then I'll be able to work if I can't sleep."

"Is your work very taxing?" Dr. Leonardi asked. "We don't want you to do anything that will create stress. It might be better for you to read a relaxing book, nothing too scary or violent. Maybe a romance. My wife reads them and says they're very good for escaping."

Charlotte forced a pleasant expression, hiding how she truly felt, as she would never, ever be caught reading a romance. A biography, yes. A history, yes. A cozy mystery, yes. Romances were for those who believed in happy endings. She didn't, at least, not anymore.

"Do you have an idea of how long you'll want to keep her here?" Brando asked.

"Another day or two, and then we can evaluate how she's doing, and how the baby is doing. If both are doing well, I don't see why Charlotte couldn't go home with you, but I'd keep her on modified bed rest."

Charlotte's heart fell. "For how long?"

"Possibly for the duration of your pregnancy."

Her jaw dropped. Three months?

Brando crossed his arms over his chest. "What is modified bed rest?"

"It's a term we use for restricted activity without the stringent dictate to remain completely confined to bed. Every doctor probably has his own definition for it. For me it means limited physical activity, and lengthy morning and afternoon rest periods in bed. I also restrict lovemaking, so no sexual activity, as sex releases prostaglandins that are similar to the medications used to induce labor."

Charlotte blushed. "That won't be an issue," she said unsteadily. "We're not having sex."

"It won't be forever," the doctor replied with a smile. "After the baby you'll need a few weeks to heal, and then you should be able to resume sexual intercourse—"

"Any other concerns?" Charlotte interrupted, embarrassed, and more than a little horrified. "Or do I just stay put for the day?"

"Just stay put, and relax, and I'll be back later this afternoon." The doctor nodded, smiled and walked out with the nurse.

Charlotte couldn't even look at Brando. Everything was so strange, and so uncomfortable. Her life seemed to be spinning completely out of control. "So there's that," she said, plucking at her covers.

"No sex for us—"

"That's not what I'm talking about," she interrupted quickly, heat rushing through her, making her feel tingly and self-conscious. "And you know it. You're just tormenting me now."

"Sex is what got us into this situation," he said mildly. "And it was good sex. Probably the best sex I've ever had."

She jerked her head up as she looked across her room at him. He was leaning against the wall, one shoulder resting against the window trim, sunlight pouring in, haloing his head with golden light. He had a hint of a smile, and there was a glint in his silver eyes that made her tummy flip and her pulse quicken. He was tall and lean, and incredibly handsome.

And he was hers...or had been for one night.

Two days ago he suggested they marry, which meant he could be hers forever.

Would he be happy, though? Would she?

"We were talking about something important when Dr. Leonardi walked in," he said now, his smile disappearing, his expression turning serious. "Let's finish that conversation."

"I don't remember what we were saying—"

"You'd just said you couldn't do this alone, and you didn't want to." Brando repeated her words back to her, almost exactly as she'd said them. "So what do we do?" he added. "What is our next step?"

Her mouth dried and her pulse jumped, beating too hard in her veins. "You tell me."

"I want to hear it from you. We both already know what I think."

She swallowed hard, her mouth feeling as if she'd been sucking on a cotton ball. It took forever to form words, but Brando waited, saying nothing, just watching her with those piercing eyes of his. "You think...you believe...you said, we should... marry."

"And what do you think?" he said bluntly.

She felt another sharp twinge in her chest. "I think we do what's best for the baby."

"Which is?"

He wasn't making this easy, was he? She drew a deep breath, feeling tender and shy. "We get married."

"When?"

Her shoulders rose and fell. "Whenever we can?"

Brando needed to head to the Ricci headquarters for a meeting that couldn't be postponed, but he promised to be back for a late lunch. He returned two and a half hours later with lunch and her briefcase and her vanity bag. She didn't know if she was more excited at being able to brush her hair or check her email.

Again Brando's chef materialized with lunch, and after lunch was cleaned up and put away, Brando opened his laptop and worked, while she worked on hers. She handled the most urgent emails, and then sent emails to others letting them know that she was taking the next few weeks off for a personal matter, but hoped to be working again by the end of the month.

It wasn't until she got a flurry of email responses from her clients asking if everything was all right that she realized her wording was problematic. Normally Charlotte was an expert at handling sensitive matters but she certainly wasn't handling her own situation very well.

She didn't realize she'd muttered any of her frustration out loud until Brando asked what the matter was.

She sighed and rubbed at her temple, trying to make the headache go away. "I think I've made a mess of things," she said. "I reached out to my clients and let them know I'd be taking some time off, and it's backfired. Everyone is asking if I'm okay, and if there is anything they can do." She grimaced. "Someone just now wanted to know how they could help. This is exactly what I didn't want to happen."

"Read what you wrote."

"I said I was taking the next few weeks off for a personal matter, but hoped to be back at work by the end of June." She looked over at him. "I shouldn't have said 'personal matter,' should've I?"

"You could have said 'wedding and honeymoon' and every-one would have been delighted, instead of worried." He saw her expression and shrugged. "It's the perception of things, isn't it? One sounds as if you're in the midst of struggle and sorrow, whereas 'wedding and honeymoon' sounds festive and celebratory."

"I can't tell my clients I'm getting married!"

"Why not? You are. Why not let them be happy for you?"

"But we don't know when we'll get married. It might not be for months."

"*Cara*, we're marrying soon. I'm determined we marry be-fore our son is born, and since he seems to want to arrive early, I don't think we should wait."

She closed her laptop and pressed it to her chest. "How soon?"

"As soon as it can be arranged."

Brando was still with her when Dr. Leonardi returned late af-ternoon to check on Charlotte but stepped out while the doctor examined her, returning when it was over.

"Everything still looks good. I think she's out of the woods, but I want her on bed rest for the next few days, and then modi-fied bed rest Friday."

Charlotte glanced hopefully at Brando. "Does that mean I can leave?"

"Perhaps tomorrow."

"But if everything looks good, can't I just rest at home?" she pressed.

Brando's gaze swept the sterile room. "I'd prefer for her to rest at my home. I'm not a fan of hospitals, and Charlotte is right, it's not very restful here. It's noisy and chaotic and I'm not sure how this is the best environment for her, or the baby."

"But we have nurses here, staff here. Equipment here," the doctor answered.

"Can't I get the same equipment for the house? Couldn't I hire a nurse to be with her at home?"

"That's a huge expense—" The doctor broke off when he saw Brando's expression. "But yes, she could be monitored at home. It's essential, though, that she rest, or you'll be right back here, and I don't know if we would be successful stopping labor next time."

"We have no intention of being back until the baby is full term," Brandon said.

Dr. Leonardi nodded. "I'll sign off on her leaving tomorrow. I still want her here tonight, but remember, no stress, no excitement. There isn't to be any drama or pressure."

"Understood."

Charlotte had imagined they'd be going to Brando's city house when she was discharged the next day. Instead the helicopter was waiting to whisk them back to the *castello*.

"There is more fresh air, more peace in the country," Brando said as they made the fifteen-minute trip by air.

Now that she wasn't in pain, Charlotte enjoyed the trip, thinking the Tuscan hills looked like a striking quilt from the air, patches of light green and dark green intermixed with squares of pale gold, which turned out to be villages and *castellos* like Brando's.

On landing at his estate, Brando swept her into his arms and carried her back to the house, despite Charlotte insisting she could walk partway. He ignored her completely, and made short work of the distance, carrying her up two flights of stairs as if she weighed nothing at all.

She'd wondered about the third flight of stairs, and it wasn't until they reached a different bedroom that she realized Brando wasn't returning her to the bedroom she'd had before, but moving her into his room. "What are you doing?" she asked lowly as she was settled onto the enormous bed.

"Keeping you close," he said. "Doctor's orders."

"I thought you were getting a professional."

"I am, for the day. But at night, you'll sleep with me so I can keep an eye on you."

"And you don't think that will be a source of stress or excitement?"

"I think it will be a greater source of stress and excitement if I come check on you three or four times a night."

She pulled herself up, sitting a little taller. "You don't need to do that. I can just shout."

"Right." But his lips twisted. He'd caught her attempt at humor.

She appreciated that, and him. More than he'd ever know. "I don't know that I can sleep in here with you."

"Why not?"

"I don't sleep well with others."

"Build a pillow wall."

"Can I really?"

"No. I need to be able to see you—"

"Nothing is going to happen! I'm not going to disappear in the night or give birth in ten seconds. Everything is fine. I just need to stay put—"

"In my bed."

"Brando, you're causing me stress and excitement."

"*Bella*, you're causing stress and excitement by arguing with me. Accept the inevitable. You're stuck with me." And then he closed the distance, bent down and kissed her, in a long, tender, melting kiss that made the hair rise on the back of her neck and her nipples peak and tighten. By the time he lifted his head, she felt like he'd poured warm honey into her veins. "It won't be all bad, though," he murmured, his lips brushing across hers in another slow, maddening kiss that had her squirming and breathless. "You just have to relax," he murmured, kissing her cheek and then just beneath her earlobe. He'd found an incredibly sensitive spot there, and then another one just beneath her jaw.

She sighed, and arched, pleasure suffusing her. "I'm not sure the doctor would approve," she whispered.

"I promise not to give you an orgasm."

She laughed softly, and the husky laugh turned to a smothered moan as his teeth scraped the side of her neck, setting her on fire, and sending hot sparks all the way down to her toes. She reached for him then, her hand wrapping around his nape as she buried her fingers into his thick, crisp hair. "If your kisses send me back to the hospital, I will—"

"Never forgive myself," he answered, lifting his head, to gaze down into her eyes. He pushed back a heavy wave of her hair, tucking strands behind her ear. "I know you showered at the hospital earlier, but would you like a bath now that you're home? I can send one of the girls up to draw you one."

"I don't need anyone to draw me a bath, and I don't want you to fuss over me. It's enough to know that you're here in case something goes wrong, so please go do whatever it is you need to do, and you can relax knowing I'll be here taking my first nap of the day."

Charlotte was relieved when Brando left the room. Her luggage had already been moved from her bedroom into his, and one of the maids brought up her briefcase and bags from the hospital. Once she was alone, she locked the bathroom door, stripped off her clothes and took a long soak in the deep tub. She washed her hair, rinsed and conditioned it, before climbing out and patting herself dry. With her long hair still wrapped in a towel, she climbed back into bed and fell asleep, grateful to be in a quiet room. Charlotte slept for over an hour and when she woke up, she discovered someone had placed a water bottle and glass next to the bed for her, plus a bowl of fresh fruit and a small plate of biscotti. But that wasn't all. Leaning against the lamp was a tall leather-bound book with a sticky note.

Charlotte, pick out your favorite.

She recognized the handwriting. Brando had written the note and she reached for the book and positioned it on her lap before opening the luxurious soft cream leather cover. *The Ricci-Baldi Bridal Collection*, the title page read.

Puzzled, Charlotte quickly flipped through the pages, from beginning to end. There were maybe twenty gowns in the book, and the entire book consisted of couture bridal gowns, exclusively designed by Livia, Brando's sister, and Livia's designer husband, Luca Baldi.

Brando wanted her to pick out her favorite bridal gown. Was this really happening?

She suddenly wasn't sure she could go through with the wedding, at least, not like this. She was scared, and troubled. Exhaling in a rush, she closed the design book, carefully replacing it where she'd found it, leaning against the glass lamp on the side table.

Intellectually she understood why marrying Brando was a good idea. But emotionally she couldn't see herself wearing a formal white gown, never mind a couture gown from one of Italy's top design teams. She wasn't having a dream wedding. The wedding was business, and the ceremony was for legal purposes. She and Brando were choosing to be responsible, and practical, and she didn't need a formal gown, or veil, or even flowers for that. She could wear a suit, or a smart dress, and Brando would wear one of his tailored suits, and they'd be married quietly, privately, by a government official without fuss.

It was better they not start their marriage under any illusions that this was a love marriage, because she had to manage her expectations, or beautiful, brilliant Brando Ricci would break her heart.

Brando returned from the winery to discover Charlotte had moved herself back to her bedroom.

He entered her bedroom with the briefest of knocks, annoyed that she'd go against his wishes. "What are you doing? Moving things around? Coming to rooms where you'll be alone at night?"

Charlotte drew the duvet up higher, hiding her breasts and bump. "I don't want or need constant supervision. I'm not a child. I'm having a child. Quite a significant distinction, Brando. And I didn't move anything but myself. Your staff carried my things, and I just took my time and walked back here."

He paced around the bed. "And what if something happens at night?"

"I'll call you. We both have phones. We're lucky to live in the age of technology."

He glared down at her. "I'm not amused. You're taking risks—"

"And you're being hopelessly overbearing," she interrupted, "as well as an alarmist. Dr. Leonardi said everything looked better, normal—"

"He never said 'normal.' He wanted you in the hospital. I was the one who insisted you would be able to rest better if you were at home. But I promised you'd be supervised."

"And I am. The midwife starts coming daily tomorrow. I'll have a quiet evening tonight. Just send a tray up for me and I'll have an early dinner, and will make an early night of it, too. I think having some downtime would be good for both of us."

Brando seemed about to protest when he thought better of it. He nodded shortly. "Fine." He started to leave, then turned in the doorway. "Did you see anything in Livia's designs that appealed to you? She's offered to come this weekend for a fitting."

The last thing Charlotte wanted to do was discuss the wedding, or a dress made for her by his famous sister, but she didn't want to offend him tonight. "There are so many beautiful designs, I couldn't even narrow the options down."

"No problem. I can look through them with you tomorrow."

"I don't need help looking at bridal gowns."

"Happy to give you my opinions."

"I'm sure you are. Good night, Brando."

"*Buona notte*, Charlotte."

CHAPTER EIGHT

A BREEZE RUSTLED the leaves of the citrus trees in the ornate terra-cotta pots on the terrace, and the moon, even though only a quarter full, winked white in the purple-black sky.

Brando leaned back in his chair at the table and let the beauty of the night distract him from Charlotte's lengthy explanation of why they didn't need a proper wedding, never mind a reception after.

She'd spent the last ten minutes giving detailed reasons why a formal wedding was a bad idea, and he let her talk as he sipped his after-dinner coffee. It was his favorite kind of night, warm, fragrant, without summer's sultry heat. He'd had a good day in the wineries, and Charlotte looked particularly beautiful tonight, too, wearing an ice-blue sleeveless blouse paired with crisp white silk trousers. Her long hair spilled over her shoulders, and she wore simple sapphire drop earrings that matched the blue of her eyes.

She was stunning and smart, and he felt fortunate that she was to be the mother of his children. She'd be a good mother, a good partner and wife. If she'd just stop fighting him on the wedding. His family celebrated marriages, just as they celebrated births and anniversaries and other special moments.

"I want a proper ceremony, followed by a proper dinner,

and a proper cake," he said. "This is our wedding. It should be special."

"Do we need the fuss, as well as the expense?"

"As this is the only wedding I will ever have, *yes*. It should be beautiful. Music, flowers, table decorations, all of it."

"A big wedding, Brando, really?"

"I didn't say 'big.' In fact, I want a small, intimate ceremony here at the *castello* chapel, followed by a reception in the courtyard. That way there is no traveling, no fuss, nothing to stress over, nor would you have to be on your feet very long."

Charlotte listened to his plans, and didn't know how to argue against them, especially as he offered to handle most of the arrangements so she didn't have to be stressed by anything. He did insist on her selecting a wedding dress, or at least, pointing out a few in the design book that she liked, and Livia and Luca would make up something special just for her.

"Your family knows, then?" she asked, careful to keep judgment from her voice.

"Only Livia so far. I will share the news with the rest once we have a wedding date."

Charlotte toyed with her dessert spoon. "What are you telling them?"

"That we're getting married and we'd love them to join us."

"Nothing about the pregnancy?"

"It's not the first thing I'll tell them, no." He lifted a brow, his expression slightly sardonic. "Would you prefer me to share the news about the baby first?"

"No." She glared at him. "And I don't want to wear a dress that screams 'pregnant bride,' either."

"I'm sure some of Livia's designs will flatter your figure. No matter what you'll wear, you'll look beautiful."

Charlotte's eyes suddenly smarted and she blinked, clearing her vision. "I feel rather lumpy at the moment, and I dread people talking. There will be gossip, you know. I know you don't care, but I'm not there yet. I'm still trying to figure out how to navigate this new world. My success stems from my reputation as someone who doesn't make mistakes. I fix other people's mistakes. And yet look at me—" She broke off, and bit into her lower lip, holding back the flow of words.

"Starting a family is a beautiful thing. We're excited. Remember that."

"You don't think your family will judge?"

"They'll be happy for us. They know you. They like you. Livia is thrilled to be making your dress."

"And your business associates? My clients?"

"They'll think the best, not the worst."

"Which is?"

"That we're head over heels in love and eager to start our new lives together." His silver gaze met hers and held. His voice dropped, and deepened. "And who is to say we're not? Who is to say that this marriage isn't something we both want?"

Her heart did a funny double beat, and butterflies filled her middle. She couldn't look away from the flare of desire in his eyes, the heat radiating out, wrapping around her. "Marriage wasn't on the agenda," she said.

"Maybe not, but you know I want you. If I could have you now, I would. Desire is not an issue between us."

She could see heat and interest shimmering in his stunning pewter eyes. She felt the intense physical pull. She craved it herself, feeling isolated in this strange new body of hers, facing a different future than she'd ever imagined. "Then kiss me," she whispered. "Make me remember why I lost my head over you."

He drew her from her seat, up into his arms, one hand sliding beneath her hair to cup her nape as the other settled low on her hip. His lips covered hers, claiming her, his mouth warm, and firm. He smelled of that spice he wore and as well as a hint of wine. She welcomed the pressure of his mouth, her lips parting beneath his, his tongue tasting, teasing, sending shivers of pleasure through her. He kissed her until she felt boneless and mindless, kissing her until she forgot to breathe and she ached between her thighs, wanting pressure there. His knee moved between her legs, his hard thigh pressed to that place where she was so very sensitive. His hand ran up the length of her, over her hip and waist to cup her breast and then play with the tight, tender nipple, strumming the peaked tip so that she arched, grinding herself against him.

Pleasure screamed through her, bright, hot, intense.

She was so close to climaxing. Just another pinch of her nipple, another rub against his thigh, and she'd come. She wanted to come, craved release, but an orgasm could set off the contractions again.

Panting, Charlotte pulled back, feeling shameless and frustrated all at the same time. "I want you," she breathed, tears of vexation filling her eyes. "But I can't have you."

"You can, but not for a while."

"This is awful." She knocked away the tears, feeling wildly out of control. "We can marry but we can't have sex."

"We'll have sex again, I promise you. But you're right, we can't take any chances now. It's not worth the risk."

Charlotte couldn't fall asleep that night. She was spending so much time resting, so much time in bed, that she felt restless and trapped. The surging hormones didn't help. The relentless desire didn't help, either. She'd never felt sexual, but now, being so close to Brando, desire and awareness hummed through her night and day.

But what she felt for him was so much more than desire, and the feelings were growing stronger by the day. They hadn't even married and yet she felt bonded. Wed. Was it the pregnancy making her feel so connected to him, or was it the way he was treating her...as if she were special...priceless...irreplaceable?

And yes, right now, he was focused on her and the baby, but was it only because of the baby? How would things be after the baby was born?

Would Brando be as attentive? Would he still want her? Would he try to make her feel special?

She pictured Louisa—gorgeous, sexy, fun-loving Louisa—and felt a wave of insecurity. Charlotte hated feeling insecure. She'd had enough of that growing up in her family. It was impossible to get her parents' attention, impossible to get anyone's attention. She'd act out just to force one of the nannies to focus on her, hoping they'd take her to her parents, and yet when she was hauled before her parents, it never resulted in the outcome she'd wanted.

They had no time or patience for her when she was good, and they had even less time and patience when she was naughty. Gradually she learned not to look to others for affection, or validation. She would take care of herself, and learn to be happy and secure through her own actions and achievements. Once she stopped wanting her parents' love and approval, she discovered herself, and became the person she wanted to be.

Since arriving in Tuscany she felt lost, though, and wasn't sure who she was anymore.

She wasn't sure about marriage and forever, either. In her family marriage didn't equal forever. Marriage was just a source of friction and tension, with the friction growing worse until someone threw in the towel and initiated divorce.

The idea of marrying to divorce made her heartsick.

But being married to a man who didn't want her, and might have clandestine relationships on the side, would break her.

Charlotte couldn't escape her thoughts, or the panic rising in her, and she left bed and then left her room and headed upstairs to Brando's bedroom. It was well past midnight and she doubted he was awake but she needed to see him, needed to hear from him that they weren't making a terrible mistake.

She knocked lightly on his door and then opened it an inch. "Brando, are you sleeping?"

"Come in," he said, his voice deep and sleep roughened. "Are you unwell?"

"I'm fine," she said, stepping into his room, leaving the door slightly open behind her. "Everything's fine. I just can't sleep and my brain won't turn off and I'm getting myself worked up."

"Over what?"

"What if you don't like being married to me?" she whispered.

"Come here," he said, drawing back the covers, and patting the bed. "Crawl in with me."

She did, needing his warmth, craving security. He gave her a pillow and then pulled her close, her back to his chest, his arm wrapping around her middle, before bringing the light feather duvet over both of them.

"Do you want to talk?" he asked, his deep voice husky.

"Will you regret marrying me?"

"We're making a family. I will never regret having a family."

A lump filled her throat. It wasn't quite the reassurance she needed. "What about me, though? Will you regret marrying me?"

He kissed her bare shoulder. "Never."

Her chest squeezed, air bottling in her lungs. "Promise?"

"It will not always be easy between us. We're two strong people. But we can make it work, if we want to make it work. Does that make sense?"

"Yes."

He pushed her hair aside and kissed the back of her neck. "We will find our happiness, *cara*. I am sure of that."

And wrapped in his arms, and in his assurances, Charlotte fell asleep.

The wedding plans moved forward quickly, with the date set for the last Saturday in June, which was less than two weeks away.

Brando handled the arrangements, but he ran his ideas past her, making sure she approved. She liked his ideas and agreed with him on virtually everything, appreciating his logic, his tastes, as well as his decisiveness. Her only real objection was marrying in the historic chapel. Charlotte asked if maybe they couldn't say their vows outside, perhaps in one of the gardens, with a view of the valley.

He agreed with her suggestion for a simple outdoor ceremony, and shared his idea for a reception in the inner courtyard, which could be illuminated with strings of white lights, and torches attached to the stone walls.

Ten days before the wedding, Livia arrived to take measurements for Charlotte's dress, but before they could discuss dresses, there were other things Livia wanted to know. "You and Brando did not seem to like each other very much during our meetings. Clearly the rest of us did not know what was really going on behind closed doors."

Charlotte blushed. "Nothing happened during our work together. He and I did have some issues—"

"Too much chemistry, hmm?"

"There were sparks, yes," Charlotte admitted. "But nothing happened while I was under contract. I wouldn't do that to you, not while working for you. It happened New Year's Eve. He'd invited me to Enzo's big party. That was the first time—and the only time—we got together."

"One night and you're pregnant?"

Charlotte grimaced. "We used protection, too. He did, I did." She gestured helplessly to the bump. "But this one wanted to be born."

"That's a Ricci for you," Livia answered with a wink. "Prepare yourself. You're going to have your hands full. Now let's get your measurements and discuss the kind of dress you'd like for the wedding."

"I don't actually have a preference," Charlotte admitted. "I prefer clean, sophisticated designs, which is what you do. Can I just leave it to you to make whatever you think would look best on me?"

Livia embraced her, and then kissed her on each cheek. "It would be my pleasure. Leave it to me."

* * *

A week passed, and the wedding was just days away. The guest list had swelled, with most of Brando's family electing to stay overnight at the *castello* rather than make the drive back to Florence. All the decisions had been made for the wedding, too. Musicians and photographer were booked, flowers ordered, and Brando's chef from Florence was coming to assist the *castello* chef and kitchen staff for the wedding weekend.

All the decisions that needed to be made were done. But Brando, who wasn't a worrier, had concerns. The wedding, while still intimate, was no longer as small as he'd hoped, and the family and friends coming would be up late into the night, celebrating. Brando had wanted a special night for Charlotte, a wedding they'd both remember for years to come. He just hoped that it wasn't going to be too much for her. The last thing they needed was Charlotte being rushed back to the hospital at the end of their wedding night.

From her room Charlotte could see the preparations for the ceremony and reception this weekend. The villa staff swept and scrubbed the courtyard, wiping down stones and the dozen columns supporting the arches of the inner courtyard. Planters were refreshed, topiaries pruned, and long strings of white lights were run across the courtyard, creating a tent-like canopy.

The morning of the wedding, tables were set up in the interior courtyard, and then covered with white cloths. Flowers arrived, and antique silver candelabra lined the long tables, the heavy silver candleholders matching the ornate silverware.

Livia was there to help her dress, and after her hair and makeup were done by a stylist Livia had brought from Florence, Charlotte carefully stepped into her gown.

Her gown was exquisite and what made it so beautiful was that it was perfect for her. It was her style—modern, clean and yet classic. The white silk gleamed in the sunlight, and the luxurious fabric molded to her full breasts, hugging her torso and bump, before forming a full, sophisticated skirt. There were even pockets in the skirt, a touch she adored. Normally she would have avoided such a deep plunging neckline, and yet the dramatic neckline, paired with the wide shoulder straps, looked chic, and drew the eye from her bump to her shoulders and face.

With her hair pinned up, and a long white veil attached to the chignon, she looked like a true bride—radiant, glowing, excited.

Livia walked around Charlotte, adjusting her skirt, and then the floor-length veil. "Perfection," she said approvingly. "Even the pearl earrings. Elegant, classic, discrete."

Charlotte reached up and touched one pearl stud. "My mother's."

"Is she coming?"

Charlotte shook her head. "She couldn't make it. Most of my family couldn't make it. One of my sisters is on the way. She's coming from London with her husband. They're not here yet, but I think they should arrive soon."

"Not to worry. You have lots of family here," Livia answered. "The Riccis are here. You are one of us now."

In the end, Charlotte thought her wedding was impossibly beautiful, although it wasn't as small as Brando had intimated. Her sister and brother-in-law arrived moments before she walked down the aisle, and of course, all of Brando's family was there—his mother, his mother's sister, his brothers and sister, cousins, so many cousins, plus other guests, people who were "like family" to the Riccis.

They said their vows in the garden overlooking the valley with the gently rolling hills, dark green vineyards and views of the tiled roofs of the village below, and then moved to the *castello*'s courtyard for the dinner and music. The flowers on the table matched her bridal bouquet—the palest pink roses hand-tied with a wide pale pink satin ribbon.

She felt beautiful in the dress Livia had made for her, and Brando looked impossibly handsome in his black suit with the white shirt and dark tie. His hair was sleekly combed back, highlighting his strong cheekbones, jaw and lovely mouth. Her hand had trembled in his as they'd said the vows, but his voice was deep and steady, and he'd held her gaze the entire time, promising to honor and protect her for the rest of their lives.

During dinner Brando insisted she stay seated at the head table, asking guests to come to her. She wondered what he'd said to them as no one seemed surprised, or questioned why she left her chair only to cut the cake, and have a first dance with Brando. The song from the first dance was the same song they'd danced to on New Year's Eve, "At Last" by Etta James. Charlotte was surprised he'd remembered, but also touched. Dancing with him beneath the stars and moon and strings of white lights was probably one of the most romantic moments in her life. Brando might not love her, but he'd gone to great pains to make tonight special. To make her feel special.

"You take my breath away," he said, as the song came to an end.

"Thank you for a beautiful wedding, and a beautiful night," she answered.

His head dropped and he kissed her, there in front of everyone. The kiss filled her with warmth and hope. Their families and friends applauded. Brando lifted his head and grinned. She blushed and smiled.

And then before she knew it was all over, Brando was saying he needed to carry his bride away, and he encouraged everyone to eat and drink and dance as late as they wanted as there were no neighbors nearby to disturb.

Brando literally carried her away, too, sweeping her into his arms and carrying her through the courtyard doors and up the central staircase to his room on the third floor.

She'd been here before but she'd never seen it like this. Tonight, the master bedroom glowed with dozens of white candles. They were everywhere—on the mantel, on tables, on windowsills. There were roses, too, countless white roses, and across the bed lay a delicate ivory satin nightgown with an ivory satin-and-lace robe.

"A gift from Livia," Brando said, putting her down next to the bed. "She said every bride needs something special to wear for her wedding night."

Charlotte suddenly felt overwhelmed by the beauty of the day, and the kindness of Brando's sister, as well as everyone's goodwill. Their guests had been happy for them, celebrating their marriage with toasts, hugs and laughter. "Livia has completely spoiled me," she said, reaching to lightly stroke the satin nightgown. "I hope she knows I'm so very grateful."

"She does." He watched her from the foot of the bed. "How do you feel?"

"Good. A little tired. But happy." She looked at him, and smiled, tears in her eyes. "Thank you for tonight. It was beautiful, all of it, and I'm—"

"Grateful," he interrupted, finishing her words for her. "Yes, I know." His mouth quirked. "But I didn't do this for your gratitude. This was for us, and our son, so we'd have memories and photos to share with our children and grandchildren, and then they can say, *Oh, you were so young!*"

She smiled. "Well, thank you for giving us memories." She glanced down at the shimmering satin nightgown. "I guess I should change."

"Let me help you out of your gown, and then I need to get something from the library and I'll be back."

She turned around and he made quick work of the dozens of small hooks hidden in the seam of her gown. The bodice fell away and she caught the silk, pressing it against her breasts to keep from exposing herself.

"I have seen you naked before," he said, a hint of amusement in his deep voice.

She blushed. "Not like this. There is so much more of me now."

"I think you're absolutely beautiful pregnant."

She didn't know what to say, and so she stood up on tiptoe, and kissed him. He caught her by the arms and pulled her closer, his mouth claiming hers, hunger and heat and possession in the kiss. Desire shot through her, bright and fierce. She wanted him badly, wanted the pressure and sensation, wanted touch and release. Everything in her craved more of him—more of his time, more of his attention, more of his heart.

She loved him, and yet she feared the love because she didn't know how she'd ever survive this marriage if he didn't love her back.

Brando lifted his head, gazed down into her eyes, before pressing the pad of his thumb to her full, tender lips. "There are so many things I want to do to you. It's incredibly difficult to keep my hands off you."

It wasn't a declaration of love, but it was something, she thought, as he left the room and she removed her veil, and unpinned her hair, brushing it smooth before taking a bath and changing into her satin nightgown, the delicate fabric impossibly soft and light as it followed her every curve.

Brando returned, and his dinner jacket was off, and the tie gone. He'd unbuttoned his dress shirt, exposing the upper planes of his muscular, golden chest. He was carrying a bottle and two crystal flutes. "Come," he said, going to the French doors and opening them onto his private balcony.

She followed him out, smiling as he popped the cork from the champagne and filled the two flutes. "Just a sip," he admonished, handing her one flute. "Just for a toast."

She took the pretty flute and glanced down at the pale gold champagne, the bubbles rising and popping.

"To you," he said, lifting his glass. "To your beauty, to your amazing mind, to the miracle you carry. I'm lucky to call you my partner, and wife."

Her eyes burned and a lump filled her throat. "Thank you," she whispered, lightly touching her glass to his.

As she sipped her champagne, a loud popping sound came

from the corner of the castle, and then fireworks filled the sky, a dazzling display of light.

She could hear their guests cheering below, and Brando reached for her, and kissed her as the dark sky lit up with all the colors of the rainbow. It was an extraordinary surprise, and a wonderful way to cap a magical evening.

He'd given her absolutely everything this evening but his heart.

CHAPTER NINE

THE *CASTELLO* WAS still full of guests the next day, with Brando's friends and family staying over to enjoy a leisurely Sunday morning brunch before an afternoon departure.

Charlotte came downstairs for the late breakfast, hoping to see her sister Alice, but Alice and Philip had already left to catch their flight back to London. Charlotte felt a pinch of disappointment, aware that she'd exchanged only a dozen words with her sister last night, but at least Alice and Philip had appeared to be having fun, sitting at the same table with Brando's brothers, and talking the evening away with Marcello and Elena, Marcello's wife.

Elena and Livia were together, drinking coffee, and Elena waved Charlotte over now. "Last night was beautiful," Elena said to Charlotte as she joined them at their table. "And those fireworks! Did you know?"

"No, it was a complete surprise," Charlotte answered. "I was shocked, but I shouldn't have been. Brando did most of the planning for the wedding and it went off perfectly."

"It did," Livia agreed. "And you were the most radiant bride. Brando couldn't keep his eyes from you."

Charlotte grimaced. "He watches me constantly, afraid that I might go into labor." She saw her sister-in-laws' confused expressions and explained, "We had a scare a couple weeks ago. If Brando hadn't flown me back to Florence in his helicopter, who knows what would have happened. But fortunately we got there quickly and the doctors could stop the labor. That's why he's so protective of me now. We want the baby to stay put as long as possible."

Elena glanced at Livia, murmuring, "Aren't you glad Brando married her, and not the other one? That would have been awful."

Livia gave her head a slight shake, discouraging Elena, before smiling warmly at Charlotte. "We've been hoping he'd settle down, and so very glad it's you. We're already quite fond of you."

"And we also know you're not after his money like the other one," Elena added. "Thank goodness Marcello convinced Brando to take a paternity test before the wedding—"

"The wedding?" Charlotte interrupted. "Was Brando engaged before?"

Elena looked at Livia. "Would you call it an engagement, Liv? I don't think it was that formal. She was pregnant and he was going to marry her. Wasn't that pretty much how it was?"

Charlotte's heart fell, and her insides went icy cold. She clasped her hands together, feeling chilled to the bone. "When was this?"

"A couple of years ago," Elena answered. "I don't even know what's happened to her—"

"I thought the flowers were gorgeous last night," Livia said, cutting Elena off. "They were roses and peonies, weren't they?"

Charlotte nodded vaguely, unable to focus on the question. Brando had been through all of this before? He'd nearly married another woman because he thought she was pregnant, and apparently, all his family had known.

And here he was, years later, going through it all again. No wonder he was good at planning weddings. The whole celebration last night had been a show...a sham...

My God, what had his whole family been thinking last night as they watched him marry her? Charlotte put a hand to her middle, suddenly feeling as though she might be sick. "I think I need to get some food," she said unsteadily, rising. "If you'll excuse me, I'll see what I can find."

She waited until late afternoon and everyone had gone before approaching Brando about what she'd learned from Elena and Livia. She found him in his ground-floor study so lined with antique volumes that it probably was a former library. He was at his desk, reading through a document, looking relaxed and bronzed as if he'd spent his afternoon swimming.

He looked up with a smile as she entered the room with its golden paneling and rich wood accents. "How was your rest?"

"Boring." She took a seat across from his desk. "Not very restful." She hesitated, trying to figure out how to broach the subject that had troubled her all day. The more she'd thought about it, the more upset she became. "I heard a story today," she said carefully. "Elena told me. But Livia was there and verified it. Apparently they nearly got a different sister-in-law a couple of years ago. Elena says they didn't like her much. Thankfully she likes me more." Charlotte stared at a button on Brando's shirt, unable to meet his eyes. "It was a bit embarrassing to realize you've been through all this before—"

"I haven't."

"Apparently, you have. You get a woman pregnant, and you marry her."

"I've never been married before. There have been no weddings, no engagements, no babies. You're the first."

"But this other woman… You would have married her if it had been your baby?"

"Yes."

Her heart did that awful freefall again, plummeting all the way to her feet. Charlotte wasn't special. He had no real feelings for her. Brando was just going through the motions.

"But Charlotte, it wasn't mine. We didn't marry. None of this is relevant," he said, leaning forward in his seat. "You can't let Elena upset you over something so trivial—"

"Trivial?" Charlotte interrupted. "Marriage changes everything, and marrying you has turned my life inside out. Having a baby would have been a significant change, but this...becoming your wife...moving to Tuscany... I've given up everything I am, and everything I've known, for you—"

"Not for me, for our child, for our family."

"No, Brando," she corrected, getting to her feet, hands clasped tightly together. "I agreed to marriage because I would be marrying you. Just for clarification, I wouldn't have married anyone else. I married you because it's you."

She left his study then, and headed outside to walk the rose garden, and then circle the *castello* grounds, ending up near the fountain in the historic walled garden.

Brando found her in the walled garden, pacing around the gravel like a caged animal. "The walking doesn't seem to be calming you."

She shot him a look of reproach. "I'm not calm, no."

"You're getting yourself agitated over nothing. Charlotte, there was no one else—"

"Oh, Brando, please. Don't say that. Let's not pretend there has never been anyone before me. Your bed is never empty. You never lack for female company."

"When I'm in a serious, monogamous relationship, it's serious and monogamous."

"Define 'serious relationship,'" she said, hands on her hips as she faced him.

"Affection, attachment, respect, monogamous."

"Is that what we have?"

"You're my wife. My family."

His words were beginning to make her feel a little mad. "Yes, but you feel affection, attachment, respect for me?"

"Yes."

"We're to be faithful to each other?"

"Yes, absolutely."

"And this is what you offer your significant others? This is the most you offer? Affection, attachment, respect?"

His jaw set, his eyes narrowed. "Last night you were content with me, and hopeful about the future. Today, you throw it all back in my face? Because Elena thoughtlessly mentioned someone from my past?"

Furious tears burned the back of her eyes. "I'm not a replacement bride—"

"No, you're not. But I don't know what you want from me, Charlotte. I don't even know how to talk to you right now. We had a beautiful wedding last night. We had our friends and family here. You thanked me last night for making it a special day, but suddenly, based on something Elena said, it's not enough?"

She didn't know how to explain, but she felt as if there was an injustice here. In marrying him, she'd lost everything she'd known—her home, her name, her identity, her independence. And he'd lost nothing other than his ability to sleep with whomever he wanted. Because he hadn't really given up anything. He didn't have to change, or even feel too much, because he didn't feel too much.

"This was a mistake," she said hoarsely, mouth dry, stomach in knots. "I didn't marry out of duty. It's not why I agreed to this."

"We're doing this for our son," he answered.

"This marriage will make us miserable. I refuse to raise a baby in a home where we're miserable."

"I'm not miserable."

"Because you don't love. You lust—"

"Charlotte."

"Where are your emotions? And what do you really feel for me? Affection...desire?"

"Yes."

"It's not enough."

"Our attachment will grow."

She was already attached, though. She already cared. What was she supposed to do, wait for him to catch up? Hope he might one day have more feelings for her?

"I don't want this marriage," she said lowly. "I don't want to be part of any of this. You're not who I thought you were. We don't have what I thought we have."

He closed the distance between them, hands settling on her upper arms. "You're working yourself up over nothing. Adele meant nothing to me. I swear—"

"Isn't that the whole issue?" she cried, looking up into his face. "You don't care about any of them you've been with. You love sex, the act of sex, but you don't love the women you're with, and you will never love me." She tried to pull away but he didn't release her. Charlotte pushed his chest, and still he held her. "See, it's already a trap. I'm trapped. I knew this would happen. It's what marriage does... It changes people...changes the power balance between two people."

He gave her a gentle shake. "Nothing has changed, Charlotte."

Her chest burned and her heart was beating so fast she couldn't catch her breath. Her emotions were chaotic, her control splintering. Where was the Charlotte who was so capable of dealing with crises that she could virtually do it in her sleep? She needed that Charlotte to show up, right now. "I shouldn't have agreed to marry you. I shouldn't have let you convince me it was the right thing to do. It's not, and I can't pretend like you, can't fake happiness." She struggled to pluck his fingers from her arm. "I can't live with you. I won't live with you—"

"The baby—"

"The baby will be fine. I promise you I'll make sure of that." She reached up and pressed a hand to her eyes to hold back the tears. She wouldn't cry now. She had to keep it together. "I'd like to return to Florence. I'll get a small apartment for the rest of the summer—"

"That's absurd."

"I'll be close to the hospital should anything happen," she added, continuing as if he hadn't interrupted. "I promise to keep you informed. I won't take any risks. You won't have to worry about me."

"I don't understand any of this."

"That's the problem, Brando. You don't understand this, because you don't understand me. I didn't marry you to give the baby your name. I didn't marry you to do the right thing. I married you because—" She broke off, tears filling her eyes. "I married you because I wanted to be with you."

"And that's changed?"

She couldn't hold the tears back. *"Yes."*

"Why? Because you've heard some story about Adele and her pregnancy that had nothing to do with me?"

"You were prepared to marry her. You would have married her—"

"It wasn't my child. I didn't get her pregnant."

"It doesn't matter. What matters is that we're all interchangeable in your eyes. You love making love, but you don't really love, and then when you're faced with the consequences, you think you're doing the right thing, but marriage isn't the answer, not when there's no love."

"It's a little late for regrets, though. We've said our vows, we've made a commitment. There's no backing out of it now." He released her then and she took a step back, and then another, her chin high, spine straight.

For a long moment she just held his gaze, expression defiant, before regally turning around and walking away from him, aware that his gaze followed her every step of the way.

Brando watched Charlotte return to the *castello*, gut on fire, head throbbing. What the hell had just happened?

How had everything gone sideways?

She'd been happy last night, radiant in her bridal gown, and breathtaking in her shimmering satin nightgown. He'd slept with one arm around her last night, savoring her warmth, her softness, feeling overwhelmed with his desire to protect her. And then the baby kicked, right against his hand where it rested on her belly, and he'd known then that he would sacrifice everything for them, his wife and son. They would want for nothing. They would always have him, a devoted husband and father.

All day he'd felt renewed. Purposeful. There was a reason now for him to work harder, to push to be more successful. Everything he did would be for them... And yet Charlotte now wanted none of it.

And nothing from him.

He was baffled, but also angry. Angry that she didn't trust him. Angry that she would judge and condemn him. Angry that she'd be so selfish that she'd put her needs before their son's needs...before the needs of the family.

Apparently, he didn't know her.

Apparently, she wasn't who he'd thought she was, either.

There was no honeymoon, and they spent the next week living like strangers in the *castello*. Charlotte moved out of the master bedroom and back into hers. He never once commented on her decision.

After she returned to her own room, they still had dinner together twice, but each evening they barely spoke, the atmosphere tense, so severely strained that Charlotte couldn't manage a bite. After the second miserable dinner, she told him she couldn't eat with him anymore, it was too upsetting, and it was true. After that last dinner, she threw up after crying so hard. This wasn't the life she wanted. This wasn't the marriage she'd agreed to.

Days passed and the first week of July had come and gone, the summer heat making the air hot, and heavy. The heat gave

Charlotte a headache and she stayed in her room, in the dark, heavy coral silk curtains drawn to keep her room cool and dim.

She felt listless and lost, confused as to why she was here in this place, living this way. Brando didn't seem to care that he never saw her anymore, either, and he came to her room only after hearing she hadn't gotten out of bed again one day.

He didn't bother knocking. He opened her bedroom door, stood on the threshold, gaze sweeping the room, before crossing the floor and drawing back the heavy silk drapes, allowing sunlight to pierce the darkness. "Are you having contractions? Is there pain?" he asked brusquely.

"No," she whispered.

"Then what are you doing still in bed?"

"I'm on bed rest, Brando."

"The midwife said you should get up and walk a little. She said you need fresh air."

"I'm fine."

"You're not fine." He crossed to the side of the bed, narrowed gaze raking her, the curl of his upper lip revealing disdain.

"I want you to get up."

"Why?" she asked, rolling onto her back to look up at him.

"Because this isn't good for you, or the baby."

She hated his tone, hated his arrogance, hated his superiority. She pushed herself up, the covers heavy on her legs. "Do you only care about the baby?"

He rolled his eyes. "That's absurd, and you know it. I care about you. I'm concerned about you. You can't keep this up. It's not healthy, and it's not good for any of us—"

"You don't seem overly troubled by it. You've gone about your life this past week without any trouble."

"I was giving you space."

"Thank you for the profound emptiness."

"I was respecting your wishes."

"You don't know me at all, do you?"

"I don't play games. I didn't think you played them, either."

"You're above all of this, aren't you? How nice not to have emotions—"

"Charlotte, I'm genuinely worried about you. You're clearly having a breakdown of some sort."

She stared at him in wonderment. "What is your solution to the problem, then, Brando?"

"Get some sun, go for a swim, take short walks, read something interesting, take the focus off you." His broad shoulders shifted carelessly. "You're not the only one whose life has changed. We both have adjustments to make."

"And yet this is your house, and your country. You are surrounded by your family and your employees, and your friends. The only thing you have lost is your ability to bed new women." Her lips curved, but it wasn't a smile. The pain inside her was blistering and raw. "Is that your hardship, Brando?"

Brando couldn't remember the last time he was this angry. He felt as if he'd married a stranger. Who was this woman in his house? What had happened to the Charlotte he knew? Where was the woman he'd been so enamored with? "Do I need to call the doctor?" he asked, struggling to contain his temper. "Should I make an appointment for tomorrow?"

She averted her face. Her lower lip quivered. "I'm not sick."

"Something is clearly wrong, though. You're not yourself. If you don't try to pull yourself together, then I'll find help."

"You don't need to find 'help,'" she said, still not looking at him. "I'll be fine once I'm away from here. I need a break. I need to go somewhere for a while. I'm suffocating here."

"No, I'm not going to let you go 'somewhere.' You're not running away. You've made a commitment. We both made a commitment, and we're going to honor the commitment."

Her head jerked around. Her gaze met his, eyes flashing fire. "You're not my father. I don't work for you. I don't belong to you, which means you don't get to tell me what to do, or how to behave."

"You're my wife. That gives me some authority—"

"Authority?" she laughed. "Oh, that's fascinating, but also wrong. You have no authority over me, and you trying to manage me will backfire. It'll destroy everything I feel for you."

"Obviously, you feel very little if you're already determined to leave me."

"Speaking of feeling very little, Brando, just because you throw huge sums of money around doesn't mean you're being kind or loving. It means you're paying for things, but I don't need your money, and I don't need you to buy things for me, and you can't buy me. Maybe everyone else is taken in by your extravagance and generosity but I know the truth. You dazzle with your gifts and your generosity, because it's all you offer. Our elegant wedding…the dinner reception…even the fireworks… It was to make up for the fact that you don't love me, and you will never love me. Instead I'm supposed to be satisfied—"

"You don't know what you're saying." His hands balled into fists. He was at the end of his tether.

"No? Then tell me about one woman from your past that you deeply loved. Tell me how it broke your heart when it ended, and you didn't think you'd ever be able to continue without her."

"This is ridiculous. You're hysterical. It's not good for you, and it's not good for the baby. Clearly you need space, space I'm happy to give to you. I'll be heading out to the vineyard near Greve and then having dinner with my winemakers. I'll have my phone with me. Call if there's an emergency. Otherwise I'll check in on you after I'm back."

Hands bunched in the covers, heart thudding hard, Charlotte watched him leave her room, and listened to him close her door, firmly.

Part of her wanted to fling pillows at the door. Part of her wanted to hurl insults at him, because who was he to tell her anything? Who was he to lecture her on behavior? He was the one who'd slept with legions of women, never truly caring for any of them. But on the other hand, she'd known who he was when they went to bed together. She knew he was a powerful, sexual man who had no intentions of settling down.

If she wanted to cast blame, she could only blame herself for falling for him, and worse, allowing herself to become so terribly attached. The attachment, the love, the passion... It was what made her hurt now. It was maddening that she felt so much for him, and he felt nothing at all.

The dinner with his winemakers went later than he anticipated and the *castello* was dark when he returned. Brando locked the front door and headed upstairs, hesitating on the second landing, wondering if he should still check on Charlotte at this late hour.

There was no light shining beneath her door and he remembered their fight earlier. Perhaps it was better to let her sleep. She needed sleep, and so did he. He'd have breakfast with her in the morning and begin working on untangling their knotted relationship, because ignoring her, and their problems, hadn't worked so far.

The next morning Brando asked his housekeeper if Charlotte had requested a breakfast tray yet. The housekeeper looked at him, expression bewildered.

"She left yesterday, signor," she said. "A car came for her a little after you left."

Brando didn't believe it. He went through his room, and then her former bedroom, but all traces of her were gone. He called her but her phone was turned off, and he was sent to voice mail. Brando struggled to stay calm as he threw his things into his leather duffel to return to Florence.

He spent the drive to Florence trying her phone—still off—before making some calls. She wasn't at his house in Florence. She hadn't checked back in at the hotel she'd stayed at before. Florence was a city filled with hotels. She could be anywhere.

He called a half-dozen hotels while he drove, and none of them had her under her name, or even his.

His frustration mounted with every call. This was ridiculous. Such a waste of time, as well as dangerous for her and their son. She was supposed to be on modified bed rest, not running off somewhere making it difficult for her to be found.

In Florence, he went straight to his house, asked his staff to help make discreet calls, but even after two days no one could find a trace of her. Brando was certain she wouldn't try to fly, not in her condition, but where had she gone? And why? Why go through the motions of marrying him, if she'd never intended to stay?

Those questions haunted him over the next week and continued to trouble him for the rest of the summer as it seemed Charlotte had vanished completely.

CHAPTER TEN

TWO MONTHS WENT by, two months without a word from Charlotte, months that passed with agonizing slowness for Brando.

Where had she gone?

And why had she cut him out so completely?

He knew she'd seen Dr. Leonardi at least three times over the past eight weeks, because ten days ago Brando had cornered the doctor and demanded information. Dr. Leonardi didn't know where Charlotte was staying, but he confirmed that she'd come in for her regular appointments and all was well.

So Charlotte was in the area still—that was a plus.

But where, he didn't know, and he couldn't find her, despite repeated searches. Knowing she'd remained in Florence helped calm him, though. He still didn't understand why she'd leave, but he was grateful she wasn't taking unnecessary risks by traveling.

The baby's due date was September 24. If it wasn't harvest season, he'd be permanently in the Florence town house, but as harvesting had begun, he was at the *castello* in Chianti, waiting for word, should word come that she'd gone into labor.

Word arrived far earlier than he expected, though. It was just the first week of September when Brando received a call from

Livia telling him to get to the hospital immediately, that Charlotte had gone into labor.

It was on the tip of his tongue to ask how Livia found out, but instead he hung up and drove straight to the hospital. Thankfully it was the middle of the day and there was no traffic, and he made it to the Florence hospital in under an hour.

Brando was met in the emergency waiting room by Livia. "There are complications," Livia said bluntly. "They've taken her to surgery."

"The baby?"

"Is fine. He's here, small, but healthy. It's Charlotte. She's hemorrhaging. They're trying to save her now."

Brando shook his head. "What do you mean, *save her*?"

"Her blood pressure dropped very quickly. Her heart—"

"You're not making sense."

"Because you're not listening. Charlotte is in critical condition, and I was told to prepare you—"

"Prepare me for what?"

"She might not make it, Brando. The surgeons are going to do the best they can, but there was a lack of blood flow to her vital organs."

"I need to see her."

"You can't. She's in surgery."

"I'm her husband, Livia."

Livia gave him a pitying look. "And what will you do once you're there? How can you do anything to help her?"

"You don't think I should be with her?"

"Where have you been all summer?"

He froze, and then slowly turned to stare at his sister. "What do you know about this?"

"I've taken care of her all summer." Livia lifted her chin. "She's been with me."

"I've been to your house. She wasn't there."

"She's been staying in the apartment over my studio. I've been taking her meals and making sure she gets to her doctor appointments. My daughter has been helping, too, keeping her company so she wouldn't be lonely when I had to work."

"You never told me."

"Charlotte asked me not to."

"Why?"

"She was terribly unhappy. She needed a friend."

"I am her husband."

"Yes, but not her friend."

Livia's reproach stung. His hands knotted. "You shouldn't have gone behind my back."

"What would you rather I did? Turn my back on my new sister, pregnant with your baby? Tell her I don't care? But I care, and I took her in, because I know somewhere in your hard heart, you care."

"I do not have a hard heart, and I have always cared. I was never unkind, never impatient—"

"But was there love?"

"Of course there was love. She's my wife, the mother of my son."

Livia sighed. "Brando, you're so very shrewd in so many areas, but you don't understand women, and you don't understand Charlotte. Charlotte loves you, so much so that I think she's dying because her heart is breaking."

"She's not dying."

Livia's shoulders twisted. "Fine. You know best. You know everything."

Her icy, dismissive tone gave him pause. "You're not being dramatic?"

She shot him a look of scorn. "You have a newborn son, and a wife dying. Why should I be dramatic?"

"I don't know," he admitted. "Maybe I'm in shock."

"Then prepare yourself. It's probably going to get worse."

His chest tightened, his pulse felt heavy and slow. "She can't die. We have a son—"

"You'll find another wife. It'll be fine."

Brando drew back, appalled, sickened. "What in God's name?"

"Her heart stopped, Brando. It will be a miracle if she makes it. But you'll find someone else to marry and raise Charlotte's son—"

Brando walked away from her then, going to the nurses' desk and demanding to be allowed into the surgical room. "I'll scrub in. I need to be there. My wife needs me."

"That's not permitted, signor. I'm sorry—"

He dropped his voice, speaking in measured words. "I am one of the largest benefactors for this hospital. I'm not asking to participate in surgery, but to be allowed to be in the room. I will not interfere with anyone. I just need to be near her."

The nurse said she'd check, but she couldn't promise anything.

Brando refused to look at his sister while he waited for the nurse to return. Brando watched the hands on the clock slowly move. It seemed to take forever for the nurse to return, but it was maybe just five minutes.

"They're just finishing now. She's to be taken to ICU, where they will monitor her recovery. I'll take you to her once she's there. It will be another ten, maybe fifteen minutes."

"So, she's okay? She's stable?"

"I wasn't given any information about her condition, only that she's to be closely monitored." The nurse hesitated. "Would you like to see your son, though? I can take you to him until you're able to join your wife."

Brando stood at the window of the neonatal intensive care unit staring at his son in the Isolette. His son looked tiny and red-faced, swaddled in a blue-and-white blanket with a little blue knit cap on his head.

A nurse joined him outside the window to explain that the incubator was protecting the baby from infections, allergens and excessive noise. He'd had a stressful delivery and the hospital was doing what it could to regulate his environment with optimum oxygen, humidity and warmth. "It's a lot to go from his mother into the outside world," the nurse said with a smile. "But overall he's doing well." She shot him a side-glance. "It's his mother we're worrying about. How is she?"

"I don't know yet. I'm supposed to go to her once she's in recovery."

"Let me make a call."

The wait again felt endless, and Brando stared at his son, unable to imagine his child growing up without his mother. Without Charlotte.

He couldn't imagine life without Charlotte. She was meant to be with him, part of everything. She was part of him. How could she go? How could there be a future without her?

Brando's gut burned, and the fire spread to his chest, creating a searing pain. None of this made sense.

How had they even gotten to this point?

And yet how had he thought this would turn out?

The nurse returned. "I'll take you to her."

Charlotte might have been taken to recovery from surgery, but she wasn't awake. She lay utterly still, her skin so pale that it looked like alabaster. Tubes were attached, as well as machines that monitored her.

Her long hair had been gathered into a side ponytail, the vivid gold strands the only color against the white sheets.

The nurse who'd walked him to ICU stood next to him for a moment. "She'll remain sedated for some time," she said quietly. "Don't expect anything."

Brando gave a brief nod that he'd heard the nurse, but he couldn't look away from his wife. He still couldn't process it all. That she'd been with Livia all this time. That his family had been taking her meals and keeping her company. That even his mother had been to see her.

Everyone had been with her but him.

The nurse silently slipped out and Brando drew a chair close to the bed. He watched the shallow rise and fall of her chest, watched the pulse at the base of her throat, watched the monitors measuring her every breath and beat of her heart.

She looked so small and fragile. So terribly alone.

Regret filled him, regret and pain. He'd caused her pain, and everyone could see it, and everyone could feel it, and everyone wanted to do something about it…everyone, it seemed, but him.

Brando slipped his hand through the tubes and cords and covered her hand with his, careful not to bump or disturb anything attached to her.

Carefully, gently he squeezed her hand. Of course, there was no response, and yet her very lack of response drove home how vulnerable she was. How vulnerable they all were.

"We made a beautiful baby," he said to her, voice low and rough. "He's in the nursery where they're taking good care of him. But he needs you, *cara*. You are his everything. You're the only one he knows. You're the only one he loves. He trusts you. He depends on you. Don't leave him, Charlotte. Don't break his heart."

There was no response from her, no flicker of her eyelids, no movement in her fingers. She was so still it was as if she was no longer there.

And yet she was here. She was somewhere in there, resting, quiet, waiting.

Waiting for what?

He thought of Livia's words. *But was there love?*

He'd answered that of course there was love. He married her. He was starting a family with her.

Charlotte loves you, so much I think she's dying because her heart is breaking…

But that didn't make sense. He loved Charlotte. It's why he'd followed her to Los Angeles. It's why he wanted her in his life—forever. How could she not know how he felt? How could she not believe he cared deeply?

He stood up, and leaned over her, gently kissing her forehead. "It's not just the baby that needs you, *cara*. I need you," he whispered, his lips brushing her cheek, and then her lips. "I love you. I always have. I always will. Now come back to me. You've made your point. I'm paying attention. Give me a chance to make it right."

She woke late that night, groggy and weak, but her eyes opened, and she saw him and for a long moment just stared at him. "The baby?" she croaked, voice raspy. "How is he?"

Brando left the chair he'd been in all day, all night, and stood next to her. "Good. But he'll probably be happier once he's with you."

"He's really all right?"

"Yes." He could see the fear in her eyes as well as the extreme fatigue. She'd been given transfusions, but she was still pale, dark shadows etched beneath her eyes. "You're the one we're worrying about."

"I'm fine."

And yet her voice sounded hollow and there was no light in her eyes. She wasn't fine. She hurt. She didn't feel safe, didn't feel loved. He felt an ache in his chest, hating that all this time he'd caused her so much pain. "I have missed you," he said. "I looked for you everywhere. I called everyone in your family. No one knew where you were."

"Hiding right beneath your nose," she answered.

"I've been worried sick."

"I took no risks. I kept all my doctor appointments. Your family has been really good to me."

He felt another lance of pain. "I should have been the one taking good care of you."

"I don't think we belong together—"

"But we do," he interrupted quietly, firmly. "I haven't expressed my feelings properly, and I apologize, and vow to become better, and more communicative, but you must know that just because I struggle with words, doesn't mean I don't feel, and don't care. Charlotte, I love you. I care for you so much that

I can't imagine a future without you in it. I don't want a future without you in it. You are my future."

Her head turned and she looked up at him, her eyes slowly filling with tears. "You have your son now. You don't need me. I did my job. I gave you what you wanted. Now I just want you to let me go."

"*Cara*, baby."

The tears shimmered in her eyes, turning the blue irises aqua. "I can't live like this anymore." Her eyes closed, and a tear spilled. "I don't want to live like this. Let me go."

"I love you, Charlotte."

"Don't lie to me."

He bent over her and wiped away the tear before kissing her near the corner of her mouth. Her lips trembled. "I love you, Charlotte."

Another tear slipped free. He wiped that one, too. "I love you, Charlotte," he repeated.

"They're just words."

"But they're the words you needed to hear, and I should have told you. I should have said them before, not just once, but over and over, until you felt safe, and loved. Because you are loved. You are my heart, Charlotte. Come back to me. Stay with me. Give me a chance to show you I'm the one for you."

Her mouth quivered as she gave her head a faint shake. "I can't do more pain."

"There's no more pain. We've done that part already. It's time for happiness. Time for love. Time for change. I promise. I swear. I give you my word."

Her eyes slowly opened and she looked at him. "I don't want your word. I want your heart."

"You have it, *cara*. You have all of it."

"Why do you feel now, but you didn't before?"

He used the pad of his thumb to dry her cheek. "I feel. I've always felt things, sometimes so strongly that I keep those emotions under lock and key."

"Why?"

He shrugged. "I was the youngest in a big family. Everyone else was important. Everyone else had a voice. I was the baby, dismissed as shallow and silly, a boy with a pretty face. I learned to hide things, especially the things that affected me deeply. It's become a terrible habit, and I promise to never again shut you out."

Her hand reached for his. Her fingers circled his. "I need to know how you feel. We need to know, your baby and me."

"Our baby," he corrected. "And, yes, I agree."

CHAPTER ELEVEN

IT WAS A week before she was released from the hospital but now they were all back at the *castello*, a family having come home.

The grapes were close to being harvested, and the days were long and warm. During the morning and early afternoon, Brando was in the fields, and with his winemakers, but late afternoon he always returned to her. Now Charlotte drowsed in the lounge chair beneath an umbrella by the pool, their newborn asleep on her chest, while Brando swam laps. She could hear the lazy hum of bees in the flowers in the big terra-cotta pots and the warble of a distant bird. Now and then she opened her eyes to watch him swim, marveling at the ripple of bronzed skin and muscle against the sparkling water.

He was magnificent.

And he was hers.

Finally.

The baby stirred against her and Charlotte nuzzled him even as she rubbed his tiny back. He smelled heavenly. Of milk. And love. He was so very loved.

"You know, we really need to give him a name," Charlotte said as Brando climbed from the pool before wrapping a towel around his lean waist. "We can't just call him 'the baby' forever."

"Why not?" Brando retorted, leaning over them, to drop a kiss on her mouth and then on the back of his son's head. "I was called 'baby' for years in my family."

She laughed softly, appreciating his humor. Brando grinned down at her, white teeth flashing, silver eyes filled with warmth.

"Aren't we supposed to name him after one of your father's brothers or something?" she asked. "Remind me again of the Italian tradition? I find it very confusing."

"Don't worry about the tradition. I don't think we need to follow any rules. We should give him a name that we think will suit him, a strong male name, as he's a strong boy."

"A miracle boy. He was determined to come into the world."

Brando nodded. "Determined to be made."

Her heart turned over. "Determined to bring us together."

Brando crouched next to them and kissed her again. "And he did. Our miracle. Our angel."

Charlotte's eyes met his. "Angel. Angelo."

Brando was silent a moment and then kissed her, and then the baby's cheek. "We love you, our Angelo."

Charlotte's heart was so full. She blinked back tears as she reached up to caress Brando's hard, chiseled jaw. "And I adore you, Brando. Thank you for loving me. Thank you for giving me this amazing family."

"And thank you, *cara*, for being mine. I love you."

"I know." And she did.

EPILOGUE

September, two years later

IT WAS HARVEST season and life at the *castello* was unusually busy, with two babies and a very busy husband who spent more time in the vineyards than he did at the house, but Charlotte understood and was almost as excited as Brando about this year's harvest.

After feeding the newest addition to the family, another boy, seven-month-old Joseph, Charlotte left the contented babies in care of their day nanny, and put on a hat, and left the house in search of her missing husband.

She hadn't gotten very far before she saw him approaching. He was on his way back to the *castello*, his white shirt damp and sticking to the hard planes of his chest.

He smiled when he spotted her. "Where are you going?"

"I was looking for you."

"Is everything all right?"

"Everything's perfect, and I thought maybe, just maybe, I could steal you away from work… But only if you've time."

"It depends on why I'm needed."

She loved the teasing light in his silver eyes and the husky note in his voice. Everything about him was so impossibly sexy.

"I've had lots of time with the children, but I could use some adult time." She gave him a pointed look. "I could use some of you."

His smile widened, and he lowered his head to drop a warm, melting kiss on her lips. The kiss was full of promise and she pressed herself closer to him, desire flaring, hot and hungry. "You can use me all you want," he said against her mouth.

"Good. I intend to."

Brando wrapped an arm around her, holding her firmly to his chest and hips. She could feel the hard ridge of his erection through his work jeans, the ridge of his shaft rubbing her right where she was sensitive. "You still make me crazy," she whispered, arching against him, wanting all of him. "You make me want you morning, noon and night."

"Which is probably why we have a second baby already."

She smiled. "I have a feeling we're going to end up with a big family."

"As long as there are no more difficult pregnancies, I'm good with that."

"Last one was easy."

"Yes, it was. Thank you, Joseph." Brando swung her into his arms and cut across the gravel path, making a swift detour to the gated swimming pool.

She hummed with excitement and that electric heat that always crackled between them. "Where are you taking me?" she asked.

"Somewhere we can get some privacy." He pushed open the gate, and carried her into the pool house, and locked the door behind them.

The shutters were closed and the inside of the small stone building was dark and cool, smelling of lavender and citrus. Brando stripped Charlotte's clothes off and walked her backward to the oversize chaise, before nudging her down. He dropped to his knees, and kissed her right knee, and then the left, and then higher, up her tense thigh.

She sighed his name, her breath no longer steady. He pressed between her thighs, parting them wider, making room for his body, but instead of filling her, he kissed her, there where she was so wet and tender, where every flick of his tongue created licks of fire. Her hips danced of their own volition, her body desperate for him. These kisses were maddening. His flicking tongue was maddening. What she wanted was the heavy weight of him, the consuming pleasure that only he could give her. She needed him, needed him desperately, now and forever.

Brando never tired of the taste of his Charlotte, or her soft urgent cries. He loved the feel of her in his arms, the silk of her pale gold hair, and the shimmer in her eyes as she reached for him. Her passion for him was matched only by his need for her. He loved how much of herself she gave, whether they were making love, or being a family. As he made love to her on the chaise, he didn't just give her his body, he was giving her his heart. Making love was more than sex, more than sensation. It was a pledge between them, to always put their love and family first.

Charlotte was still independent, and strong, but he'd come to understand that what she needed most was loyalty, commitment and stability. She needed hope and family. He wasn't perfect but he understood these things, and knew that this was a promise he could keep. To protect his Charlotte. To protect their children. They were his life now, and he cherished this life with them because it was full of hope, and love. Always love.

And maybe another baby.

* * * * *

The Playboy Prince Of Scandal

Susan Stephens

Susan Stephens was a professional singer before meeting her husband on the Mediterranean island of Malta. In true Harlequin style, they met on Monday, became engaged on Friday and married three months later. Susan enjoys entertaining, travel and going to the theater. To relax, she reads, cooks and plays the piano, and when she's had enough of relaxing, she throws herself off mountains on skis or gallops through the countryside singing loudly.

For my readers

There's nothing better than reading and music to lift the mood. I hope you enjoy reading this book even more than I enjoyed writing it, and that the happy-ever-after ending gives you the type of happy feeling that stays with you until you pick up your next romance.

With my love to you,
Susan xx

CHAPTER ONE

*The Winter Palace of Prince Cesar Romano di Sestieri
Ardente, Isla Ardente*

'SOFIA ACOSTA? Are you serious?' Cesar speared a look at his
long-suffering equerry, Domenico de Sufriente. Dom had been
reading out the proposed guest list for Prince Cesar's annual
banquet celebrating the start of the polo season, to be held at
Cesar's *palazzo* in Rome.

'Signorina Acosta should be invited with her brothers,' Dom
pointed out, 'or you risk insulting the entire Acosta family.'

Cesar frowned. That would not do. He planned to play exhibition matches in aid of charity with the Acosta brothers'
Team Lobos in various locations across the world. Working out
a way to exclude his least favourite woman without offending
her brothers was impossible. It couldn't be done.

Dom cleared his throat to attract Cesar's attention. 'You expressed a wish to field a mixed team for your next charity
event. Having grown up in competition with her brothers, Sofia
Acosta is—'

'Don't mention that woman to me!'

'One of the finest riders of her generation,' Dom ventured.

'But not a professional rider like her brothers,' Cesar pointed out.

'True, but there are few who can match her on the field of play.'

After the furore she had created, Sofia would pull in the crowds, Cesar silently conceded. The exhibition matches would benefit all his charities. 'Her skill on horseback is undeniable, but I'll never forgive her for what she did.' Using his hand like a blade showed his feelings on the matter.

'The article?' Dom proposed mildly.

'Of course the article.' What Sofia had written was the most florid pack of lies, and with her by-line brazenly plastered over the rubbish in a newspaper belonging to Cesar's old adversary Howard Blake. He'd been at odds with the man since their schooldays, when Blake had stopped at nothing to get some innocent fellow student to take any blame directed at him—until he'd tried it on with Cesar. That hadn't gone too well for Blake, Cesar recalled.

What was the relationship between Blake and Sofia? Was she another innocent dupe, playing a role in some new tactic Howard had thought up to bring Cesar down to repay him for policing Blake during their years at school? Was it possible Sofia hadn't realised the harm the article could do to her family and to his? Why target him at all? They met in passing at polo matches, so why had she set out to destroy his reputation?

He only knew the woman through her brothers, though he'd registered Sofia's face and figure, as both were outstanding. Was she in cahoots with Blake? Without knowing the facts, he could rule nothing out. There was only one certainty, and that was that he refused to dignify her smut with a response.

'I will deal with Sofia Acosta in my own time.'

'Yes, sir.'

Dom bowed his head, but not before Cesar had caught sight of the expression on his equerry's face. 'Why are you looking so smug, almost as if this pleases you? You're lucky that you still have a job—that anyone in the palace has a job. Sofia Acosta tried to bring us all down, so please don't suggest she has any finer qualities. She's a typical over-achiever, dipping her snout into multiple troughs because she can't bring herself to keep it out. I applaud dynamism, but not when the only possible motive is profit.'

'She rides like a demon,' Dom reminded him.

'Perhaps you would too, if you'd grown up in a horse-mad family.'

'I doubt it,' Dom murmured beneath his breath as he straightened his perfectly straight tie.

'Regrettably, she would be an asset to the team,' Cesar added, musing out loud. 'She'd draw the crowds based on her scandalous nib-dipping alone.'

Money-grabbing siren, he raged inwardly. Sofia Acosta might have the face of an angel, and a body made for sin, but it seemed to him that she'd stop at nothing, even bringing down a country, if it stood in the way of her lining her pockets.

A warm breeze chose that moment to steal in through an open window. It went some way to softening his tension, by reminding him of what lay outside the palace. However luxurious—and Palazzo Ardente was exquisite—a palace was just a set of rooms, static and unchanging, while the ocean and the beach were fresh and new every day.

'Just don't put that woman anywhere near me,' he instructed as he left his desk.

'The banquet will be held at your *palazzo* in Rome where there is a very long dining table...'

'Excellent. I will sit at the head, while Sofia will be at the far end with my mother and sister.' The hint of a smile tugged his hard mouth. 'I'd like to see Signorina Nib-Scribbler lecture them on the error of my ways.'

Sofia Acosta, outstanding polo player, amateur artist and sometime journalist, had famously written an article about European royalty, mostly featuring Cesar, though she had also taken a passing swipe at her brothers. The headline banner had screamed, 'Is Royalty Necessary in Today's World?' The piece had caused a storm on social media. As an ex-Special Forces, polo-playing billionaire prince, Cesar had been put under the microscope—Sofia's fantasy microscope. His reported success with women, according to her, had made him sound more like a rampaging satyr than a dutiful prince.

She'd found numerous archive shots, showing him in every form of undress: playing polo bareback, barefoot, in banged-up jeans, topless, with a bandana tied around his head, making him look more like a kickboxer on vacation than a serious-minded working royal. There was even one of him naked beneath a waterfall, slicking back his hair as if he had nothing better to do than idle away his time in a tropical lagoon.

Granted, a few shots showed him in his official capacity, but always with an array of different women on his arm.

Had there really been so many?

The upshot of it was that a playboy billionaire, more intent on womanising and indulging in a hedonistic lifestyle than leading his country, was as far away from the man he was as it was possible to imagine. Duty came first. Now. Then. Always.

Not to say he had no appetite for pleasure, but that was then and this was now, and he always looked forward. Sofia Acosta had dredged up the past, embroidering the facts until they could only cast doubt in people's minds. What he found almost harder to believe was the way she'd dragged her brothers through the same mire. So much for family loyalty!

Why should he forgive Sofia Acosta for making him and his friends of many years the butt of her argument when she hadn't given him the courtesy of seeing her words before they had gone to print? The effect on his pride might have been fleeting, but the longer-lasting effect on his country, and on the trust of his people, was what he cared about. Had she thought of that before she had put pen to paper? He doubted Sofia Acosta had thought of anyone but herself.

And now he was expected to sit in the same room as this woman and make small talk with her?

'Sofia Acosta won't be the last unwanted guest you are forced to welcome,' Dom pointed out, reading Cesar's mind with his customary ease. 'Think of this as a trial run for the many unpleasant duties you'll face in the years to come.' Dom turned the page in his notebook. 'You requested a meeting with Sofia's brothers and your sister Olivia after the formal dinner?'

'Correct.' Anything to avoid dancing with the twittering princesses his mother and sister had no doubt seen fit to invite.

'And Sofia Acosta will be included as well?' Dom pressed diffidently.

'She will have to be included,' he reluctantly agreed. He frowned. 'That's supposing we can drag Signorina Acosta away from her hippy commune.'

'The facility is more of a retreat,' Don ventured as he handed over a report, 'funded entirely by Signorina Acosta.'

'With money inherited from her parents?'

Don confirmed this.

'So, the demon rider has some redeeming features,' he murmured as he scanned the report Dom had offered for him to read.

'This is my decision,' he stated. Unfolding his athletic frame from the chair, he went to stand by the window. 'I will meet with the Acostas, including Sofia Acosta, and my sister Olivia, after the state dinner while the other guests are enjoying dancing to the orchestra.'

'A wise decision, sir.'

Dom had his head down, but why was he smiling? What was his equerry thinking? Recently, Cesar had begun to doubt Dom's advice, because something had changed in his manner. His equerry wasn't as open as he had used to be.

Before he could progress his thoughts, a pair of sparkling black eyes invaded his mind. They belonged to a voluptuous woman who could throw any man off his game. It was hard to avoid Sofia Acosta when they attended polo matches across the world, and when their paths crossed there was always fire between them.

There'd be no fire at his dinner. Sofia must learn that she could not profit from rumour and stolen, off-duty snaps. She knew nothing about him. He knew even less about her. If Dom handled arrangements for the dinner correctly, that was how it would remain.

Sofia Acosta's rustic rural retreat, deep in the heart of Spain, where Sofia's brother Xander is tired of sitting for his portrait

'If you could stop painting for a moment and speak to me!' exclaimed the magnificent brute on his towering black stallion. 'I should never have agreed to this!'

'If you would stop ranting for a moment and keep still,' Sofia soothed, 'maybe I could finish this...'

Paintbrush high, she checked her work, and silently admitted that it was nigh on impossible to capture the darkly glittering glamour of a man who overshadowed everything in his immediate vicinity, including the stallion he was mounted on. 'Against all the odds,' she declared as she laid down her brush, 'I've finished. Come and see, if you like—I'm sure you'll love to see yourself blazing like a comet, fiercer than your stallion Thor.'

'Which is exactly the impression you intended to convey, I imagine,' Xander commented in a husky drawl as he eased his neck. 'Why must everything be sensational in your world, Sofia? Why can't you settle for calm?'

'If that's a reference to the article—' She stopped speaking as hurt overtook Sofia's natural desire to defend herself. Xander was her eldest brother, and the only one of the four prepared to listen to her defence when it came to an article that had appeared in print under her name but had been written by someone else. As of now she had nothing to back up her claim.

'You're a talented woman,' her brother insisted as he dismounted. 'You have your retreat, your riding... And you're a passable artist,' he remarked grudgingly as he scanned the canvas she'd been working on. 'You don't need to add journalist to your quiver of accomplishments. Be content with what you've got. Settle down. Enjoy life.'

'Like you?'

Xander ignored this reference to his continuing bachelor state. Having had responsibility for the entire family thrust upon him when their parents had died, he'd never loosened up and allowed himself to live.

'Why this pressing urge to see yourself in print, Sofia? I'm guessing it must have paid well.'

That was what all her brothers thought—that she had sold her soul to the devil in return for a hefty pay-out. The truth was rather more complicated. She had never wanted to see her name in print, but the offer of lots of money to write 'something harmless' had proved irresistible. There were so many people she wanted to help at the retreat she had created. Without a constant flow of funds that was just impossible.

Since her mother's death, Sofia had lived her life as she believed her mother would have wanted her to, which included building a haven where others could escape for a while to recover from their difficult lives. Never in a million years had she imagined that once the article was written it would be changed, or that her brothers would be put under the same distorted spotlight.

Both they and Prince Cesar did so much good in the world, and yet some sleazy scribe had altered Sofia's words to make it seem that they and Cesar showed one face to the public, while living scandalous lives. If she didn't keep her mouth shut, there would be more articles, she had been promised, and these would be worse than the first. To protect her brothers she couldn't say anything, not even to Xander, though the article had done irreparable harm to their relationship.

Finding pony nuts in his pocket, Xander gave his stallion some treats before handing him over to a waiting groom. Turning around, he dipped his head to confront Sofia. 'Who wants to read everything in the garden of the super-rich is rosy? Was that your thinking? I don't understand you Sofia. Why didn't you come to me for money, instead of selling your cross-eyed opinions to that scurrilous rag?'

Because the damage had been done. The article she had written in good faith had already been changed.

'If you need money so badly I'll make you a loan right now—'

'No. Please!' Xander was always ready to save the day, but she had to do this to prove the article was a lie. The threat of a second article appearing under her by-line, mentioning trumped-up charges involving financial shenanigans between Cesar and her brothers, was enough to secure Sofia's silence.

'There's something you aren't telling me,' Xander stated with certainty.

This was the moment she should tell him the truth, but from the moment they had been orphaned, Xander had taken all the responsibility on his shoulders. She had to sort this out. 'I'm not a child any longer. I appreciate everything you've done for me, as we all do, but you must let me stand on my own two feet.'

'Your stubbornness will be the end of you,' Xander snapped as they left the barn. 'I can't understand why you picked out Cesar for special mention. He's done more good than you know, and yet you appear to have gone out of your way to undermine him. You put a country at risk with a few thoughtless words, making out that Cesar is a playboy prince when nothing could be further from the truth. I expected better of you, Sofia.'

She expected better of herself and, knowing she deserved every stinging word, she remained mute.

'Cesar would never discuss the good he does,' Xander continued, frowning, 'and I've no doubt some of the readers will believe your piece of smut. The way you dwelled on him, anyone would think you were half in love with him and jealous of the life he leads.'

'Which only shows how little you know me.' She sounded defiant, but she was broken inside. Xander thinking so little of her hurt like hell. The article had paid well, and every penny of the money had gone to her retreat. The demand for places had expanded so rapidly she'd desperately needed additional funds. Naively believing that what she wrote would be printed word for word, the chance to write an article for a national newspaper had seemed too good to be true. And guess what?

As for falling in love with Cesar... The little she'd seen of that magnificent monster had convinced her that she could never fall in love with such a hard-bitten individual. She'd tried love and had found it a pallid substitute for the romantic novels that had informed her teenage years. That had been when she had been unable to secure a date. Having four high-octane brothers, overlooking her every move, had hardly been an incentive for likely suitors. Rubbing paint-covered hands down her paint-covered, overall, she took Xander to task on the subject of Cesar. 'Every single time I've met the man he's seemed insufferably superior.'

'I think you're harking back to one time when I had to remind you to curtsey when Prince Cesar visited our family home to trial some ponies. You were sixteen years old. Cesar was twenty-four. You may have noticed that over the years that he's changed. You've both changed. He's a hard man because he's had to be.'

Cesar had almost had the throne snatched from under his nose, she remembered. According to the press, a self-seeking man who cared nothing for the Queen, her family or the country had somehow weaselled his way into court, where, with a great deal of flattery and false promises, he had set about making himself indispensable to the Queen—a polite way of reporting he had been her lover. Having uncovered the truth and banished the conman from the kingdom, Cesar had stayed on at court to support and comfort his mother. Sofia heaved a sigh. So he wasn't all bad, just autocratic, aloof and way beyond her reach.

'You will accept the Prince's invitation,' Xander stated firmly. 'His banquet will be your first step towards rehabilitation before you appear in the match.' She had to drag her mind back to the present as Xander continued, 'It's the least you can do. If the public sees you playing polo with the Prince, it will reassure them that things are back to normal.'

Whether it did or not, the thought of seeing Cesar again both chilled and excited her. As compelling as a human cyclone sweeping along on a wave of testosterone, Prince Cesar of Ardente was perfect hero material for susceptible females, but Sofia was neither susceptible nor was she in the mood for trembling in awe at a royal prince's feet. There was nothing more tiresome, in Sofia's opinion, than a six-foot-plus titan lording it over her, as she, with four self-opinionated brothers, was well placed to judge.

'We will attend Cesar's banquet as a family.' Xander stated in a tone that brooked no argument. 'He has requested a meeting with all of us, including his sister Olivia, after the banquet to discuss the upcoming charity polo matches, in which, I presume, you'll be playing.'

'Of course.' Sofia's retreat was one of the charities that would benefit. She could hardly refuse. Neither would she refuse the invitation to Cesar's banquet, though it meant confronting the man she had supposedly slammed in print. That was the best reason for attending she could think of. She'd see her brothers again, and if Cesar really thought so little of her, she had no further to fall.

CHAPTER TWO

HIS STAFF HAD outdone themselves. Never could he remember such a glittering scene. The dining table at his *palazzo* in Rome seated more than a hundred and each high-backed seat, sumptuously covered in night-blue velvet, was occupied tonight. Chandeliers sparkled like diamonds overhead, bouncing light off the jewels of those bound by wealth, power, pedigree, as well as an abiding passion for horses and polo. He was the only mongrel in the room.

His father's son by his mother's handmaid, Cesar had the Queen to thank for raising him as her own. She had plucked him from an uncertain future when Cesar's birth mother had abandoned him in favour of her latest lover. Romano born, he would now be Romano bred, the Queen had decreed. Though as soon as he was old enough to understand the implications of becoming heir to the throne, the Queen had insisted that Cesar must curb his wild streak. She was still working on that.

'Is everything to your liking, sir?' his equerry asked.

'I can't thank you enough, Dom. Please convey my appreciation to the staff.'

Staring through the forest of crystal and silver ablaze like fire on a ground of white damask, his attention fixed on one woman. Sofia Acosta seemed confident and happy and was certainly animated as she chatted easily to his sister Olivia and to his mother, the Queen. His plan to spike Sofia's journalistic guns by seating her with the two women in the room who were strongest and most loyal to him appeared to be foundering. They were clearly enjoying each other's company.

He couldn't have seated Sofia Acosta far enough away, he reluctantly accepted. Even in another room, she would claim his interest. Cesar wasn't the only man present to have noticed the most fascinating woman in the room. What made Sofia so intriguing was the way she chatted so easily with his mother, and achieved what he would have believed impossible at a formal banquet, which was to make his mother laugh.

'You seem distracted.'

Sofia's brother Xander was seated next to him.

'My sister has not done something else to upset you tonight, I hope?' Xander suggested with concern.

'I've moved past that article, and we avoid each other whenever possible.' He hadn't spoken more than a curt hello to Sofia since she'd arrived at the *palazzo*.

'How will this distance between you work when you're playing in the same mixed polo team?'

'The match is in aid of charity. We'll forget our differences and concentrate on that.'

'That's very generous of you,' Xander commented. 'I'm not sure I could be quite so understanding.'

They shared a look. Both men were warriors; neither was understanding.

Cesar shrugged. 'Sofia's your sister and you are my close friend. I won't sully our friendship by carrying on a public feud with your sister.'

Xander raised an amused black brow. 'And this distance you talk of will be enough for you?'

'There's the entire length of a table between us tonight. And when we play our matches, the length of a polo mallet will suffice.'

'Just don't hurt her—emotionally hurt her, I mean. Sofia acts tough but she's always ready to be hurt, and that makes her vulnerable.'

'What do you take me for? I've no interest in her in that respect.'

'Don't you?'

Beyond the fact that Sofia would play an important part in the matches, no, of course he didn't. Who was he trying to kid? Cesar asked himself grimly as Sofia, together with his mother and his sister, threw back their heads and laughed.

How had she won them over so easily? He recalled his mother saying that royal life could be much improved if only people had the courage to express an honest opinion. He imagined Sofia had no trouble doing that. It had become obvious to him tonight that she was a natural communicator. But was she also a natural snoop, using this occasion to fuel another article?

The way to his mother's heart had always been unconventional. Sofia personified quirky with her abundant black hair cascading down her back in a shimmering waterfall of natural waves. Some attempt to tame it had been made. She'd tied a band of brightly coloured flowers around her forehead. Who did that at a royal banquet? He had to admit that the coronet of fresh blooms teamed perfectly with the summery, ankle-length gown Sofia had chosen to wear. With its intricate embroidery, jingling trinkets and happy, summer colours of yellow and pink, the dress perfectly mirrored the smile on her face.

A mix of anger and lust flashed through him. Sofia had the brass neck not only to outshine every other woman present but to sit amongst his guests as calm as you like. She'd clearly charmed the two people in the world who mattered most to him. Of course, his mother was notoriously tender-hearted, a thought that led him to study Sofia again. Was she as amusing and straightforward as she appeared tonight, or was Sofia Acosta a wolf in a rather attractive sheep's clothing?

Decision made, he excused himself from the table. Sofia exclaimed with surprise when he reached her chair. Bowing to his mother, the Queen, he dipped his head to murmur in Sofia's ear, 'I need you to come with me right now.'

Her eyes turned wide and curious. 'Are you throwing me out?' A smile was hovering around her mouth.

'Just come with me, please.'

They had attracted the attention of his mother. He smiled quickly for her sake.

'Is it time for pudding?' Sofia addressed herself to the Queen. 'Do we have to change places?'

His mother was laughed warmly. 'No, we do not change places between courses here.' She spared a sharp look at him. 'I believe my son would like to speak to you alone. Am I right, Cesar?'

'Correct,' he rapped, though his mother had managed to make it sound like a romantic assignation when nothing could be further from the truth. He was determined to address the issues between him and Sofia before the business of the meeting began.

He caught a whiff of some delicate wildflower scent as Sofia left the table. With a pretty curtsey for his mother, she thanked the Queen for a wonderful evening.

'Come back to us,' his mother said, with a warning look to him.

'Don't we have a meeting after dinner with Sofia and her brothers?' his sister Olivia drawled with a knowing smile in his direction. Olivia was taunting him with the fact that, as she very well knew, more lay behind his desire to take Sofia from the table than business.

'Don't let us keep you, Sofia,' she added silkily. 'My brother appears to have something pressing on his mind.'

As well as on the placket of his evening trousers, he grimly recorded.

'A stroll in the garden?' he gritted out as soon as he and Sofia were out of earshot.

'You make it sound so appealing,' she murmured.

'Fresh air, and a chance to relive old times,' he proposed.

After what she'd done, he expected Sofia to at least have the good grace to pale at his challenge, but instead she firmed her jaw, inviting, 'Lead the way.'

'Life is more exciting when you say yes,' he remarked with irony.

'In some instances,' she countered.

'In all,' he insisted, striding on.

It was his eyes that made him irresistible, she decided as Cesar led her through the open glass doors and into the garden. Well, almost. *She* would resist, of course. Black sable in colour, they delivered a message no woman in charge of her senses could misinterpret. He had a particular mix of intensity and easy confidence that held the promise of sensational sex.

Brutally handsome, Cesar was savage on the polo field, which was why her brothers often fielded him on their team. And even before the infamous article the media had hinted at Cesar's extraordinary prowess in bed. Did every palace bedroom have a reporter sitting on the windowsill? Were there paparazzi in the bushes even now? she wondered as he led her deeper into the black, fragrant night.

What did Cesar want with her? Why was she here? Where sex was concerned, he was betting on a loser. She might be twenty-four, but her experience to date was incredibly limited, involving inept fumbles in a car, several lunges in the stable, subjecting her to an assortment of acne, halitosis, sloppy kisses and inept, searching hands. This was hardly the stuff of which dreams were made, and was definitely not sufficient preparation for a night-time encounter with Cesar.

'*Sprigati!*' Cesar urged as her footsteps lagged. 'Hurry up, Sofia!'

This was no romance, only impatience in his voice. So what was this about? Did he plan to rant about the article? He should. She deserved it. He'd probably warn her off ever writing about him again. She could handle that. She hadn't wanted to write about him in the first place.

'It's private enough here,' she stated firmly, refusing to take another step.

'Not private enough for me,' Cesar informed her curtly.

She sucked in an involuntary breath as he swung around to stare at her. Formidable by moonlight, and backlit by flickering torches, Cesar was an awesome sight. Sweet-smelling jonquil and delicate sprays of white star jasmine scrambling up a nearby wall, threatened to weaken her with their scent. Lifting her chin, she confronted him. Entirely by chance, she'd chosen the most romantic spot to stand her ground. Far beyond the palace walls the lights of the city provided a fitting backdrop for a man whose darkly glittering glamour rivalled even that of night-lit Rome.

Cesar's response was the lift of a brow. 'Well? Why have you stopped here?'

'I would like to know the purpose of this meeting.'

A humourless huff was her answer. 'You'll find out,' he called over his shoulder.

'Life is more exciting when you say yes.' Cesar's words banged in her brain. But what had she said yes to?

What was this woman doing to him? He could take his pick. Countless beauties vied for his attention. He wanted none of them because they were obvious and Sofia was not. She simmered with sexuality, yet retreated if he so much as looked at her a beat too long. Was she a virgin? Was that even possible at Sofia's age? Remembering her brothers, he thought it more likely than not. Which rubbished his thoughts on seducing her. The idea of bedding an innocent was inconceivable to him. He preferred older, more experienced women who knew the score, women who used him as he used them, for casual pleasure with no strings attached. His dealings with Sofia Acosta would, from this moment on, be solely restricted to business.

Things did not go entirely according to plan. Having led Sofia into a secluded, lamp-lit pavilion where they would be quite alone until the meeting with Sofia, his sister and her brothers began, she was immediately on guard. Angry and affronted as he was by what she'd done, he had no intention of terrorising her. To this end, he switched on the light and left the route to the door clear, while Sofia stood in the centre of the pavilion, staring at him with a multitude of questions in her eyes.

'What do you want of me, Cesar?'

He kept his distance, but her intoxicating scent had joined them by some invisible alchemy. Bringing the article to mind, he dismissed the magic with a cutting gesture of his hand. 'An explanation would be a start.'

'I'm so sorry, it was—'

'A mistake?' he queried, finding he couldn't contain his anger. 'A mistake that threatens to damage my reputation and that of your brothers?'

'How many times can I apologise?'

'I'm listening.'

'It wasn't what you think—'

'So it wasn't an appalling exposé?' When she didn't answer, he lost it completely. 'If you accepted my invitation to attend the banquet tonight so you could carry on "snooping" for another article, let me warn you that my legal team will take the newspaper down, and you with it.'

There was silence for a moment, only broken by the sound of the Acosta brothers laughing and joking as they approached. For a moment he saw surprise, even anger in Sofia's eyes, as if she'd forgotten the purpose of the meeting, and perhaps thought he'd orchestrated a confrontation with her brothers to get to the bottom of her reasons for writing the article.

Frowning, she confirmed these thoughts. 'I thought our meeting with my brothers and your sister Olivia was scheduled to start after the banquet?'

'It is,' he agreed. 'Can't you hear the orchestra? The dancing has already started.'

They stared at each other while electricity between them sparked like a living force. It was a force that would find no outlet tonight.

'You could help put out the agendas,' he suggested. 'Clipboards? Now?' he proposed when she continued to stare at him in bemusement. 'The charity matches?' he prompted. She lifted her chin with an expression so like his sister Olivia's he could have laughed. The two women shared many characteristics—combat being only one of them. Excellent. He loved a good fight. 'Well? What are you waiting for?'

'For you to say "please",' she suggested mildly.

'*Please* sort out the clipboards,' he ground out, to end the impasse.

Gathering up half of them, she thrust them into his hands. 'Two work faster than one,' she explained, braving his astonished glance coolly. 'Shall I pull these tables around so we can face each other at the meeting?'

He could think of nothing he'd like less than to sit facing Sofia Acosta. Concentrating on anything else would prove impossible. 'This is an informal gathering when friends, who are also teammates, can snatch time in their busy schedules to discuss our upcoming matches.'

'We need clipboards for that?' she queried.

'Are you going to question every decision I make?'

'Only if I think it necessary.'

That level stare into his eyes again, and yet she seemed so calm and logical. The urge to see her wild with lust would have to keep for another time.

'My schedule is cast in stone,' he intoned icily. 'I've laid out an agenda so there can be no unnecessary mistakes in dates or overlaps in commitments.'

She pulled a wry face. 'I'm sure my brothers will love that.'

'I've already checked to make sure our schedules are in synchrony, and they agree with my plans.' Why was he even telling her this? he wondered as a brief wistful look swept over her features. Of course, since the article, he was closer to her brothers than she was. Was that his fault too?

'I'm glad my brothers are happy,' she said at last, with obvious sincerity, 'but does that mean anyone involved in the matches must sacrifice previous appointments to accommodate you?'

'Are you're talking about yourself?'

Her face paled but her lips firmed. 'I was thinking about your sister.'

'Ah, Olivia.' He huffed an ironic laugh. 'She wouldn't allow anything to stand in the way of riding with your brothers. As for you...'

'Yes?' Sofia's eyes narrowed in unmistakable challenge.

'I imagine you'd do anything to heal the rift you've created in your family.'

Perhaps that was a little harsher than he'd intended.

Sofia lowered her gaze but rallied fast. 'I'll study your agenda and let you know.'

As he quirked a brow, she queried, 'Men rule and women obey in your world?'

'You've met my mother and sister. Do you think that possible in my family? But playing in a team is different. Someone has to be in charge or chaos will ensue.'

'And that someone is you?' she challenged. 'Sounds as if you mean to be more dictator than team leader.'

Right on cue, his friends and fellow players, the Acosta brothers and his sister Olivia, came into sight in arrow formation, with Xander spearheading the group.

'I look forward to hearing your explanation of why you felt it necessary to cause such trouble with that article,' he told Sofia before they arrived, leaving her in no doubt that it hadn't been forgotten but had merely been postponed.

CHAPTER THREE

THE CHANCE TO ride with Cesar and her brothers was a lure Sofia would always find impossible to resist. How much more so under present circumstances? Having brothers breathing over her shoulder used to annoy her, but now she missed the closeness more than she could say. The change in their relationship since the article seemed irreparable sometimes, and determination alone wouldn't heal that rift.

She had to find a way to make her brothers believe her, but without being able to tell them everything for fear of them hitting out at Howard Blake, and him hitting out even harder, she was uncharacteristically powerless. Loyal to a fault, her brothers would see the false rant printed in the newspaper about Cesar, with Sofia's by-line proudly displayed at the top, as a blow against all of them.

In trying to save her retreat, she had only succeeded in alienating those she loved most. The upcoming matches were the best chance she'd get to ride with her brothers on neutral territory. She hoped the physical demand of the matches would help to restore at least some of the camaraderie between them.

Her feelings where Cesar was concerned were conflicted. She was a moth drawn his very fierce flame. Cesar was shrewd, sexy and keenly intelligent. His body kept her awake at night.

Dreams were safe. Reality was far more complicated. If she were foolish to offer herself up, as a waiter might offer a canapé, Cesar would swallow her down, lick his lips and move on. Leaving her where, exactly?

Embarking on a voyage of sensual discovery with Cesar would be like casting a minnow into a shark pool. She'd be saved that embarrassment as he couldn't have made it clearer in the pavilion, before her brothers and Olivia arrived, that he would never forgive her for what she'd done.

As the meeting went on, Cesar didn't attempt to include her in the discussion, while her brothers gave her thin smiles when they looked at her at all. Only Olivia pressed her lips together in a reassuring smile, as if she, at least, wanted to believe better of Sofia.

'Are we done here?'

She jumped to attention as Olivia spoke.

'I have a rendezvous later,' the Princess revealed.

'A *rendezvous*?' Cesar demanded icily. 'With whom, exactly?'

'A friend.' That was as much as Olivia was prepared to divulge. This seemed to amuse Sofia's brothers, though for the sake of Cesar they confined their feelings to sideways glances. What were they hiding now? she wondered.

She didn't have to wait long to find out.

Xander was as heated as Cesar when it came to issuing instructions. 'Make sure you're never on your own. Don't do anything that might put you at risk.'

'Isn't that rather the point of a rendezvous?' Olivia drawled with amusement, sliding a conspiratorial glance Sofia's way.

This was one situation she didn't want any part of. Breaking the stand-off, she moved to the door. 'I should get back to my room to log all these dates in my calendar.'

'We can walk back together,' Olivia agreed, seeming as keen as Sofia to escape the mounting tension.

When five autocratic individuals thought they could manipulate the lives of two young women, they had another think coming. Both Sofia and Olivia had endured brotherly smothering as children, and neither of them was prepared to roll over and accept a command simply because one of the titans had uttered it.

'Not so fast.'

She stared at Cesar's hand on her arm.

'We haven't finished talking,' he informed her.

She moved away from the doorway to allow everyone else to leave. 'What do you want to talk about?'

'I think you know,' he insisted. 'You speak and I listen.'

'And then you judge me?' She was trembling inwardly, but that was something he didn't need to know. Could anyone be more attractive, while appearing so hard and autocratic, than Cesar Romano? Cesar was as huggable as an iceberg, and as distant as a faraway sun. 'In my world conversation flows back and forth.'

His stern expression didn't change by as much as a flicker. 'I will evaluate your excuses when I've heard them.'

'So I'm already guilty in your eyes?'

'I have the evidence in print.' He said this with an easy shrug. 'If you can have something that might reverse my conclusion that you are a cold-blooded, money-grabbing traitor to your kind, then please let me know.'

'My *kind*?' she repeated tensely. 'Do you think I imagine myself as lofty as you?'

'I have no idea what you think, but I do know I find it hard, if not impossible, to contemplate working with you on the team unless I have some understanding of what drove you to be so condemning in print. In case you're in any doubt, the only reason you're on the team is because of your prowess as a rider, and the attention your notoriety will bring to the match.'

She had no excuses to offer. Desperate to raise money for her retreat, she'd been tasked with providing details of life behind the glamorous polo scene, little realising she was going to be manipulated by a newspaper mogul called Howard Blake. There was no point now in wishing she hadn't taken that call. She'd been naïve, thinking the polo scene, with its royal connections and appeal to various celebrities, would be something people wanted to read about. She hadn't realised that in writing a harmless article she had inadvertently provided Blake with enough detail to flesh out, making his lies seem perfectly believable.

Now she wondered if Cesar had been his target all along. Prince Cesar certainly had the most to lose when it came to reputational damage. Her brothers could shrug it off. Though that wasn't what they'd told Sofia, of course. In truth, any attempt to tarnish their reputation only enhanced it, for with the exception of Dante, who was now a happily married man, her brothers prided themselves in being the bad boys of polo.

'What?' Cesar pressed, jolting her out of her reveries. 'Not a word of explanation?'

None that she could tell Cesar. First she must find a way to curb Howard Blake's bullying ways. His next victim might be more vulnerable than she was. Blake had already threatened to bring down her brothers if she went public with the fact that he'd changed her words and, goodness knew, there was enough rumour and scandal to damn them. With Sofia's relationship with her brothers already stretched to the limit, she couldn't risk it taking another blow.

'I have no excuse,' she said flatly. 'The invitation to write the article came at a time when I needed money badly, so I wrote a story I knew would sell.'

'*You* needed money?' Cesar demanded with incredulity, no doubt thinking about her brothers' massive combined wealth.

'I have no part in my brothers' tech empire. I launched the retreat with my own money. It grew to a point where I needed a much wider-ranging roster of staff, and that requires proper funding.'

'You couldn't ask your brothers for money?' Cesar exclaimed with disbelief.

'Of course not. I stand on my own two feet.'

'This one defamatory article will keep your retreat running for how long?' His stare pierced her. Cesar's mind was already made up. She was guilty as charged.

'You don't know me, yet you set yourself up as my judge and jury and, if you had your way, executioner.'

Cesar's expression turned as black as thunder. 'And you only know what you've read about me,' he fired back.

She couldn't deny it.

'Gutter journalism,' he derided. 'Aren't you ashamed, coming from a family as proud and as upstanding as yours'?'

Cesar was viciously opposed to everything she stood for. She had to keep her nerve. She could so easily make things worse with careless words, and that would mean losing that closeness with her brothers for ever.

'I imagine you made a pretty penny out of the rubbish that was printed.'

'It wasn't *my* rubbish. It was heavily edited—'

'Rubbish,' Cesar supplied. 'It's easy to deny you had any part in it now.'

'Believe me or not, that's your prerogative. I had no say in the finished article, and every penny I was paid went to support my retreat.'

Disbelief was written all over Cesar's face. 'I'm giving you a chance to clear your name,' he stated harshly. 'This may be your only chance. I suggest you think hard and long before you walk away from me tonight.'

'I don't think anything I say will make you change your mind, so I see no point in staying.'

'I'm sure not,' he agreed.

His short laugh chilled her. She glanced at the door. 'I should be getting back.'

'We both should. I will escort you. Far be it from me to see harm come to any woman, even you. I can only think you're a cuckoo in the family. Regardless of what you've done to them,

I know your brothers would do anything to protect you, and I respect their wishes.'

A now familiar blaze of shame burned through Sofia's veins. But one thing was nagging. There had been detail in that finished article that even she hadn't known. So who had? She would have to find out to stand a chance of making peace with her brothers and Cesar.

'I thought you might have more pride,' Cesar remarked as they walked side by side through the gardens to the palace. He made it sound as if she'd disappointed him.

'I have no pride,' she said honestly. 'If I have to wash dishes to keep my retreat going, then that's what I'll do.'

'In between selling more stories on those you profess to help?' he bit out.

The calm she was fighting so hard to maintain was shattered. Trust was perhaps the most vital element in a sanctuary where people came to recover and rebuild their lives. The thought of disclosing even the smallest detail she'd been told by one of the guests was as shocking to Sofia as seeing her brothers and Cesar damned in print.

'At least you have the good sense to appear ashamed of your actions,' he commented as they slowed on their approach to the open doors to the banqueting hall.

Shame was the least of it. This was the first time that she had been faced by the fact that Howard Blake might target her retreat. He must be stopped, but to do that she'd need help. Powerful men like Cesar and her brothers were the only individuals she knew with sufficient clout to curb Blake's bullying, but the truth would have to come out.

Cesar gave her a brief sideways glance. 'You appear confused.'

'Not confused,' she assured him. Suddenly everything was crystal clear. 'I need your help,' she admitted.

'So you're every bit as self-seeking and as selfish as I thought? *You* cause the damage, and now *you* need help?'

She was determined not to show her feelings. Hiding how stung she felt had been second nature growing up. She'd soon learned not to blub in front of her brothers.

'I made a mistake,' she confessed. 'And now I want the chance to make things right.'

'Why don't you take some well-earned respite at your retreat?' he demanded sarcastically. Whirling on his heel, Cesar made to peel away. 'You can find your own way from here.'

She caught hold of his arm. 'Cesar, please...'

He didn't shake her off, and his expression was calculating. The punch to her senses was extraordinary. 'Are you sure it's rehabilitation you're looking for? Or do you have something else in mind?'

She sucked in a sharp breath, but desire never came first for Sofia. She squashed her feelings to concentrate on others, but now she must forget her pride, forget about being a cool-headed woman, and just this once risk everything for the chance to make things right.

He couldn't have been more surprised when Sofia stood on tiptoe to brush a kiss against his lips. 'I'm sorry,' she whispered.

Feelings rampaged inside him at the realisation that Sofia wanted more than to apologise. He knew the signals. This was unusual play for a woman who had betrayed him, and betrayed her brothers, yet for all her bravado there were shadows behind her eyes, and that set up doubt regarding her guilt. He had to know more before he took things further.

Did he care enough to find out?

'Aren't you in enough trouble?' he demanded harshly. 'Go back to the ballroom. There should be more than enough distractions there to keep you occupied.'

'Cesar, please...'

Tension swirled around them as she clutched his arm. Reluctantly, he admired her grit.

'I need to talk to you, Cesar, nothing else, I promise.'

He gave her a cynical look to find her eyes pleading and her lips tempting. He was no saint. She matched him like a tiger, kissing him fiercely as she thrust her body against his. It was as if some force beyond their control had taken them over, Sofia especially, until they were bound together in a dance as old as time.

But something was off kilter. Was desperation driving Sofia's passion or were her feelings for him genuine? Would he ever know? Concluding that deciphering her motives was beyond him right now, he pulled back.

'Did I do something wrong?' she asked, staring up with confusion in her eyes.

'You did nothing wrong.'

She had tasted of honey and innocence, so if anyone was at fault he was. Her mouth was swollen and red where his stubble had abraded it, and her eyes were bottomless pools of distress. *But was that an act too?*

'Why are you doing this?' she asked, rubbing the back of her hand across her mouth, as if to hide the evidence of how much each of them had invested in one single kiss. 'Why kiss me at all?' she demanded. 'Why not ignore me and wait for the evening to end? Then you wouldn't need to see me again until we ride in the matches.'

'I might ask you the same question,' he pointed out.

'You don't want this,' she said with sudden certainty, shaking her head. 'I forced myself on you.' Her face crumpled. 'How you must hate me.'

The idea of Sofia forcing herself on him made him want to laugh, but he couldn't be that cruel. 'Hate is a powerful word,' he commented mildly instead.

'But I can see fire burning in your eyes,' she claimed. 'So why kiss me, Cesar? *Why?*'

'I could say you started it.' He kept his hands loosely looped around Sofia's waist. She made no attempt to break free. 'And you kissed me back. So why did you do that?' he asked with genuine interest.

She was silent and then her eyes cleared as she admitted with faint surprise, 'I couldn't stop myself.'

Appearing seductive, as she most certainly did, yet vulnerable might be part of Sofia's script. She had caused more trouble than could be imagined. Proving he was worthy to rule was a lifelong task, and an article hinting at financial irregularities in his past, however fictitious, did him no favours. He'd embraced responsibility for his country gladly. His countrymen would always come first, and Sofia Acosta would not be allowed to distract him.

'Seems to me you were consumed by that same impulse to kiss me.' Growing embarrassment reddened her cheeks.

He shrugged off her suggestion. 'Everyone's entitled to a momentary lapse.'

'Even me?' she asked.

If he could forget all the doubts and half-truths and uncertainties currently swirling around them, Sofia was perfect, and he wanted her. His body was aroused to the point of pain, but it was the challenge in Sofia's eyes that made her irresistible. Her lustrous hair, tumbling in wild profusion to her waist, glinted like black diamonds in the muted light, making the temptation to fist a hank, so he could draw back her head to taste the soft skin of her neck, was overwhelming. But why give her that pleasure?

'Perhaps that stupid kiss was a lapse we should both accept and move on?' she suggested.

Sofia Acosta was beyond infuriating, yet he loved the way she could rally so fast and come back fighting. Her dark gaze brightened as she intuited his thoughts. Or was that a scheming light? Maybe her only reason for kissing him was to soften his mood in order to dig up more dirt to use in another article.

'Who are you, Sofia?' Holding her at arm's length, he dipped his head to stare into her eyes. 'I can't decide if you're a rogue member of the Acosta family, who cares nothing for your brothers' love or your family's reputation, or if you're under some form of duress?'

Was he imagining it, or did she flinch when he said that? 'If there's something on your mind, please, tell me.'

He was so certain she was about to say something revealing, but Sofia's hesitation suggested she thought him as dangerous as whatever was causing the shadows behind her eyes. *Dios!* Would he never find out the truth about this woman?

There was only one certainty here, and that was the heat rising between them.

'Is this what you want?' he demanded.

'Yes!' she exclaimed, eyes closing, lips parting as his hand found her.

'Then I suggest you find someone else to ease your frustration. I don't play games with dangerous little girls.'

CHAPTER FOUR

CESAR STALKED BACK towards the palace, leaving Sofia standing on her own. She couldn't catch her breath, let alone order her thoughts. Kissing him had been a huge mistake that had left her feeling embarrassed and humiliated. Giving in to wild impulses would only ever lead to trouble. Judging by his expression, she couldn't have sunk any lower in Cesar's opinion.

Not only did he believe her to be a gutter journalist but someone who held her body cheaply, like a counter to be played when it suited her. What irony that nothing could be further from the truth. Her body might ache for Cesar's touch, but not like this, furtively and wildly, but passionately, truthfully and openly. With a long, shaking sigh she dragged herself back into the moment. It was vital to clear her head before returning to the party.

She found it easier than expected to remain in the gardens, where the scent of blossom soothed her. It was quiet and removed from the upbeat atmosphere inside the brilliantly lit palace ballroom, which gave her chance to search her mind for a solution to keep her retreat afloat.

On top of that, she had to keep her brothers and Cesar and any future victims safe from a blackmailing tyrant. Cesar was the most obvious ally. No one wielded more power than he did, but she'd lost his trust. He couldn't have made it clearer that he despised what she'd done, and despised the person he believed she'd become. He wasn't alone in that. Right now she hated herself, but it was no use crying over spilt milk. She smoothed her hair. This was a time for action, not brooding. It would take too long to try to win back Cesar's trust by small increments. She had to be bold, and the only way she knew how to be bold was in the saddle.

The retreat she had created, on land left to her by her parents, was another gentle, contemplative setting, created specifically to house those who badly needed help to rebuild their lives. She could see now that her paintings had been her way of escaping reality, but what was needed going forward was Sofia in warrior mode. There could be no more missteps or hesitation. She had always looked out for herself, and her next task was to convince one of the most commanding men on earth to join forces and help her defeat a bully.

Well, that should be easy, Sofia reflected as she made her way back through the night-fragrant garden. Her body burned with arousal after the encounter with Cesar, while her mind was burning up with embarrassment. Cesar didn't trust her. He didn't like her. And though he needed her to ride in his charity polo matches, he almost certainly wouldn't shed a tear if he never saw her again. But since when had life been easy? There was always a new hurdle to jump. This one just happened to be higher than most.

Having studied Cesar's famous agenda, it was immediately clear that where anything was connected to him, money was no object. First-class travel arrangements had been made for all, including the horses. With influential contacts across the globe, Cesar naturally anticipated that everyone's path be as smooth as his. He could alter the destiny of a country at a stroke of his pen, for goodness' sake, and all she needed was for Cesar to help her end the bullying tactics of one wicked man.

First she'd have to win back his trust and change his opinion of her. The feat loomed ahead of her like an insurmountable wall.

Then it was a wall she'd go around, or go through, Sofia determined.

She paused before entering the ballroom to allow her heartbeat to steady. She would need every bit of her composure to confront Cesar again. Most important of all was to hide her feelings for him. Attraction had no part to play in this. She had a job to do.

Dannazione! Where had she gone? Where was Sofia? Had she fled the party? Gut instinct said no. Sofia wasn't the type to run away from anything or anyone. She'd had to be gutsy to survive four hard-living brothers—and him, Cesar reflected as he unconsciously swiped the back of his hand across his mouth where her lips had touched his.

Only one Acosta brother had found love. He turned to look at the team's fitness trainer, Jess, whose husband was Dante Acosta. Jess was a down-to-earth farmer's daughter and a trained physiotherapist, who had helped to heal her husband when doctors had practically given up on Dante submitting to the months of treatment required. They somehow managed to combine Jess's career with Dante's business and polo-playing schedule, and quite obviously their love for each other was blooming, as Dante had confided that family life came first.

Dante had been lucky finding Jess, but lightning never struck the same place twice, and neither Cesar nor Sofia's other brothers had even come close to finding a soul mate.

'Cesar...'

Sofia! He swung round. 'I thought you might have left the party.'

'Is seeing me a good surprise or a bad one?' she asked coolly.

It was impossible not to notice how beautiful she was, and how appealing only she could be with a coronet of fresh flowers in her hair. 'What do you want?' he asked, impatient with himself for feeling this way about her.

'Bad surprise, I take it,' she said.

He frowned.

'I'm here to apologise,' she explained. 'There's no mileage in you and me being enemies. We have to work together during the charity polo matches so we can raise as much money we can. Why not declare peace now?'

He shot her a cynical look. Sofia had many things to apologise for, but he didn't feel inclined to drive her away. 'Why don't you find somewhere to sit and enjoy the party while you can?'

'While I can?' she queried. 'Do you expect something to go wrong imminently?'

Ignoring that, he offered to find her a seat. He scanned the crowded ballroom.

'I can find my own place to sit down,' she assured him, 'but thank you.'

'I could deliver you back to my mother.'

'Like a missing parcel?' she suggested, starting to smile.

He shrugged. 'It would be the polite thing to do.'

'In that case, I accept.'

But she trembled at his touch. Her expression, however, remained carefully neutral.

'You're too kind,' she told him when he brought her in front of the Queen.

'I'm not kind at all,' he murmured in Sofia's ear, 'and you would do well to remember that.'

Then his mother took over, smiling at their approach. 'Ah, Cesar, I was wondering how long it would be before you asked Sofia to dance.'

'Dance with Sofia?' He couldn't hide his surprise.

His mother glossed over his lapse in good manners by drawing Sofia forward to kiss her on both cheeks.

'You've been far too kind,' she told his mother.

'Nonsense,' his mother insisted. 'I notice Olivia is dancing with one of your brothers. Well, Cesar,' his mother pressed, 'why are you keeping Sofia waiting?'

Why indeed?

'If Cesar doesn't feel like dancing—' Sofia began to protest, clearly not keen to feel his arms around her.

'Nonsense. Of course he does,' his mother the Queen insisted in a tone he'd never heard her use before. 'How can my son refuse to dance with such a beautiful guest?' This query was accompanied by a long, hard stare at him.

Sofia slid him a withering look. This was no puling princess touting for a crown, or some celebrity social climber with vaunting ambition, but a real woman with genuine feelings and a history that he could never forget. Any interaction between them was bound to be tense and awkward.

'Cesar?' his mother prompted.

'I can refuse you nothing,' he told his mother sincerely.

'Good!' the Queen exclaimed. 'I shall increase my demands in future.'

'I have no doubt of that,' he murmured, exchanging an amused look with a woman he held in the very highest regard.

'Well?' she urged. 'What are you waiting for? I'm sure Sofia is longing to dance with her Prince.'

If looks could kill he would be dead. His mother, usually keenly observant, had missed the opposition to this idea on Sofia's face. 'This is no easier for me than it is for you,' he assured Sofia once they were out of earshot. 'One dance and then we're done.'

'Until the matches, when we'll be thrown together again,' she reminded him with a rueful slant of her mouth.

'When that happens, you'll do your job and I'll do mine,' he stated firmly.

'To the very best of my ability,' Sofia promised with a long, fearless look into his eyes.

He gave a cynical huff, but it was hard not to believe her. No one could accuse Sofia Acosta of entering into anything in half-measures. When they reached the edge of the dance floor, in deference to his rank the other couples stopped dancing and stood back. If he refused to dance with Sofia, there would be food for gossipmongers the world over. The orchestra struck up a waltz in keeping with their splendid surroundings.

'I've heard of dancing with the devil,' Sofia murmured dryly.

'Are we taking it one step further?' he suggested.

'The demon on horseback dancing with the devil?' she remarked. 'At least we should march to the same beat.'

But they didn't march, they danced as closely as two people could. 'Relax,' he suggested. 'Unless you aim to cause comment.'

'More than I already have?' Sofia countered. 'Just by being here I've caused comment. No one has forgotten the article.'

'Including me,' he assured her, 'but I choose to rise above it, and this is a wonderful opportunity to stop the rumourmongers in their tracks.'

'Is that the only reason you agreed to dance with me?'

'Can you think of any other?'

Noticing how many people were covertly using their mobile phones to take pictures of them, he drew Sofia even closer. He might have expected her to pull away, but at least in that she had more sense. 'Let's play their game,' she said, surprising him.

'Why not?' he agreed, softening a little towards her as she smiled into his eyes.

Playing the game turned out to be more arousing than even he could have imagined. Who was dancing with the devil now? Devil Woman was an apt description of the siren in his arms. Sofia managed to be both sensual and tasteful as she moved in time to the music, leaving no one in any doubt—apart from him—that they were completely reconciled. More couples joined them on the floor and were courteous enough to allow them a degree of privacy.

'When did you learn to be such a good actress?' he murmured, his mouth very close to her ear.

'Am I acting?'

It wasn't just her voice that trembled now, her body quivered against his like a doe at bay with a rutting stag in the immediate vicinity. 'I hope you are,' he dismissed, pressing home his advantage. 'I know I am.'

'And I thought you were a gentleman,' she told him in the softest, most pleasing voice, 'but now I know you're just a prince.'

'Ouch!' He barked a laugh at the punchline. 'Not all princes are the same, and please remember this is just for show.'

'Hmm, I noticed,' she commented.

Why was he surprised when she brushed her body against his? Hadn't he touched Sofia intimately and left her hanging?

'Is this just an act?' she whispered, no doubt referring to his rapidly expanding erection.

'No act,' he assured her. 'You are an extremely provocative woman.'

Her black eyes sparkled with challenge. 'As you are an extremely provocative man. Shall we keep on dancing, or cause comment by standing here in the middle of the floor?'

Couples were revolving around them like spokes around the hub of a wheel. 'Forgive me,' he said dryly. 'I had quite forgotten the need to dance.'

'*I* distracted you?' she asked with a sceptical lift of one brow.

'You...surprise me,' was the most he was prepared to admit.

'So you're allowed to touch, but I'm not?'

'You must follow your instinct,' he advised as they swirled in time to the ironically carefree strains of a Viennese waltz.

'That might get me into trouble,' she said, pushing her lips down as if that didn't worry her too much.

'Past experience suggests you can handle it,' he countered, 'though I've noticed that you can say one thing while your body responds quite differently. I'd love to know what's really going on in your head.'

'Like you, I'm trying to give the impression that everything is rosy between us,' she assured him. 'There's nothing to be gained by the charities we support if rumour suggests we're at each other's throats.'

'Friction between us might draw even more crowds,' he observed.

'Better to leave your guests with an air of mystery, to add intrigue to what they've seen tonight, don't you think?' she asked as phones were pointed in their direction.

The fact they fitted together perfectly was enough for him for now. Sofia's clean wildflower scent beguiled his senses, while her hair felt like silk as it brushed against the hand he had lodged in the small of her back. Her breath was a cool, minty draught that made the urge to plunder her mouth rise like madness inside him—which would be a sensation too far for his guests. As a man gossip didn't faze him, but as a prince he was forced to curb his natural instincts. It was enough to give the impression that all was well between him and Sofia, so as far as onlookers were concerned he had forgiven her and all was well.

'Don't you like the music?' Sofia probed as they danced on.

'Why do you say that?'

'You seem preoccupied.'

Remembering to smile for the sake of the watching guests, he conceded, 'I am preoccupied.'

'Is it anything I can help with? Have I made things awkward for you?' she added as he huffed a short laugh.

'You?' he queried.

'Okay, I get it. This is an act, and you'd prefer it if I said nothing at all.'

'No. Please speak,' he encouraged. 'Conversation between us will reinforce the impression that we like each other.'

'When nothing could be further from the truth?' she suggested.

He knew better than to answer that. 'Don't overdo it,' he warned as Sofia gave a cynical laugh. 'A happy expression on your face is enough, though you could try to relax a little more.'

'You make that so easy,' she responded sarcastically as the orchestra segued into another popular Viennese melody. 'At least the conductor thinks you're enjoying yourself.'

'My master of music can't be expected to read my mind.'

They danced on until a question occurred to him. 'Do you have enough material for your next article?'

Forgetting the act they were supposed to be playing, Sofia pulled back with a gasp of surprise. 'I'm here because you invited me to the party.'

'A necessary evil to avoid offending your brothers,' he said bluntly.

'How gracious you are,' she murmured beneath her breath, growing stiff and unyielding in his arms.

He was pleased to see she managed to smile, as if there was nothing she would rather be doing than dancing with him. Sensibly, he maintained a distance between them, and throughout the dance there was an expression of enjoyment on his face. It wasn't all hard work. Forced to bring Sofia close in order to avoid collisions on a packed dance floor meant intimate contact with the soft contours of her body was inevitable.

Sofia was a good dancer. Fit and supple, she moved instinctively to the music. The gown she had chosen to wear was of such a fine fabric it did little to conceal her form. Her hand was tiny in his, but her grip was firm. He had one hand lodged in the small of her back so he could feel her trembling. Careful not to adjust his fingers by as much as a millimetre, he took her around the floor. There would be no subtle messages between him and Sofia tonight.

'That must have been torture for you,' she observed when they finally stopped dancing.

'I've known worse.'

'Will you join me in the garden?' she surprised him by asking as they approached the French doors.

She was looking across the room to where guests were spilling out onto the balcony to enjoy the still balmy evening. The romantic setting in a lovely garden, beneath a black velvet sky peppered with stars and lit by the light of a silvery moon, was surely unparalleled. And would therefore be completely wasted on a couple like them. 'Why?' he asked suspiciously.

'Why not?' she countered. 'How are we supposed to become effective team members if you and I remain at daggers drawn? And,' she added, glancing around, 'people are still watching us, and I think that walking outside for a breath of fresh air after dancing is the most natural thing to do.'

She was right in that a fragrant breeze was drifting in from the gardens, but he'd done his duty and felt no urge to do more.

'Please,' Sofia whispered, putting a hand on his arm. 'I'd like the chance to start making things right between us.'

'Another new approach?' he suggested cynically.

Her cheeks flushed red, as she no doubt remembered them kissing earlier. 'It's important to break this deadlock between us,' she insisted. 'We're going to be working together.'

'To heal that gulf would take more than a moonlit stroll,' he informed her, and with a curt bow he left Sofia to enter the garden on her own.

CHAPTER FIVE

SHE MIGHT HAVE known Cesar would reject her olive branch. He'd made up his mind that she was guilty. Dancing together had been nothing but a necessary evil, as far as the Prince was concerned. While for her it had been thrilling. At least his guests had seemed convinced the trouble between them was over. Wasn't that all that mattered?

Apart from the fact that he had left every part of her tingling with the memory of his touch?

She had the rest of the evening to fret over going too far. Trust took time to establish, and she'd waded in with her hobnailed boots. And was so quickly lost, she reflected with a glance at her brothers. The rift between them made her desperately sad. The article had done more harm than she could mend in a single night, and she longed to make things right.

That opportunity might come at Cesar's training camp, which was where they were heading next. She might have felt more confident about that if Cesar hadn't ignored her for the rest of the evening. Deciding to sleep on the problem, she took her leave of the Queen and kissed Princess Olivia on both cheeks. She was fast coming to see Olivia as a kindred spirit.

'Sleep well, my dear,' the Queen said kindly. 'And, please, don't be a stranger.'

As they exchanged warm glances Sofia found it hard to imagine that such a poised and beautiful woman as the Queen could fall into the clutches of a conman. According to the press, that was exactly what had happened. Stricken by grief after the death of her husband, Queen Julia had searched for company online, but what had appeared to be the concern of a handsome stranger had turned out to be nothing more than a wicked plot to seize the throne. Evil always seemed to strike when a victim was at their lowest ebb. Sofia felt a great wave of sympathy wash over her as she said goodnight to the Queen.

'And remember,' Olivia said as Sofia turned to go, 'if you're still hungry Cesar's kitchens are open twenty-four seven to accommodate his huge appetite.'

Sofia didn't want to consider Cesar's appetite, huge or otherwise, but she thanked the Princess warmly, and felt lighter at the thought that the seeds of friendship really were growing between them.

First she went to her sumptuous suite of rooms to draw a great steadying breath. The suite overlooked a lake beyond the palace gardens, and had been designed to imbue a guest with a feeling of relaxation.

Most guests, Sofia's reflected. Her mind was churning with unanswered questions. And that made her hungry. Untying the laces on her dress, she allowed the glorious fabric to drift to the floor. Seeing herself in the free-standing mirror in just a flimsy thong and bra, with her hair flowing free and a coronet of fresh flowers on her head, she decided with a wry smile that she was only short of a waterfall to act the part of water nymph, with perhaps a rugged stranger riding by—one who felt compelled to rein in his horse to take a closer look.

Quickly followed by a team of brothers with towels and sarcastic remarks.

So much for daydreams!

She took a quick shower and then changed into jeans and a casual top before exploring downstairs in the hope of finding the kitchen. Guests were milling about when she came down the sweeping mahogany staircase. No one would be in a hurry to bring such a successful evening to a close, she guessed as the orchestra struck up a fresh tune.

There would be snacks at dawn, her brothers had informed her with relish. Big men with big appetites, goodness knew where her brothers were now. Cesar's *palazzo* had become a hotbed of passion, judging by the number of couples entwined in the shadows of the great hall. Not for this Acosta, Sofia reflected wryly as she followed a waiter through some grand double doors. She was hungry for food and nothing more.

Until she saw Cesar, stripped off to a pair of jogging pants and a form-fitting top, with his wild black hair only partially tamed by a red bandana.

'The party over for you too,' he said as he took a bite out of a king-sized burger. 'Hungry?' he enquired.

'What about your guests?' she asked, speaking on autopilot while she tried to get over the shock of seeing him dressed down and casual while the elegant party was still in full swing.

'It's the host's prerogative to take a break if he wants.' His shoulders eased in a careless shrug. 'My guests can join me down here if they like, though I doubt they're missing me. Burger smell good?' he said as she stared at him. 'I can recommend it.'

'Coming right up,' the young chef on duty offered with a smile.

'I don't want to put you to any trouble,' Sofia insisted.

'No trouble,' the young man insisted. 'Onions?'

'When in Rome...' She glanced at Cesar.

'I think she's saying, yes, please,' Cesar interrupted.

'Sorry. Yes, please,' she echoed, with an apologetic grin for the chef.

Cesar remained lounging back against the wall. 'Are you sure you don't mind my being here?' This was his *palazzo*, his kitchen, his chef.

'Be my guest,' he invited. 'But I forgot,' he added, 'you are my guest.'

'And most grateful for your hospitality.'

'Don't overdo it, Sofia,' Cesar warned with dry amusement.

Making peace with this man wouldn't be easy, but when had she ever embraced easy?

'Take the rest of the night off,' Cesar told the chef. 'Others can take your place. You've put in some long hours today. I appreciate it,' he added as the young chef handed over Sofia's burger.

'That was nice of you,' she commented as they munched.

'You could try not to sound quite so surprised.'

'You're as bad as my brothers!' she exclaimed as Cesar stole the rest of her bun from her plate.

'Worse,' he assured her.

She hummed agreement. 'I remember a time when you were imperious.'

'Never with my staff, though I do remember one incident when I had to deal with an infuriating tomboy on an *estancia* deep in Spain.'

Her jaw dropped. 'So you admit it?'

'On that one occasion? Yes. You were a pest.'

'And you were an imperious prince, taking up space in my stable.'

'You never had a sense of what was good for you.'

'Maybe because what's good for me has never been uppermost in my mind.'

'Does that bring us back to the article?' Cesar suggested with a long sideways look.

She sighed. 'That was a mistake. I should have known. I'm no good being at anything but what I am.'

'Clearly,' Cesar agreed. 'Though there's not much you're afraid of, is there?'

Wrong. She was desperately afraid of losing her brothers'

trust, and her own self-belief, if she couldn't clear her name. Losing Cesar's regard would be yet another blow.

'Let's take that stroll in the garden,' he said when they'd rinsed their hands and cleared their plates away.

This was a pivotal moment when her life could change for better or worse, but at least they were talking.

Inviting Sofia into the garden only proved that damping down his feelings where Signorina Acosta was concerned wasn't as easy as he had supposed. He should refuse to have anything more to do with her, but like a wood nymph beckoning him ever deeper into the thicket of her life Sofia was irresistible.

When he'd suggested the walk, Sofia's surprise had betrayed the fact that she hadn't believed he'd want to spend time with her. When her gaze darkened and her cheeks flushed pink, he knew her answer would be yes. The electricity was sparking between them again. He'd worked out in the gym then showered and changed after leaving the banquet, with Sofia a constant in his mind.

And now, with her long hair still damp from the shower, and silky corkscrews of baby hair arranged like a filmy crown around her brow, she was beautiful. She'd washed off her makeup but not the smudge of chocolate on her neck. The urge to lick it off was overwhelming.

'Snacking on treats in your bedroom?' he guessed. In area, at least, she found temptation irresistible. All his guests were supplied with everything they might need, including ingredients for a midnight feast.

'How do you know?' she demanded, frowning.

'Elementary, my dear Watson. You have chocolate on your neck.'

She relaxed enough to smile. 'Aren't you concerned that your guests might see you in the garden dressed like this, and wonder what you're up to in the garden with me?'

'My guests have everything they could possibly need, and

I'm sure they're quite capable of amusing themselves without my assistance.'

'I'm sure they are,' she agreed, 'but—'

'But what?' he interrupted. 'Don't you trust yourself alone with me in the garden?'

She hummed and gave him a look.

'You find me irresistible?' he proposed.

'Do I?'

'Don't worry, I'll keep a tight rein on you.'

'That might work,' she agreed huskily, on what sounded like a dry throat.

'As you so rightly say,' he pointed out as they moved off, 'we're going to be together, so we might as well clear the air.'

Was there anywhere on earth more beautiful than Cesar's Roman garden? Lit by moonlight, marble statues stood in silent repose like elegant ghosts from ancient times that at any moment might step down from their pedestals to join them. Beyond the vast expanse of garden the lights of Rome sparkled like precious gems. Floral fragrances teased her senses, lending a soothing quality to the setting they had chosen to have this talk that was at odds with the tension between them. But when a band was stretched tight it had to snap at some point. She was acutely aware of Cesar at her side. For some reason, she was drawn to the now deserted pavilion. The door was unlocked and yielded easily. She walked in, and Cesar followed.

'This is our chance to talk,' she said.

Cesar closed the door behind them. Leaning back against it, he stared at her. 'Is this what you want?'

It took a single step in either direction to answer his question. She stepped forward.

Cesar dipped his head and brushed her lips with his. 'You'd better not take advantage of me,' she whispered.

'I'd say the shoe was on the other foot.'

But he made the next move, moving in for a gentle, lingering kiss, and as he teased the seam of her lips apart, an over-whelming surge of hunger consumed her.

The moment was right. Reaching up, she linked her hands behind his neck.

Looping her hair around her fist, Cesar drew her head back. 'I've always loved chocolate.'

'It must have melted in my hand,' she admitted between whimpers of pleasure.

'I don't care how it got there,' he assured her, lavishing kisses on her neck, her chin, her cheeks, and finally her lips. 'Only that I get to lick it off.'

Her answer was to press her body against his. Leaning into him, she parted her lips, inviting the invasion of his tongue.

Cesar unleashed a tiger inside her. The fact that she was in-experienced, and definitely playing with fire, meant nothing to her now. All she could think of was keeping him close so he deepened the kiss. Their bodies acted independently, seeking each other greedily and fiercely, while throaty sounds of plea-sure flew from her lips.

'I think you want this,' Cesar observed as he teased her with more and more kisses.

'You think?' she whispered as she began to undress him.

There was a moment's pause when they stared at each other as if for the first time, and then clothes were flying everywhere.

Cesar was even more beautiful than she had imagined, though in a harsh and rugged way. With a lazy smile, he mapped her breasts, delivering exquisite pleasure that left her incapable of speech. Sounds of encouragement flew from her throat when he tormented her nipples into tight buds of sensation.

'You have magnificent breasts,' Cesar commented matter-of-factly.

'I'm glad you approve.'

He laughed in a way that made sensation travel from her breasts to the sweet spot between her legs. 'Your nipples are so responsive—like the rest of you, I'm guessing?'

SUSAN STEPHENS

'You wouldn't be wrong,' she admitted.

Cesar's voice was a seduction in itself, and made her hungry for more. Naked skin to naked skin was all she could think about. Instinct said Cesar would pleasure her as no one else could.

Swinging her into his arms, he carried her across to a well-padded banquette. But seduction was not on his mind. 'You wanted to talk to me?' he prompted.

Cesar's swift change of pace was a reminder to keep her wits about her, or this opportunity to talk would be wasted. Having proved he could seduce her with little or no effort at all, Cesar had put that one aside in favour of interrogation.

'I don't have all night,' he said, confirming this.

'I apologise for the article, but there was a very good reason for it.'

'What reason could there possibly be?' His voice was cool, his expression unyielding. 'Did you expect me to seduce you and then forget what you'd done? Is that why you agreed to come with me into the garden?'

'That was never my intention.' Her voice was heated, and she had wanted a civilised talk. Why could they never meet without passion of getting in the way? 'I was just grateful to have an opportunity to talk to you. Please believe me when I tell you that everything is not as it seems.'

'So you didn't write the article, as you didn't kiss me just now?'

'If you only knew the truth,' she protested.

'How I'd love to know the truth, but as you show no sign of sharing your version of it any time soon—'

'My version of it?' she exclaimed. 'And now you're leaving?'

'Why should I stay?' Cesar demanded from the door.

'Please, I—'

'You what?' he said coldly.

'Please listen to me,' she begged softly. 'I needed that money for my retreat.'

'Which I already knew. I thought you had something new to say.'

'I was invited to submit an article to a well-known newspaper.'

'A scandal sheet,' Cesar derided. 'And that's not news to me.'

'Read by millions,' she countered firmly.

He dismissed this with an indifferent gesture.

'That means it paid well,' she explained. 'I don't expect you to understand what it feels like to be short of money.'

'Oh, really?' Cesar demanded cuttingly. 'That only shows how little you know me.'

And how would she ever learn, when Cesar was notoriously reserved about his past? 'I can't pretend to have suffered as a child,' she admitted, 'Which was why it was so hard for Xander when our parents were killed. We had an idyllic childhood, and you think that's going to go on for ever. I never imagined it could end so abruptly.'

'Yet you suffered this loss, and went on to discard the principles your parents must have instilled in you. How could you do that, Sofia, just to raise money? I find it hard to believe that, with the Acosta name behind you, banks didn't flock to help. Or was it glory you were seeking? To see your name in print at any cost?'

'The banks had already helped as much as they were prepared to. I'd reached my limit,' she explained. 'I thought it would be easy to write an article with mass appeal—no details, no scandal, just a taste of the glamour that follows you and my brothers around. I didn't see any harm in it—'

'Until it was too late?' Cesar interrupted. 'By which time you had banked the money.' He held up his hand when she started to explain. 'For the sake of the charities we must move past that. Including you in the team will swell the crowds. They'll come to see how things have worked out between us, so we'll put on an act as we have done tonight. It shouldn't be so difficult. We've had our dress rehearsal, but don't ever mistake good manners for forgiveness. Do I make myself clear?'

'Perfectly.'

'Then I'll bid you goodnight.'

The ringing silence inside the pavilion seemed to last long after Cesar had gone. They were no closer to understanding each other than they had been at the start of the evening, but she had exposed how she felt about Cesar, only for him to turn and walk away.

CHAPTER SIX

TEAM LOBOS AND their associated staff left Rome for Cesar's breeding and training ranch in the far north west of Italy the day after the banquet. There were no unnecessary frills in this residence, though everything was of the highest quality. The facility was entirely dedicated to the well-being of the horses. As well as countless other animals, Cesar allowed as a pack of his favourite dogs circled his legs, looking for fuss and for treats. He didn't disappoint them. Kneeling down so he was at their level, he lavished affection on his most loyal friends.

'You still have some admirers, I see...'

His hackles rose at the sound of Sofia's voice. She was like a cork that never stayed down for long.

'Ready for battle?'

This was the far more welcome voice of Sofia's brother Dante. 'Dante!'

He sprang up and they embraced fiercely. The other Spanish Acosta brothers took their turns. Fearless, and loyal to a fault, it was a shame their sister failed to share the same brand of loyalty.

He stood back. 'You all know my sister Olivia...' Olivia raised a laugh as she gave a mock bow. 'And Jess, Dante's wife.' At his prompt, an attractive redhead joined Cesar and Dante in the centre of the arena. 'Jess is also a top-flight physiotherapist and trainer, and I know we're all going to enjoy her punishing exercises.'

Jess acknowledged the chorus of catcalls with a lopsided grin. 'Thank you for the glowing recommendation, but we have to win the tournament before I believe your praise. Until then, all I can promise is hard, relentless training.' She waited for the comic groans to die down before revealing, I'll be working in tandem with another person here... Sofia...?'

As Sofia stepped forward, Cesar ground his teeth. What the hell?

'What is the meaning of this?' he demanded.

'The meaning?' Jess enquired, laughing, no doubt thinking he was joking. 'I don't know anyone better than Sofia for building team spirit. I've seen her work with her brothers, don't forget. And Sofia's organisational skills are second to none.' Jess looked at him with surprise when he failed to stifle a scoffing huff. 'That's why her retreat is such a success,' Jess continued doggedly, with a piercing look at him. 'Anyone who has experienced Sofia's retreat can tell you the benefits. They learn to live life to the full again, and they learn to trust.'

'Excellent,' he bit out. He'd heard enough of the nonsense. Only the calming presence of Dante at his side, and the grimly set faces of those of Sofia's brothers who didn't care to hear her praised went some way to soothing his frayed temper. 'We're relying on you, Jess,' he emphasised, 'for our training regime in the run-up to the matches.'

In his peripheral vision he saw Sofia stiffen but Jess continued, undaunted. 'Without complete trust between team members you can ride the best ponies in the world and field the fittest, sharpest players, but if there isn't proper communication between each member of the team—the kind of communication that doesn't need anyone to shout for the ball, or make it clear that their horse is tiring, because your fellow players know exactly where you are, how you stand, and who best to shoot the ball to—your play will never be as dynamic or as fluid as it needs to be.'

Jess talked good sense, but he still failed to see what part Sofia had to play in this. 'I invited you to become a member of this team for the duration of the charity matches,' he murmured in Sofia's ear, 'but I don't recall hiring you to help with training.'

'You didn't have to hire me,' she informed him pleasantly. 'I'm here because Jess asked me to help her, which I'm more than willing to do.'

The irony was that as Sofia didn't work for him, he couldn't fire her, even if he wanted to. No wonder he preferred binding contracts where anyone who failed to meet the mark could be let go without a fuss.

Sofia began to address the group as cool as you like. 'We're lucky to have this chance to practise together. I know how busy you all are. Knowing your team members inside out, so you're aware of their strengths and weaknesses, as well as how they play the game, will give us the advantage we need.'

He was rocked back on his heels by the sight of two women taking centre stage, as if he were a newcomer to the game. 'That's enough talking,' he decreed with a closing gesture. 'This is nothing we don't know. We're professionals. We adapt. And now we work.'

Jess worked them hard. Truthfully, Sofia was finding it hard to keep up with Cesar and her brothers, but there was no way she going to let the side down. Olivia and Jess were as determined as she was to prove their worth to the team. Jess managed to make training fun. Galloping at full stretch, leaning over the side of her pony to snatch up a can that appeared to have invisible legs was something Sofia hadn't done since she was a child. No one fell off, though noisy hilarity and catcalls released a lot of the initial tension. By the time that morning's session was over, Sofia could do little more than slide down the side of her pony in exhaustion. But neither could she remember enjoying herself so much in a long time.

'Can I help you with that?'

She turned to see Cesar lounging back against the wall, watching her. Removing tack from a spirited pony was normally a straightforward operation, but today the bridle seemed to weigh a ton and her mount was overly keen to be turned out into the field.

'You look as if your knees are about to buckle,' Cesar remarked as she almost lost her footing.

'I can manage, thank you.'

'But you don't have to,' he pointed out, and taking the saddle out of her arms he led the way to the tack room where the others in the team were waiting. 'I've arranged entertainment for later,' he announced when everything was safely stowed away.

'So long as it doesn't involve moving,' Olivia groaned. 'I don't need *entertainment*. I need a long, hot bath.'

'You can have both,' Cesar promised.

Olivia grunted disbelievingly but Jess exclaimed, 'Wonderful!' as she linked arms with her husband.

Infected by Jess's enthusiasm, Sofia smiled too. 'If I don't fall asleep in the bath, I'll be there,' she promised.

'I'll save you a place,' Cesar offered, surprising everyone, not least himself, Sofia suspected when she caught the brief flash of surprise on his face.

If she'd hoped for something more—a glimmer of warmth in his eyes, for instance—she was disappointed. There was nothing in Cesar's expression when he looked her way but the same coolness and suspicion.

He sluiced down in the yard. Everyone else had retired to their rooms to rest, clean up and prepare for the evening ahead. His grooms had taken charge of the ponies, but he chose to check everything twice. The ponies had worked as hard if not harder than their riders, and also deserved a reward.

Raking his hair back, he slung his top over his still-damp shoulders and entered the state-of-the-art building where his beloved animals were kept. He prided himself on the fact that this accommodation was as good as that of his guests.

'Sofia?' He might have known.

'Cesar!' She seemed equally shocked. 'I was just checking the ponies were settled for the night,' she explained.

'I'd have put a top on if I'd known you were here.'

She angled her chin to stare at him boldly. 'Would you?'

Silence fell as they stared at each other. In fairness, Sofia had worked as hard as anyone and yet here she was, tending to the horses when she could have been indulging in a long, hot bath.

Must she moisten her lips like that?

He held her stare. 'Don't you want to rest before the evening entertainment? "Freshen up"?' he suggested.

She grinned. 'Was that a hint?'

He ignored the comment. 'In honour of your family I've brought over a group of flamenco dancers from Andalucía.'

'That was very nice of you. Just don't let my brothers sing,' she warned with a slanting smile.

It was almost nothing, perhaps a brief window into another side of Sofia: a fun side, a family side, a carefree side of a woman he hadn't seen so far.

'Best leave singing to the professionals,' she said.

'How about you?' he asked. 'It's your tradition. Will you dance?'

'Flamenco?' she exclaimed. 'You just try and stop me.'

He had no intention of doing so, he mused as Sofia struck a pose. She looked so beautiful—alluring beyond belief. The sight of her wreaked havoc on his groin. 'Tonight promises to be one to remember.'

'For all the right reasons, I hope?' she countered.

He stared into her eyes. She pleased and infuriated him in equal measure. How could she appear so frank and open after everything she'd done? If he judged Sofia by right here, right now, he'd say she was a free spirit who loved nothing more than to ride hard and live to help others. What had happened to change that? Surely she couldn't have turned into a self-serving schemer overnight?

She shrugged when he didn't answer and ended on a flippant note. 'I'll try hard not to disappoint you,' she promised with one last flashing glance.

He watched as she walked away. What was she playing at now? Sofia Acosta was as sharp as a bag of monkeys, and twice as resourceful. She was determined to keep her retreat afloat, and had already shown she would stop at nothing to do that.

Yet still he wanted her.

Why not? he mused as he watched as Sofia met his sister Olivia halfway across the yard and fell into conversation with her. Both women were beautiful, and as spirited as his most challenging mare. With a back view as impressive as her front, he loved the way Sofia strode out. He loved the sway in her shapely body. Not for the first time, he thought her perfect. Would he sleep with the enemy? Why not? But first he must unravel the enigma that was Sofia Acosta. In spite of everything that had gone before, he wanted to know her both in and out of bed.

Nope. She hadn't packed a party dress suitable for a flamenco party. All she had in her zip-up case were numerous pairs of jodhpurs and jeans in varying stages of disrepair, a stack of clean tops, two spare pairs of PJs, toiletries and comfortable underwear that could in no way be described as glamorous. This was a training camp after all. Not that it was a typical training camp. Everything was high quality and practical, but the suite of rooms Sofia had been directed to, for instance, contained enough tech to satisfy even her brothers. There was also every muscle-easing balm and potion known to man in the bathroom, which she intended to take full and luxurious advantage of. A separate room was devoted to massage, and there was a sauna, as well as a steam room and an ice bath. The latter she was determined to swerve.

She chose bubbles.

The bath was huge. The warm water was plentiful, and the selection of fragrances mind-blowing. She could happily have remained soaking all night, without the prospect of a party. Would Cesar be relaxed in an informal setting or would he still be cool and unreadable? Numerous images flashed through her mind, but for this one night she was going to forget the damning article and have fun.

Which meant sorting out an outfit for the party.

No problem, Sofia reflected as she towelled down. She had a tongue in her head and an exuberant group of *gitanos* had arrived from the mountains of Andalucía to entertain them. She could hear them in the courtyard now. There was a possibility they might have heard of her mother. Keeping the tradition of flamenco alive required a tight-knit if widespread community.

It had been on a night similar to this that Sofia's aristocratic Acosta father had met his future wife. Sofia's mother had danced for him and, according to her father, the firelight had not been able to compete with the fire in her mother's eyes. It remained to be seen if tonight would be a damp squib for Sofia, or whether the traditional music and dance would thrill everyone with its upbeat message.

Sofia was welcomed into the *gitanos*' fold like a long-lost sister, daughter, friend. She was deeply touched by how many women clustered around to help her pick out a gown. Cesar had housed the performers in some of the most luxurious accommodation so there was plenty of room for all the women and Sofia to gather, and plenty of room to prepare properly, which was fortunate as Sofia's hair alone took a good deal of taming and grooming before it could be confined in the severe style worn by all the women. The last touch was an ornate comb for her hair, decorated with sparkling paste jewels, which held a flowing black

lace mantilla in place. There was only one problem, in that Sofia's new friends seemed to think that she would be one of the
star performers tonight. 'Your mother's talent was legendary,'
the head dancer told her. 'You can't refuse.'

Neither would she. 'Of course I'll dance,' she agreed with a
flutter of nerves.

She tried out a few steps, and it was a relief to find that the
childhood lessons from her mother had not deserted her.

'And you must use a fan,' one of the older women insisted.
'The language of the fan is universal.'

And dangerous, Sofia reflected as she stared at the glorious
bright red fan the woman wanted her to use. Flamenco was a
sensual dance that ebbed and flowed as smoothly as silk, with
rhythmic stamps to punctuate the dancer's movements. This
built tension and excitement, while a fan allowed grace and style
to soften the repeated clatter of heels on wood. But a fan must
always be used with discretion, Sofia remembered her mother
telling her, as it increased the charm of the dancer's spell.

She was taken aback when she caught sight of herself in a
mirror, and thanked the women who'd helped her profusely. 'I
can't believe the transformation!' she exclaimed, as she took
in the sight of her hourglass figure in a tight-fitting black and
white dress. With its frills and ruffles—which she never, ever
wore normally—the costume made her feel like a different
person, one who was bold and who never suffered from doubt.

What would her brothers make of seeing her on stage? Whatever their differences, she was confident they'd cheer her on.
She was an Acosta. They were family, and it was this deep and
abiding love that would always protect her. Her brothers might
think she had abused that love, and she could only hope that
one day they would forgive her.

And Cesar? What would he think when he saw her on stage?

When he entered the room her stomach clenched with nerves
at the thought of performing in front of him.

CHAPTER SEVEN

'I'VE COME TO make sure you all have everything you need,' he said, taking in Sofia's much-changed appearance with interest. 'If there's anything more I can do for you,' he added, 'please let me know.'

The soft whir of the spurs on her fan as she opened it drew his attention. 'I didn't expect to find you here. Are you performing tonight? I have to say the costume suits you.'

'This is all thanks to my new friends,' she explained as the women who had helped her watched on. 'My mother's people,' she explained, remembering how her mother had told her to take compliments gracefully and always be proud of who she was. Composing her features into something less wistful, she raised her chin and said, 'Thank you.'

'So I will see you dance tonight,' Cesar concluded.

'You will,' she confirmed, thinking him so rampantly male it would be hard to concentrate on anything while he was watching. But behind that compelling persona she saw genuine interest fire in his eyes. This was a chance to make her mother proud, and her brothers too. She couldn't influence Cesar. His thoughts were up to him.

She was surprised when he waited behind to escort her. 'Will you allow me?' he asked.

'Do I have a choice?' she teased.

He linked her arm through his. 'None,' he confirmed.

The party was being held outside, where a huge bonfire lit up the night. The stage was set at a safe distance in front of it, backlighting the performers with soaring flames. A backdrop of mountains and a soundscape of owls could lead some to think this a romantic setting. Not Sofia, who had so much to prove, though it was certainly rare to have a flamenco performance in this part of Italy, with Apennine wolves howling in the background, as if they agreed that she'd better not mess this up.

'Did you organise the wolf chorus especially for Team Lobos?' Dante enquired with amusement as he and Jess came over to greet Cesar and Sofia.

'My friends never disappoint me,' Cesar confirmed dryly. 'They are no doubt as curious and as excited as we are, especially as we're so close to their mountain home.'

It was an elemental setting, Sofia realised as she looked around, and as such was the perfect setting for Cesar.

'Are you dancing tonight?' Dante asked, taking in her costume.

'That's the price I have to pay for borrowing one of these fabulous dresses,' she admitted, 'though I hope I can remember the steps our mother taught me.'

'You will,' Dante said confidently.

She had to now.

'No one persuades Sofia to do anything she doesn't want to do,' Cesar commented, which earned him a look and a shrug from Dante. 'Enjoy the party,' he added.

Just how much she would enjoy the party remained to be seen.

There must have been something in the air that night, or maybe it was the fabulous red fan, casting its promised spell. Surrounded by her mother's people, Sofia felt able to express herself fully and freely, perhaps for the first time since she'd lost her mother. Tears rolled unchecked down her cheeks at one point while she danced, for all the things they could no longer share, and when the final chord sounded and the main dancer came on stage, she took Sofia in her arms to whisper, 'Your mother would be very proud of you. And remember that as we cry when we lose someone, we live on in their honour to laugh and make love, and live fully again.'

And then the crowd went wild, and called for an encore.

There comes a point at the end of an impassioned flamenco solo when the dancer, having expended every last drop of emotion, cries out, *'Duende!'* and drops to the floor. He was waiting at the side ready to give his congratulatory speech once Sofia had finished dancing when that moment occurred. Sofia struck her final pose, and then allowed her limbs to soften and her face to relax as she sank to the ground.

'Duende!'

The audience rewarded Sofia with rapturous applause. Duende perfectly expressed the heightened emotions he'd witnessed on stage, and he was cheering with the rest. There couldn't be a single person present she hadn't touched in some way.

Sofia was an extraordinary performer. The story she'd told through the medium of dance was one that everyone could relate to at some point. The mask she showed to the world had dropped away, leaving Sofia totally exposed and vulnerable. He might have had every reason to mistrust her in the past, but what he'd seen made him want to re-evaluate what he knew of.

'Congratulations!' he exclaimed as he raised her to her feet.

'I have my mother to thank.' Her eyes were shining with happy memories as she looked back into the past. 'My mother believed in the power of dance, saying music is a power for good.'

'Your mother was right, and you certainly convinced everyone here,' he admitted as he led her forward to take another bow. 'You surprised me tonight,' he confessed once they were out of the spotlight.

'Well, we don't know that much about each other, do we, Cesar?' she said as she lifted her chin to search his eyes. 'All we know is what we see now, and what rumour suggests is fact. Who knows how many more surprises are in store?'

'Just don't write another article,' he cautioned with a lift of his brow.

Her face fell, making him wish he hadn't said it. Couldn't he even allow her to enjoy this moment of triumph?

'I promise I won't,' she said in all seriousness.

'Forget it,' he rapped, angry with himself for being so crass. 'Take your applause. You've earned it.'

He left Sofia with her newly won admirers, most of whom were young dancers dressed in traditional costume, all wanting autographs and selfies with Sofia.

'I'll be with your brothers if you need me.' He jerked his chin towards the crowded bar area, feeling vaguely discomfited as he accepted he could have handled this better.

'I felt like a fraud,' Sofia told him some time later when she had returned to his side.'

'I don't know why,' he said as he drew her away from the boisterous crowd to find a quieter spot.

'I haven't done anything like this in years,' she admitted. 'Not since I was a little girl, in fact.'

'Then perhaps you should do more,' he suggested.

'I'll bring you up on stage next time,' she threatened.

'You may regret that.'

'I'm prepared to chance it,' she shot back.

'Well, now...'

'Now?' she pressed.

'I must get back to the rest of my guests. If you will excuse me?'

'Of course,' she said faintly. And was that regret?

* * *

Sofia barely had chance to speak to Cesar for the next part of the night. It was a great party, so many people to talk to. Her brothers were swept up in a good-natured crowd, relaxing and enjoying themselves, and it felt so good to Sofia to relax and unwind. Escape the web of intrigue into which she'd inadvertently become embroiled when she'd written that article. Doing nothing more complicated than talking and laughing and dancing, she couldn't have enjoyed herself more—or so she thought until Cesar stepped forward to make a short speech.

'We've had a wonderful night of entertainment, for which I'm immensely grateful,' he declared. 'And now it's time for everyone to enjoy themselves, performers and guests alike. So I invite you to party, but not too hard because tomorrow the real work on match fitness begins.'

The usual chorus of groans greeted this statement, though it didn't seem to stop anyone enjoying the party.

'But before we start training again,' Cesar added, 'I'm claiming my right to dance with the star performer.'

Me? The thought of Cesar's body enfolding hers, and without the need for pretence this time, made Sofia's heart riot. She had to remind herself that this was just an innocent dance, and when it finished she'd return to her quarters, take a shower and go to bed.

Who was she kidding?

Difficult questions could wait until later.

Her body melted from the inside out when Cesar took her into his arms. Heat fizzed through her veins, bringing everything into sharp focus. Her awareness level soared. They fitted so well together, which didn't make sense when Cesar was twice her size. But it was a fact, she realised as he led and she followed. 'Don't get used to shepherding me around the floor,' she warned with amusement born of nerves.

'I don't notice too much resistance,' he remarked. 'You're an excellent dancer, and I enjoy using my body.'

Her senses were in freefall now Cesar's rampantly male body was aligned with hers. The urge to move and rub herself against him was constant—one she knew she had to resist.

'Relax,' he murmured, drawing her closer still. 'Or stop dancing. It's your choice. We're not acting now so there's no need to pretend, if you don't want to.'

He was giving her an out she didn't want. Up to now her hand had remained unmoving in his, while her body was as unresponsive as she could make it, but the thought of leaving Cesar and walking away forced her fingers to ease in his as she consciously relaxed her shoulders. Cesar responded by linking their fingers, which she found both intimate and exciting. His other hand was lodged in the small of her back, his fingers resting on the topmost swell of her buttocks.

Waves of want flooded her. They were so close they shared the same breath, the same air, but was this sensible or would it leave her with more unanswered questions? 'We've got training tomorrow,' she reminded them both. 'I should be thinking about bed.' The insistent rhythmic strum of guitars called her a liar. She wanted nothing more than to stay and dance with Cesar.

Releasing her as the music reached a crescendo and finally stopped, Cesar stepped back. 'I'll see you back to the house.'

'You can't leave your guests,' she pointed out.

'I doubt anyone will even notice that I've gone,' Cesar insisted as he steered her away.

So speaks the man who has no idea of the effect he has on people, Sofia reflected as she noticed how many of their fellow dancers glanced at Cesar as they left the improvised dance floor. His type of machismo could electrify a room. 'I don't need you to take me back,' she insisted, avoiding his gaze. She glanced at the last place she'd seen her brothers. They would normally take her back, but they weren't even looking her way.

'Just tell me what you want,' Cesar prompted.

His grip on her wrist might be gentle but the look in Cesar's eyes was not at all safe. What did she want? What was he offering? To be alone with him? The connection between them fired as they stared at each other.

Just for one night. That's all it would be.

They didn't make it as far as the ranch house or even the guest quarters. The hay barn loomed. The building was in darkness when they arrived. Before she could lift the latch, Cesar had swung her round, and with his arms bracketing either side of her face he kissed her hungrily and she kissed him back.

'No,' he rapped as her body enthusiastically took the lead. 'Not here. Not with you dressed like this. '

He was right. The mantilla she was wearing was held in place by a large, ornate hair comb, and the flamenco dress fitted her like a second skin.

Sweeping her into his arms, Cesar shouldered the door and carried her inside the shaded interior where the air was warm and fragrant, and countless dust motes danced on moonbeams. There was nothing to compare with the scent of stacked hay, unless it was the scent of Cesar, Sofia concluded as he set her down gently on a sweet-smelling bed of clean hay.

'You should never tie your hair back,' he said as he removed the comb and mantilla with dextrous skill. 'There should be a law against it.'

She couldn't believe how carefully he rearranged her severely drawn-back hair, finger-combing it until it hung in its usual tumbling disorder. Was this a man she could confide in, or was she fooling herself again? History showed her to be woefully lacking when it came to good judgement.

She needn't have worried. With the removal of her clothes tension between them gradually relaxed and in its place came playful intimacy. Nothing that had happened in the past seemed relevant. Only this moment mattered. Until he hit a sweet spot on her neck.

'You're like a highly strung pony, always ready to bolt,' Cesar observed huskily.

'Where would I bolt to?'

'Back to the party?' he suggested.

'In my underwear?'

'What remains of it,' he commented with amusement. 'What am I going to do with you, Sofia Acosta?'

'Didn't you bring your clipboard?'

Cesar stared at her for a moment then laughed. 'Tell me what you want,' he insisted.

Her heart was thumping. The menu was tempting. Cesar was dressed in low-slung, snug-fitting jeans that displayed more than a few tantalising inches of hard, toned flesh. No wonder her body was responding by aching and yearning.

She didn't move when he settled himself over her, braced on muscular arms.

Where to start?

'Kiss me?' she suggested.

CHAPTER EIGHT

SHE COULD NEVER have predicted what a simple request to kiss her would entail. Starting with her feet, Cesar kissed the soles, her ankles, her calves and finally her thighs, until she thought she would go mad with waiting. Locking stares, he moved past her thighs. If the attention he'd given the rest of her legs was anything to go by...

A soft cry escaped her lips when he murmured, 'Look at me.'

Staring into his eyes was the most erotic experience of her life. It was as if Cesar could see through her to every thought and feeling she had. When he found her and cupped her, she almost lost control, but his touch was so light, too light, and she wanted more. Covering his hand with hers, she demanded more. It wasn't a question of boldness now but more a lifesaver like the air she breathed. It only took a moment and she was lost.

'Greedy,' Cesar murmured as she bucked uncontrollably in the throes of a most powerful release. Unable to control her cries of pleasure, she could only respond by instinct, grateful that he used one hand to palm her buttocks and hold her in place, while he extended her pleasure with his other hand.

'More?' he queried with low, husky, sexy amusement when she was quiet again. Her answer was to reach for the waistband of his jeans. Dealing with the belt first, she ripped it out of its loops and tossed it aside. Next came the zipper, but Cesar took over and dealt with that with efficient speed.

'I need you to do something for me now,' he said.

'Anything,' she offered fiercely.

'Your task is to do nothing at all. Your only goal is to float and feel.'

As he spoke, Cesar removed her bra, only pausing to lavish attention on her breasts before removing her tiny thong. Stripping off his jeans, he moved over her.

Moving between her legs, he teased her with the tip of his erection. But just when she was sure she was ready, he drew back. Resting her legs wide on his shoulders, he pressed her back onto the hay. 'Remember what I told you?'

A ragged sigh escaped her as Cesar dipped his head. After that first release it was a surprise to discover how easily he could make her needy again. She fell quickly, screaming into ecstasy, and the drowning waves of pleasure went on and on. 'How do you do that?' she asked when she had the breath to do so.

Laughing softly, Cesar cupped her buttocks to raise her to his mouth.

He took her gently because Sofia was inexperienced. It rested on him to set the pace. Left to herself she would scramble all over him, and it would be done in moments. He wanted more for her than that. Delay was the servant of pleasure, and Sofia was like a flower unfurling, a process that should never be rushed.

Giving her more, and then a little more still, while she clung to him, her eyes telling him everything he needed to know. She was apprehensive but eager. She wanted him, wanted this, but wasn't quite sure if she could handle it, handle him. He was so big and she was so small. He could practically see these thoughts flashing through her mind. To help ease her concerns, he spoke soft words of encouragement in his own tongue, until gradually she relaxed enough for her hands to stop gripping him like vices. They would soon close on him again when she urged him on to give her the greatest pleasure of all.

When she rested her arms above her head in an attitude of complete trust, he knew she was ready. Protecting them both, he enclosed her wrists in one big fist and cupped her buttocks with his other hand to guide her onto him. Nudging her thighs apart, he sank a little deeper, and then a little deeper still.

'Relax... *Rilassati, tesoro... Non aver paura. Non ti farei mai del male...* Don't be frightened. I would never hurt you.'

'I'm not frightened,' she assured him, though her breathing was hectic and her voice was unsteady, which told him the exactly opposite.

Easing Sofia's fear was paramount. Releasing her wrists, he made sure she made the transition from tension and concern to hunger and need within the space of a few well-judged strokes.

'Ah, yes, yes!' she exclaimed, and, exactly as he had anticipated, she reached for his buttocks to urge him on.

He rested deep, and waited to allow Sofia to become used to the new sensation. Then he gently massaged her by rotating his hips. That was her flash point. She lost control immediately, falling with excited screams of pleasure as she experienced the new and hugely increased sensation of release while he filled her. Her inner muscles attempted to suck him dry, but he had control to spare when it came to Sofia.

'*Non ancora, il mio piccolo micio*—not yet, my little wildcat,' he insisted, holding her still as she battled to bring him release.

'When? You have to! It's amazing,' she insisted on a great exhalation of breath. 'I mean, I realise that you know that, but—'

'But?' he queried with amusement as he began to move again.

'Don't expect me to speak now,' she protested on a ragged breath.

'I don't. I expect you only to—'

'Float and feel,' she remembered, heaving another great sigh of pleasure as he moved faster, the finish of each stroke a little firmer each time.

When she fell again he laughed softly against her hair. She took an age to come down. 'You are the greediest person I've ever known.'

'I don't want to know about *others*,' she assured him with all the old fire.

'What others?' he demanded, lifting his head to stare her in the eyes. 'There is only one Sofia.'

Wasn't that the truth? Sofia accepted as reality raised its ugly head—or in this case multiple beautiful heads, all perfectly coiffed and exquisitely made up, as befitted the women in the life of one of the world's most eligible bachelors.

So why was Cesar with her? Was this revenge? Was he proving a point? She hoped not, because for her this was so much more. It was an exercise in trust.

Searching Cesar's eyes, she found what looked like genuine concern, but she didn't want his pity. She'd had enough of being petted by her brothers as if she were their favourite puppy, only to be kicked out without a chance to explain her misguided actions. She longed for a man who treated her as his equal, and who would expect her to account for what she'd done. A man who would listen and maybe understand. She wanted to believe that man was Cesar, and was forced to remind herself that sex was second nature to Cesar, like eating or breathing.

'You will sleep with me tonight,' he decreed.

She stared up with surprise. 'I'll sleep in my own bed,' she stated. 'We both have to work first thing.'

A smile tugged at one corner of his mouth. 'Are you saying that if you stay with me no work will be done?'

'Not the right type of work,' she said as she reached for her clothes.

Capturing her hands in his, Cesar nuzzled her neck, her mouth, her cheeks with his sharp stubble, until she couldn't bring herself to leave. She wanted to stay with him, so they could grow closer in every way there was.

There was a rustle of foil, and then he turned her so her back was to his chest. 'I promise you'll sleep tonight,' he murmured, the sexy smile in his voice, encouraging her, as before, to lose control.

Had she really chosen her bed over his? Had that encounter in the hay barn really happened?

Determined to cling to reason, she reasoned that Cesar had made no attempt to prevent her leaving. He took his pleasure where he found it—no strings, no consequences, and she was a fool if she read anything more into it than that. But reason wasn't enough to stop her hurting and wanting, or longing for a different type of closeness with Cesar. Leaning back against her bedroom door, eyes tightly shut and with her body still singing with remembered pleasure, she could only rail silently against yet another missed opportunity for them to talk.

Had Cesar been looking for conversation?

She hadn't exactly been talkative herself. If things had been different, if the regime they'd embarked on in preparation for the matches hadn't been so demanding...

If only, if only, if only. But would you have stated your case and taken the consequences, whatever they might be?

If there was a major fallout between them, it would impact the whole team, and with the charity matches coming up fast none of them needed more ripples right now.

So you're burying it? What about the plan to thwart your blackmailer?

Grinding her teeth, as if that would shut out her inner critic, she determined to keep a tight rein on her emotions, and only tell Cesar the whole story when launching preventative measures against the blackmailer would have minimum impact on anyone else.

What about all those people you're supposed to be protecting? The people at your retreat, your brothers, Cesar?

A soft yelp of desperation escaped her throat. Her retreat was full to capacity with vulnerable people. She'd been looking for ways to open another—

And now?

Pulling away from the door, she headed out.

She found Cesar in the deserted kitchen, drinking coffee and demolishing a pizza. 'I'm sorry to disturb you.'

'You're not.'

The flatness of his statement pinned her to the spot. There was no warmth in his eyes and no recollection of remembered pleasure, as far as she could tell. Cesar had sated one of his needs and now he was sating another...with pizza.

So retreat or advance. Your choice.

She moved deeper into the room. 'I'm not here for the reason you suppose.'

'And what is that?'

Holding his black stare was a challenge she met gladly, though there was no hint of the generous lover Cesar had been only a short time before.

'What am I thinking?' he pressed.

'That I've changed my mind about spending the night with you?'

A few long seconds passed, during which Cesar drank more coffee and ate more pizza. 'Why would you do that?' he asked, his sharp gaze suspicious. 'The little I know about you says you only do what you want to do, when you want to do it.'

The sudden realisation that Cesar thought her as coldblooded as him came as an unpleasant shock, but what else could he think after reading the article she had supposedly written?

The one thing she must not do was risk turning this into a confrontation. She needed help, and couldn't be too proud to ask him. 'I need to talk to you—really talk to you,' she explained.

'Now would be good, if that's okay with you? It's important, Cesar,' she stressed when he shrugged.

'Have you finally decided to apologise for the article?' he suggested with a keen, sideways look.

'I can explain how it came about, and was then changed without my knowledge before it went to print.'

'That's some story. You want me to believe you're an innocent dupe,' he suggested. 'Forgive me if I find that hard to believe.'

'Cesar, please—'

'You must excuse me.' He pushed away from the counter. 'I'm heading off to bed. I suggest you do the same. As you mentioned before, we have training tomorrow.'

She stared at the door long after Cesar had closed it behind him. Explaining her actions wouldn't be easy. Cesar wasn't easy. But what in life was? She would just have to find another way.

He couldn't forgive her, and had only firmed his resolve. Everything about Sofia fired him up—to anger, to passion, to disgust. She might be the first member of the team to arrive each morning for training, and the last to dismount when each day's demanding session was over, but she hadn't needed to write that article, and had clearly given no thought to the harm it would do.

It was still possible to enjoy her. They enjoyed each other. That was something separate. It was a simple arrangement between them, with no demands beyond those of mutual pleasure on either side.

The next day's training went well, though he'd had a sleepless night. Judging by the dark circles around her eyes, Sofia hadn't slept well either. Each time their stares clashed, electricity fired between them. It was only a matter of time before he had her again. Primal hunger needed an outlet. She knew that as well as he. As dutiful about training as Sofia undoubtedly was, she was also a hot-blooded woman and the thought of sinking deep into her exquisite warmth provided him with the most delicious torture throughout a satisfyingly testing day.

He was alone in the stables when she found him after training. The topic she chose to open with was not what he had expected. 'You want to talk about the article?' he queried, pulling his head back with surprise.

'And this time have you listen,' she insisted.

He raised a brow.

'Sorry. That sounded harsh.'

Sofia taking an unusual tack shouldn't surprise him, but the fact that her heated glances had either meant nothing or he'd imagined them, which was unlikely, irritated him. Continuing to check his pony's legs, he waited to hear what she had to say.

She joined him in the stall, where there was no sound apart from his mount contentedly munching. Their teammates were already refuelling in the ranch house, so they were alone.

'I want to explain. I have to,' she insisted. 'I can't stand this tension between us. And what's the point of waiting for the right time when the right time never comes?' She caught hold of his elbow when he stood up to go. 'Cesar—'

He pinned her with a cold glance. 'Well? What do you want to say to me?'

As they stared at each other something changed in her eyes. Her body softened, and the words she had been about to say froze on her lips. 'No,' she whispered huskily, keeping eye contact.

'Yes,' he argued softly. He'd never had a problem in recognising or responding to the needs of his body.

'We must talk,' she insisted in a breathy whisper.

Her eyes were black, her lips were swollen, and her breathing was growing increasingly rapid. 'All you need to say is yes,' he insisted in the same low tone.

She was instantly in the moment when he found her with his hand. Her heat reached him through her breeches. 'This is what you need,' he explained as his fingers went to work. But she hadn't finished with surprises yet.

'This is what we both need,' she insisted, eyes blazing a challenge into his.

When she was done, she sank against him, spent. She'd used him. That was okay with him. Kissing her, he undressed her. She saw to the button at the top of his jeans. Wrapping her hands around him, she smiled and voiced her pleasure, as if he had provided her with all the delights of the world in one jutting member.

Having protected them both, he thrust forward. They exclaimed with relief. After a moment or two of basking in sensation, he lifted her, so she could lock her legs around his waist while he pounded into her. From there it was a crazy, furious ride towards the goal they were both seeking, and when they reached it, it was stunning in its ferocity for both of them.

'Again?' he suggested as Sofia groaned and writhed in his arms, biting her fingers into his muscles.

Her answer was to work her hips greedily against his, but to his surprise this felt like more than sex, more than even he had anticipated. It was a glorious coupling, both unsettling and complicated. This was life as he wanted it.

CHAPTER NINE

FEELING LIKE THIS about Cesar resulted in clear thinking, forward planning, even sensible behaviour flying out of the window. The power of her feelings for him allowed for no modification or delay but, as always, once they reached the summit there was only one way down. Uncertainty beckoned.

They dressed quickly. She covered the evidence of outrageously good sex with a fast smoothing of her hair and a few deep, steadying breaths. Cesar made no adjustments. His hair remained as wild as ever, while his breathing had remained steady throughout. For him, sex was an exercise, probably not entirely dissimilar in his mind from the body-stretching workout they undertook on horseback in the ring. And now exercise time was over, and he was ready to move on.

That was how much it had meant to him.

Her mind was made up. There could be no more self-indulgence. Incredible sex with someone who was starting to mean far too much to her was a luxury she couldn't afford. She had to find a way to curb want and replace it with enough confidence to make Cesar hear the truth.

She left first, striding ahead of him to the ranch house. She cared about the people there, and those currently staying in her retreat must be kept safe. Her feelings had to be put aside.

Loading her tray at the counter, she joined her brothers and Jess at a long table in the centre of the comfortably furnished wood-panelled room. There was a moment of readjustment by those of her brothers who weren't remotely on Sofia's side. Raffa and Xander exchanged glances before carrying on with their meal, heads down. They'd always been so easy together, and now she felt like an unwelcome stranger. Yes, they'd always teased her. That's what brothers did. But deep down they were there for her. Not any more, thanks to her supposed betrayal of them, and Cesar. She had to mend that rift before it became too wide to bridge.

Jess and Olivia were the only ones to greet her with genuine warmth, perhaps sensing there was more to Sofia's story than they knew. When Cesar had collected his food and joined them, there was another discernible rustle of interest around the table, but everyone was too cool to comment. He soon put them at ease with easy banter, culminating in, 'I'll take any seat.' Which just happened to be thigh to thigh with Sofia.

It was hard to breathe. How hard would it be to fall in love with him? She covered her concerns with a grin as she turned to Jess. 'Work us harder tomorrow.' Exhaustion might help. Something had to.

Jess winked, as if she understood everything. 'Don't worry, I intend to,' she promised.

'Good.' Cesar was the only one at the table who responded. Pushing his chair back, he stood up. 'We'll all benefit from another good workout tomorrow.' He glanced at Sofia. 'I'm going to take a sluice down in the yard.'

Sofia flicked a quick glance at Jess. It felt good to have an ally. She had no idea how much Jess knew, but she could feel her sympathy coming in waves across the table.

Was she expected to join him? Sofia wondered when Cesar paused at the door. Turning away, she continued her chat with Jess. They had a lot to talk about. They both had to put up with her brothers.

Her gaze strayed out of window. Cesar was tipping well water over his head. She clenched and unfurled her fingers, remembering how he'd felt beneath her hands.

Droplets of water went flying from his thick black hair when he shook his head like an angry wolf. His torso was gleaming and wet. How was she supposed to feel nothing for this man?

'Sofia?'

She turned to face Jess. 'I'm sorry... Forgive me. I was distracted.'

Jess grinned. 'Who wouldn't be? Anyway, I was just saying, prepare to be exhausted tomorrow. There's less than a month to go before the first match. These might be exhibition matches, but you know as well as I do that when your brothers and Cesar are playing against a rival like Nero Caracas, there's no such thing as a friendly game.'

Jess wasn't exaggerating. Nero and his team Assassin were their closest rivals. 'Work us hard. Give us every advantage you can. The rest is up to fate, and how we play on the day.'

Placing her hand over Sofia's, Jess gave it a squeeze as she whispered discreetly, 'I know how worried you are, but you don't need to worry about Cesar. He's overcome mountains before, and knows how to handle himself. Concentrate on looking after yourself.'

'Thank you.' *For being my friend* didn't need to be said.

Sofia glanced through the window at Cesar. Another lonely night beckoned, and then a new day with all that that entailed.

'Need a leg-up?'

She looked around to see Cesar standing behind her. Feelings swamped her.

'No, thanks. I can manage.'

'Please yourself.' With a shrug, he sprang into the saddle and cantered into the arena.

Jess placed Sofia behind Cesar in the line, which taunted Sofia with the sight of a back view as good as his front. Powerful and unyielding, Cesar's mighty shoulders and straight spine could have been a metaphor for the way he lived.

Her heart clenched at the thought of any harm coming to him during the matches. They would be rough, they would be hard; neither side would give way without a fight. And then there was the blackmailer she had to deal with, which was like coping with a virus, sneaky and unpredictable, working in the shadows to bring a victim down—

'Sofia, are you with us?' Jess was calling from across the ring. 'Change direction now!'

Sofia wheeled her pony around just in time to avoid a collision with Xander, who blasted her with a derisive look as he cantered past.

In the unlikely event that Cesar spares the time to actually hold a conversation with you, how likely is it that he'll jump at the chance to help you with your blackmailer?

She had to hope pretty high. Like her brothers, Cesar was a man of principle—

'Sofia!' Jess rode up alongside. 'Do you need to take a break?'

'No. Sorry. I'm on it.'

'I hope so. Carelessness leads to accidents at this level of training.'

'It won't happen again, Jess.'

Just as she would never, *ever* write another article. Now all she had to do was persuade Cesar of that, and that the original article had been so heavily doctored she'd hardly recognised it.

Well, that should be easy, she reflected as Cesar gave her a black look for reckless riding.

Easy or not, it had to be done.

Her chance came at the end of the afternoon session when everyone left to freshen up. Sofia's legs felt like wood. She couldn't remember working so hard on a horse, and for the first time in her memory she stumbled when she dismounted.

Cesar was at her side in an instant, steadying her with one hand firmly lodged beneath her arm. 'Too much for you? You made a bit of a mess of today's training. Maybe don't ask Jess to make things harder tomorrow?' he suggested dryly. 'Was there any particular reason behind your request to make things hard for you?'

She chose to ignore that question. 'Training's hard for all of us. I can take it.'

Cesar gave her a critical look. 'Can you?'

Ignoring that too, she focused on the one thing that mattered. 'I have to talk to you—and I mean talk. To clear the air,' she explained when Cesar remained silent.

'It will take more than a chat to do that.' He was already turning away. 'Barbecue this evening,' he announced.

'Cesar, please,' she insisted, grabbing a moment alone as soon as he'd finished spelling out the details. 'We can't go on like this, not if we hope to play well as a team.'

He stared at her hand on his arm. She stood back. Good enough for sex, she wasn't good enough for Cesar to engage in conversation apparently. Now she was mad. Which was unfortunate timing, as the stable hands had arrived to take charge of the ponies.

'If only you were so caring about your human counterparts,' Cesar observed, holding the door for her to pass through as they left the building.

She always spelled out her pony's preferences, and mentioned any worries she might have about the animal's condition after hard training.

Her heart lurched as their hands brushed. How was she ever going to concentrate when that was all it took? She had to. She must. She couldn't lose her brother, and she couldn't lose Cesar. 'There's something you need to know.'

'Sounds intriguing.' He speared her with a stare until it was hard to believe she had any secrets left.

'Can we talk now?'

He shrugged. 'I can spare you five minutes.'

She'd take it. 'Thanks.'

'Follow me—'

'No.' She shook her head. 'I need you to follow me.'

Without looking back to see if Cesar was following, she led the way to what had quickly become Sofia's favourite place on Cesar's ranch. It was a secluded spot by the river, where she could read and think, not that she got much spare time to do either. Her destination was a woodland grove where she could sit, sheltered by a copse of trees. It was an idyllic spot on the banks of a fast-flowing river, but it wasn't easy to reach, which was half of its attraction. Few made the effort, so it was completely private. Brambles on the ground threatened to trip unwary visitors, but for someone brought up in the country like Sofia, who was accustomed to trekking over difficult ground, it was a hidden treasure.

She could hear Cesar's long strides behind her. He had to hear her out, then he could send her home if he wanted to. Either way, she had to make a stand.

'My mother used to being me here,' Cesar revealed when they stood on the banks of the fast-flowing river. 'It was part of my introduction to a brighter world, she'd tell me. A world where things are clean, and clear, if you remain still and allow yourself to hear.'

Would he? Would he allow himself to hear? With all her heart, she hoped he would.

'When I was older, I'd come here on my own to think.'

'Did it help?' she asked, wanting to open this window onto Cesar's early life wide.

'Five minutes,' he reminded her, closing off. 'So you'd better be fast. What do you want to talk to me about?'

If that was the way he was going to play it, she'd be just as blunt. 'I'm being blackmailed.'

Obviously shocked, Cesar recovered fast. 'Go on,' he prompted.

'I signed up to write a light, fluffy piece for a fee I could plough into my retreat. At the time I had no idea Howard Blake was such an unscrupulous man, or that he would seize the opportunity to take my material and doctor it beyond all recognition. Now he's threatening to publish more articles under my name. I'm guessing they won't do you or my brothers any favours. I don't know why he's got it in for you. I do know my reputation will be ruined, but that's nothing in comparison to losing the love and trust of my brothers, and causing you more harm. If I could wind back the clock, and change things, I would, but...'

Cesar was staring out across the stream in silence. 'Did you hear me?'

'Every word.' he assured her.

She couldn't believe how calm he was, though alert like a wolf on point.

'Your five minutes are up.'

There was no warmth in his voice as he swung around to head back up the bank. 'But—'

'I promised you five minutes,' he said, briefly turning. 'You've had that and more.'

'But, please, I—'

'Don't,' Cesar warned quietly. 'How could the chance to see your by-line above an article in a national newspaper prove such a lure you were prepared to throw your brothers under a bus and me along with them?'

'Weren't you listening? It wasn't like that. Those weren't my words.'

'So you say. What I read was invented scandal. Maybe you dressed up the facts until they provided outrageous amounts of click bait with no basis of truth. How do I know? How can I be sure of you, Sofia? The dates on which your accusations were based were entirely accurate, but the events you wrote about never happened.'

'Because I didn't write them!' she exploded, growing increasingly frustrated. 'Believe me, Cesar. Have I ever given you cause to doubt me before?'

'How well did I know you before?' he countered.

'Do you seriously believe I would hurt those I love—or, almost worse, those vulnerable individuals recovering at my retreat? If you think so little of me, I'm wasting my time.'

'Maybe you are,' he agreed.

'I need help,' she admitted grimly as she clambered up the bank to join him. 'What started out as what I thought was a normal relationship between an enthusiastic amateur journalist and a newspaper mogul quickly turned sour. If Blake can do that to me and get away with it, how many more people are at risk? He has to be stopped, and I can't do this on my own.'

There was a silence she thought would never end, and then Cesar said the words she had hoped and prayed he would. 'This is not something you can handle on your own,' he agreed. 'I know Blake from our schooldays together. We attended the same boarding school. He was the class bully, picking on younger boys with no one to defend them.'

'So you defended them,' she said.

A grim smile firmed Cesar's lips as he thought back. 'It was a full-time occupation.'

'And one he never forgave you for,' she guessed.

Cesar nodded briefly. 'Blake was the type to bear grudges. I always suspected him of being behind the swindler who tried to steal the throne by cosying up to my mother. There have been numerous attacks over the years.'

'Of which I'm just the latest?'

'Don't beat yourself up,' Cesar said, to her surprise. 'You couldn't know how devious he was, or how he would use you to get at me.'

Hope surged through her. 'So you believe me?'

'I'm giving you the benefit of the doubt,' Cesar prevaricated.

'I handed him ammunition on a plate.'

'To help your retreat.'

'Yes.' Still reeling from the thought that Cesar might believe her, and that he might help after all, she asked the obvious question. 'Why have you never hit back at him before?'

'Make myself as small as him?' Cesar shook his head. 'There are other, more efficient ways to deal with a bully like Blake, subtle ways that will keep him in a moral cage.'

CHAPTER TEN

CURIOUS TO HEAR MORE, Sofia continued with her explanation. 'To start with, it seemed as if fate had dropped an opportunity into my hand. 'Writing "a piece of fluff" for the features page was how Lord Blake put it. It seemed such a good opportunity to bring in much-needed money to support the expansion of my retreat.'

'Easy money?' Cesar challenged. 'There's no such thing. You should have been suspicious right away.'

'It's easy to be wise in retrospect,' Sofia argued, 'but when you've spent months casting about for ways to keep things running, you're open to any idea that seems remotely feasible.'

'Writing an article exposing the antics of the super-rich seemed feasible to you?'

'That wasn't how I phrased it. There was no mention of "super-rich". I wrote about humorous incidents that happened on the world tour. None of them were scandalous or libellous. I certainly didn't depict you as an "elitist degenerate", which was one of the descriptions used. What I wrote made you and my brothers seem approachable. It was supposed to make people laugh, not cause trouble.'

'Blake couldn't have doctored the piece without your ready supply of facts,' Cesar pointed out.

'But that's just it. Some of those facts I didn't even know. How could I? I don't have access to your diary. So now do you see why I need your help?'

As Cesar's thoughtful gaze rested on her face, she felt a great sense of weariness at her seemingly endless attempts to try to explain what had happened. Why wouldn't he take her at her word? She'd never knowingly told a lie, and had believed that as soon as she opened up, Cesar would believe her.

It didn't take much for weariness to turn into anger. Staring at Cesar's back as he made his way home was the final straw. Catching up, she stood grim-faced in his way. 'At least have the courtesy to let me know what you think.'

Lifting her aside, he moved on.

'I expect a fair hearing, and all I get is ignored? How do you expect anyone to stop Howard Blake if you turn your back and walk away?'

'I'm not ignoring you, but this is not the time,' he said, striding on.

'Not the time?' She caught up. 'What do you mean? What else is going on?'

At least he stopped walking.

'You're the only person I know who wields as much power as Howard Blake,' she pressed. 'Maybe more. Definitely more. If anyone can stop him, you can. Cesar, if your back was to the wall, wouldn't you do anything to make things right?'

'I've never been in that position.'

'I'm glad, but please have sympathy for those who aren't so lucky. I have to believe you can stop Blake hurting anyone else.'

She was puzzled when he didn't answer. 'Is there something you're not telling me?'

'It was a very different situation. A member of my family was under attack.'

Lifting her chin, she braced herself and ignored the sting. 'Family loyalty is paramount to me too, which is why I would never intentionally hurt my brothers. Blake will dig and dig until he finds something to use. He has to be stopped. You must be thinking I've got a cheek, asking you for help, but who else can I turn to?'

'Your brothers?' Cesar suggested in a dead tone.

'I've always wanted to stand on my own two feet. I caused this problem, so it's up to me to sort it out.'

'But you're asking for my help,' he pointed out impatiently. 'I don't see the difference.'

'You have a certain reputation when it comes to dealing with difficult people. Didn't you mention subtlety? I'm calling on your expertise.'

'Save your flattery.'

'I'll stop at nothing to prevent Howard Blake causing any more trouble. If I involve my brothers and they bring in the weight of the Acosta lawyers, this could run and run, doing more harm than good. I'm trying to avoid that.'

'You must have a record of the original article on your computer to prove that it was changed?'

'Conveniently, my computer was stolen when burglars targeted my home.'

'Stolen from your retreat?'

'Yes.'

'Do you vet the people you allow in? Your brothers tell me there's very little security.'

'That was the whole point. I wanted people to feel free, not trapped.'

'Oh, Sofia, Sofia.' Cesar gave her a long, considering look. 'I'm beginning to think that you tried to do your best—'

'If you're going to be patronising—'

'Stop,' he commanded.

She tensed at the touch of his hand on her arm.

'Sometimes a warm heart can put you at a disadvantage.'

Cesar's tone was gentle, but she had no intention of being treated like a child. Bringing Howard Blake down would take both of them equally.

Giving herself a moment, she refocused her mind. This wasn't about pride or personal considerations, but getting a job done. 'How did you stop him last time?' she asked briskly, turning to stare Cesar in the eyes.

'Money talks?' He sounded faintly amused, as if he had accepted both her stand and the fact that massive wealth could be useful in a number of ways. 'My last run-in with Blake involved a member of my family, someone else with a kind heart, falling into Blake's clutches. It was necessary to step in to protect that family member.'

'Your mother?' Sofia guessed.

Cesar was too protective and too discreet to answer her question, both of which counted in his favour.

'Howard Blake was silenced, and that's all you need to know. He got to keep his publishing empire in a deal that suited us both.'

It was hard to imagine Blake, a man who had bullied and hectored *her*, turning over meekly, though coming up against Cesar would be daunting, she imagined, even for a man as unscrupulous as Howard Blake. Her brother Xander had once referred to Cesar as being the most resourceful and determined individual he'd ever met, adding that Cesar always protected those who needed him. 'I never thought I was Blake's first target, and I'm sure I won't be the last. I'm strong enough to take the consequences, but what about the next person he picks on?'

'So what's your plan?'

'From what you've told me, and from personal experience, we know Blake can't stop himself targeting those weaker than himself. It's like an addiction. You've already dealt with him successfully, and I'm lucky to have you onside. I do have you onside?' She went on before Cesar had a chance to answer. 'We can't hang his future targets out to dry. We can't turn our backs. We have to stop him. Someone has to bring him to account.'

'You?' Cesar interrupted with a cynical lift of his brow.

'I can't do this without your help,' she said honestly.

'So you propose co-operation between us?'

'Is that so bad?'

Sofia's voice was quiet and intense. Her stare remained fixed on his face. How could he remain unsympathetic when Blake had targeted both his mother and his sister? His mother had taken a lover, a conman planted by Blake, he now thought, and there was a sex tape featuring Olivia. These were Blake's weapons of choice. Rage roared inside him as he recognised Sofia as an equally attractive target for a bully. Desperate to keep the retreat that meant so much to her going at any cost, she was exactly the type of victim Howard Blake loved to prey on. Sofia must have been a prized victim, giving Blake direct access to the Acosta brothers and his old enemy Cesar. How he must have gloated, thinking he could send them all down like a line of dominoes.

'Cesar?'

Fury must have been written on his face. Most would shrink from it, but not Sofia. She stood to confront him and barred his way, 'We'll call him out,' she said fiercely.

He raised a brow. 'How do you propose to do that?'

'We'll set a trap. We'll feed him false information and then expose it as a lie.'

'He'll see that coming a mile off,' he reflected out loud. 'The confrontation has to be face to face. So I'll deal with him.' He held up his hand when she started to argue. 'I don't want you anywhere near him. This is something I will handle alone.'

Even as he was speaking, an idea was niggling at his brain. There was no time to waste. He had investigations to make. 'Is that it?'

Sofia reached out a hand as if to stop him, but then she withdrew it and lowered her gaze in a way that made her seem suddenly fragile. 'You go on,' she said. 'I'd like to stay here for a while.'

'Be back before dark. Remember the Apennine wolves. They roam freely in the forest.'

'I won't forget. I can look after myself. Remember?'

She stared up, her eyes luminous and unblinking. He didn't move. He couldn't move. How could he leave her alone in the forest? The light was fading, and there was more than one wolf on the prowl. Sofia had made a dangerous enemy in Howard Blake, and Cesar would take no chances. 'You're coming with me so I know that you're safe.'

'A few minutes ago you'd have liked to throw me in the stream,' she commented with amusement.

'Never,' he assured her. 'I'd only have to jump in and save you.'

'I'd save myself,' she insisted, lifting her chin.

'And how would you do that?'

'I'd do it somehow,' she assured him stubbornly.

Somehow wouldn't help her with Howard Blake. 'I do need you to do something for me,' he revealed as they started to walk back.

'Tell me.'

'The best way to show Blake he can't hurt you, let alone destroy your brothers and me, as he seems to think he can, is by making sure we win those matches and raise more money than even Howard Blake can dream of for our charities.'

'You're cutting me out,' she said with affront, having read the subtext behind his words. 'You can't do this alone. Cesar— what are you going to do?'

'It's better that you don't know. That no one knows.'

'Don't you trust me?'

She was hurt when he didn't answer right away, but his mind was made up. Keeping Sofia safe, saving her brothers and even a country from the spite of Howard Blake, was more important than explanations. 'Be the best you can be,' he advised. 'That's your revenge when it comes to Howard Blake.'

There were tears in her eyes, he realised when he turned to look at Sofia. She had guts but a tender underbelly, reminding him that emotions did matter, whether he liked it or not. 'Don't worry about Blake. I'll deal with him, so he never hurts anyone else. And when this is over,' he added in an attempt to turn her mind from the dark side to something lighter, 'I'll commission a portrait of the winning team.'

For a moment he thought his offer had missed the mark. In fairness, contemplating the evil of a man like Blake then switching to the prospect of the quiet contemplation involved when Sofia picked up her brush and paints was quite a stretch, but one Sofia had to make if she was ever to sleep easily again.

He should have known she was equal to the task.

'The winning team had better not be Nero Caracas and the Assassins,' she said, smiling in a way that touched him somewhere deep. 'I don't have enough black paint.'

It had been good to walk back to the ranch house with Cesar with some ease at last between them. It made her hopeful that other things could change for the better.

But now, back in her room, without the beauty of the countryside surrounding her, she had started to worry again—primarily about Cesar. His promise to 'handle things'. What did that mean? If Cesar could deal with Howard Blake help without putting himself at risk, that was one thing, but she had never intended him to do this on his own.

Getting ready for dinner involved showering before changing into clean jeans and a casual top for the promised barbecue. Staring at her reflection in the mirror above the sink, she craved the chance for them to continue getting to know each other outside sex. They'd made a small start down by the river, but would he take things further? It took two to form a relationship, and Cesar's wishes were one thing determination alone couldn't influence.

Cesar hosted the barbecue. He got on so well with her brothers. Jess and Olivia came straight over to welcome her. 'Okay?' Jess asked. 'Nothing aching too much?'

Only my heart, she thought, smiling. 'I'm fine.'

Olivia came up with some startling news. 'I've seen the looks that pass between you and my brother. Jess and I have been talking, and you don't need to tell us that Howard Blake set you up. Jess knows everything about my run-in with Blake, so if you need allies, look no further.'

'Thank you.'

'Take my advice,' Olivia continued. 'First find the mole.'

'The mole?' Sofia frowned.

'Someone filmed me secretly. I don't know if you heard about the tape?' Olivia pressed. 'Anyway, it was explicit,' she continued, sparing Sofia the need to answer, 'and somehow it found its way to Howard Blake. That someone is almost certainly the same person who supplied the dates and details you couldn't. Someone helped Blake doctor that article. I know it wasn't you, and it most certainly wasn't me.'

An unseen enemy was one to fear the most. Fear tightened around Sofia's heart. She drew a deep breath, and pushed it aside. 'Do you have any suspects in mind?'

'I do,' Olivia confirmed, 'but I can't prove anything yet. We'll speak again,' she promised.

Sofia's mind was spinning as Olivia moved away. Cesar's sister had left her with more questions than answers. Cesar's bottomless resources would open many doors, but now Sofia wished she hadn't asked him for help. The thought of putting Cesar in danger was the worst nightmare imaginable. She had to put things right. Quite how she was going to do that, she had no idea yet. Olivia only proved that caution must be her watchword.

'I thought it was me you wanted to talk to, not my sister,' Cesar remarked dryly as he loaded Sofia's plate with food.

'Steady. Am I not allowed to speak to your sister? No more food,' she insisted, laughing as he continued to stack it on her plate. 'You're not feeding my brothers.'

'I'll take your plate to the table,' he offered.

Everyone else was seated by the time they arrived. Sofia sat on a bench facing her brothers, while Cesar straddled the end of it, so he was facing her.

'Olivia is a hothead,' he informed her. 'Don't believe everything she says.'

'Even if what Olivia says makes sense?' Sofia queried.

Cesar shrugged. 'Just don't allow her to draw you into one of her ill-thought-out schemes.'

'What makes you think I don't have schemes of my own?'

'If you do, I must insist you run them past me first.'

She almost choked on her burger. Chugging down a glass of water, she shook her head. 'I can't believe you sometimes. You mentioned co-operation? I get that. Putting safeguards in place is only sensible, but to defer to you on every decision I make?'

'I'm trying to keep you safe, Sofia.'

'And I'm trying to keep you safe,' she reminded him. Glancing around, she tried to work out who the mole might be. Each group was an island separate from the rest, but could any of them be guilty of betraying Cesar's trust? It seemed unlikely.

'I have a lot of things to put right and I don't expect you, or anyone else, to do that for me,' she stated firmly. 'I may not have your seemingly limitless resources, but neither am I incapable.'

'Or as experienced as me at dealing with sharks like Howard Blake,' Cesar pointed out.

'I'm a fast learner.'

'Fast learners listen to advice.'

Sitting back, she closed her eyes briefly. 'Do you have any idea how annoying you can be?'

Cesar flashed a quick and, oh, so welcome smile. 'Some.'

'Well, just forget I said anything. I shouldn't have asked you for help.'

'That's a matter of opinion. Howard Blake is a slippery character.'

'All the more reason to stop him.'

'But not on your own.' Cesar articulated each word in a low, fierce tone.

With a laugh she pushed her plate away. 'Anyone would think you care.'

'I do care,' Cesar insisted, surprising her, but just as happy surprise leapt onto her face he added, 'I'm not looking for more tangles to unpick before the match. The clock is ticking. None of us can afford to be distracted. You expected something more?' he enquired, when she couldn't hide her shock.

Recovering fast, she said coolly, 'Why would I?'

'We can't talk here,' Cesar said, frowning. 'It's too noisy. My study...' He stood.

She'd seen his study. Desk. Floor. Rug. Hard chairs. Easy chairs. Inviting sofas. All options open. But to persuade Cesar not to do anything that might put him danger, was this the best chance she'd get?

CHAPTER ELEVEN

LEAVING THE TABLE, she joined Cesar as they walked the short distance to the ranch house. Once inside they went straight to Cesar's study, where he directed her to an easy chair. He remained standing with his hip propped against the desk. 'So talk,' he invited.

'I've got nothing new to say. I just don't want you doing anything on my behalf that puts you in danger.'

'How much of your own money have you put into your retreat?'

'Every penny. And I mortgaged the property,' she admitted. 'I had to so I could take on more people.'

Cesar's look grew cynical. 'Were you planning to write more articles to fund this expansion?'

'No! Of course not! How can you even think that?'

'I'm curious as to how you intended to support yourself going forward.'

'I thought selling my paintings might help.' That sounded so lame now. How did she know anyone would buy them? So far she'd had a commission from her brother and the sniff of a promise from Cesar. That wouldn't be enough to support her retreat.

'How much do you need?' Cesar asked bluntly.

'I don't want a loan,' she said. 'I'll find the money.'

'You have a money tree?'

'I'll listen to any suggestions you care to make, but I won't sit on my hands while you go into battle on my behalf.'

'It's time to accept that you can't carry the world on your shoulders. I'm sure your brothers would be only too eager to help you if you didn't push them away.'

'I haven't pushed them away. It takes them all their time to speak to me.'

There was silence for a while and then Cesar reflected, 'I guess it must have been hard as a teenager in a household of over-protective brothers.'

'You have no idea,' she agreed, relaxing enough to smile as she thought back.

'I think I do,' Cesar argued. 'My sister was left without a father, and when my mother recovered from her grief she was... distracted, shall we say? I was in the Special Forces, and it was only when Olivia alerted me to trouble—and, believe me, Olivia seeks help from no one—that I left the army to save the throne from an unscrupulous man. So I'm not exactly out of practice when it comes to dealing with problems. I'd go as far as to say I'm your best hope.'

Maybe her only hope. 'Okay, but we do this together or not at all.'

'Too many chiefs,' Cesar cautioned.

'You're not suggesting I leave it all to you?'

'It's not a suggestion,' he assured her.

'Not my way either,' she said, firming her jaw.

Cesar went to stare out of the window. 'My mother grieved long and hard for my father,' he said without turning around. 'Years passed and then she took a lover. Howard Blake's press were all over it. I was still in the army when the palace made an announcement that this man from nowhere, no history, no relatives, no obvious experience to make him a suitable candidate to support the Queen in her duties, planned to join her on the throne.'

'As your mother's equal?' Sofia asked with surprise. 'I didn't realise it went that far.' The throne should rightfully pass to Cesar, and she could only imagine how he must have felt, or how delicately he'd had to handle the situation without upsetting his mother, who must have been very vulnerable at the time. That, as well as protecting Olivia from a scandal, made her wonder if Cesar ever spared a thought for himself.

'What's your plan?' he asked as he swung around.

She didn't want to talk about herself, or what *she* was going to do. She wanted to talk about Cesar so she could try to understand this deep and complex man. In short order, Cesar had lost his father, found himself head of a prominent family, and been thrown into the turmoil of fixing his mother and sister's lives. He could only do that by pushing his feelings aside. Joining the Special Forces might have given the wild youth an anchor, but he'd been forced to give that up. Cesar's recent life seemed to have been one of constant sacrifice, and now she was throwing up yet another hurdle.

She understood his mother's reasons. Grief could throw anyone off kilter. Sofia had always tried to live up to what she believed were her dead parents' expectations of her, but this time, like the Queen, she'd gone too far. If she'd called a halt when she'd built a small retreat with limited places, none of this would have happened. But so many had applied to go there. How could she choose who could stay and who to turn away?

'So what next, Sofia?'

Cesar was waiting for her answer. He had the world on his shoulders already, and now he expected her to load him down with more.

'Sofia?' he pressed.

'I plan to turn my fledgling investigative skills on Howard Blake,' she revealed.

'Hoping he has an Achilles heel?' Cesar guessed.

'I have to hope so,' she confessed. 'But it's more than that. I want to understand his jealousy towards you and the way he'll stop at nothing to destroy you, even using me.'

'I can't argue with that,' Cesar admitted. 'I've thought the same thing myself.'

'So we do agree on something?' she said wryly, hoping she was right.

When Cesar didn't answer, she decided it was time for bed. Getting up from her chair, she said, 'If I do find out anything else that might be helpful, I'll let you know.'

'You do that,' Cesar agreed. 'Goodnight, Sofia.'

'Goodnight.'

He didn't call her back or come after her. And, of course, she was glad about that.

Was she?

The sound of the door closing behind Sofia rang in Cesar's ears for some time. Not that she was angry, or even disappointed he hadn't pulled a rabbit out of a hat to show her when it came to his plans for Howard Blake. When he did decide what to do, he'd be the only one with that information. It was safer that way.

External influences hadn't made Sofia leave in such a hurry, he concluded, but the pull between them had done the damage. They'd shared a look. She'd moistened her lips. Her cheeks had flushed pink and her breathing quickened, but instead of taking things further he'd made it clear that wasn't going to happen, at which point she'd left the room. Sex was the answer to a lot of things, but not this.

Exhaling a long, steady breath, he sat back. What was this woman doing to him? When things looked as if they might become complicated by feelings, he always pulled back. Capable of feeling the deepest emotion, he also knew how to hide it well, thanks to understanding the cost of love. He had idolised his father, the strongest and noblest of men, but still found it hard to accept that a fall from a horse during training could have brought such a well-lived life to a sudden and unalterable end.

He and his father were the same in that they solved problems and found solutions. His father's tragic death was the first time Cesar had been faced by a catastrophe he could neither change nor soften. The end of one way of living and the beginning of another, quite different life had been brutal. One minute his father had been laughing and joking, poised and confident as he'd cantered around the arena, and the next his horse had stumbled, throwing him over its head. And that was it. The end. Over. Never to move, breathe, speak, or offer loving advice again.

Everything had changed on that day. His mother had been hysterical, his sister numb with shock. From a confident, hard-living youth, home on furlough from the army, he had been catapulted into a world where caring for people was more important than crowns. Stability for family and country had become his guiding light from that moment on, just as personal feelings had become a complete and utter irrelevance. All that mattered had been putting things back on an even keel.

The bombshell of the King's death had spread a shroud of fear across the citizens of Ardente Sestieri as people had wondered what would come next. Prince Cesar, the wild youth whose exploits had entertained them, was surely not fit to be King? Cesar's lifestyle hadn't mattered to his people when his father had been alive, but for such a solid and reliable presence on the throne to be replaced by someone unknown had taken a lot a lot of living down. The trust he'd won since then could be lost in a heartbeat.

At one point he'd wondered how his mother would survive the loss of his father. They had been two sides of the same coin. How would that one, lonely side of the coin weather the wear and tear of ruling, with only one face, one opinion, one decision-maker to hold the reins, with no one to advise, curb or recommend? His mother had needed him to step up, and he'd answered her call gladly. With her so-called suitor dismissed, the Queen would rule alone with Cesar as her chief advisor. Nothing must stand in the way of that.

It was in everyone's interest to bring Howard Blake to account. But there was another reason. Sofia had shown him her vulnerable side. He couldn't walk away from that. This was a time to keep her close. He had to, if he was to keep her safe.

What other reason could there be?

Pushing his chair back, he left his study to track her down.

He found her in the empty stable where she had gone to sort out her thoughts. Whatever else was going on in her life, animals always soothed her. Cesar lost no time in delivering his broadside. 'I can't let you approach Howard Blake on your own. I won't allow it!'

Brain and body moved as one for Cesar, and he was in front of her in a heartbeat. Scrambling to her feet, she faced him down. 'Cesar—'

'Yes, Cesar!' he cut across her. 'Who the hell else do you think would chase you down to stop you walking blindfold into danger?'

He really cared? She could see the concern in his eyes. How did she feel about that? Thrilled. Surprised. And also keenly aware that Cesar's concern could stand in the way of her setting things right.

'I'm glad you came,' she said, quickly marshalling her thoughts. 'I wanted to let you know what I've done so far.'

'What you've done?' Far from this enticing him to back off, Cesar's expression was thunderous. 'Without telling me first?'

'My plans are still in the very early stages,' she explained in what she hoped was a soothing tone. 'I won't need an army or strong-arm tactics—'

'Just tell me what you've done,' Cesar bit out.

'I just made a call.'

'Who did you call?' She'd never seen him like this. She could only describe it as anguished. 'Tell me what you've done, Sofia. I hope you haven't put yourself in danger?'

'I called a woman who lives at my retreat, the same woman who passed on the original request from Howard Blake for me to write an article. I trusted her. Dante always says I trust everyone too quickly. Now I must face the possibility that Dante's right, and this woman and Howard might be in league.'

Cesar frowned. 'But how would she know the dates in my diary?'

'Maybe there's more than one conspirator,' Sofia allowed. 'Howard Blake's pockets are deep enough to hire an army of moles. All I offer is a haven until people are ready to face the world again, while he offers a lot of money. Who could blame her if she was tempted?'

'I could,' Cesar said coldly. 'You're far too soft, Sofia.'

'I'm not soft at all,' she argued, 'but I do know what it's like to feel you've no control over your life, and to wonder and fear what's coming next. Seizing back even a little bit of control in those circumstances feels good.'

Cesar dismissed this with an impatient huff. 'You credit the person who quite possibly betrayed you with finer feelings than they deserve. If you have a suspect you should let me follow it up. I have the resources,' he pointed out. 'And whatever our differences, I would never allow someone to harm you and get away with it.'

'But you have enough to do.' Having asked Cesar for help, she was having second thoughts. He did have enough to do, and she had only made things harder.

'You don't know what you're up against,' he said with an impatient gesture.

'But I do, and I also have a theory as to why this is escalating. Jealousy,' she declared. 'I know it makes no sense when Blake's as rich as Croesus, but for some people even too much is never enough.'

Cesar didn't argue, but holding his stare for any length of

time was never a good idea. Her body was always ready to seize the smallest cue, and this was not the right time to do that. This felt like the first time they'd ever talked, really talked, and both of them had listened. Surely that was something worth preserving and treasuring? All she'd wanted had been to build the connection between them and hopefully watch it turn into something deeper and more meaningful. Yes, her body burned to feel his touch again, nothing had changed where that was concerned, but now her heart yearned for company.

'You will not do this on your own. Understood?'

Cesar's instruction jolted her out of gentler thoughts. 'Don't forget I survived a house full of brothers,' she reminded him.

'Howard Blake is nothing like your brothers, and I shouldn't need to tell you that.'

'You don't,' she said, 'but if you think I'm going to sit on my butt, doing nothing, you're wrong. You have a country to consider, as well as a mother and sister to protect. Your duty lies there. I got into this mess, and now I'm going to get out of it.'

'I won't release you from your training,' Cesar told her with a closing gesture of his hands.

He wasn't used to being countermanded, let alone be taken out of the game, but Sofia was in no mood to give ground. 'You can't stop me,' she said. 'We're here because we choose to be here, not because you commanded our attendance. All of us are successful in our own right—some more successful than others,' she conceded with a shrug, 'but seriously, Cesar, you can leave this to me.'

'Seriously, Sofia,' he mocked with venom, 'that will never happen, so put it out of your mind.'

He swung her round so fast the air was sucked from her lungs. The time for calm reason had gone. 'Do you seriously think I'll allow you to risk your life? Don't you realise there's a kingdom at stake and that's what he's after? Blake tried once with my mother, dangling a gigolo in front of her. Do you think he'd care what happens to you? You'll be collateral damage—

just another counter for Blake to play and discard when it suits him. I won't allow you to do that—for your sake, and for the sake of everyone who cares about you. Your life is worth nothing to Howard Blake. *Nothing!* Don't you get it?'

Cesar's face was very close. His eyes scorched hers. She'd never seen so much passion in one man. Perhaps because Cesar never showed emotion it seemed all the greater now. Whatever it was she felt, it was not the urge to pull away or even to stand on tiptoe to give him a kiss—*definitely not that*. What she felt, deep down, through every fibre of her being was the urge to reassure him. Cesar had been through enough. 'I'm not your responsibility, and I promise I won't get hurt. I'll be back to play in the matches before you know it. And we'll win—in every way there is,' she added with icy resolve.

He couldn't believe what he was hearing, and frankly he'd had enough. Sofia appeared convinced that fairy-tales could come true and that good would prevail over evil. She refused to see the danger. Whatever he said fell would fall on deaf ears. Fortunately, he'd cut his teeth on an equally wilful sister so he was in familiar territory. 'I'll bar you from leaving the kingdom if I have to. I'm not joking, Sofia.'

But the sterner his tone, the brighter grew the gleam of amusement in Sofia's eyes. 'What's wrong with you?' he demanded. But he knew. He'd seen the same thing on the battlefield. In a hazardous situation humour often showed itself, as if to thumb its nose at danger. That was the case here. Sofia thought she knew the person she was dealing with, but he really knew.

'Whatever it takes,' he warned as he took hold of her arms. His mouth was so close to hers now they shared the same breath, the same air. Her eyes held challenge, and however much he glowered back she smiled at him, until the laugh she'd been smothering broke free. 'You think this is funny?' he demanded. 'Or are you addicted to playing with fire?'

Her expression changed. Her eyes filled with an expression

he rejected, not need or passion—compassion. 'Stop looking at me like that,' he warned.

'Someone should,' she said coolly.

'What are you talking about?' Letting her go, he stood back.

'It must be lonely in your ivory tower. I was hoping I could pay a visit and get to know you.'

'Isn't that what we've been doing?'

She slowly shook her head. 'So far you've lectured me and I've listened, but now I'm going to tell you what I'm doing next.'

'You think?' he scoffed.

When reason failed, his instinct took over.

CHAPTER TWELVE

As Cesar drove his mouth down on hers, she knew that if there hadn't been so much pent-up longing inside her she would have... *What? Pushed him away?*

Not a chance. Caring and hunger mixed in one fiercely compassionate need to be close to him. Pulling his head back, he stared down and smiled. 'Must you always choose a stable for your amorous encounters?'

'I didn't invite you to join me,' she countered, challenge firing in her eyes.

'Didn't you?' Cesar queried as he smoothly dispensed with her clothes. He was in even more of a hurry than she was, and she was desperate for release. Every part of her ached for him and rejoiced when he lifted her so she could lock her legs around his waist. Breath escaped her lungs in a long-drawn-out sigh as he plunged deep.

'Excellent,' Cesar growled, throwing his head back in ecstasy as he slammed her against the wall.

Ripping his top out of the waistband of his jeans, she rested her face against his hard, warm chest and made a comment of her own.

'Your wish is my command,' Cesar informed her, losing no

time before thrusting her screaming and bucking with pleasure into the abyss.

Grinding her fingers into his buttocks, she urged him on.

'Good?' he asked much, much later when she was quiet again.

She smiled up. 'What do you think?'

'Once is never enough?'

She laughed. Cesar had made her greedy. 'I swear, if you stop now, tease me, or make me wait, I'll—'

'You'll what?' he demanded in a low growl.

Nuzzling her neck, he whispered encouragement in his own language, which stole what little control she had left. 'Yes! *Yes!*' she begged, as breath shot out of her when Cesar plunged deep.

One powerful release stormed into the next. Rotating his hips made her more sensitive that she could ever have believed. Speech was impossible. Breathing was hard. Fractured shrieks of enjoyment was the best she could manage, while Cesar made sure he held her where he wanted her.

'I can't hold on,' she wailed at one point.

'You're not supposed to,' he said as he encouraged her to work her hips to the same greedy rhythm as his. 'Wildcat!' he approved when she dug her fingers into his shoulders.

'Faster! Harder!' Would she ever get enough?

The next climax came out of nowhere. She was powerless to resist. It was bigger, and far sweeter in its intensity than anything that had gone before. It seemed like for ever before the pleasure waves subsided, and when they did she was as helpless as a kitten, resting limp in Cesar's arms.

'Don't tell me I've finally exhausted you,' he remarked wryly as he lowered her carefully to the floor.

'I doubt you could ever do that,' she admitted, feeling warm and safe as he wrapped her in his arms and dipped his head to brush tender kisses against her mouth. 'But was that just to calm me, so I'll do anything you say?'

'Calm?' he queried. 'Are you in a different realm from me?'

'Answer my question.'

He held out his hands...the same hands that had held her safe and pleasured her until she could think of nothing else. 'What more do you want me to say, Sofia?'

'Reassurance that I haven't fallen for some sort of charm offensive,' she said bluntly.

'Surely you're not that insecure.'

Who knew what they were until they were tested? she wondered. Since getting together with Cesar everything mattered so much to her, too much maybe.

'Just tell me this didn't happen because you threatened you'd do whatever it took to bring me into line?'

'I have needs, just like you,' he dismissed.

'That's not an answer. Is that all it is?'

'Should there be more?'

Holding her breath, she closed her eyes briefly. Cesar could shut himself off completely whenever she tried to get close. What gave her the belief that she could break through his impregnable shell?

'Of course there's more,' he stated as he raised her chin to stare into her eyes. His hands remained resting on her shoulders. She was unused to tenderness. Her brothers' idea of affection involved a not-so-gentle pat, and it had been a long time since she'd felt the loving touch of her parents. Cesar had caught her unawares, and now it was too late to hide the tears in her eyes.

He seemed puzzled. 'Is it so hard to believe that someone outside your immediate family cares what happens to you?' he asked. 'Or that a man wants you as fiercely as I do?'

'At least you're honest,' she said as she pushed a smile through her tears.

'Always,' Cesar promised, but within a moment he was back to his unemotional self. 'Come on, it's time to go.'

Face facts. Apart from the mind-blowing sex, she didn't know him that well.

* * *

How could he prove to a woman as strong and yet as fragile as Sofia that he meant her no harm?

By doing something together that didn't involve sex.

Thanking his inner voice with a silent two-word curse, he returned his attention to Sofia.

'Something wrong?' she asked as he pressed his lips down in thought.

He was only surprised at the unexpected interruption from an inner voice that had lain quietly dormant for years. Maybe nothing had happened in that time that had required it to speak up, the thought occurred to him. 'Do you play chess?'

'Chess?' Looking at him as if he'd gone mad, Sofia smoothed her hair, which required plucking quite a bit of hay out of it. 'Yes, I play chess,' she confirmed. 'Is that relevant?'

He shrugged. 'I don't see why not. We could go back to the ranch house, grab some food and a couple of beers, then engage in the age-old game of strategy. I find it clears the mind.'

'And you think it might help me?' she asked, curbing a smile.

'I don't see why not. It always helps me to focus and think clearly.'

'Something I need?' she suggested.

'Something civilised,' he confirmed,

'Civilised?' Sofia exclaimed on a laugh. 'When I play chess with my brothers it's like all-out war. If they even come close to losing, there's always a possibility they might upend the board and storm out.'

His lips tugged with amusement as he pictured the scene. 'Sounds reasonable.'

'Not to me,' Sofia assured him good-humouredly. 'But if you promise to behave, I'm happy to give you a game.'

'Come with me,' he invited.

There was a chessboard in his study. The room was quiet and warm. He sat on one side of the chess table and Sofia sat on the other. He set out the pieces. 'Ready?'

'Are *you* ready?' she challenged, dark eyes blazing with a competitive light.

'Are you sure it isn't you who upends the board if you lose? Just checking,' he soothed when she shot him one of her looks.

Doing something together that didn't involve sex turned out to be harder than expected. Sofia was a smart and merciless chess player. He knew the moment she asked to play the black pieces that she'd go for fool's mate.

Foiling her plan, he sat back.

'Okay,' she conceded, viewing the board through narrowed eyes. 'You got me.'

'Not yet,' he admitted. 'But I will.'

Maybe it was the heat they had created between them, or the recent memory of what had happened in the stable, but he was finding it increasingly hard to concentrate. Had she intentionally picked up the bishop and stroked it? After touching the piece, should he commit her to that move?

To hell with chess! His groin had tightened to the point of pain.

Having completed her move, Sofia tapped her fingers on the table.

'Would you like to use a timer for each move?' he asked.

'No.' She angled her head to study him. 'I like it when you take your time.'

'Be careful what you wish for.'

'Oh, I am,' she assured him in a tone that led him to wonder at what point Sofia had decided that moistening her lips with the tip of her tongue might be a good idea.

'Are you deliberately trying to distract me?'

'What makes you say that?' Her eyes widened in an expression of pure innocence. When she closed them again, perhaps to hide her amusement, he noticed how a fringe of black lashes cast a crescent shadow on the perfectly carved line of her cheekbone. Dragging his gaze away, he focused on the game. Too late, as it happened.

'Check,' she said crisply.

Leaving his seat, he turned away from the board to rub a hand across the back of his neck in an attitude of abject defeat. He allowed Sofia to bask in her triumph for all of two seconds and then, smiling faintly, he turned back.

Confident of triumph, Sofia was studying him when she should have been continuing to study the pieces. Leaning over, he moved his queen. 'Checkmate,' he said softly.

Sofia made a sound of disgust. 'Who's the fool now?' she exclaimed. 'Well played,' she offered sportingly.

'Do you want to play another game?'

'Best of three?' she suggested.

'I suggest we play something else.'

Electricity flashed between them. No words were needed. Linking their fingers, he led her through the silent house. They mounted the stairs to his bedroom—or, more accurately, they almost reached the first landing. Pausing to kiss her was his downfall—their downfall. One kiss led to another and then they were fighting to rid themselves of clothes.

'I promise myself that one day I'm going to have you in bed,' he growled as she reached for him.

'Pillows? Covers? The whole nine yards?' she suggested.

'Depend on it.'

He took her to the hilt in a single thrust. There was no finesse about this mating. It was wild and fierce, and deliciously intense. As if the more they gorged on each other, the more they needed. One question remained. Would they regain reason in time to continue with everyday life? It didn't seem likely right now. Their lives were complex. His was eaten up by duty and responsibility, while hers was eaten up by concern for others.

Did she ever lavish time on herself?

'Again!' she insisted.

'Hey,' he soothed. 'Remember what I said? Next time in bed.'

This was true intimacy, Sofia mused contentedly as she lay replete in Cesar's arms on his enormous bed. Had there ever been a more unselfish lover? She doubted it. Cesar was sleeping. She should be too. They had training in the morning. Or, rather, he did.

Slipping out of bed, she ran to the shower, freshened up, and then dressed while she was still half-damp. Speed was of the essence. But she couldn't leave without imprinting every moonlit inch of Cesar on her mind. Naked he was glorious. Clothed he was glorious. Sleeping he was beautiful and strong. There was no tension on his face now, no weight of the world resting on his shoulders. She felt a quite ridiculous urge to go back over to the bed to pull the covers over him and give him one last kiss. Until the next time, she promised herself. This wasn't goodbye, it was just a temporary break. She wouldn't risk waking him. She'd do anything to protect him. And she would.

Stopping by Cesar's study, she quickly scribbled a note. She'd be back in time for the match and would spend every spare minute she had in training. She didn't expect to have many spare minutes, but she didn't want Jess or the team worrying about her fitness level.

Turning at the front door, she gazed around the hall and up the staircase, then back into Cesar's study, all the different places where they'd made love and grown closer.

They had grown closer. Cesar was slowly changing from the cold individual she'd first met into a man who gave her everything she needed. Cold was no longer a word she could associate with him. Cesar was hot and funny and caring. They hadn't exactly shared words of love, but silent communication could be more effective than words. Actions certainly were, and action was in her immediate future.

Closing the front door noiselessly behind her, she drew on the closeness that had grown between them to buoy her up and convince her that this was the right thing to do. There had been many moments of trust between them and, whatever happened next, she would never forget this time with Cesar.

She'd called a cab to take her to the airport so she could fly home to Spain. When she arrived back at her retreat, she'd root out the truth. Someone had to be liaising with Howard Blake. If she couldn't uncover the truth in Spain, she'd fly to London and confront Blake at his office.

Tears stung her eyes at the thought of parting from Cesar, but she had a mission to complete before they'd meet again.

The cab she'd requested was waiting at the gate. She turned to look at the sleeping house one last time before climbing into the back of it. A few lights were beginning to show in the windows of the ranch house as people woke up, though the sun had only now crept over the horizon. Dawn was breaking on a new day. Cesar would wake to find her gone. 'Forgive me,' she whispered.

CHAPTER THIRTEEN

THE AIR RANG blue with curses, leaving no one in any doubt that Prince Cesar of Ardente Sestieri was beyond furious.

'Understandable, Your Royal Highness,' Dom placated as he bent to remove the newspaper from Cesar's desk.

'Leave it!' Cesar thundered. 'My apologies,' he added grimly. 'This is not your fault.'

With a brief nod of acknowledgement at a rare climb-down by the Prince, Dom made himself scarce at the back of the room.

And still his presence continued to irritate Cesar. Maybe it was Dom's excessively obsequious behaviour lately. Royalty had staff. That was a given. Trusted staff were party to every aspect of Cesar's life. It was a boon he never took for granted, though right now he wished himself back in the army where he could trust his comrades with his life, and where he could take out his frustration on a daily basis with mind- and body-stretching exercises, without anyone knowing what he was thinking.

'The article is…upsetting,' Dom ventured from the shadows.

'You think that piece of garbage upset me?' he asked his aide with incredulity.

Snatching up the tabloid, he flung it down again in disgust. He'd skim-read the article that claimed to have been written by Sofia Acosta. In her spare time, presumably, which he happened to know had been non-existent. Blake had gone too far this time. But where the hell was she? It was Sofia's absence that was sending him into a rage. Concern for her that made his blood boil. The article was nothing more than a scurrilous piece of filth that he refused to dignify with a comment.

Why had she left without telling him where she was going? Why hadn't she woken him?

'It's hard to believe Signorina Acosta would write something like this,' Dom murmured at a level where he had to strain to hear him.

'Impossible,' he snapped.

Where was his control? What had happened to regal manners? All the niceties of life had deserted him around the same time as Sofia. As for the article, the author, whoever that might be, had gone for the jugular this time, crediting Cesar with a harem of imaginary lovers to rival the seraglio of Genghis Khan. It would take around three lifetimes for him to satisfy so many women. And, no, he refused to give it a try.

Whoever had written the article had stepped well over the line, insinuating that his relationship with Sofia was nothing more than a ruse planned by Sofia to ensnare him. She would never write such trash. The florid tone employed in the article was enough to clear her of guilt. No, this had come from the pen of some evil fantasist with a grudge and expensive tastes. The claims were so ridiculous they suggested that whoever was behind the plot to discredit him was fast becoming desperate.

'File a flight plan to Spain,' he instructed Dom. 'I'm leaving today.'

'In the middle of training?' Dom enquired with surprise.

'I'll be back before you know it.' The man was really starting to annoy him. Dom had never questioned Cesar's decisions before.

'But the newspaper owner lives in Mayfair,' Dom pointed out, staring at him keenly.

'He's next on my list.'

'May I ask who's first?'

'No,' he said flatly. He'd had enough of Dom's intrusive change of manner. 'You may not.'

'Okay. Hand it over,' Sofia demanded as she took in the scene in the ranch house kitchen.

Cesar's aide, Domenico de Sufriente, was seated at the table, pounding his laptop, and leapt up guiltily when she walked into the room. He must have been confident she was on her way home. In fact, the cab ride to the airport had been long enough to figure out that there was another possible leak for Sofia to investigate, and that it was much closer to home.

Drawing himself up with affront, Dom pursed his mouth 'Hand over what, may I ask?'

'Your laptop,' Sofia said briskly.

'I beg your pardon?' Straightening his tie, Cesar's equerry laughed, and it was a mean, sarcastic little laugh, Sofia registered. 'I don't think so,' he sneered.

As he was standing, she took her chance to glance at the screen. 'Howard Blake?' she queried, heart pounding as her suspicions were confirmed. 'You're sending an email to Howard Blake?' She pretended incomprehension. 'What on earth for? What can you possibly have to say to him? Were you perhaps warning him that I was on my way?'

'Is it customary where you come from to read people's mail?' he enquired cuttingly.

'I don't think I've ever done so before,' she admitted, 'and if you've nothing to hide, I can't see why you're making such a fuss.'

'Why should I have anything to hide?' Dom asked defensively as he slammed the lid of his laptop down. 'Your imagination has got the better of you. Personally, I'm surprised you've got the nerve to come back after the trash you've written about Prince Cesar.'

'Those were not my words, as you well know.' Dom's reddening cheeks suggested she'd caught him out. 'I wrote one article, which was changed completely. I'm not a career journalist. I'm a rider and a painter and a—'

'Philanthropist?' Dom suggested with an evil snigger, as if no one had any right to be kind to people, least of all Sofia.

'If you're referring to my retreat, it helps those who need it, and that's all I care about. You can deride it all you like, but you won't destroy it. I won't allow you to.'

'You think I'd waste my energy on destroying your pathetic little retreat?'

Judging by his expression, the only thing Dom would like to destroy was Sofia, she realised, feeling the first ice-cold frisson of fear.

Only fools don't feel fear, her brothers had told her, and Dom's small black eyes had turned as hard as marble. This was the other side of the smooth courtier's coin. It showed a man eaten up by jealousy for a prince who was twice the man he was, and for his Queen, who was vulnerable and kind, and now, incredible though it might seem to her, Sofia. 'I know you did it,' she said calmly.

'Did what?' Dom demanded in a disdainful tone.

'You're the only person who could possibly know the details that appeared to back up those scurrilous comments in the article. You're the only person with access to Prince Cesar's diary. You know all the dates and the events he attends. I ran through everyone else it could possibly be in my head on my way to the airport, and realised that no one else knows as much about the Prince's diary as you.'

A look of triumph sprang onto Dom's face. 'Are you admitting the details are true?'

'I'm not admitting anything. I'm saying you embroidered the facts to suit you and your master, Howard Blake, and I'm accusing you of colluding with Blake to introduce a suitor for the Queen's hand into court when Her Majesty was at her lowest ebb. You, above everyone, knows everything about the royal family, and how best to hurt them.'

Dom stiffened. She'd made a lucky guess but, having shown her hand, she was now in danger. Her brothers were out riding, and there was no sign of the SUV Cesar used on the ranch. He must have gone out somewhere, and there was no doubt that Dom, like his master Howard Blake, would stop at nothing to complete his mission of destroying everyone she loved. And she was alone with him in a kitchen full of potential weapons.

Contrary to popular belief, men could multi-task. On his way to the airport, speakers in his muscle car read out his texts. There was nothing from Sofia. While he was confirming that, he was calling up his security team on a second, secure line. The first thing he'd done on waking and finding Sofia gone had been to ask his team, comprised entirely of ex-Special Forces, to institute a full-scale search for Sofia to make sure she was safe. Whatever had pulled her out of bed that morning had to be serious. Sofia was a serious-minded woman.

When she wasn't wild and abandoned in his arms.

He got an update from his team leader and smiled faintly. Nothing about Sofia could surprise him. 'This has only just happened?' he confirmed as he slowed the car.

His next call was to the airport, where his jet was ready and waiting. 'I won't be needing it,' he told his people.

His last call was to check the facts. He was a meticulous man.

An impersonal voice on the other end of the line informed him that the aircraft due to take Sofia home to Spain would board in around an hour, though as yet there was no sign of a Señorita Acosta on the checked-in passenger list.

Burning rubber, he screeched into a tyre-flaying U-turn and headed back the way he'd come. The road was straight and empty. He was driving a car with a top speed of over two hundred miles an hour. It would be rude to ignore the vehicle's potential.

As fast as it was, he still had time to think. If Sofia did something unusual, there was a good reason behind it. She'd slept in his arms. That was unusual. How had that made her feel? It had made him feel too much, which in itself was unusual. She'd trusted him, and that had touched him. What grabbed at his heart now and twisted it in knots was that whoever had their claws into Sofia wasn't ready to let go. And that put her in danger.

Howard Blake was another matter. He'd been dealt with. Cesar was not just meticulous, once he'd made up his mind he moved fast. He couldn't wait to tell Sofia that a cast-iron, signed and sealed document from Cesar's lawyers had landed in his inbox a couple of hours ago. His legal team had been working through the night to draw up a contract that would secure the financial future of Sofia's retreat for as long as it existed, thanks to an unbreakable trust that had been set up by none other than Howard Blake. Under Cesar's instructions.

To make doubly sure Blake's teeth were pulled, Cesar had purchased his newspaper empire, so Sofia was free to paint and ride to her heart's content, as well as help as many of those who needed her arm around their shoulder as she could.

The journey home was exasperating as possibility and probability jostled for position in his mind. Had Sofia read the second newspaper article yet? Would she laugh or cry when she did? His brain refused to stop whirring. Was she having second thoughts about sleeping with him? Not that much sleep had been involved. Was that why she'd left his bed? If she'd never reached the airport, but had returned to the *estancia* because she had guessed, as he had, that the trouble lay right there, then she could be in danger. Concern hit him like a punch in the gut. He put his car to the test. Two hundred miles an hour was not only achievable, but vital in this situation.

The black beast didn't let him down. The car did all but take flight.

* * *

'What are you going to do about this discovery of yours?' Dom sneered at Sofia as they faced each other in the kitchen. 'Do you plan to tell Cesar? Do you really think he'll believe you, after this second article? He might pretend not to believe you wrote it, but does he really know? Won't he doubt your honesty?'

With each question asked Dom moved a step closer. Sofia was backing up. They had almost reached the door. She planned to take her chances and escape as soon as she reached it. 'Of course I read the article on my phone,' she confirmed—anything to keep him talking. 'It was full of accusations, and insinuations about events supposedly taking place at the training camp.'

The lies had churned her stomach. With Sofia's by-line at the top of the piece, it had made her relationship with Cesar read like a sting, calculated to trap him and prove him unworthy of the throne. If he believed those lies Cesar would cut her out of his life with surgical precision. Her brothers would never speak to her again. Funding would dry up for her retreat. It would have to close, leaving those she cared for with nowhere to go. She'd be a pariah, but that was nothing compared to the effect the damning article could have on a man who was brave and strong and principled, and who led by example, a prince who would one day be King. 'Where is Cesar?' she queried, heart clenching with lurid possibility. 'What have you done with him?'

'Me?' Dom touched his crisp, tailor-made shirt just short of where his heart should be. And then he lunged for her.

Dom's hand around her neck was removed so fast Sofia had no idea what had happened. One minute she was fighting a murderous opponent, and the next Dom was flat out on the kitchen floor with Cesar looming over him.

'Cesar!' It felt as if she'd shrieked his name but it sounded like a croak. He was at her side in an instant with his arm around her shoulders, bringing her so close in a clasp of relief that she could hardly breathe. 'Help—'

He released her in an instant and, holding her at arm's length, he stared down with relief, as well as something warmer and deeper. 'The conventional phrase, I believe, is, "Thank you".'

'When have we ever been conventional?' she managed hoarsely as she clutched her throat and coughed. 'But thank you.'

'Stop thanking me,' Cesar commanded in the softest whisper she'd ever heard. 'You landed a good blow there, making things easy for me, or why was that monster grabbing his crotch with one hand while attempting to strangle you with the other? If he'd had both his hands free—'

'But he didn't,' she soothed. 'And, anyway, you laid him out.' She'd checked.

'I've always been a bit of a scrapper,' she admitted. 'Four brothers?'

'I should have been here.' Cesar was in no mood for humour. Summoning his security team, he told them to remove the prisoner and lock him up.

'You got here as soon as you could,' Sofia argued. 'You came looking for me. That's all that matters.'

'I had to,' Cesar reflected grimly. 'I know you well enough to be confident you wouldn't leave the house without good reason. When I worked out what that reason could be, I knew I had to find you fast or you'd take things into your own hands. Are you sure you're okay?'

The look in his eyes touched her somewhere deep. 'I'm fine.' She stood back as two military types dressed in black entered the room.

'We have a lot to talk about,' he said.

'You read the article.' She knew he must have and felt a flutter of alarm.

'Of course,' Cesar confirmed.

'How did you know to find me here?'

'How do we know anything?' He frowned. 'Intuition? The assembly of known facts into a recognisable picture?'

Now the initial shock was over, her knees had turned to jelly. Cesar's steadying hand beneath her arm was more than welcome. It was one thing to be at the peak of physical fitness, and another to be attacked by someone who meant her harm, Sofia had discovered. She might have accepted that Dom was not the silky courtier he appeared, but his vicious lunge for her throat had really shocked her.

They went into Cesar's library. It was a cosy, reassuring room, with wood-panelled walls and comfortable seating.

'Take a seat on the sofa,' he invited. Crossing the room to a well-stocked bar, he poured a generous slug of fine brandy into a crystal glass. 'Here. Drink this...'

'I don't—'

'You do,' he insisted. 'And then we'll talk.'

She sipped and put the glass down, only then realising that the newspaper with its damning article—the same article that someone had *kindly* sent to her to make sure she didn't miss it—was lying open on the low table between them.

Closing her eyes, she exhaled shakily. 'How can I ever—'

'Don't.' Cesar raised his hand, palm flat. 'Let's get one thing straight. This is not your writing, not your fault, and nothing to do with you.'

'Without me, the campaign to discredit you wouldn't have got started,' she argued. Picking up the newspaper, she scanned the article she'd already read as if hoping it would somehow change into something she could read without feeling sick to the stomach that anyone could write such trash.

Cesar shrugged off her comment. 'Blake would have found someone else to do his dirty work.'

Breath shuddered out of her. She didn't want to be let off the hook so easily. 'The article appears under my name and will seem totally plausible to anyone who reads it. My brothers will read it and they can only think I'm betraying you again.'

'Then I'll set them straight, though I believe you're worrying unnecessarily. Do you really think they don't know what's been going on between us?'

What is going on between us? she wondered in the few seconds it took for Cesar to supply an answer to his own question but not to hers. 'I've known your brothers a long time—too long for them not to have picked up the vibes between me and their only sister. They're probably laughing their heads off right now as they read this garbage over the breakfast table.'

'Thanks. I'd rather not think about that, not when this could be so serious for you.'

'Believe me, I'm not taking it lightly,' Cesar assured her.

'And then there's your mother and sister. What will they think? This is so unfair, especially when it's clearly untrue.'

Maybe she had expected Cesar to argue this point, and say that there was something between them and that it was so deep that it transcended cheap gossip, but he remained silent, while she couldn't seem to stop words pouring from her mouth.

'All this rubbish about secret liaisons between us, and the things we do—' Her cheeks blazed red. 'With my by-line at the top of the article, it makes it seem I set you up.'

'But we know you didn't.'

'Of course I didn't, but this article is dangerous for you. You can't take it lightly.'

'I haven't,' Cesar assured her.

His eyes were cool and calculating. She knew instinctively that he would be reviewing plans he'd already made. Why didn't he share those plans with her? This cut right to the heart of why she wanted more from their relationship.

Her pulse jagged as Cesar shifted position, but it was only to ease his massive shoulders in a careless shrug. 'So everyone knows,' he observed, lips pressing down. 'What of it? Does it embarrass you to be linked to a prince? Or would you rather not be linked to me?'

'That's not it at all,' she protested, shaking her head with frustration.

'Then how about this?' He pinned her with his black stare. 'What if that prince asked you to marry him? Would you be mortified? Or relieved?'

'Relieved?' she asked incredulously. In her fantasies perhaps! 'I'd be horrified.'

Cesar's eyes narrowed. 'Should I be insulted?'

He didn't look insulted. Hand pressed to his chest, and with his black eyes scorching her face into an even hotter shade of red, Cesar appeared to be amused.

'I take it you're joking?' she said on a dry throat.

'Am I?'

Cesar managed to imbue those two words with so much heat and promise her body went wild. Her mind, however, was by now firmly back on track. 'If I were a drinker I'd ask for another brandy. I could never be princess material. You need someone—'

'What?' Cesar queried. 'Someone like me, do you mean, from a rarefied background raised on a diet of riches and privilege, while you were a raggedy tomboy, dragged up in a stable? It may surprise you to know I was an urchin, filthy and starving, plucked off the streets of Rome after being abandoned by my birth mother. I have a wonderful woman to call my mother, and to thank for hunting me down. The Queen saved me. It's as simple as that.'

Nothing about Cesar was ever simple, Sofia reflected, though she kept silent as he talked on. 'The Queen is the only real mother I've ever known. Her heart was big enough to make a home for the bastard son of her handmaid and the King, and she went on to bring me up as her own.'

For once Sofia was lost for words. Cesar had never opened up about his past. However bad things got between them, the fact that he had chosen her to confide in meant a lot. 'I had no idea,' she said softly.

'About so many things,' Cesar confirmed, 'such as you can trust me with your life. Which brings me to repeat my question: Will you marry me?'

'I have to understand why you're asking me first,' she admitted.

'What is there to understand?'

'I understand why you bottle up your emotions, Cesar. To be abandoned at such a young age was bound to have repercussions—'

'I don't want to talk about me. I want to talk about you,' he insisted.

'By not talking about how you feel inside, you're letting the past win.'

'The past is the past. I've treated you badly.'

'And now I deserve a reward?' she asked, frowning.

'You're not one of my horses.'

'I'm glad you realise it.' A smile crept through.

'We're making progress?' he suggested.

'If you can express your feelings...'

'I do feel lots of things—especially when it comes to you. I feel lust, passion, frustration, tenderness...but most of all I feel an overwhelming certainty that I can't share my life with anyone but you. I love you, Sofia, with all my heart, my soul, and my body too. Marry me and let me keep you safe for ever.'

'You love me?' she whispered.

'How can you doubt it?'

Her head was spinning. She didn't have an answer right away. There was so much to take in that her heart felt as if it was in a vice. She'd barely recovered from the shock of Dom's attack, and then there had been the shame of seeing yet another newspaper article written in her name. Now she was faced with Cesar's bombshell proposal of marriage. 'I've said it before. I'm just not princess material, let alone queen.'

'Which is precisely why I think you'll be the most marvellous addition to the royal family,' Cesar insisted. 'You're what my people deserve—someone who will genuinely care for them and who's prepared to get their hands dirty. Not forgetting you'll have to put up with me.'

She searched Cesar's eyes for some hint of humour and found none. The past half an hour had brought about great change. Cesar had found her, saved her, and they'd confirmed the treachery of his aide. What was she waiting for? For the doubt demons to leave? Life was full of uncertainty. How you dealt with it was what mattered. The one thing you could not, must not do was to turn your back and walk away from the chance of happiness. 'Is this a serious proposal of marriage?'

'I would never joke about something so important,' Cesar promised with a steady look.

'But there's been no lead up, no hint of what you were thinking, no preparation—'

'For life?' he asked gently. 'How much preparation do you need? Seems to me you've been doing pretty well up to this point, and I believe this is the perfect solution to silence the critics following any fallout from the article. The Playboy Prince is ready to settle down—'

Just when she was ready to believe he could change and grow in the emotional sense, he slashed her belief into tiny pieces.'

'There's no point in dragging things out,' he said.

Life drained out of her but she was a fighter, which meant refusing to give up, especially when that meant giving up the man she loved. She wasn't going to let him go without a fight. 'What about tracing a possible path for our future first?' she asked crisply. 'What about describing your vision of the path we'll be walking down together. Or is this marriage just another business deal for you? Maybe it's a way for you to get your people onside. After all, everyone loves a royal wedding.'

Cesar looked shocked.

Grief, hurt and shame collided inside her. Receiving the proposal she'd dreamed of all her life in what amounted to bullet points was unbearable. She didn't need to be told that she wasn't a likely choice of bride for Prince Cesar of Ardente Sestieri, but to be made to feel that she was nothing more than a convenient solution for Cesar hurt like hell.

And then he made it worse.

CHAPTER FOURTEEN

'I AM A brutally honest man,' Cesar conceded with a grudging grin, 'but I'll admit that what I'm thinking doesn't come out the way I intend.'

'I get that, but it's what you're feeling too that needs expressing,' Sofia observed, 'and not just clinical thoughts when it comes to something as precious as marriage. What I don't want is for you to say something you don't mean.'

'But I do mean it,' he insisted with a hard stare. 'Every word.'

'With eyes as hard as flint?' she said, breaking up inside. 'Please, don't lie to me, Cesar. I don't understand how you can love me so much that you want to spend the rest of your life with me when I'll never be princess material.'

'That's the very reason I want to marry you. Haven't I told you that before?'

'Why can't you stop pretending that the marriage you propose is anything more than a convenient solution?'

'What do you want me to say, Sofia? I thought this was what you wanted.'

Tears sprang to her eyes. 'A marriage proposal that sounds more like a business deal?' she asked incredulously.

'Don't do this to me.' Cesar pulled back when she longed for him to move forward. 'I'm trying to be fair,' he insisted.

'So your future plans include a quirky horse-riding artist, said to have written defamatory articles about you? No smoke without fire,' she reminded him grimly. 'Does that sound like the perfect royal match to you? Will your countrymen go for it? Will the Queen stand and cheer when you tell Her Majesty our news?'

'Please, be calm,' Cesar insisted in a way that made her madder still. 'I've told you about my past so you know I'm not obvious prince material. Yet, here I am, not so very different from you. I wouldn't be asking you such a vital question if I thought you were a typical princess, spoiled, indulged, entitled, but none of those words describe you, Sofia.'

'No. I'm just the mug who fell in love with you,' she admitted, when she could finally draw an easy breath.

'You love me?'

'Of course I do!' she exclaimed heatedly.

'A fact that makes our marriage even more likely to succeed,' Cesar declared, without returning the compliment. 'So now we've got that sorted out, I'll give you a list of things to do in the lead up to our wedding.'

'No clipboard?' she asked heatedly. 'Don't tell me you forgot to bring it with you?'

Cesar appeared to be genuinely surprised. 'I'm sorry you think marriage to me such a dreadful prospect.'

Feelings erupted inside her. She wanted to go to him and hold him close, kiss him and drive the ghosts of the past away. Surely he could see that marriage between them was impossible. 'It's not a terrible prospect,' she protested. 'It's impractical. It wouldn't work. I've told you I love you—to which you showed no reaction at all. It's as if you don't value my love. '

'Nothing could be further from the truth,' he insisted. 'And I'd like to know what you base your conclusions on. I've made it plain from the outset that I'm not too grand for you. In fact, you come from a far more stable background. There must be another reason for your refusal. What is it, Sofia? What's holding you back?'

'I can't be with such an emotionless man. If this proposal of marriage is just a duty for you it wouldn't be honest of me to accept. I'd be selling your people short. We both would. They deserve more than a reluctant princess and a cold-hearted prince.'

'Cold-hearted?' Cesar queried frowning. 'Haven't I made it clear that you can have anything you want?'

'But I don't want material things. I want honesty, truth and love. Where are your feelings, Cesar? Where are you hiding them? Why can't you express them? Or do you think it's weak to show emotion?'

'Of course not.' He was growing heated now. 'I have deep feelings for my people, my family, and especially for you. What do you want me to say, Sofia? I know what I want. Marry me. Give me the chance to make you happy. You've nothing to fear from me. You're free to leave this marriage if you're unhappy, and of course that would be with a pension for life.'

That was the worst thing he could have said. Hope died inside her. It was as if her heart had shrunk until it resembled a walnut, shrivelled and dry.

'Haven't you listened to a word I've said?' she asked quietly. 'I don't want or need a pension for life. You make it sound as if I'm to be rewarded for deceiving your people.'

'I would never deceive my people,' Cesar protested, incredulous.

'With a grand royal wedding and a smiling bride?' she suggested. 'What would you call it? When I get married it will be for love, not for what I can get out of it. The era for business-like marriage mergers is long past!'

'But you'll be safe with me,' Cesar insisted, as if he couldn't believe what she'd said. 'I've bought up Howard Blake's empire so he'll never trouble you again. My former equerry Dom is currently in custody and will be judged by the highest court in the land. I intend to live my life protecting you and my people in every way I can. If you have even a gram of the renowned Acosta honour, surely you'll support me in this?'

'By marrying a man who cannot share his true feelings with me?'

It was tragic to think Cesar did have feelings, deep feelings, but he was incapable of expressing them in a way her heart could accept. In that, she supposed when she thought about it, they were both guilty.

'I'm sorry I've got no pretty words for you,' he said at last. 'That's just not who I am. Rest assured, I have no intention of forcing you to do anything you don't want to do. I'm relying on your good sense to get you through this.'

'You make it sound as if I must survive some unpleasant illness that can be dosed with a spoonful of sugar. I want so much more out of marriage than that. Love dies if it's all one-sided, and I couldn't bear—'

'To be abandoned again?' he suggested gently.

She took a moment to refocus, as he added, 'Losing your parents has left a gaping wound, and it's important for you to know that I understand. It will take time to prove I can help you heal, but I need the chance to do that.'

A tsunami of emotion threatened to overwhelm her. She had no doubt now that Cesar was sincere. Marrying him was a dream that could so easily become reality. All she had to do was say yes. But she wanted the best for Cesar too. He was a king amongst men, strong and principled, sincere, and she'd never find anyone like him again. Her heart yearned for nothing more than to twin with his. She truly couldn't fault him. And, of course, she loved him with all her heart.

'Maybe I could have said things better,' he conceded in the silence, 'but I'm not an orator, and I didn't plan to win your heart with words. I can see now that I've rushed things, but once I see a goal I go for it. There's been no time to woo you as you deserve, but I'll try to make it up to you. Most importantly, I'll care for you and keep you safe. Anything you need for the wedding can be ordered online,' he added, frowning as he compiled his mental list. 'If you need people to help you to prepare, call them now and put them on standby. Transport will be arranged for everyone who attends the ceremony. Make that clear to anyone you invite—'

'Cesar!' Her shout stopped him in his tracks. 'There can be no wedding. Have you listened to me at all?'

'The ceremony can take place in one week's time on my private island of Isla Ardente,' he said, unwittingly supplying the answer to her question.

'You're making plans for an event I have no intention of attending,' she pointed out.

'But that's the neatest way,' he insisted. 'When we're married we'll draw even bigger crowds to the charity matches. You'll need a ring, of course,' the man she loved with all her heart added, frowning, 'So why don't you browse the internet and choose something you'd like?'

For a moment the plastic rings that came in Christmas crackers flashed into her head. They would be perfect for a sham wedding.

'Better still, leave it to me!' he exclaimed, 'I have contacts at all the top jewellers—'

'Of course you do!' she interrupted. Doubt crept into the mix as she imagined all the expensive trinkets Cesar must have purchased over the years.

'There's no real urgency for an engagement ring' he added thoughtfully, 'though I expect you'd like something to show off at some point—'

'Show off?' she burst out.

'Whatever you like,' Cesar countered, with a smile that proved he was oblivious to her mounting frustration. 'Though we'll concentrate on finding a wedding band for now. We can sort out more jewellery later—'

'Stop this,' she exploded. 'Is this what your proposal boils down to? A sparkly stone and a pair of handcuffs disguised as a wedding band? Believe me, I'm not that desperate to get married. I'd sooner wed a walrus and feast on sea cucumbers than marry a man who opens his wallet without opening his heart.'

'But you want me,' Cesar stated flatly.

'If you're asking whether I like having sex with you, why not say so? I do. You're an amazing lover. Would I like to have more sex with you? Yes, of course, but having sex is very different from planning to spend the rest of your life with someone.' It hurt to even think those words, let alone say them. Being intimate with Cesar had meant *everything* to her. She'd given herself completely, freely, trustingly and lovingly, but had it meant the same to him?

'Perhaps you see things differently,' he suggested.

'I see you clearly.' She drew on every bit of control she had to keep her voice steady and her eyes direct. 'The unexpressed feelings you have are possibilities waiting to happen. You get angry when you can't express yourself, but I don't need flowery words any more than I need expensive gifts. I just want you to be honest with me—with both of us.'

Cesar frowned. 'Are you frustrating my plans?'

'There you go again,' she said with a hint of desperation in her voice. 'We should be getting married because we want nothing more than to be together. Not because it suits your agenda. Open your heart, Cesar. Let me know how you truly feel.'

'But we could save a country together.'

'As well your reputation,' she observed shrewdly.

'Not to mention yours,' Cesar countered. 'Just tell me what you want. Name your price.'

'Name my price?' she repeated in a strangled whisper.

'Clumsy words,' he admitted, raking his hair with frustration. 'I told you I'm no good with words.'

But the damage had been done.

'This marriage will lift the mood of my people—'

'You can't even call it *our* marriage,' she burst out, unable to keep silent any longer.

'It would instantly make a mockery of the article,' Cesar continued as if she hadn't spoken. 'Despite what the writer suggests, there was no seedy liaison between us at the training camp but an unfolding love story that will now have a beautiful ending.'

'Is that what you truly believe?' she asked. Hope pushed its way through the tangle of weeds like a green shoot.

Only to be trampled on.

'I've told you to name your price, Sofia, so please tell me what you would like to make this marriage happen. Please, appreciate that this is a difficult situation for both of us and time is short.'

She shook her head sadly. 'Not for you. You seem to have it all worked out. Would you like my bank details for a money transfer or will you pay me in pieces of silver?'

'Stop it,' Cesar advised calmly. 'If you think about this logically, you'll come to agree that nothing could be more uplifting for my people than a wedding between us.'

How could they be so far apart? She hid an agony of disillusionment behind another question. 'Have you discussed this with my brothers?'

'I thought you were old enough to make your own decision.'

'As I thought you experienced enough in the ways of the world to know what's right,' she fired back. 'What you're proposing is a marriage of convenience—convenient for you, that is.'

'All I want is for you to be happy and safe.'

'You have a strange way of showing it.'

'Do I?' Cesar asked, seeming perplexed.

'Asking me to be your wife surely requires me to say yes before arrangements can be made? A little more thought and preparation generally goes into these things than the advice to "Browse the Internet".'

Cesar raked his hair. 'But you can have anything you want.'

'*Things* don't matter.' She waited, and then waited some more while Cesar stared at her as if she was speaking a foreign language. 'I give up,' she said at last. 'Seduction might be your forte, but when it comes to wooing a woman you have zero idea. It takes more than a vault full of priceless jewels to build trust, and more than pomp and ceremony to impress me. If you had suggested a small, informal barefoot wedding on the beach of your private island, with just a band of twine around my finger and some fresh flowers in my hair—'

'Done! That's an excellent idea.'

'What?' She stared at Cesar in horror.

'I'll get my team on it right away, and then I'll present my beautiful bride to our people at a formal blessing in the cathedral in the capital sometime later.'

'Best find yourself a bride first,' Sofia advised before she left the room.

Well, that went well. Cesar paced up and down, frowning, long after Sofia had slammed the door and disappeared. Her final words had been like a well-aimed blow to the chin, but instead of knocking him out they had knocked him into a different mind-set. He'd been so preoccupied, facing the threat to him and Sofia, that he had instinctively moved into leading and planning mode, which on this occasion had involved a wedding ceremony, when Sofia had needed proper reassurance that he loved her before, not after, a proposal of marriage.

He had assumed she would realise that his offer was heartfelt, but now he realised she'd thought it a ruse to distract his people from the latest gossip. The thought of marriage to Sofia had struck him like a bombshell, mainly because marrying anyone else was unthinkable. That nightmare was only exceeded by the thought of Sofia marrying someone else. He loved her with all his heart, he realised now, but had he left it too late?

Years back, when he'd been in the army and his comrades had been getting married one by one, he had envied them for the love they shared, and for the company they could look forward to with someone who loved them unreservedly. Marriage had once seemed an elusive possibility for the so-called Playboy Prince, but he had longed for nothing more than to settle down and build a family...if only he knew how.

Sofia had made that achievable. She was no spoiled, milksop princess, staring haughtily down her nose at his people while acting as everyone's friend. He wanted a real woman with real character, someone who would take him to task, and here she was, but had he messed up the best chance he'd ever have?

He had to find a way around this. He wanted Sofia to be his wife, not to smooth over the cracks of the article or because it made sense but because he adored her and he wanted her in every way there was. It was hard to express his feelings, but if he kept on trying, maybe he'd get better at it. He had to or he'd lose her for good. And there would never be another Sofia.

Time was short, and the task ahead of him was not just demanding, but would normally take months to complete. How long did it take to woo a woman? He had no idea. It had never been necessary in the past. He prided himself on being a meticulous organiser, but where this was concerned he was in the dark. How long would it take to convince Sofia she could trust him completely when he was starting his campaign from such a low base?

Happiest when he was doing something, he called a meeting for everyone to attend the following morning before training. Until then, guessing Sofia had had enough of his 'bulldozing ways', as she'd called them, he keep himself busy riding, working out, swimming, reading, sparring in the gym with her brothers—anything but risk speaking to Sofia before he was ready. He was good at planning and hopeless at wooing, but when it came to winning Sofia's heart, he was on a mission to succeed.

CHAPTER FIFTEEN

PUNISHING HER PILLOW for the lack of anything else to thump, she sobbed like a baby and railed against fate. How could a man who had risen like a phoenix from the ashes of his child-hood, with a brain to rival Einstein's and personal success that exceeded most people's, be so dense as to imagine that a pretty ring and the promise of riches could find their way to her heart?

She didn't want that with Cesar. She wanted new paints, a puppy and a kitten, and a bridle for her horse. She wanted time together to laugh and be silly, and plan a future that didn't in-volve self-interest and what she had to gain. There was so much she wanted to do, and all she needed was the chance to get out there and do it. The idea of extending her retreat to encompass an entire country, where no one felt left out or forgotten, would be a dream come true. And, yes, she was a bit of a dreamer, but wouldn't Cesar be the perfect counterbalance to that?

She was glad when the phone rang. Maybe that would shake her out of this noisy, messy pity party. 'Hello?'

'Sofia?'

Her heart stopped beating.

'Cesar here.'

As if she didn't know, as if her entire body, mind and soul

hadn't recognised that deep, husky voice the moment he'd spoken. A quick analysis of his tone said this was an exploratory call to judge her mood, as she was attempting to judge his.

'Are you all right? Sofia? Say something.'

'I'm fine.' She sniffed. 'A bit of a cold coming on, that's all.'

'Good. I've called a meeting tomorrow morning before training to give the official line on the latest article. I trust you will attend?'

She was confused and not a little angry. '*Your* official line?'

'Yes.'

'Don't I have a say in this?'

'I'll speak first, and then open the floor to questions.'

'Cesar...' She hesitated, frowning. 'Do you ever listen to yourself?'

'You mean playback when I've been interviewed? Sometimes—'

'No. I mean right now,' she informed him. 'If you could only come down from Planet Exalted and speak to me as an equal.'

'I do,' he protested.

'Good, because I'd like to stand at your side and give my own version of events, if that's okay with you?'

There was heavy silence for a good few moments and then he said stiffly. 'If that would make you happy.'

'It would.'

Perhaps she should be angry with Cesar but she had grown up with four brilliant brothers—brilliant in the sense of their keen, ever-seeking minds, and brilliant because they were so good to her—but they often saw no further than their noses, especially where matters of the heart were involved. 'What time tomorrow?'

Cesar gave a time. She thanked him and promised to be there. Putting the phone down, she went to stare at her reflection in the mirror. Very nice if red eyes and runny noses were your thing. Not such a good look for a woman who was about to buckle on her armour to fight for the heart of a man she couldn't bring herself to let go. Never mind what Cesar could do for her. What could she do for him?

He felt like a child on Christmas Day waking early to check that everything was as it should be when the moment came when gifts could be opened in a shower of discarded paper and laughter. A run, a ride, a workout in the gym, and a swim before his shower, and he was ready for what would be a very different day.

Dressed in riding gear, he greeted Sofia's brothers in the arena. Sofia was already there, with his favourite mutt Bran at her heels. He took it as a sign. The hound viewed him with his big, intelligent brown eyes, assessing his mood as Cesar was assessing Sofia's.

'Good boy, Bran,' he soothed as the dog trotted over to him. He dug out some treats.

'Well?' Sofia's youngest and wildest brother Xander demanded, snapping a whip impatiently against his boots. 'You called this meeting. What do the two of you want to talk about? We've got training to do.'

'Cesar has asked me to marry him.'

Sofia's voice carried clear and strong in the vaulted space. A good few seconds of deafening silence passed before Sofia's older brother Raffa commented, 'He must have enjoyed your article.'

'I can do without your sarcasm, Raffa,' she scolded.

Her brother shrugged.

The only four men in the world who could possibly, in a concerted effort, take Cesar down were staring at him as if his remaining time on earth would be short. That didn't bother him. What did concern him was Sofia's blood-drained face. She was standing in front of them at her most vulnerable. He lost no time reassuring her.

'I'm here to ask you, Sofia's brothers, to do me the honour of allowing me to ask for your sister's hand in marriage.' Pretty words could trip off his tongue when he was desperate. 'I want to do everything properly,' he explained with a long look at Sofia. 'And in case you're wondering, I've already asked Sofia to marry me and she said no. My timing was out, but I'll make that right.'

'If Sofia said no, that's an end of it,' Xander insisted, slashing a whip impatiently against his booted calf.

'No.' Sofia held up her hand as she stepped forward. 'At least do Cesar the courtesy of listening to him—as I shall.'

'So talk,' Xander growled.

'Have you engineered this proposal to spare you the accusations in the latest article?' Raffa demanded suspiciously.

'Of course not.' He could state that with a clear conscience. 'If there had never been an article, I would want to marry Sofia. For me, there's no one like her. No one remotely close. And I love her.' He had to hope he wasn't too late. 'Humble pie is not a dish I eat with any frequency,' he admitted with a self-deprecating shrug, 'but this is different, this is for Sofia, and I'll grovel if that's what it takes.'

'My sister has brought you to your knees?' Dante suggested, failing to hide his amusement.

'She did,' he confirmed. 'I've promised myself to listen and act in future, rather than the other way around. I think we all know that your sister had nothing to do with those articles. My equerry, Domenico, is the culprit, and has been dealt with, while his master Howard Blake will be funding Sofia's retreat, as well as any future retreats she cares to open, out of his substantial bank account.'

'How on earth did you get him to agree to that?' Xander remarked with a glance at his brothers.

'I bought his company with a binding agreement that ensures Blake signs away part of those funds to Sofia's retreats each year. So now all that remains is your answer...'

'Sofia?' Dante asked.

Not realising what he had arranged with Blake, Sofia appeared shocked numb, and could only nod her head briefly. 'You did this for me?' she managed finally.

'Useless with words, better with actions,' he confirmed with a smile.

'I can't believe what you've done!' she exclaimed.

'But it pleases you?' he confirmed.

'Securing the future of my work? Of course. I can't thank you enough.'

'Okay, you two,' Dante interrupted, holding up his hand as he prepared to mount his pony. 'Let's call a halt to this. We've got training to do. As I understand it, Cesar is asking our permission to court Sofia with the intention of making an honest woman of her—a princess, in fact. We can hardly deny him that opportunity.'

Sofia's brothers agreed with a knowing laugh. When they finally quietened down, Xander said, 'Have you ever asked permission to do anything in your life, Cesar?'

'Never,' he admitted bluntly. 'But this is different. This is Sofia.' And these were men of honour that he was proud to call friends.

'Are you sure you know what you're taking on?' Raffa asked with amusement.

'I've got some idea, but I'll take her in spite of her faults.' This ended in a chorus of good-natured catcalls, and then he added, 'Because I love her with all my heart.'

'Should we start the training now?' Sofia suggested, a warm note in her voice as she winked at Jess and gave him a lingering smile.

Suitor-in-training would be an accurate description for him. How good it felt. Triumph surged through him as he sprang into the saddle and wheeled his hot-wired pony around.

By the end of that day's training Sofia was mentally and physically exhausted. It had been almost impossible to keep her mind on training after Cesar's impassioned declaration. She kept glancing at him as if to make sure this new, improved Cesar wasn't a figment of her imagination. Nope. He seemed pretty real to her. Her brothers said nothing more about it, and it was a thrill to feel much of their camaraderie returning. Cesar saying she was innocent was enough to convince them. She couldn't thank him enough for that. She'd take brotherly love any day over a flashy diamond ring.

When the session ended, Cesar dismounted first. Handing his reins to a groom, he insisted on helping her down. 'You've worked so hard your legs will buckle under you.'

'My legs will obey my commands,' she insisted, stubbornly as usual.

Wrong. Her legs did not obey. They buckled. Cesar's hand steadied her, but he made no move to crowd her or do any more than set her firmly on her feet.

'See you at supper,' he said.

So much for romance, she reflected wryly, wondering how and when Cesar's idea of wooing would actually show itself.

Before cleaning up for the evening ahead, she went to check on the ponies. Bran trotted along at her heels. She stopped at one of the stalls where a pony belonging to Cesar was receiving attention. Glad of something to take her mind off Cesar, she sent the groom away to enjoy her supper and set about applying the poultice herself. Soft words and the cooling relief soon had the pony's ears pricked again.

'Problem?'

'Cesar!' She wheeled around at the sound of his voice. 'No. She'll be fine for the match if you rest her tomorrow.'

'I guess we're all feeling the strain of Jess's training,' he observed.

Sofia was feeling the strain of something. She smiled faintly. Cesar didn't appear to be any the worse for wear as he rested back against the wall of the stall. In fact, he had never looked more startlingly dynamic, with his deep tan, close-fitting breeches and plain dark polo shirt. His thick black hair was all messed up and catching on his stubble, while his eyes, his lips—everything about him... He was so hot it felt like being hit by an electric charge. She dropped her gaze, only for it to land on well-worn leather riding boots hugging hard-muscled calves. Swallowing deeply, she looked away to concentrate on the pony. 'See you in the ranch house when I've finished here—'

'Change of plan,' he announced, pulling away from the wall. 'I'm cooking tonight.'

'You're...?'

'You can close your mouth now,' he said, his lips curving in a grin. 'My mother the Queen taught me some campfire specials.'

'That seems unlikely.'

'My mother is a very surprising woman.'

'I don't doubt it.' There was something shining in Cesar's eyes—a warmth she hadn't seen before, and affection. And was that hope that she'd agree to his suggestion? A campfire supper was a small thing, but it marked a big step forward in their relationship. She wanted nothing more than to be close to him, normal with him, and what better way than singeing sausages over a campfire? Did she really mean that much to him? He couldn't have been more forthright when he spoke to her brothers,

'See you around eight o'clock—lower field,' he instructed.

She smiled inwardly at his tone of voice. Some things never changed.

Give him a chance, her inner voice insisted.

'Lower field?' she queried. That was one she hadn't heard of.

'Anyone will tell you where to find me. Don't be late.'

'I won't,' she promised softly.

Sofia rode out to meet him, by which time he'd lit a fire and their meal was cooking, though the most important ingredient had just arrived.

'Cesar!' she exclaimed as she dismounted. 'What have you done?'

'Brought an easel and paints along to join us. I thought you might be missing your painting, and there's nothing more beautiful than sunset at the river. I thought you could sketch an outline, and maybe finish the painting before you leave for Isla Ardente. That way you can hang the painting anywhere you choose—here, or in my house on the island.'

'You mean you'd seriously hang my painting in your ranch house?'

His lips pressed down as he pretended to consider this. 'If it's any good.' And when she cuffed him, he added, 'It could be your ranch house if you agree to become my wife.' She stared at the easel and paints, and then at him. 'Do I get a second chance to make this right?'

'Nothing could make me happier…' she breathed, eyes wide, lips parted seductively '…than a reunion with my easel and paints.'

A laugh cracked out of him. *'Touché!'*

'But seriously,' she added, 'this really does make me happy. Thank you.'

She looked beautiful. Her hair was loose, wild and tangled after her ride, and her cheeks were flushed pink. She'd dressed for a picnic in casual clothes—a cotton shirt in a faded check print tucked into a pair of clean jeans.

'You didn't need to do all this. You still don't,' she said. 'Putting things back to normal with my brothers is more than enough for me. I can never thank you enough for all you've done.'

'I don't want your thanks any more than you want lavish gifts. All I want is your hand in marriage, for no better reason than I love you.'

'Nicely put,' she teased, but the smile on her face was one of pure happiness. And then she dropped a bombshell. 'Though we don't have to get married. You do know that, don't you?'

His gut clenched. 'What do you mean?'

'Just that you silenced the gossips when you exposed Howard Blake and his accomplice Dom. Your country applauds you, your mother has never doubted you, and I… I only want you to be happy.'

'Without you?' He frowned. *No. No. No.* This was supposed to be perfect. An evening together in a glorious setting, away from all distractions was their chance to put the past behind them, to discard it like an old notebook crammed full of notes that were meaningless now so they could start again on a clean sheet.

'We do have to get married,' he argued quietly, feeling as if his entire existence depended on his next few words. 'I can't live without you. I don't want to try.'

'You mean it, don't you?' she asked him softly.

'Every word,' he stated firmly. 'If you can see this as base camp, we'll start our journey here. I can't promise there won't be difficulties along the way but we'll get through them. Are you up for starting tonight? See where it takes us?'

Sofia didn't speak for the longest few seconds of his life, during which the road ahead of him loomed bleakly at the prospect that she might say no.

'I'd be honoured to accept your proposal, on the understanding that this is a true partnership.'

'Of equals,' he confirmed.

'In that case…'

'Kiss me?' he suggested.

'What's keeping you?'

The meal was singed to a cinder by the time he had answered that question. Fortunately, his chefs had left him well prepared, and Sofia declared the remaining food some of the best she had ever tasted.

'And you prepared all this yourself?' she exclaimed with approval.

He would start as he intended to continue—with the truth. 'I put my name to it,' he admitted, staring up through half-closed eyes. 'I also warmed it up, which took a certain degree of skill.'

'Save your skill for the bedroom,' Sofia scolded.

He would, but restraint was killing him.

'Please thank your chefs from me, and tell them the food was delicious.'

'Don't I get any credit?'

'For that? Or for this?'

When Sofia kissed him, he congratulated himself on not following the impulse to thoroughly ravish her. True to his vow, he'd store up that desire and would suffer a straining groin for as long as it took. But not for too long, he trusted.

A welcome distraction came when Sofia went to examine her easel and paints. Even in jeans she looked like a queen, he reflected as she walked to the riverbank. His groin tightened on cue, reminding him that where Sofia was concerned there was no such thing as too much sex. To ramp up the agony, he'd chosen a setting that was perfect for lazy lovemaking. The grass was lush and deep, and it would be soft and fragrant beneath then. The night breeze would cool them— *Dio!* He wanted her. Now he knew the true meaning of agony.

'Are these artists' materials really mine?' she asked, turning to greet him as he joined her at the easel.

'They're all yours',' he confirmed, thinking how beautiful she looked with the last rays of the sun bathing her in a cloud of light. Looping his hands loosely around her waist, he encouraged, 'Go to it. I can't wait to see what you come up with.'

'I know what you've come up with,' she scolded. 'And this is only our first date.'

'But I can kiss you,' he said, starting by kissing her neck.

'You can,' she agreed. Her voice trembled with a throb of excitement so her next words were unexpected. 'But that's all you can do,' she insisted.

Unseen, he ground his teeth until he was sure they would shatter.

They cantered back together. Wind in her hair and Cesar at her side, she had never been happier. Her lips were bruised from his kisses, though the frustration of holding back from progressing those kisses was pure torture. And now the idea of marrying a prince, and therefore becoming a princess, was niggling at her. Cesar's life was so very different from hers. No way was she regal material. Born a tomboy, she was happiest and most relaxed at an easel or in the saddle. Cesar was rich and she was poor, having invested every penny of her inheritance in the retreat.

'You're very quiet,' he commented as they slowed their horses on the approach to the yard.

'Happily contented,' she said as she dismounted. That wasn't strictly true. She wanted Cesar's arms around her and his naked body, warm and demanding, against hers.

Springing down from the saddle, he led their horses to the stable. 'I'll see them settled down and then I'm going to bed. I suggest you do the same. Remember, we've got training in the morning.'

She didn't want to sleep alone, and had expected Cesar to change his mind about wooing her 'properly', she realised now. 'I hadn't forgotten, but thank you,' she called to him on a dry throat.

With one last, brief sideways glance Cesar raised an amused brow and walked away.

CHAPTER SIXTEEN

THIS WAS KILLING HIM. Taking things slowly did not suit him. Cesar ground his teeth as he led their horses back into the stable complex. Having not only read the menu but having tasted it, holding back where Sofia was concerned was up there with the hardest things he'd ever had to do. Hard being a word he wanted to expunge from his mind right now.

Taking things slowly was the sensible thing to do, he persuaded himself as he removed his horse's tack. In Sofia's case, it was the only way. But that didn't mean he had to like it or that it was going to be easy. He had never held back, whether in the army, business, polo or anything else, but having promised to court Sofia as she deserved—when what he wanted was to throw her over his shoulder, carry her off to bed and make love to her until her legs refused to hold her up—he would stick to the original plan. But if there was one thing this experience had taught him it was that celibacy was massively overrated.

She couldn't sleep that night. Things were so bad she had actually left her bedroom door open a crack in the hope that Cesar might find his way in. No such luck. Thin strands of lilac light were already pushing their way through the curtains. Everyone would be up soon, and there was no sign of him. Not even a text.

Scrambling out of bed, she took a quick shower and got dressed, ready for the morning training session. Leaving her room, she crept down the corridor. Everyone was still asleep. Her next stop was the ranch house. Running across the yard, she entered the main house through the back door with the key they'd all been given in case they felt hungry when the cookhouse was closed. Setting to, she made pancakes, something she was rather good at, if she did say so herself. Loading a tray with coffee and freshly squeezed juice, she loaded it with pancakes for two and went to say a proper thank you to Cesar.

Backing into his bedroom, she put the tray down on the nightstand by his bedside. His pillows looked as if they'd been punched into oblivion and his covers were in a knot. There was no sign of Cesar but she could hear the shower running. Her throat dried with anticipation. Would he stride out of the bathroom naked, fully clothed, or would he have a towel looped around his waist?

'Sofia!'

Naked.

Okay.

Securing her wide-eyed gaze to his, as if to prevent that gaze from straying, he reached for a robe, handily tossed onto a nearby chair, and shrugged it on.

Too late. Her gaze had already strayed. Her breath quickened and her lips parted. 'Pancakes?'

'I could do with something to eat,' Cesar confirmed, though she thought she detected a wicked smile on his wicked mouth. And was his robe left unfastened on purpose?

'You'll catch cold.'

'Not a chance,' he said, padding purposefully in her direction. Rather than reaching for the food she had prepared, or pouring a cup of coffee, he reached for her. Cupping her face in his hands, he whispered, 'You look so beautiful this morning. And what a thoughtful thing to do.'

She could have drowned in those eyes. She still might.

Bringing her close, Cesar kissed her good morning.

His kisses were like incendiary devices to her senses. Closing her eyes, she dragged deep on the heady mix of soap and warm, clean man. If she could have this for the rest of her life, she would be the happiest woman on the face of the earth.

'Coffee?'

She realised Cesar was speaking to her. 'I made the breakfast for you,' she insisted. 'It's nothing much, just another thank-you for the easel and paints, and the delicious picnic last night.'

'I have a confession to make.'

'You do?' Apprehension gripped her. She should have known this was too good to be true.

'If we're going to make this work, we have to be honest with each other. Correct?'

'Correct,' she agreed tensely.

Cesar's burning gaze lit with humour. 'I want you, and it isn't in my nature to wait.'

Laughter drove her tension away, and then their fingers brushed as she accepted the cup of coffee he'd poured. How was it she'd never noticed before how seductive the brush of a hand could be? 'Pancakes first?' she suggested.

Cesar laughed. 'Seriously?'

'Of course seriously,' she insisted, trembling with excitement inside. 'Do they look that bad?'

'They look absolutely delicious. Do your worst,' he encouraged.

Oh. She forced herself to brighten. 'Sugar?' she asked with a smile.

Cesar's answer was to yank her close enough to drown in his eyes. 'We're going to be very late for training,' he promised. But then he gently disentangled himself and started eating pancakes.

The result was a frustrating day. Sex helped to wipe her mind clear of doubt, Sofia realised, reeling with exhaustion by the time training ended. Doubt had been her constant companion since losing her parents, and it was back full force now. What if Cesar's proposal was only to prove to her brothers that his intentions were honourable? Once they left this training camp hothouse behind, and life returned to normal, would Cesar come to realise that he didn't love her after all?

The temptation to confront him with these concerns battled with her desire to squeeze every last drop of happiness out of their time together. Remembering how Cesar had touched her face so tenderly last night didn't help, and only made her realise how much she'd miss him if Cesar came his senses and realised that marrying her would be wrong. Tears stung her eyes as she walked back to the stable. Thank goodness Jess had pushed them hard. She'd had less time to think. But now—

'Hey, you!'

Cesar's call stopped Sofia in her tracks halfway across the stable yard. He was tossing a bucket of ice-cold water from the well over his impossibly magnificent half-naked self. She closed her eyes to that, and to him, or she tried to.

'Where are you rushing off to?' he asked with a frown, staring at the large, zip-up bag she was carrying. It contained all her loose possessions from the tack room. She was on her way to add it to the stack of luggage in her room.

'Hey, yourself.' Her face burned with guilt at having been caught out. She should have told Cesar before arranging her journey home, but once she'd realised the best thing to do was to give them both space, she had rushed through the arrangements, knowing that if she stopped to think too much about it, she'd never go through with her plan. She'd confided in Jess and had promised she'd be back in time for the match. Jess clearly didn't agree with what she was doing but had enough sense to keep those thoughts to herself, confining herself to comments on Sofia's fitness, saying that if she kept up her training back home in Spain, Sofia would be more than ready for the match.

'I couldn't get an internet connection in my room,' she told

Cesar now, 'so I'm off to the cookhouse to see if I can sort out something there.' She was a terrible liar, and he knew it.

'Internet?' he probed. 'Why don't you use mine at the ranch house?'

'I never thought of that.'

'Really?' He quirked a disbelieving brow.

If she stayed another hour her heart would shatter. However Cesar dressed it up, a marriage of convenience would never work between them. Her heart would break before their union had a chance.

You seem preoccupied, Sofia.'

'No.' She shook her head.

'Wistful, then.'

'Memories can do that,' she admitted.

'Live in the moment and be happy.' Cesar spread his arms wide as if to welcome her into his world. 'Don't look so worried. What you see is what you get.'

Which was not just a prince, she thought as he stared down. Cesar was a deeply principled man who wielded great power and wealth. His destiny was preordained. She'd been lucky enough to cross his path briefly, but that was all. There could never be anything more between them. She had to help Cesar to see that he must forget the idea of marrying her, and if that meant leaving him so that in time he forgot her, then that was what she would do.

Love involved sacrifice sometimes, and this was one of those times. The threat of scandal was already fading, its roots stamped out. The press had new headlines. The people of Ardente Sestieri were confident in their prince. It was just Sofia who was out of step. But the one thing she owed him above everything else was honesty. 'Is there somewhere we can talk?'

'No,' he grated out, surprising her with the harshness in his tone. 'There is not. And you're not leaving me,' he stated firmly. 'I won't let those demons from the past destroy you. You have to be brave to love completely, and I know you can.'

'Cesar—please… You don't understand. I can't do this to you. I have to leave. It's for the best.'

'Whose best? Yours?'

She lifted the bag. He took it from her. She wrestled it back. 'I'm going home. You can't stop me. I should have told you before, but—'

'There wasn't time?' he suggested. 'Forgive me, Sofia, but where is your loyalty now?'

'I won't let the team down. I'll be back for the match. We both need time to cool down and think, and then you'll see that I'm right.'

'Oh, will I?' Cesar challenged fiercely. 'When are you going to stop running, Sofia? You can't escape your parents' death, no matter how far or how fast you run.'

'What?' The bag dropped from her hands. 'Is that what you think this is about?'

'I don't think, I know it is,' Cesar assured her. 'How do I know? Because my emotions have been strangled for years. I resented you to begin with for the way I saw myself reflected in the way that you behave—the self-inflicted isolation, the determination to help others at whatever cost to yourself, the overwhelming urge to win, to race, to exhaust yourself—and it still doesn't blot out the pain.

'It doesn't work, Sofia! Because when you've finally run yourself into the ground and lie down on your bed at night the pain's still there. And it will be with you until you deal with it.'

Sofia seemed to visibly shrink in front of him. 'How do you do that?' she asked him in a small voice.

'You learn coping strategies. You remember the good times as well as the bad. I'm still a work in progress,' he admitted. 'But we can fix this together. I won't lose you now.'

'You can't stop me leaving.'

'True.' Sofia was ready to be hurt some more, he realised as her dark eyes searched his. 'I would never stop you with force,' he assured her, his voice full of understanding. 'You have to decide you want to stay, just as you have to move forward instead of constantly looking back. You can do it,' he said gently, 'because now you're not on your own, you have me.'

She exhaled on a faint smile. 'How do you know all this?'

'Because I still have pain here.' He pressed a hand against his heart. 'I just hide it better than you.'

Taking hold of Sofia's shoulders in a loving grip, he brought her to face him. 'I know how you feel because I've spent most of my life hiding my feelings. When my father was killed, when I lost comrades in the forces, and when my mother took up with a man who only ever meant her harm and I felt I'd lost her too, I hurt like hell, but I've become an expert over the years when it comes to hiding my true thoughts.' He frowned. 'I can't do that with you, Sofia. Stay with me, and I promise I'll make you happy, and we'll work through this together.'

She wanted to stay with Cesar more than anything, but if she agreed to marry him, what would happen when the training camp ended and the matches were over, and she was no longer outstanding in any way? She'd be plain Sofia Acosta again— a great rider, with some small skill in painting pictures and a retreat to run. She wasn't suited to royal life.

Cesar needed someone with style and panache, who could sit beside him, exuding elegance and grace, and who would behave properly at all times. Not some country bumpkin with grime under her nails and dog hair and slobber on her clothes. 'I'm just not suitable.'

'For what?'

Cesar's eyes had a wicked glint, and his mouth was tugging up at one corner in the way she loved. 'Don't do this,' she warned.

'Do what?'

'Seduce me with a look. Make me change my mind—' She broke off, seeing her brothers with Olivia and Jess crossing the yard. Let off the hook, she yelled, 'Hello!'

'Come on, Sofia,' Cesar insisted, reclaiming her attention.

'You're only allowed so much time to bury your head in the sand and pretend this isn't the best thing that has ever happened to either of us.'

Come on, Sofia, her inner voice echoed. *Prince or not, Cesar is the best thing that ever happened to you.*

'Dump that bag in the barn,' he suggested. 'Join everyone in the cookhouse. You must be hungry after training.'

Was she giving Cesar another chance or herself? Sofia wondered as they headed off to the cookhouse together.

For the first time he could remember, no one teased them when he and Sofia finally sat down in the cookhouse to eat their meal.

'Okay?' He took hold of her hand in full sight of everyone present and brought it to his lips. There was a moment of complete stillness, but no one commented, and after a moment or two the buzz of conversation started up again. He wouldn't have cared whether or not they were accepted as a couple, but it felt good to have the acknowledgement of those closest to them that he was taking his wooing plans forward.

'Getting there,' Sofia whispered back with an intimate smile. 'You've given me something to think about,' she admitted. 'A lot to think about, in fact.'

'Like another date night?' he suggested.

'Only if it comes with pizza and a bottle of beer.'

'I can sort that,' he confirmed. 'Whatever your heart desires.'

'My heart isn't as sophisticated as yours'—'

'No doubts,' he interrupted. 'We're in this together, remember?'

She thought about this for all of two seconds before adding chocolate ice cream to her list of requirements for their second date.

'Deal.' He held out his hand across the table to shake hers. And never wanted to let go.

Now they got catcalls. 'Find a room,' one of Sofia's brothers bellowed.

They shut him out. The amused glance they shared said it all. Sofia couldn't have been happier to be teased by her brothers. When'd she first arrived at the training camp the relationship between Sofia and her brothers had been strained, to put it mildly, but now she was elated to find it back to normal. They should expect more of this, he accepted wryly as they rose as one from the table. Fingers linked, they walked out of the cookhouse without a backward glance.

CHAPTER SEVENTEEN

THE FACT THAT chocolate and pizza could taste so good on a dish called Sofia would bring a smile to his face for the rest of his life. Date night had started innocently enough with Sofia cutting pizza into slices while he wedged lime into bottles of beer. They talked, relaxed, laughed, and talked some more.

But the more they laughed, the more sexual tension soared between them. Fingers brushed, eyes met, gazes steadied, lingered, until something had to give. Drawing Sofia into his arms, he meshed his fingers through her hair and kissed her as tenderly as if this was the first time they'd touched.

'Why are you always so impatient?' he growled against her mouth when she moved her body seductively against his.

'Have you looked in a mirror recently?'

'So you only want me for my body?'

'We can start with that,' she teased. 'But actually,' she added, turning serious, 'I want all of you, every bit of you, even the bits you didn't know you had. I want to hold your secrets in my heart and laugh with you as we've laughed tonight. I want to grow old with you.'

'You don't want to know all my secrets,' he assured her.

'Yes, I do,' she argued in a whisper, 'but you'll tell me in your own time. There are things you don't know about me, and a lot I don't know about you, but we can find out together. And sorry to ask but do you think we could stop talking now?'

'You are a shameless hussy.'

'Thank goodness you made me that way.'

'As you're naked in my kitchen, I guess it would be rude to ignore—'

'Ice cream?' she interrupted. 'But I don't have a dish.'

'Won't you catch cold?'

'Not if you warm me. Lick it off...'

'I intend to.'

From there it was a rough and tumble that saw them end up on the floor, with pizza scattered everywhere and rapidly melting ice cream coating parts of them urgently needing attention.

'It's in my hair,' Sofia laughingly complained at one point.

Swiping ice cream from his chin, he ordered, 'Stop complaining.'

'Everything's an opportunity for you,' she scolded between shrieks of hysterical pleasure.

Rolling Sofia onto her back, he loomed over her. 'Sofia Acosta, I'm asking you again, and again, and again, will you marry me?'

'Must I repeat my answer?'

'Do you want more pleasure or not?'

'Why ask when you know my answer?'

'Because last time I didn't ask, I instructed, and I'm trying to mend my ways.'

'By proposing while I'm covered in ice cream, lying naked on your kitchen table?'

'I can't think of a better time, can you?'

They stared into each other's eyes, and then Sofia's mouth began to twitch. Once she started laughing, she couldn't stop.

'I'll go down on bended knee later,' he promised.

'I'll hold you to that,' she warned as he silenced her with a kiss.

* * *

It was a long time later, after an extremely lengthy shower, that they finally made it to his bed. 'I just want you to be sure,' Sofia told him as he drew her into his arms. 'Marriage is such a huge step for you.'

'And for you, as it is for anyone,' he argued. 'I can't pretend we won't live in the spotlight, but it's up to us to make time for each other.'

'And our family,' she whispered against his mouth.

'The balancing act won't be easy,' he agreed. 'Serving our country in the full glare of publicity while maintaining a happy family life will be a challenge, but as we both thrive on challenge I don't see a problem. We'll be stronger together than we are apart.'

'You make a good case, Prince Cesar,' Sofia teased tenderly.

'I'm fighting for a woman who is worth the world to me. If you had left me, I would have regretted it for the rest of my life—and I've got too much living to do to waste time on regret.'

Sofia's eyes searched his with concern. 'A huge royal wedding with a cathedral full of people we don't even know?'

'What about that wedding on the beach you talked about?'

'You can't. You're a prince.'

'I can do anything I want to do,' he assured Sofia. 'We can have a grand ceremony in the cathedral to celebrate the birth of the first of our many children or a formal blessing in the months after our marriage. Our countrymen are romantics at heart—they're Italian,' he reminded her. 'And we won't sell them short. We'll share our lives—good and bad—so they have an insight into the human side of our royal partnership. I know my people's generosity of spirit well enough to be confident that they will applaud our decision to have a simple beachside wedding, for no other reason than it means so much to us.'

'Saying our own words in our own way, rather than repeating words written by someone who doesn't even know us,' Sofia reflected out loud. Her eyes brightened as she saw the possibility of change for the better opening out in front of them both.

'Exactly.'

'You'd do this for me?'

'I'd do anything for you,' he confirmed. 'I'm saying I love you in every way I know. I'll always respect royal traditions, but we can still do things our way, a new way, and if a wedding on the beach is what you want, a wedding on the beach is what you shall have.'

'I can't think of anything I want more than to be your wife, to stand alongside you, whatever the future brings. I love you so much,' Sofia whispered, staring up into his eyes.

The first charity polo match was brought forward. The crowd was vast. The game was fierce. Sofia and Olivia proved indispensable members of the winning team, which was naturally Team Lobos. They defeated the infamous Argentinian Team Assassin, led by past world champion Nero Caracas, by seven goals to six. Any other result would have been unacceptable, Sofia's fiercest brother Xander told Cesar without a flicker of expression on his tough, unforgiving face.

To allow the cheering fans to see many of the world's top players in action, both sides swapped different players for each chukka, so there was a huge crowd of players and their families in the cookhouse afterwards, where warm camaraderie prevailed. What had happened on the pitch stayed on the pitch, and all that mattered now were the huge sums of money raised for their favourite charities. It was the perfect time to make an announcement.

Tapping a champagne bottle, Cesar grabbed everyone's attention. As silence fell, he announced, 'Sofia and I are getting married.'

'Does Sofia know?' demanded Nero Caracas, Cesar's arch-rival and great friend, to a chorus of raucous cheers.

'She does,' Sofia shouted, coming to Cesar's side to link her arm through his. 'And you're all invited to our wedding on the beach on the beautiful island of Isla Ardente.'

Isla Ardente. Paradise on earth. That was Sofia's first impression of Cesar's private island, and it only improved in her eyes as she walked barefoot down the firm sugar-sand beach to join her life with his.

Cesar had dressed simply in a loose-fitting white linen shirt that was striking against his tan. He had completed the ensemble with delightfully fine linen trousers in a dusky shade of taupe that would slip off as easily as he'd put them on. These things were important when you spent most of your life in tight-fitting breeches.

Sofia was wearing the wedding gown they'd chosen together. It was also flimsy and easy to remove. A dream of a dress, it was an unadorned slip of ankle-length ivory silk that moulded her body with loving attention to detail. She wore her hair down with a coronet of fresh flowers, picked that morning in the palace gardens, secured around her forehead with a floating rose-pink ribbon. Instead of a bouquet, she carried her wedding gift from Cesar. The puppy was his hound Bran's prettiest daughter. So Cesar hadn't quite kept to the rules when it came to this marriage, any more than she had.

Jess was waiting as she reached his side to take the puppy from her. Linking fingers with Sofia, Cesar brought her hand to his lips. Dipping his head, he murmured, 'I love you... How beautiful you are.' And then his lips brushed her neck, her mouth. 'I can't wait to get you alone—'

The celebrant cleared his throat abruptly, which made the unruly guests laugh, but even the minister was smiling; everyone was in the same euphoric mood.

'I do,' Sofia confirmed as the surf rustled and lapped over her naked feet.

'Time and tide wait for no man, not even a prince,' Cesar

explained with a dark smile for Sofia as a groom brought up his great black stallion.

Swinging into the saddle, he lifted Sofia into his arms, and to the cheers of their guests they galloped away for some vital private time before the wedding feast began.

EPILOGUE

'WE'VE COME A long way, *piccola amata*.'

'A very long way,' Sofia agreed, smiling as she snuggled closer to Cesar. How she loved this intimacy between them. Most of all she loved the happy family they had created amidst the pomp and duty of royal life.

Currently they were staring down with the same astonished adoration they had experienced when their twins had been born three years ago. Their latest beloved newborn was a baby girl called Thea, after Sofia's mother. Thea was sister to Nico and Tino, their three-year-old sons. The boys were currently nestled on the bed alongside them, admiring the new addition to their family.

'I bought you something,' Cesar remembered, delving into the pocket of his jeans.

'Cesar, no,' Sofia protested as he brought out a night-blue velvet jewel case. She gazed lovingly at their children. 'You've given me everything I need already.'

She could never have predicted how happy they would be. The people of Ardente Sestieri celebrated their Prince's tight family unit at an annual celebration in the castle gardens each year. This year Cesar and Sofia would share the joy of a new baby with their people, and not just with a series of photographs taken by Cesar but with new portraits of the children painted by Sofia, just as soon as she was back at her easel.

The polo matches continued to raise vast sums for charity, while Sofia's retreat had developed into a worldwide charitable foundation with outreach services, and Cesar was popularly acclaimed as the most charitable and caring Prince in his country's history.

'Aren't you going to open it?' her loving husband prompted. 'The boys are waiting. We love you so much, and Nico and Tino helped me choose the gift.'

'I'll love it whatever it is,' Sofia assured them, but Tino and Nico were more interested in their baby sister curling her tiny fists around their fingers.

'Another warrior woman,' Cesar groaned.

Sofia gasped on opening the jewel box. He helped her to remove the most beautiful diamond necklace from its snug velvet nest.

She had become accustomed to wearing the priceless, heavy and opulent gems of state. Always conscious of their history, she felt humbled wearing them, but this was a different jewel, because this was a gift from Cesar's heart.

The fine gold chain held three pure blue-white diamond hearts. 'With room for more,' Cesar pointed out.

'Do you really think these three will give us the chance to add to our family?'

'You can depend on it,' he promised.

Staring into the darkly seductive eyes of a man she trusted and loved more than anything else on earth, she believed him.

* * * * *

Keep reading for an excerpt of
Chased
by Lauren Dane.
Find it in the
The Art Of The Chase anthology,
out now!

Chapter One

At the sound of the doorbell, Liv dabbed her eyes and cursed to herself, seeing they were still red and puffy. She'd have ignored it on any other day but Cassie and Maggie were picking her up to take her to drive over to Polly and Edward's fortieth wedding anniversary party.

Letting out a resigned sigh, Liv answered her door to her friends, both dressed to the nines.

"You've been crying." With a concerned look on her face, Maggie pushed her way into the house and Cassie followed.

"I'm fine. Really. I'm nearly done, I just need to fix my eyes. I don't want you two to be late."

"I've spent all afternoon with Polly, and Cassie took care of the setup. Edward's out with Polly, he's taking her for a drive. I think they're going to make out at the lake. And that means you're going to tell us what's going on." The look on Maggie's face told Liv she wouldn't back down.

"Brody." Liv sighed, turning to the mirror so she could repair her makeup.

"Brody what? What did he do?"

"Not what. Who. That rat bastard cheated on me with Lyndsay Cole. I walked in on them yesterday afternoon at his apartment. Got off work early and brought him some dinner. I got a lot more than the thank-you I was expecting."

"He did not! She did not! That bitch," Maggie hissed. "That man-stealing bitch. I'm going to make a Lyndsay doll and stick her full of pins."

Liv snorted a laugh. "You always make me feel better. And someone was already sticking her full of something. But don't blame her. She wasn't in a relationship, Brody was. Pig."

"I hope his pecker falls off," Cassie said through clenched teeth.

"Or maybe it should get like a thousand paper cuts and then have lemon juice poured on it. And I hope Lyndsay gets a cold sore. A big one and a wart on her chin." Maggie nodded.

"With a big, black wiry hair that grows out of it and no one tells her," Cassie added.

"You two are the best." Liv grinned and turned around, finger-combing her hair and smoothing down the front of the sweater dress she'd chosen for the party. "I feel better than I have since yesterday when I found out. I wish I could say he sucked in bed, but I'd be lying. What is it about me? Why can't I find someone? Something real?"

Maggie sighed. "You found out yesterday and you're only telling us now?"

Liv shrugged. "I couldn't face anyone. I caught them and I couldn't get it out of my head. You and Kyle had a date, Shane and Cassie had only just returned from their honeymoon and Dee and Arthur just finished the move to Atlanta. She's already got high blood pressure and I don't want to make her pregnancy worse. I came home, ate too much ice cream, watched *Thelma and Louise* and went to bed.

"I know Brody and I weren't engaged or anything. I didn't think he was the one, but I thought perhaps someday... Oh I don't know what I thought but I do know we were supposed to be exclusive. It could have been right someday to move to the next step. You know, he could have broken up with me. He didn't have to fuck someone behind my back."

Cassie hugged her tight and Maggie followed. "He's a pig. He's a pig, a jerk and a dick."

"And an ass. And his nose is big," Cassie added.

"Marc asked if I wanted him to kick Brody's ass." Liv grinned.

"You told Marc? You told Marc Chase before your best friend?" Maggie's eyebrows flew up.

"It just happened. He came by this afternoon looking for Shane. Something about the party. Anyway, he came by to look at my legs and flirt a bit and he asked if I was coming tonight with Brody and it just came out. He was very sweet about it."

Maggie harrumphed but looked mollified. "Well, I suppose if you have to unburden such a shitty story to someone, it may as well be someone who looks as good as Marc does."

Liv laughed. "He does, doesn't he? Lawd, you should see the damned place every time he walks through, women coming out of the woodwork to be seen."

They all walked to the car and admittedly, Liv felt better.

"I just want someone I can trust. Someone I can come home to at the end of the day and share my life with. I want to be in love and get married and have kids. Not tomorrow or anything but I feel like I'm very far off schedule." Liv chewed her bottom lip as she pulled her seat belt on.

"Love doesn't have a schedule, Liv," Maggie said from the back seat. "And you *will* find love. You will, I promise you. This thing with Brody isn't about you at all. He didn't cheat because you were bad. He cheated because he's a jerk."

"And Matt?" Liv's heart still ached a bit when she said his name.

"Matt is a good person, don't get me wrong. But he was not right for you. He's not right for anyone just yet. She'll come along though. But you aren't her and I'm sorry because I know you wish it was different. He's not ready."

"I want what you have with Kyle. What Cassie has. What Dee has. I look at Polly and Edward and think about how they've had forty years together and I wonder why I can't have that."

"You *can* have that. It'll come."

"It's only because you're pregnant that I don't smack you for saying that. People who are so happily married it makes my teeth hurt can say that stuff awfully easily. You have Kyle who looks at you like there's not another woman on Earth. Cassie has Shane who can't take his eyes off her for three minutes."

Maggie laughed. "No one but you two and Kyle knows about the pregnancy so watch it. Polly will kill me if she hears it before Kyle and I can tell her. As for you? Lotsa frogs in this world, Liv. Your prince is out there."

Liv groaned. "Maybe I need to sign up with a dating service or something."

Cassie shrugged. "I don't know, Liv. I mean, do those things work? Maybe you just need to get out there and meet people. Or give people a second chance. You're very picky. There are some great men in this town."

"Who are all married, cheaters or quite happily single like those damned Chase boys."

"Well, there's always Marc. He's damned good-looking. Sweet too."

"Maggie Chase, Marc is way too young for me. Not to mention the fact that he goes through women like potato chips. I'm done being a potato chip."

"He is not too young for you. It's not like he's twenty or anything. But you're right about the potato chip part. Let's just look for someone appropriate then. In the meantime, you need to stop riding yourself so hard about this."

Easier said than done. Liv knew it wasn't a problem with her looks. Without vanity, she accepted that she was beautiful. The kind of woman who got second glances everywhere she went. She had a good job, a good life, she was intelligent and most people thought she was funny. She did have a bit of a smart mouth, but it wasn't like at nearly thirty-five she could change that part of herself. And she had self-respect, damn it. She would not start lying and biting her tongue just to appeal to men!

"You could always ask for Polly's help." Cassie winked as Liv groaned. "She's got her finger on the pulse of this town. She can find you an eligible man in minutes, I'd wager."

"You know, I may take her up on that if this goes on too much longer."

They pulled up out front and Liv sighed at the exterior of the house. Matt had strung white fairy lights in the trees out front and the lights inside burned out a warm, inviting glow. Truth be told, Liv missed being a regular part of the Chase family more than she missed Matt. Missed the house and Sunday dinners. Belonging to the Chase family had felt really wonderful.

"Ugh, I'm such a fucking whiner," she mumbled before joining Cassie and Maggie to go inside.

"By the way, nice tan." Liv put her arm around Cassie as they entered the foyer. "All that vacation sex really relaxed you."

Cassie laughed. "Shane, the sun, fruity drinks and lots of hot monkey love. I've never enjoyed myself more. Come on through, the present table is in the sitting room but we've set up the food in the back so that's where everyone will be."

"They're here!" Kyle yelled as Polly and Edward approached the door.

As Polly and Edward came into the house, everyone gathered shouted "Happy Anniversary!" Polly clapped her hands and started smooching up on everyone she could grab as Edward just took it all in with a calm smile.

They'd tried to plan a surprise party but Polly was too nosy and she'd found out early on. Instead, her sons and daughters-in-law had made Polly and Edward agree to let them plan the event and to stay out of the way until it was time to start.

Getting out of the way, Liv went to hang up her coat and bag before going back to the living room. She saw Polly Chase's hair first and then the rest of her as the crowd parted to let her through.

"Why, hello there, Olivia. It's good to see you, honey. I'm glad you could make it." Polly click-clacked on over in her stiletto heels, that giant, lacquered wall of hair not budging an inch as she moved.

Liv bent and hugged Polly, wishing her a happy anniversary. "I wouldn't miss it for the world. You and Edward are a fine example to the rest of us. I hope I can find what you two have someday."

"Aw, well, it's all Edward. The man is quiet, lets me have my way, doesn't say much. A good father and a good man. I'm fortunate." Polly turned and Liv followed her gaze to where Edward Chase stood with Matt.

It was hard to see him, even after a few years. There'd been a time when she'd believed Matt Chase was the one for her. He was attentive and fun, they had sexual chemistry that was off the charts and Liv kept thinking that soon he'd fall for her too. But it never happened. Sure, he had affection for her, but as they'd reached the year mark he hadn't moved even an inch toward marriage or living together. She'd tried to deny it, tried to pretend he'd change but in the end, she knew he didn't love her and never would.

Pride intact but heart broken, she'd left their relationship because it was time to go. She wanted something permanent and it wasn't fair to just spin her wheels with a man who'd never want more than a Saturday date.

Matt saw her and smiled. She waved in return.

"That boy is a fool." Polly shook her head and Liv warmed. "Tells me you're his best female friend. I said he doesn't need any more friends, he needs to settle down and if not with a beautiful, successful woman like you, who? I swear. Kyle was always the sweetest one so of course it wasn't a surprise when he ended up with Maggie. Shane, well, he's been a trial since the moment he was born but Cassie can handle him just fine. Marc doesn't think he needs forever but I think he needs it more than any of the others do. Matt though? I'm afraid he's going to be in for a rude awakening when he finally realizes just how much he let go when you left."

Fighting back tears, Liv squeezed Polly's hand. "Thank you for that, Mrs. Chase. That means a lot to me. He and I weren't meant to be. I wish that weren't so, but it is. And he is my best guy friend, even if he can be a total butthead. You raised four good boys. The last two will do fine when the right woman comes along."

"I'll have you know I have my eye out for a good man for you. I heard about that punk Brody Willitson from my Marc earlier today. Never liked him and he wasn't good enough for a girl like you, honey. Don't you worry though, I've got my ear to the ground." Polly winked. "Now get yourself a plate and have a drink, the night is young."

Liv watched, amused, as Polly ambled off to greet the next person who'd arrived when she saw Maggie with Marc.

"Hey, you two." Liv picked up a plate and began to fill it.

"Hey, Liv. I keep meaning to compliment you on that dress. Is that the one you bought online? That dark purple color is gorgeous on you." Maggie touched her arm.

"I have to agree with Maggie on that one, Liv. Now, as much as I like you in short skirts, this one is very nice. The appeal of a curve-hugging sweater that's a dress is not lost on me at all. The boots are sexy too. A little bit dominatrix. You got any secrets to share, Livvy?"

Liv laughed to cover the warm surge in her belly that always came when Marc flirted. She knew he was full of it and flirted with every woman he met, but still, it made her feel tingly all over.

"Have you seen the bench we got them?" Marc held his

arm out and Liv took it, letting him lead her out of the room, through the kitchen and out into the large backyard.

"Kyle landscaped this little alcove for it. He says the roses will bloom over the arbor in the summer and night-blooming jasmine is planted on both sides."

The bench sat in an isolated corner of the yard with a pretty white arbor over it and a fountain nearby.

"Momma saw the bench last year during the insanity after Christmas when they were planning the wedding and Cassie told Shane and it went from there. You see the plaque?"

On the back of the bench, there was an inscribed plaque with Polly and Edward's name and anniversary date.

"It's impossible to shop for them but this and the album of all the pictures we had made from the slides my daddy had have been the biggest hit yet." Marc sat down and Liv joined him.

Liv warmed at the affection in his voice. "It's really beautiful out here. Kyle did a great job at making this little place. Like an oasis for the two of them to come and sit together."

"He'll read and pretend to listen to her and she'll talk and cross-stitch and pretend he's listening when she's really just planning on getting me and Matt married off."

Liv laughed out loud at the truth of that statement. "They work."

"They do. One day, if I can have what they do, even a shadow of what they have, I'll be lucky."

Liv nodded as she picked at the food on her plate and Marc helped himself to it as well. The noise from the party wafted out on the air but their corner of the yard was an isolated haven. They didn't talk, instead just looked at the stars and picked at Liv's food.

"We should probably go back inside," Liv said, standing. She needed to get back inside before she gave in and leaned her head on his shoulder.

"Yeah, it'll be cake time soon. I love cake." He pressed

a quick kiss to her cheek. "Don't forget that you owe me a dance later."

"We'll see."

"No seeing about it, Olivia Davis. You owe me a dance and I mean to collect." Popping a stolen olive into his mouth, he drew her back into the house, letting her go ahead once they reached the porch.

Man oh man did he love to look at her. Tall, long legs, big brown eyes that always looked like she had a very naughty secret and hair as black as a raven's wing. Straight and glossy and usually in some short, stylish 'do. Her clothes were just shy of outright sexy but it was clear she was a woman who knew what looked good on her body and she dressed accordingly. Not too tight but certainly clingy enough to highlight the high, round ass and the legs. She wore heels high enough to show off hard calves and tilt her ass and breasts out just right. The blouses and sweaters lovingly showcased her perky B cups.

He adored her smile. One of those smiles women had when they knew something delicious. Her accent was nice and thick—sexy, soft Southern sin—and she always sounded on the verge of laughing.

Liv Davis was just an all-around package. Funny, intelligent, independent, very feminine but capable too. She never ceased to make him smile when he thought about her. And she was the only woman he knew who flirted as well as he did. He had to admire that.

Once they got back inside, Liv got pulled into a cutthroat game of canasta with Marc, Cassie and Shane.

"Sheesh, I was hoping your mind would still be addled with all that honeymoon nookie but you're a shark with the cards," Liv joked with Cassie.

"I don't play to lose, Liv." Cassie sniffed and tossed down some cards, reaching to draw more.

"I love it when you're vicious, beautiful," Shane said and Marc rolled his eyes.

"Stop before it starts. No cow eyes over the cards. Chase family rule."

Liv laughed. "I like that rule."

"I hear the music starting up in the other room, Olivia. You promised me a dance don't you forget." Marc winked.

"Let me just do this." Liv tossed down her last suit and stood with a smile. "I don't play to lose either."

Cassie laughed and Marc stood. "Okay then, darlin', let's dance."

Liv took his hand and let him lead her through the house to the formal living room where the music was playing.

With an artful flourish, he pulled her into his arms and against his body. They both froze a moment and moved a bit apart. Swaying slowly, they chatted about town gossip as Reba sang over the stereo speakers.

That night when she finally got home, sore feet and all, the small of her back still tingled where his hand had lain when they'd shared a dance. "I must be ten kinds of fool for even entertaining the thought," she mumbled to herself as she tossed and turned.

But her dreams had other ideas.

Subscribe and fall in love with a Mills & Boon series today!

You'll be among the first to read stories delivered to your door monthly and enjoy great savings.

WE SIMPLY LOVE ROMANCE

MILLS & BOON

JOIN US

Sign up to our newsletter to stay up to date with...

- Exclusive member discount codes
- Competitions
- New release book information
- All the latest news on your favourite authors

Plus...
get $10 off your first order.
What's not to love?

Sign up at **millsandboon.com.au/newsletter**